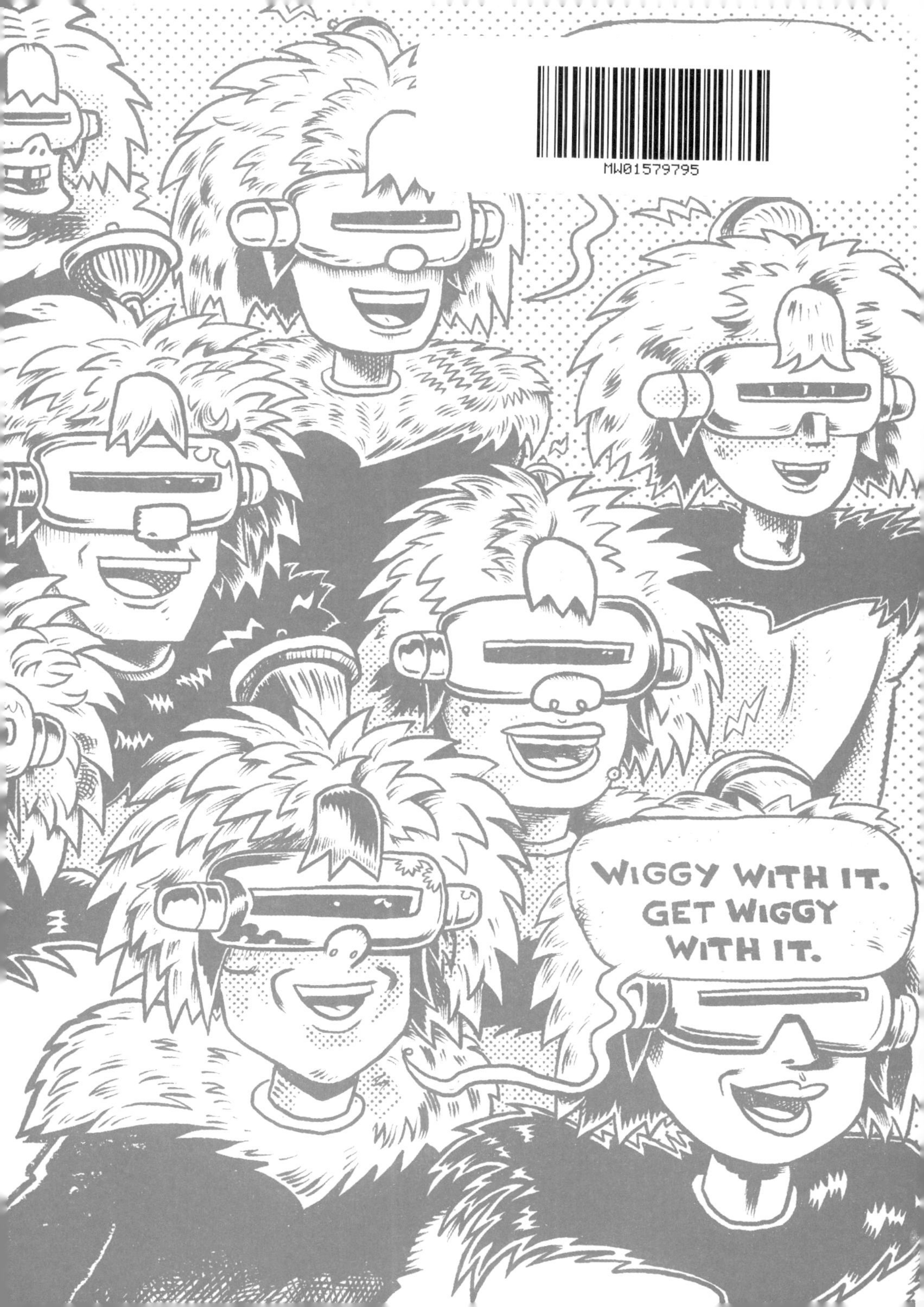
WIGGY WITH IT. GET WIGGY WITH IT.

MW01579795

FLEALIX and the Unruly HairThing

the SNIPS

Enter the WIGMASTER!

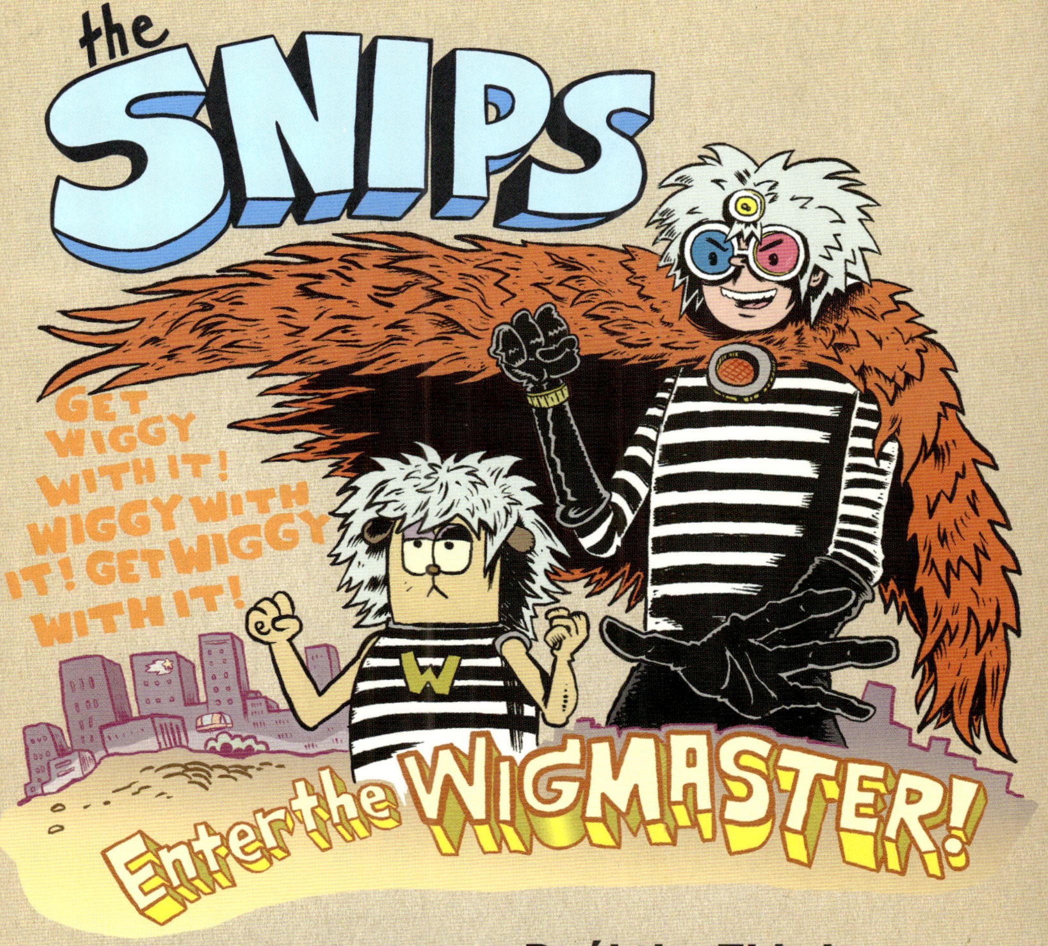
GET WIGGY WITH IT! WIGGY WITH IT! GET WIGGY WITH IT!
W

Written and illustrated by Raúl the Third

Colors by Elaine Bay

Coloring by Eleonora Bruni

Lettering by Rob Leigh

LB INK
Little, Brown and Company
New York Boston

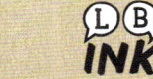

About This Book
The illustrations for this book were done in Procreate on an iPad Pro with True Grit Texture Supply brushes. This book was edited by Margaret Raymo and designed by Megan McLaughlin. The production was supervised by Patricia Alvarado, and the production editor was Jake Regier. The text was set in CC Samaritan, and the display types are Ad Lib and the author's hand lettering.

This book is a work of fiction. Names, characters, places, and incidents are the product of the author's imagination or are used fictitiously. Any resemblance to actual events, locales, or persons, living or dead, is coincidental. · Copyright © 2026 by Raúl González III · Colors by Elaine Bay · Coloring by Eleonora Bruni · Lettering by Rob Leigh · Cover illustration copyright © 2026 by Raúl González III. Cover design by Megan McLaughlin. Cover copyright © 2026 by Hachette Book Group, Inc. · Hachette Book Group supports the right to free expression and the value of copyright. The purpose of copyright is to encourage writers and artists to produce the creative works that enrich our culture. · The scanning, uploading, and distribution of this book without permission is a theft of the author's intellectual property. If you would like permission to use material from the book (other than for review purposes), please contact permissions@hbgusa.com. Thank you for your support of the author's rights. · Little, Brown Ink · Hachette Book Group 1290 Avenue of the Americas, New York, NY 10104 · Visit us at LBYR.com · First Edition: January 2026 · Little, Brown Ink is an imprint of Little, Brown and Company. The Little, Brown Ink name and logo are registered trademarks of Hachette Book Group, Inc. · The publisher is not responsible for websites (or their content) that are not owned by the publisher. · Little, Brown and Company books may be purchased in bulk for business, educational, or promotional use. For information, please contact your local bookseller or the Hachette Book Group Special Markets Department at special.markets@hbgusa.com. · Library of Congress Cataloging-in-Publication Data · Names: Raúl the Third, 1976– author illustrator | Bay, Elaine, 1976– colorist Title: Enter the Wigmaster / written and illustrated by Raúl the Third ; colors by Elaine Bay. Description: First edition. | New York : Little, Brown and Company, 2026. | Series: The snips ; [2] | Audience term: Children | Audience: Ages 7–10. | Summary: The crime-fighting barbers face off against a new villain who uses mind-control wigs to command his minions. Identifiers: LCCN 2024056012 | ISBN 9780316528955 hardcover | ISBN 9780316576918 ebook | ISBN 9780316576925 ebook · Subjects: CYAC: Graphic novels | Barbers—Fiction | Superheroes—Fiction | Wigs—Fiction | Humorous stories | LCGFT: Humorous comics | Graphic novels · Classification: LCC PZ7.7.G384 En 2025 | DDC 741.5/973—dc23/eng/20250312 · LC record available at https://lccn.loc.gov/2024056012 · ISBNs: 978-0-316-52895-5 (paper over board), 978-0-316-57691-8 (ebook), 978-0-316-57692-5 (ebook) · PRINTED IN DONGGUAN, CHINA · APS · 10 9 8 7 6 5 4 3 2 1

To Steve Crosno, legendary El Paso DJ and host of *The Crosno Hop* and *Cruizing with Crosno*. Your seemingly endless collection of wigs was always a thrill to behold.
—Raúl the Third

To our son, Raúl. Thanks for braiding my hair. I loved being your barber mannequin as you practiced for your cosmetology class in high school.
—Elaine Bay

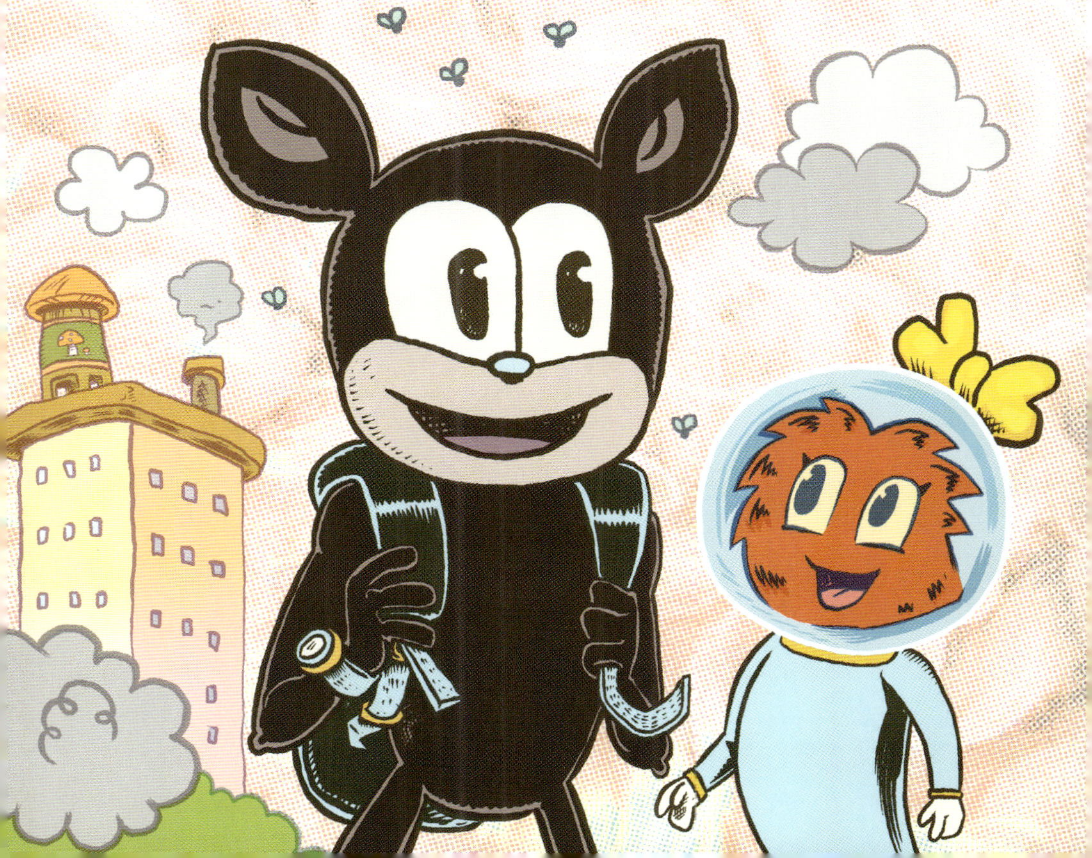

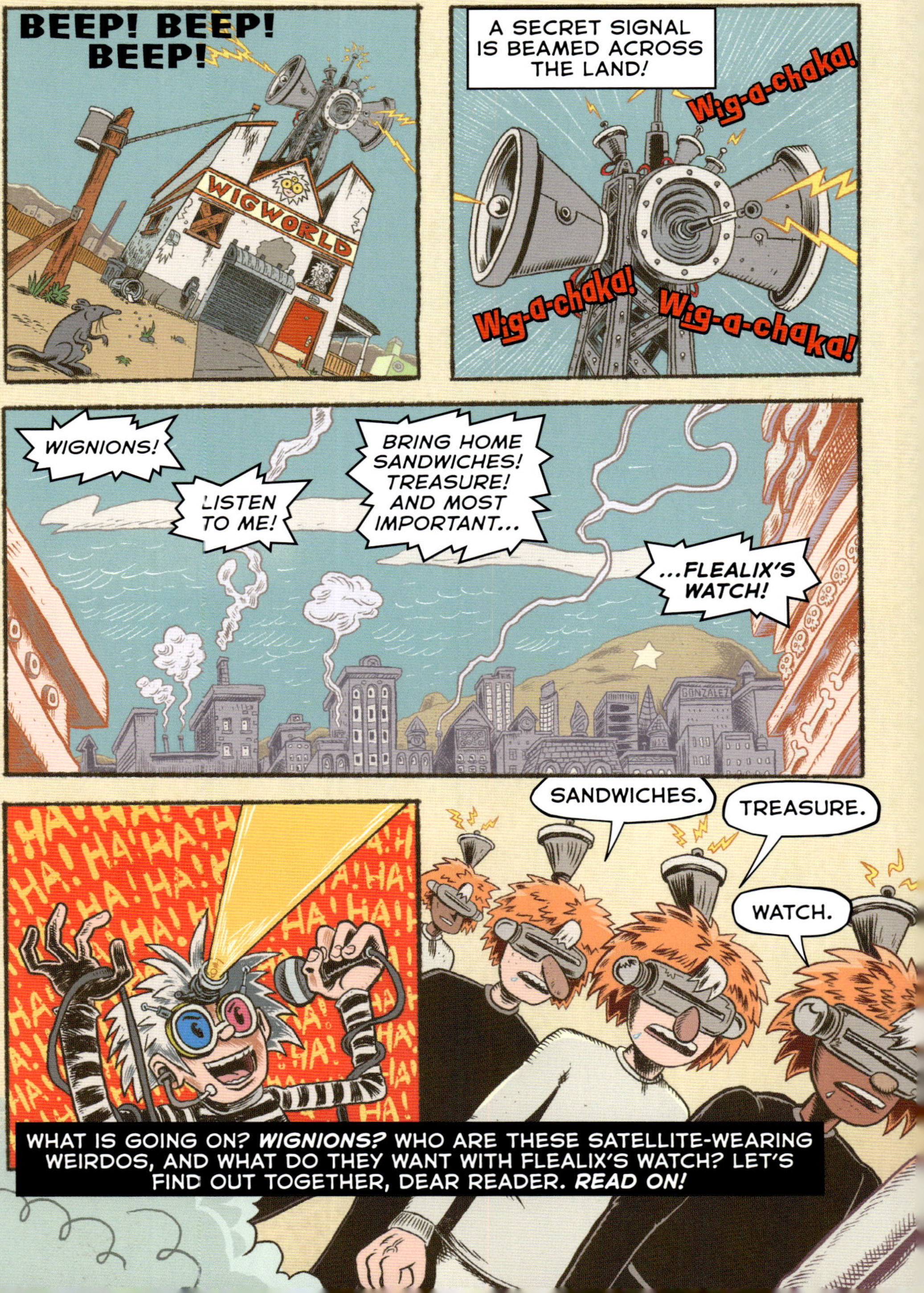
BEEP! BEEP! BEEP!
WIGWORLD
A SECRET SIGNAL IS BEAMED ACROSS THE LAND!
Wig-a-chaka!
Wig-a-chaka!
Wig-a-chaka!
WIGNIONS!
LISTEN TO ME!
BRING HOME SANDWICHES! TREASURE! AND MOST IMPORTANT...
...FLEALIX'S WATCH!
SANDWICHES.
TREASURE.
WATCH.
WHAT IS GOING ON? *WIGNIONS?* WHO ARE THESE SATELLITE-WEARING WEIRDOS, AND WHAT DO THEY WANT WITH FLEALIX'S WATCH? LET'S FIND OUT TOGETHER, DEAR READER. *READ ON!*

SUNDAY IN THE PARK WITH FLEAS!

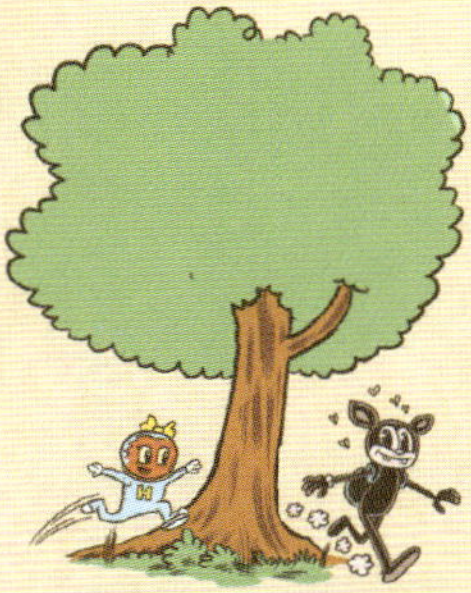

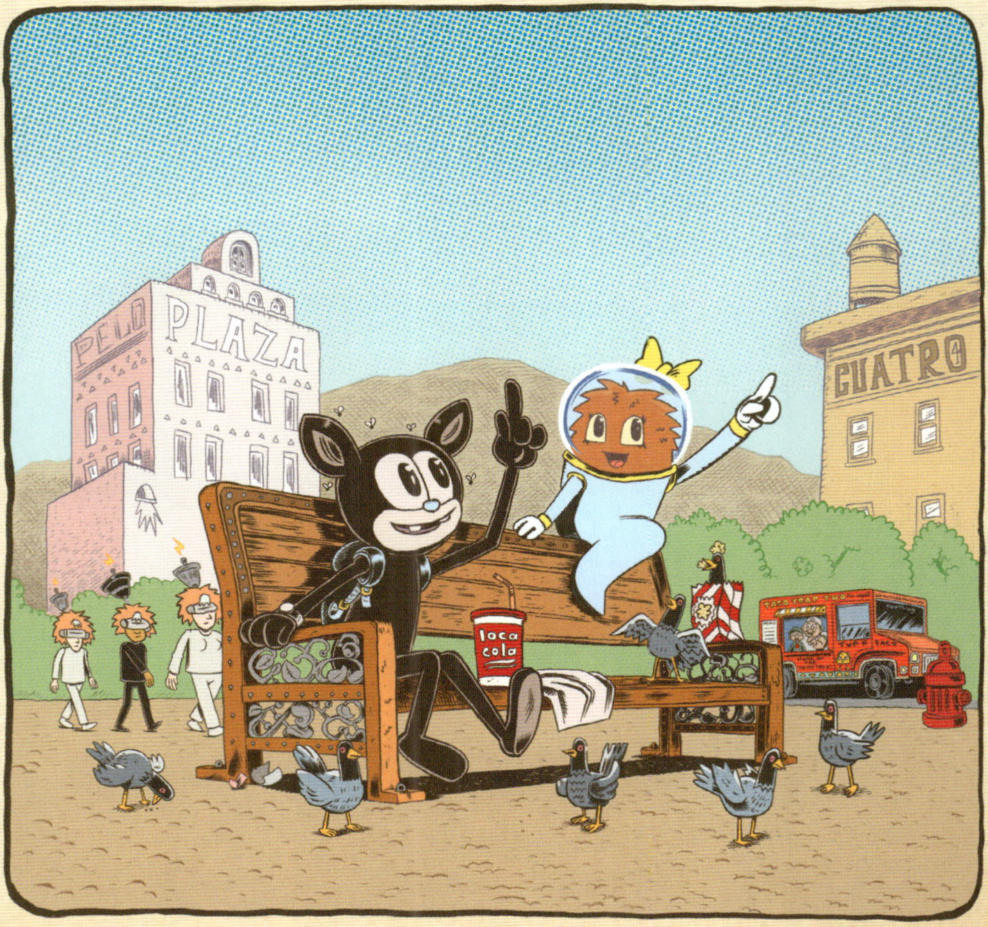
PELO
PLAZA
CUATRO
loca cola

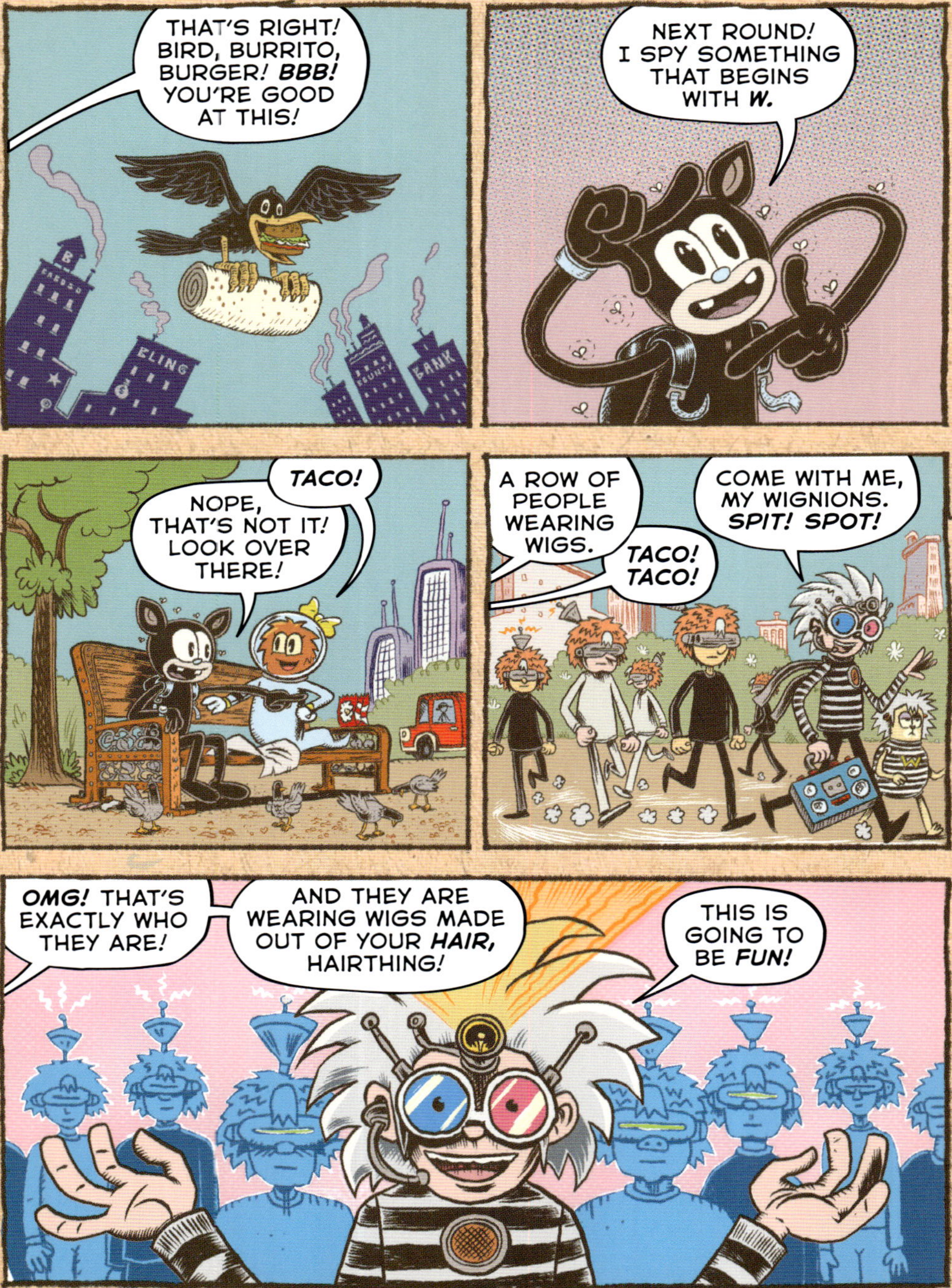
THAT'S RIGHT! BIRD, BURRITO, BURGER! BBB! YOU'RE GOOD AT THIS!
NEXT ROUND! I SPY SOMETHING THAT BEGINS WITH W.
TACO!
NOPE, THAT'S NOT IT! LOOK OVER THERE!
A ROW OF PEOPLE WEARING WIGS.
TACO! TACO!
COME WITH ME, MY WIGNIONS. SPIT! SPOT!
OMG! THAT'S EXACTLY WHO THEY ARE!
AND THEY ARE WEARING WIGS MADE OUT OF YOUR HAIR, HAIRTHING!
THIS IS GOING TO BE FUN!

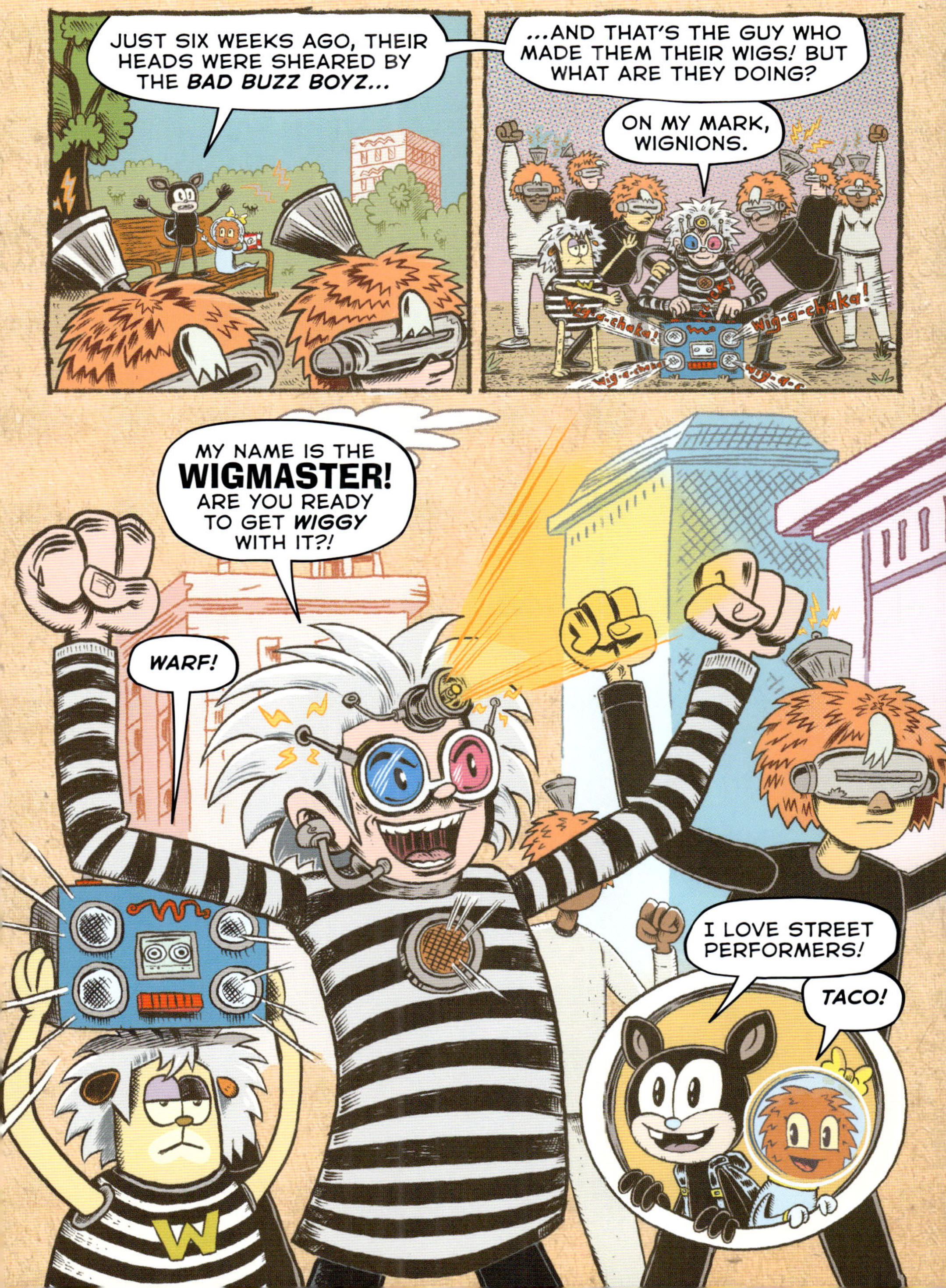
JUST SIX WEEKS AGO, THEIR HEADS WERE SHEARED BY THE *BAD BUZZ BOYZ...*
...AND THAT'S THE GUY WHO MADE THEM THEIR WIGS! BUT WHAT ARE THEY DOING?
ON MY MARK, WIGNIONS.
CLICK!
WIG-A-CHAKA!
WIG-A-CHAKA!
MY NAME IS THE **WIGMASTER!** ARE YOU READY TO GET *WIGGY* WITH IT?!
WARF!
I LOVE STREET PERFORMERS!
TACO!

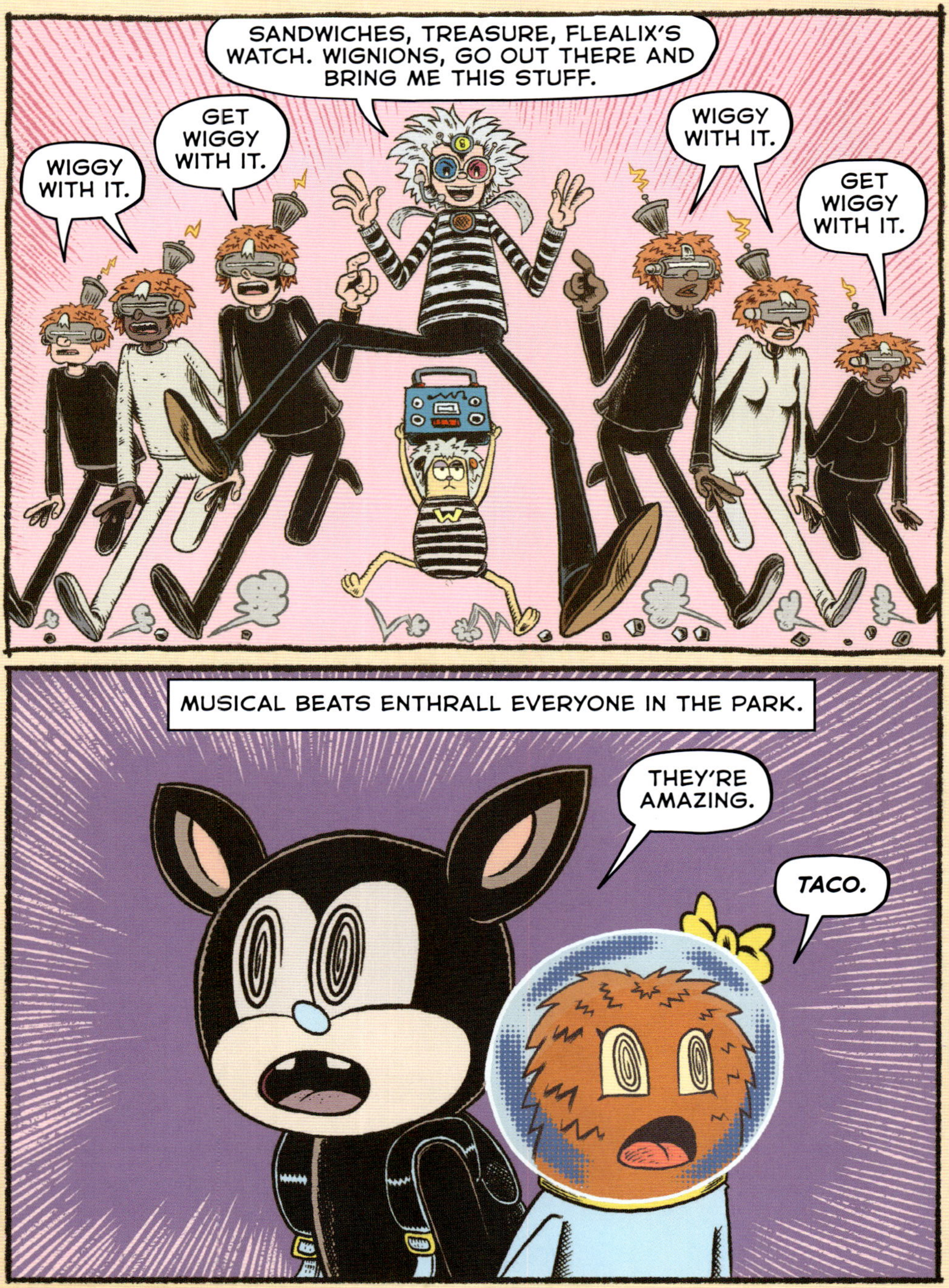
SANDWICHES, TREASURE, FLEALIX'S WATCH. WIGNIONS, GO OUT THERE AND BRING ME THIS STUFF.
WIGGY WITH IT.
GET WIGGY WITH IT.
WIGGY WITH IT.
GET WIGGY WITH IT.
MUSICAL BEATS ENTHRALL EVERYONE IN THE PARK.
THEY'RE AMAZING.
TACO.

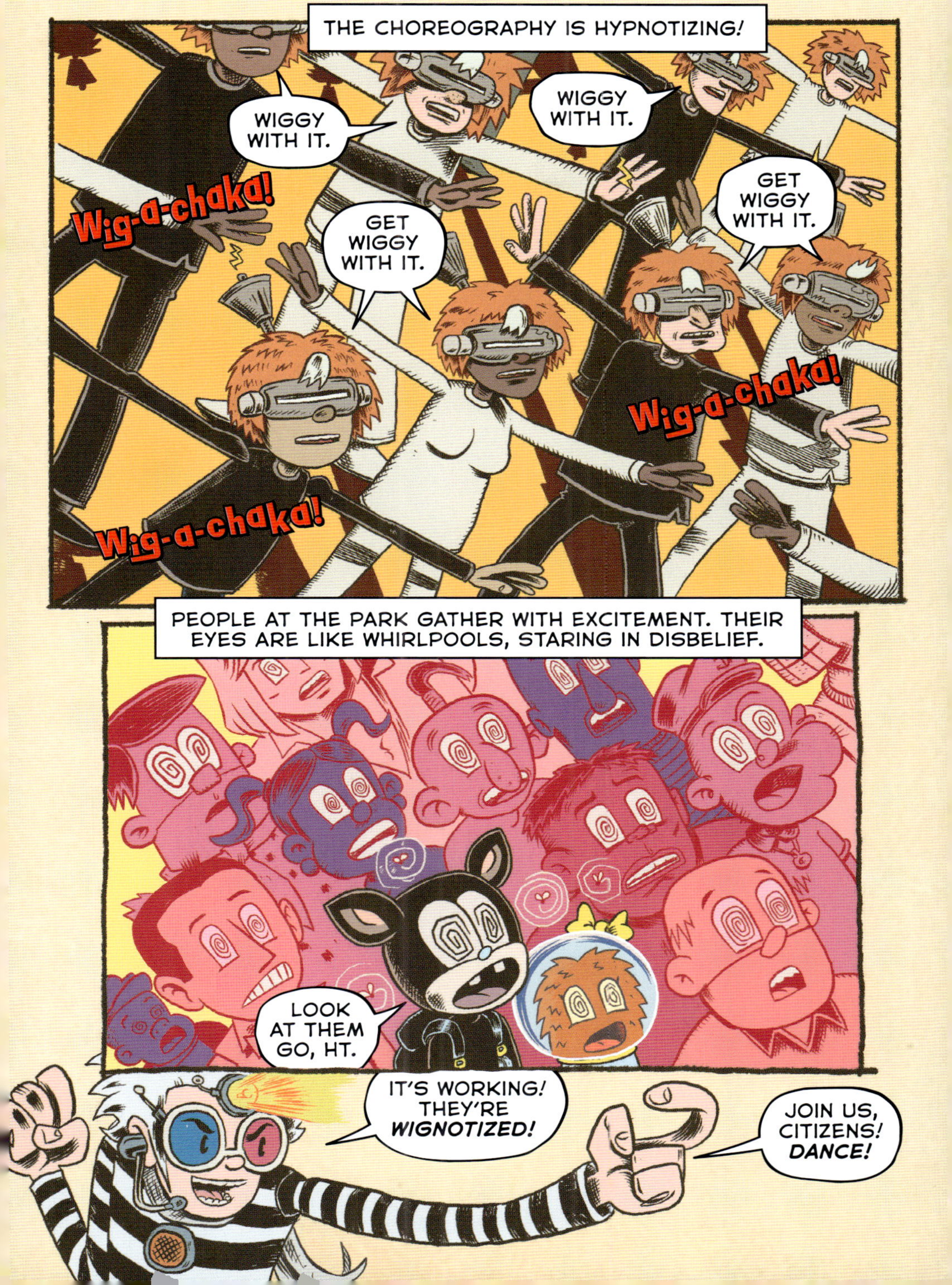
THE CHOREOGRAPHY IS HYPNOTIZING!
WIGGY WITH IT.
WIGGY WITH IT.
GET WIGGY WITH IT.
Wig-a-chaka!
GET WIGGY WITH IT.
Wig-a-chaka!
Wig-a-chaka!
PEOPLE AT THE PARK GATHER WITH EXCITEMENT. THEIR EYES ARE LIKE WHIRLPOOLS, STARING IN DISBELIEF.
LOOK AT THEM GO, HT.
IT'S WORKING! THEY'RE *WIGNOTIZED!*
JOIN US, CITIZENS! *DANCE!*

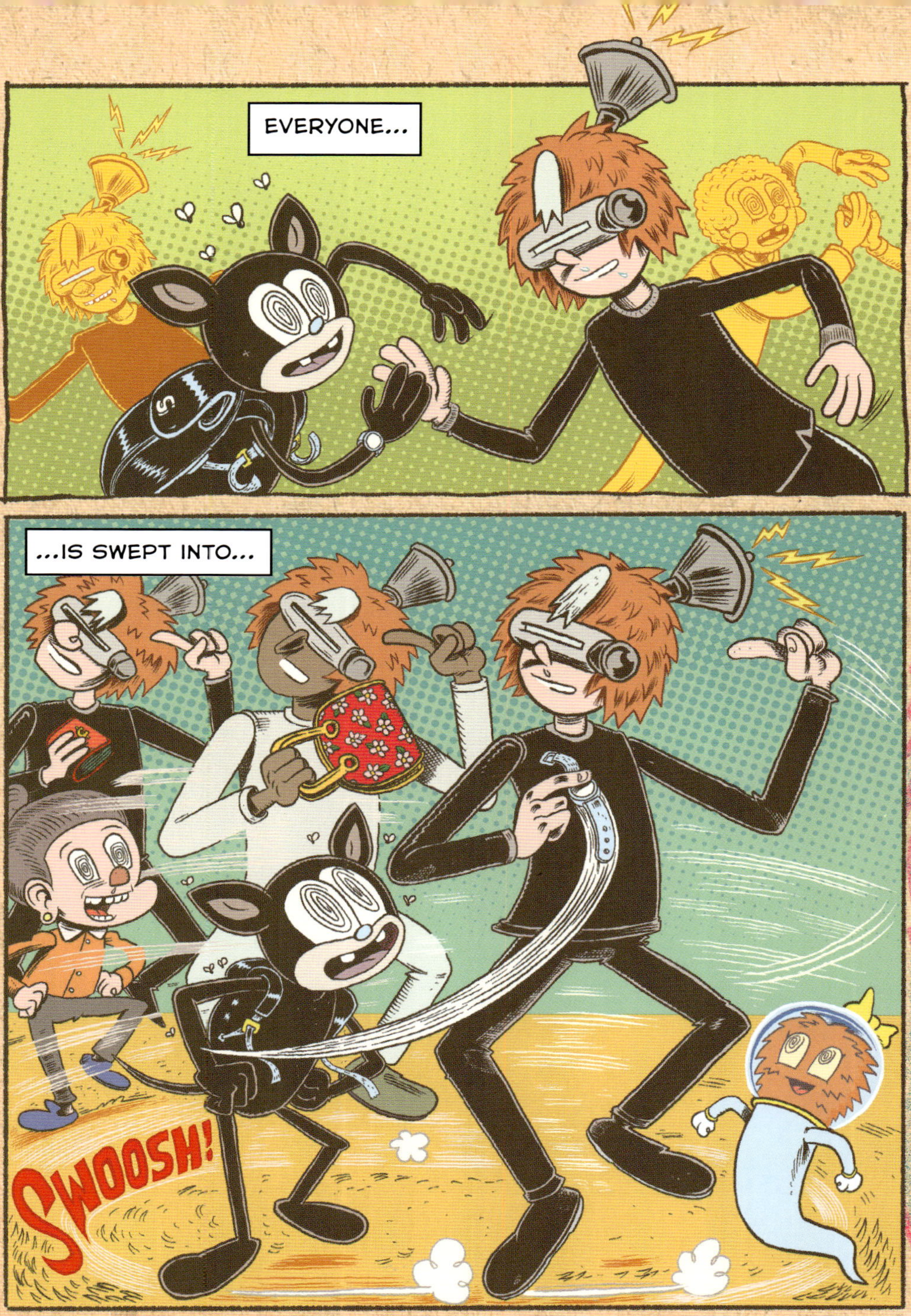
EVERYONE...
...IS SWEPT INTO...
SWOOSH!

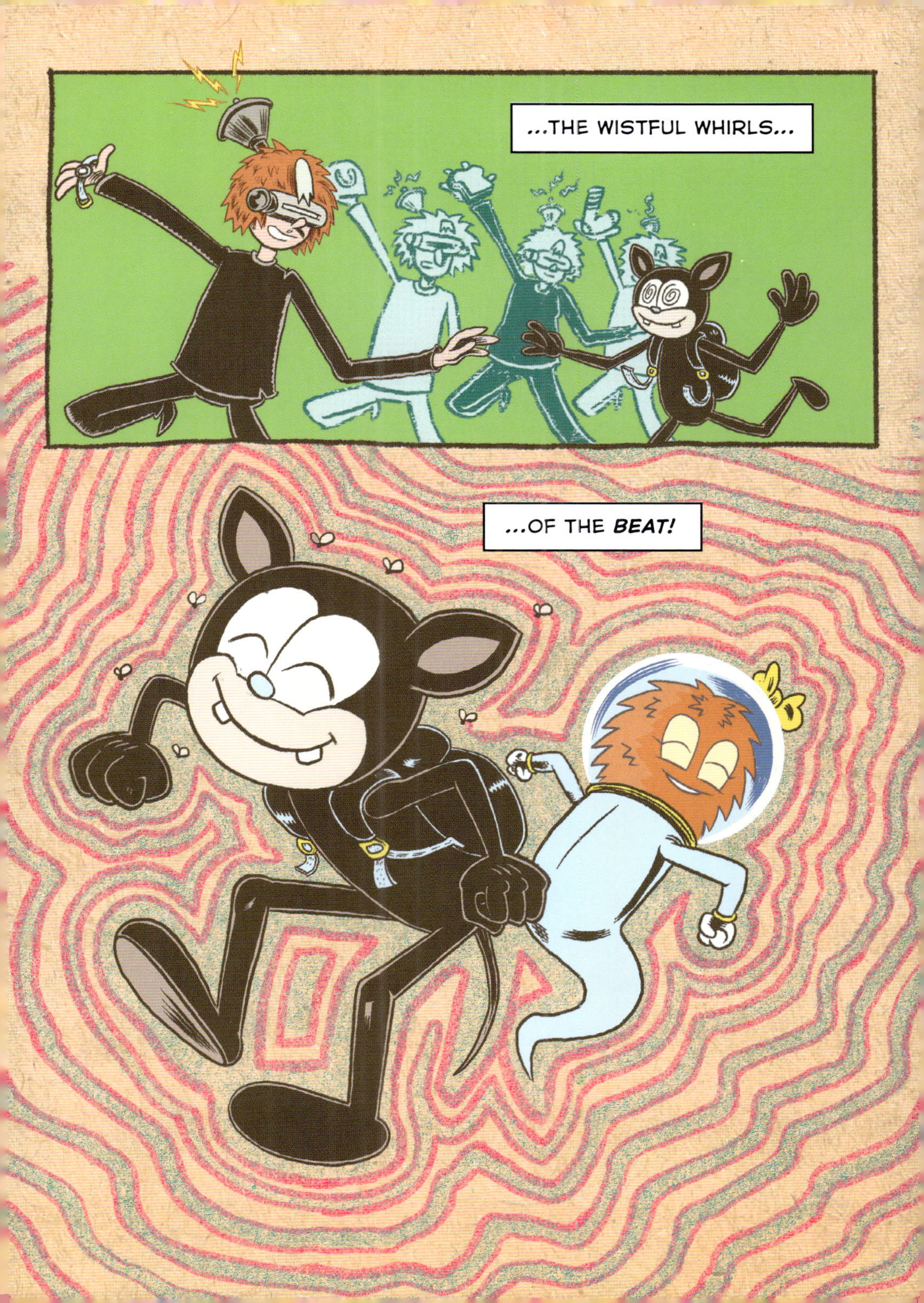
...THE WISTFUL WHIRLS...
...OF THE ***BEAT!***

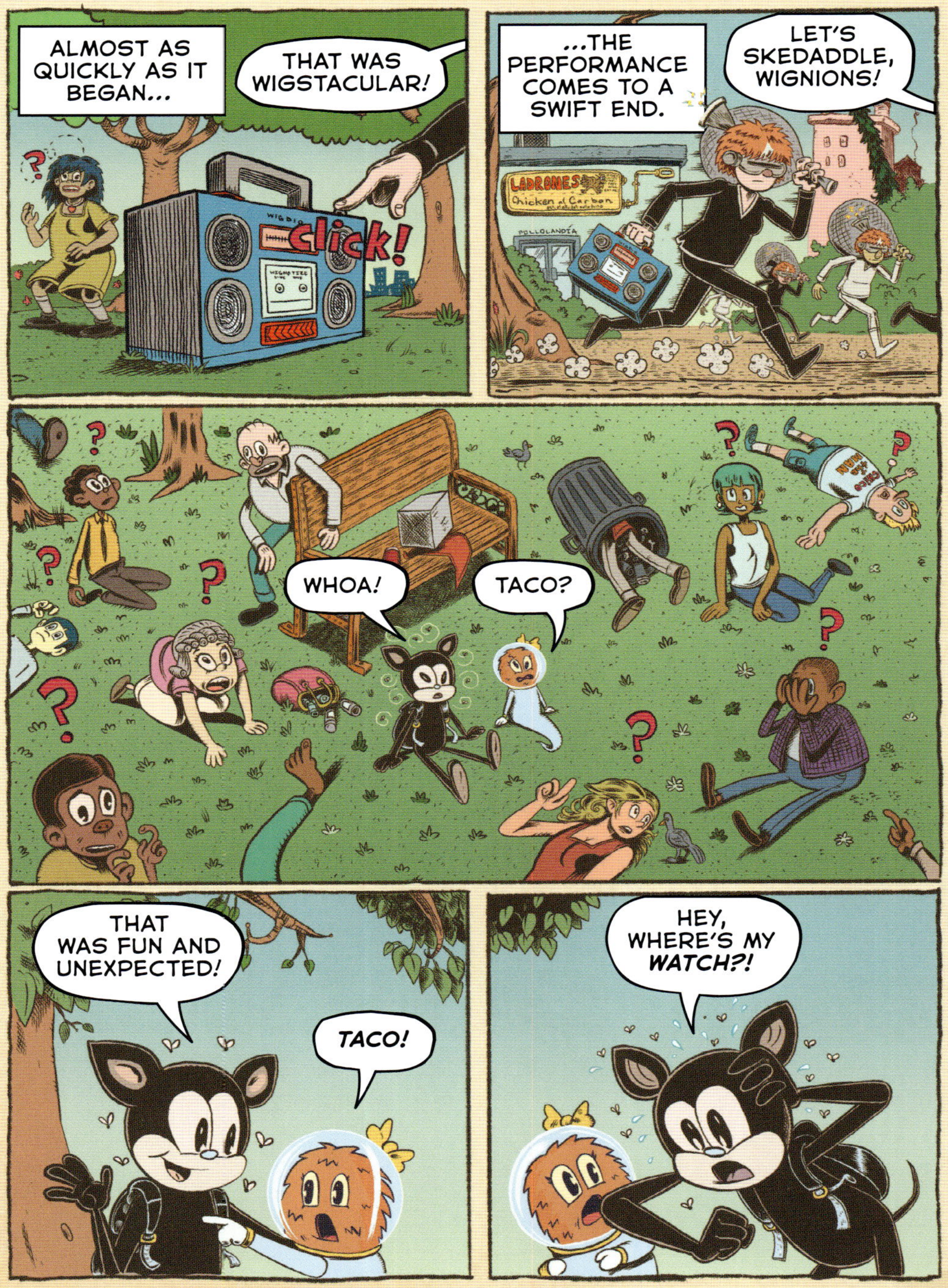
ALMOST AS QUICKLY AS IT BEGAN...
THAT WAS WIGSTACULAR!
CLICK!
...THE PERFORMANCE COMES TO A SWIFT END.
LET'S SKEDADDLE, WIGNIONS!
LADRONES
Chicken al Carbon
POLLOLANDIA
WHOA!
TACO?
THAT WAS FUN AND UNEXPECTED!
TACO!
HEY, WHERE'S MY WATCH?!

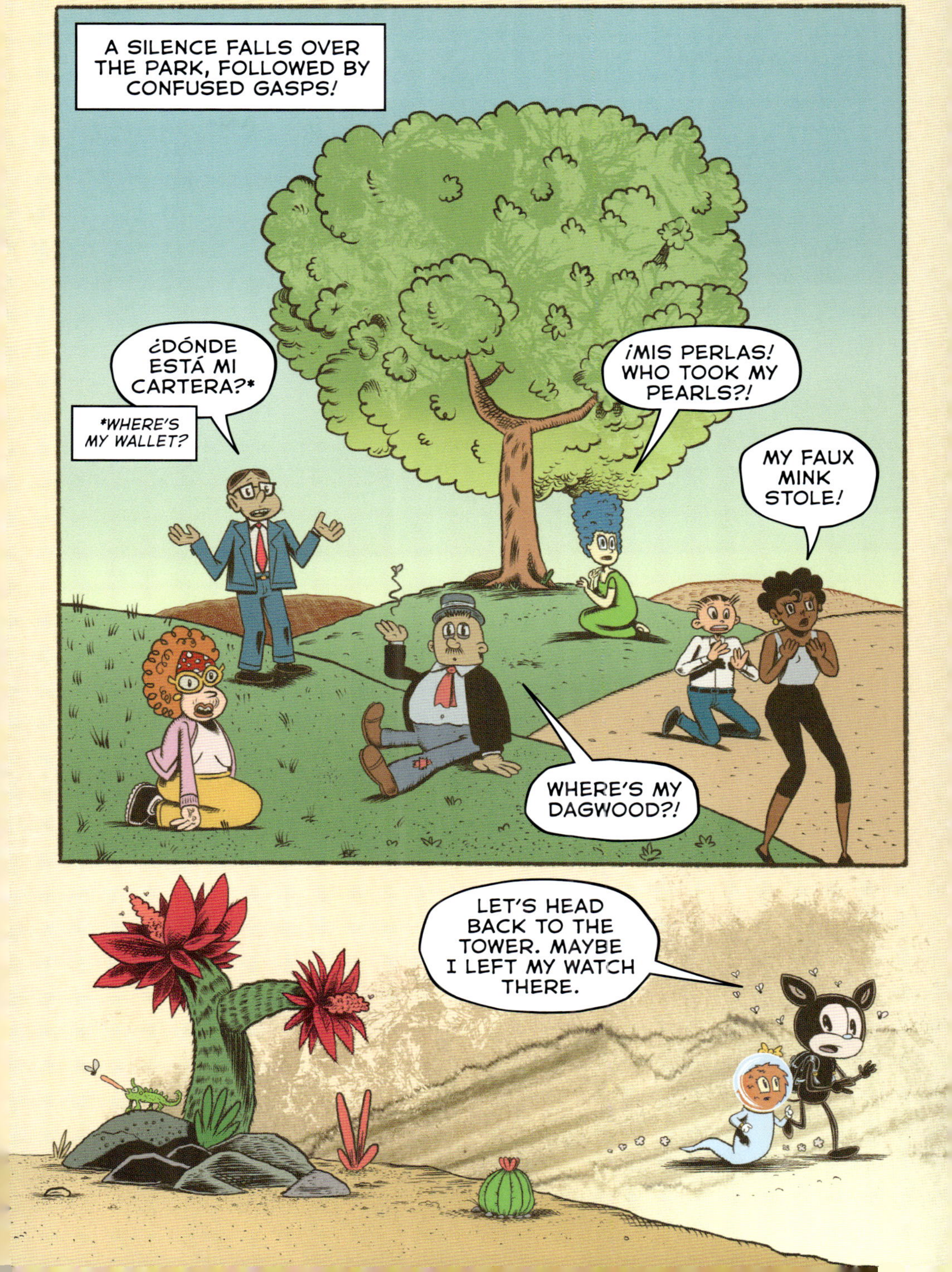
A SILENCE FALLS OVER THE PARK, FOLLOWED BY CONFUSED GASPS!
¿DÓNDE ESTÁ MI CARTERA?*
*WHERE'S MY WALLET?
¡MIS PERLAS! WHO TOOK MY PEARLS?!
MY FAUX MINK STOLE!
WHERE'S MY DAGWOOD?!
LET'S HEAD BACK TO THE TOWER. MAYBE I LEFT MY WATCH THERE.

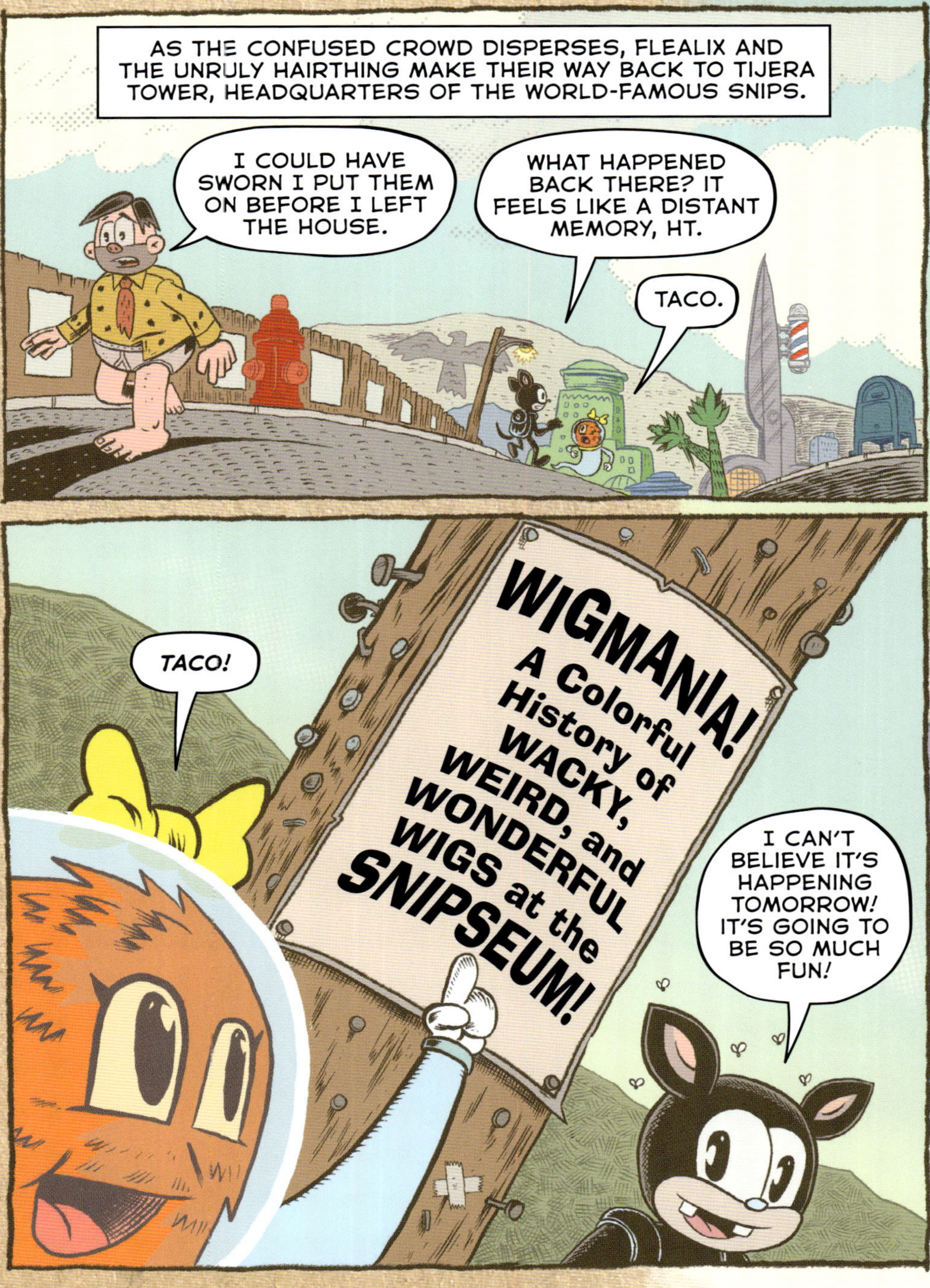
AS THE CONFUSED CROWD DISPERSES, FLEALIX AND THE UNRULY HAIRTHING MAKE THEIR WAY BACK TO TIJERA TOWER, HEADQUARTERS OF THE WORLD-FAMOUS SNIPS.
I COULD HAVE SWORN I PUT THEM ON BEFORE I LEFT THE HOUSE.
WHAT HAPPENED BACK THERE? IT FEELS LIKE A DISTANT MEMORY, HT.
TACO.
TACO!
WIGMANIA! A Colorful History of WACKY, WEIRD, and WONDERFUL WIGS at the SNIPSEUM!
I CAN'T BELIEVE IT'S HAPPENING TOMORROW! IT'S GOING TO BE SO MUCH FUN!

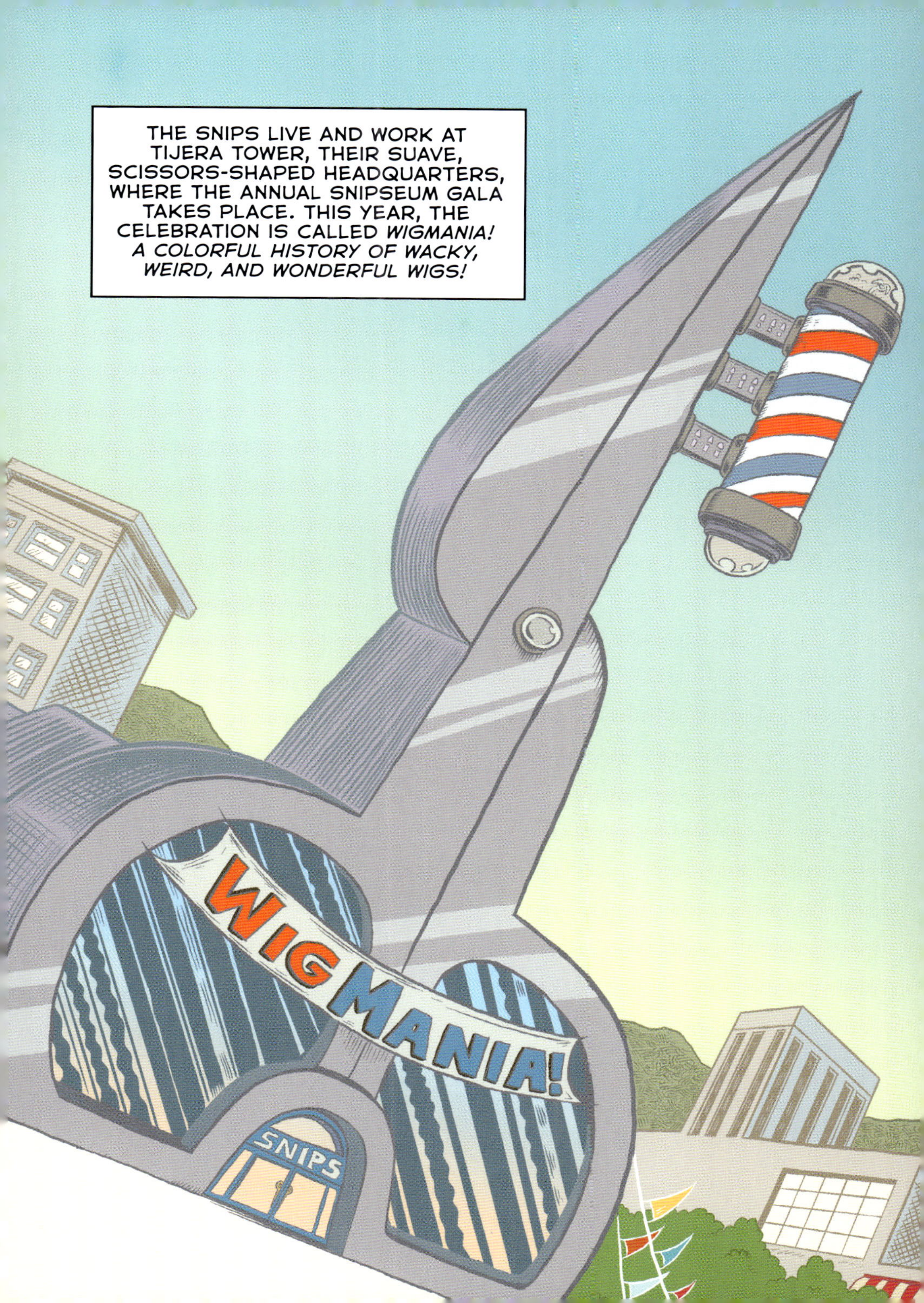
THE SNIPS LIVE AND WORK AT TIJERA TOWER, THEIR SUAVE, SCISSORS-SHAPED HEADQUARTERS, WHERE THE ANNUAL SNIPSEUM GALA TAKES PLACE. THIS YEAR, THE CELEBRATION IS CALLED *WIGMANIA! A COLORFUL HISTORY OF WACKY, WEIRD, AND WONDERFUL WIGS!*
WIGMANIA!
SNIPS

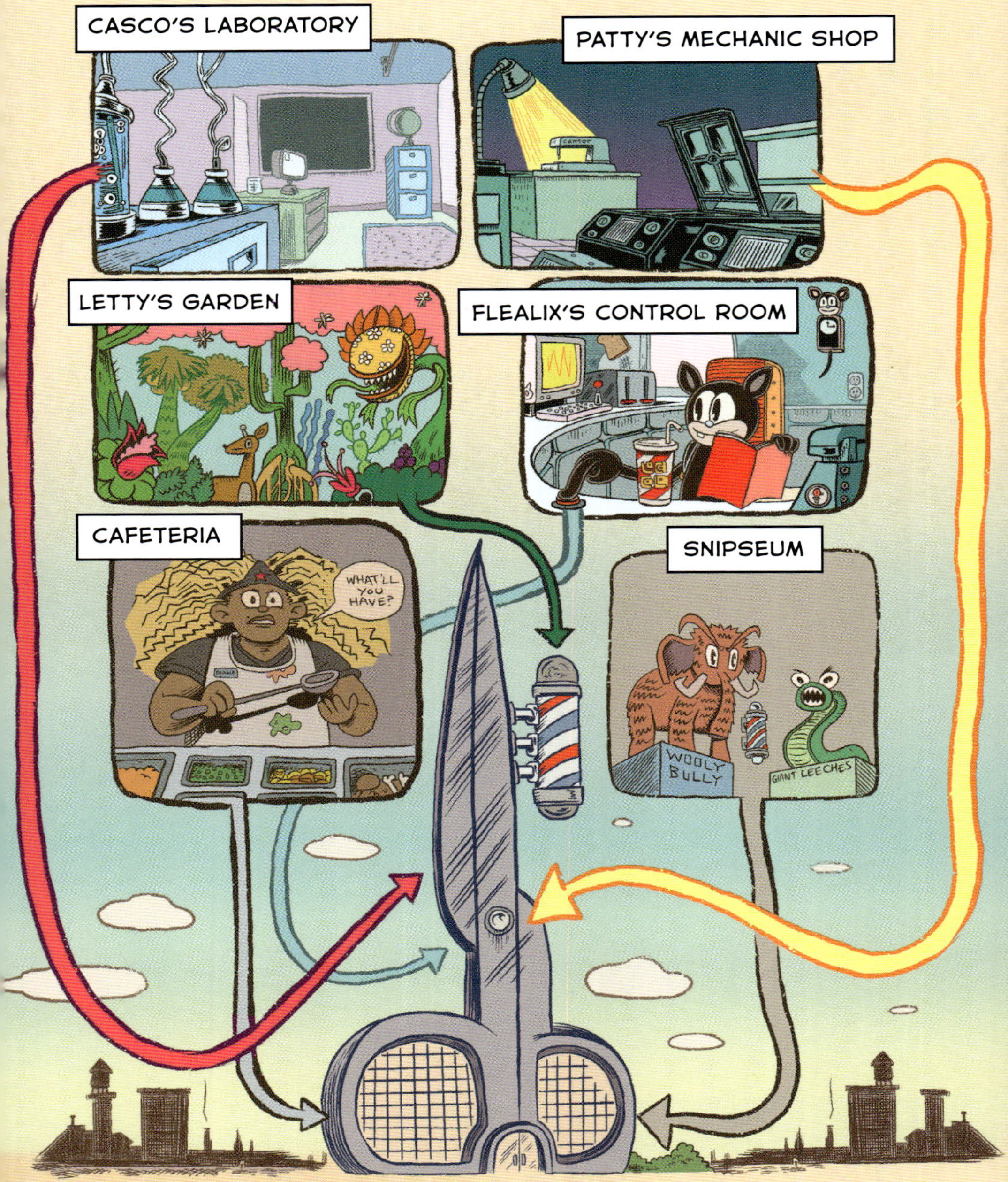
CASCO'S LABORATORY
PATTY'S MECHANIC SHOP
LETTY'S GARDEN
FLEALIX'S CONTROL ROOM
CAFETERIA
WHAT'LL YOU HAVE?
SNIPSEUM
WOOLY BULLY
GIANT LEECHES

LOOK AND SEE WHAT PATTY POMADA, NUBES CLOUDHEAD, LETTY LENTES, AND CASCO HARDHAT ARE UP TO!

PATTY IS HARD AT WORK ON HER SEWING MACHINE.

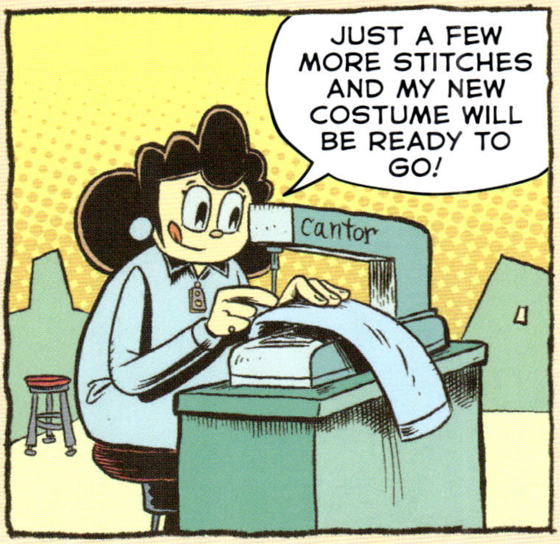

JUST A FEW MORE STITCHES AND MY NEW COSTUME WILL BE READY TO GO!
Cantor

NUBES IS MODIFYING A BARBER-POLE JET PACK.

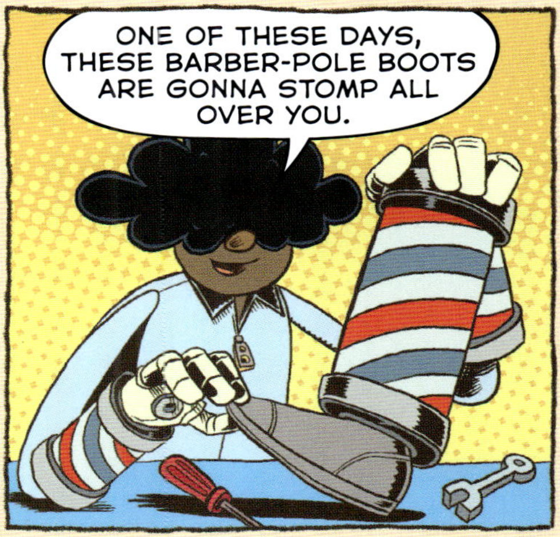

ONE OF THESE DAYS, THESE BARBER-POLE BOOTS ARE GONNA STOMP ALL OVER YOU.

LETTY IS STARING AT HER REFLECTION AND HISSING LIKE A SNAKE.

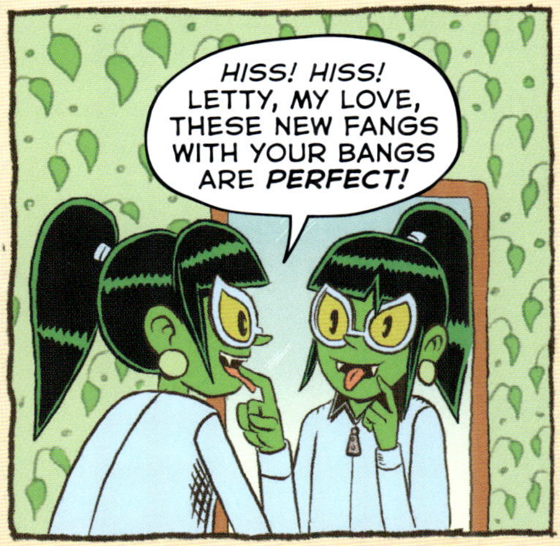

HISS! HISS! LETTY, MY LOVE, THESE NEW FANGS WITH YOUR BANGS ARE *PERFECT!*

AND CASCO IS...CASCO IS... ***HEY!*** WHERE'S CASCO?!

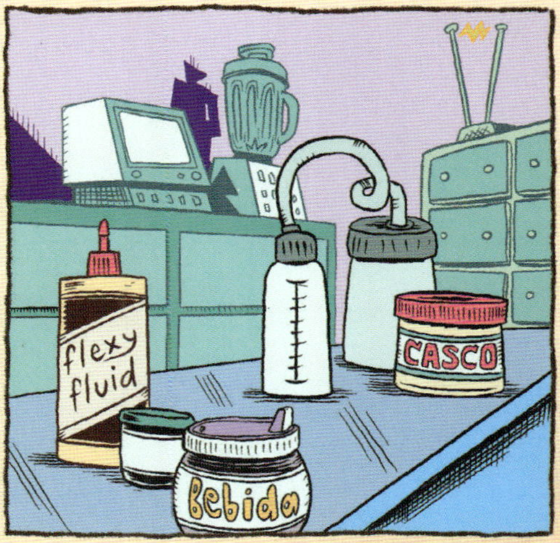

flexy fluid
CASCO
Bebida

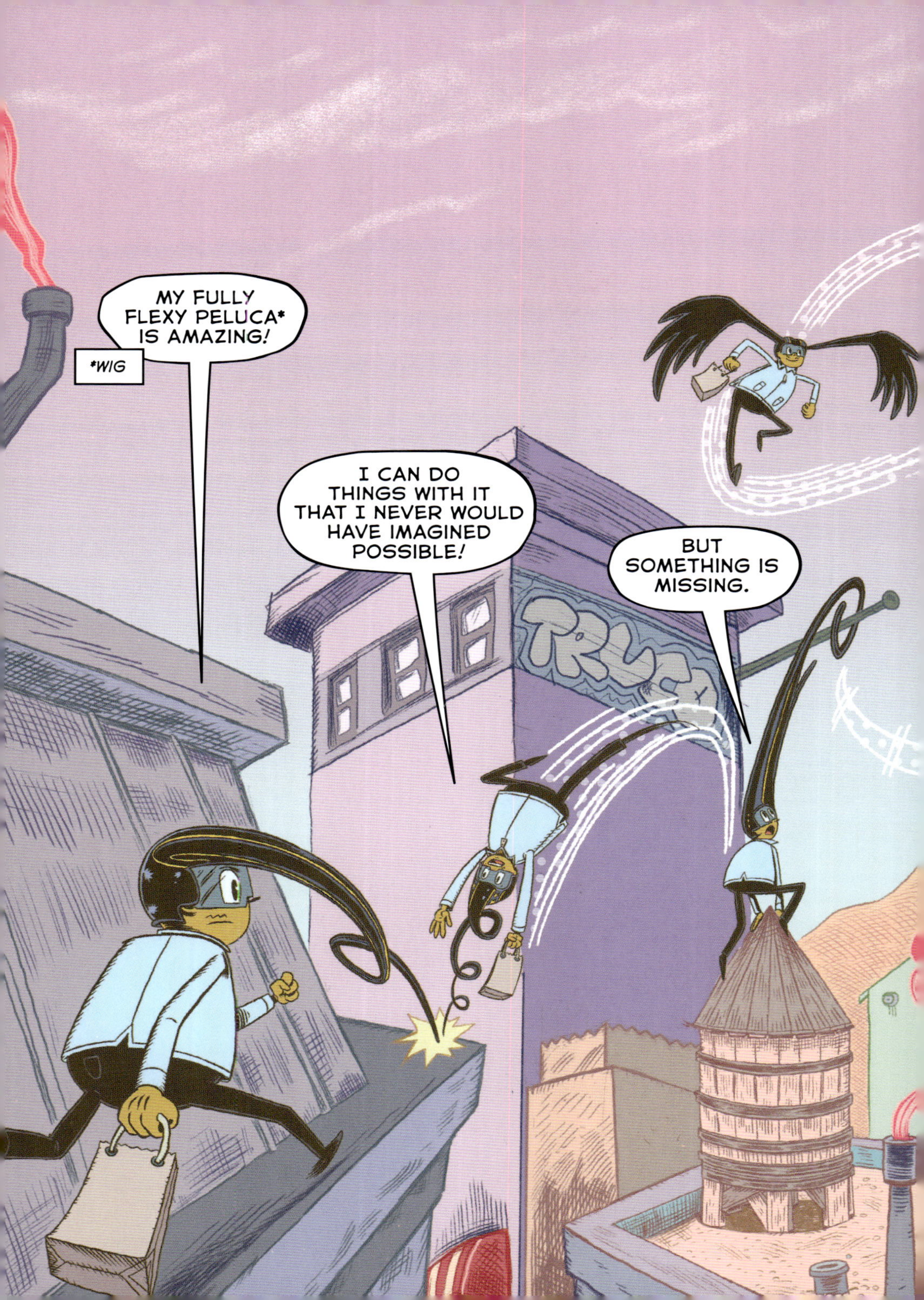
MY FULLY FLEXY PELUCA* IS AMAZING!
*WIG
I CAN DO THINGS WITH IT THAT I NEVER WOULD HAVE IMAGINED POSSIBLE!
BUT SOMETHING IS MISSING.

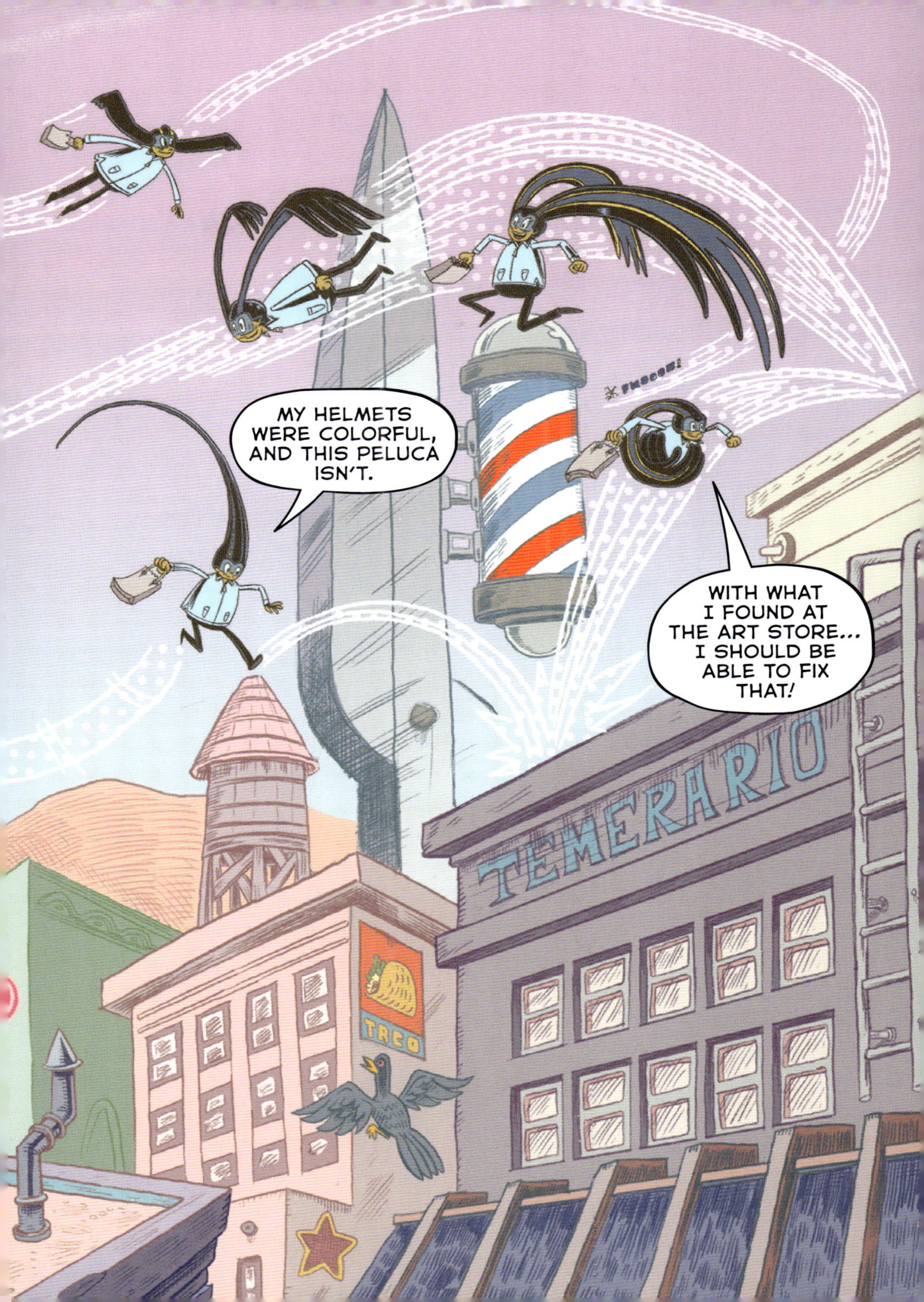
MY HELMETS WERE COLORFUL, AND THIS PELUCA ISN'T.
WITH WHAT I FOUND AT THE ART STORE... I SHOULD BE ABLE TO FIX THAT!
TEMERARIO
TACO

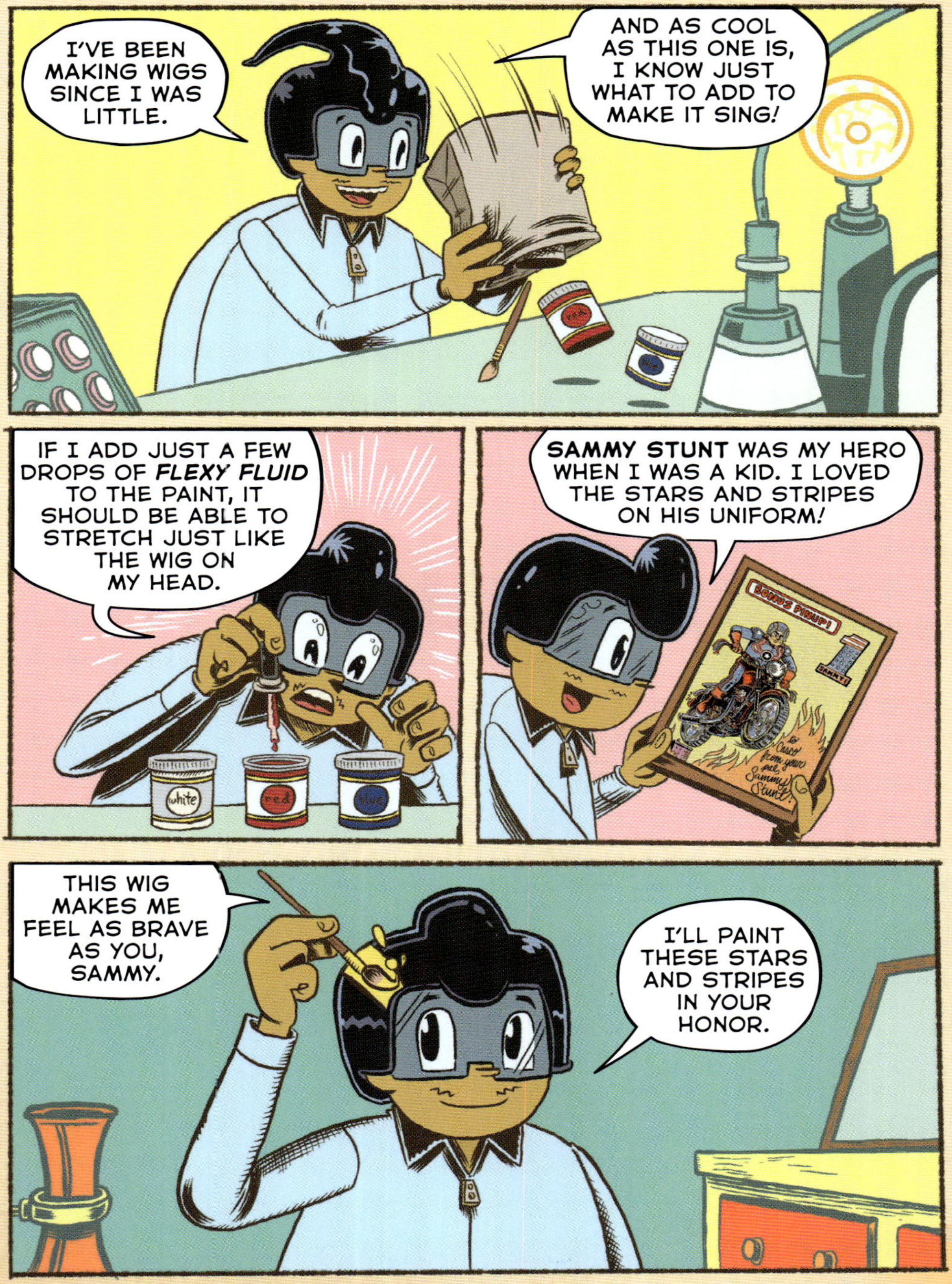
I'VE BEEN MAKING WIGS SINCE I WAS LITTLE.
AND AS COOL AS THIS ONE IS, I KNOW JUST WHAT TO ADD TO MAKE IT SING!
IF I ADD JUST A FEW DROPS OF FLEXY FLUID TO THE PAINT, IT SHOULD BE ABLE TO STRETCH JUST LIKE THE WIG ON MY HEAD.
SAMMY STUNT WAS MY HERO WHEN I WAS A KID. I LOVED THE STARS AND STRIPES ON HIS UNIFORM!
THIS WIG MAKES ME FEEL AS BRAVE AS YOU, SAMMY.
I'LL PAINT THESE STARS AND STRIPES IN YOUR HONOR.

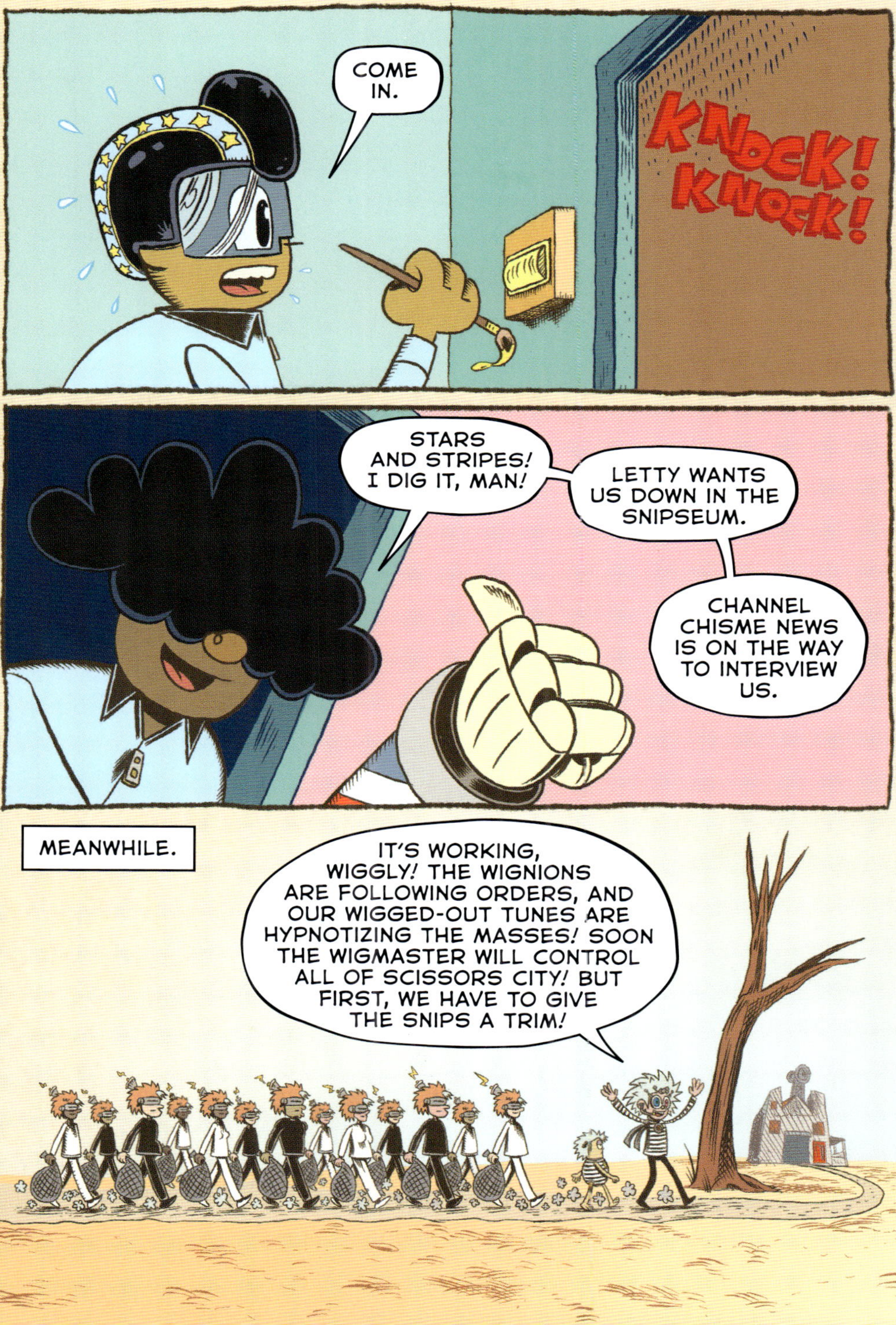
COME IN.
KNOCK! KNOCK!
STARS AND STRIPES! I DIG IT, MAN!
LETTY WANTS US DOWN IN THE SNIPSEUM.
CHANNEL CHISME NEWS IS ON THE WAY TO INTERVIEW US.
MEANWHILE.
IT'S WORKING, WIGGLY! THE WIGNIONS ARE FOLLOWING ORDERS, AND OUR WIGGED-OUT TUNES ARE HYPNOTIZING THE MASSES! SOON THE WIGMASTER WILL CONTROL ALL OF SCISSORS CITY! BUT FIRST, WE HAVE TO GIVE THE SNIPS A TRIM!

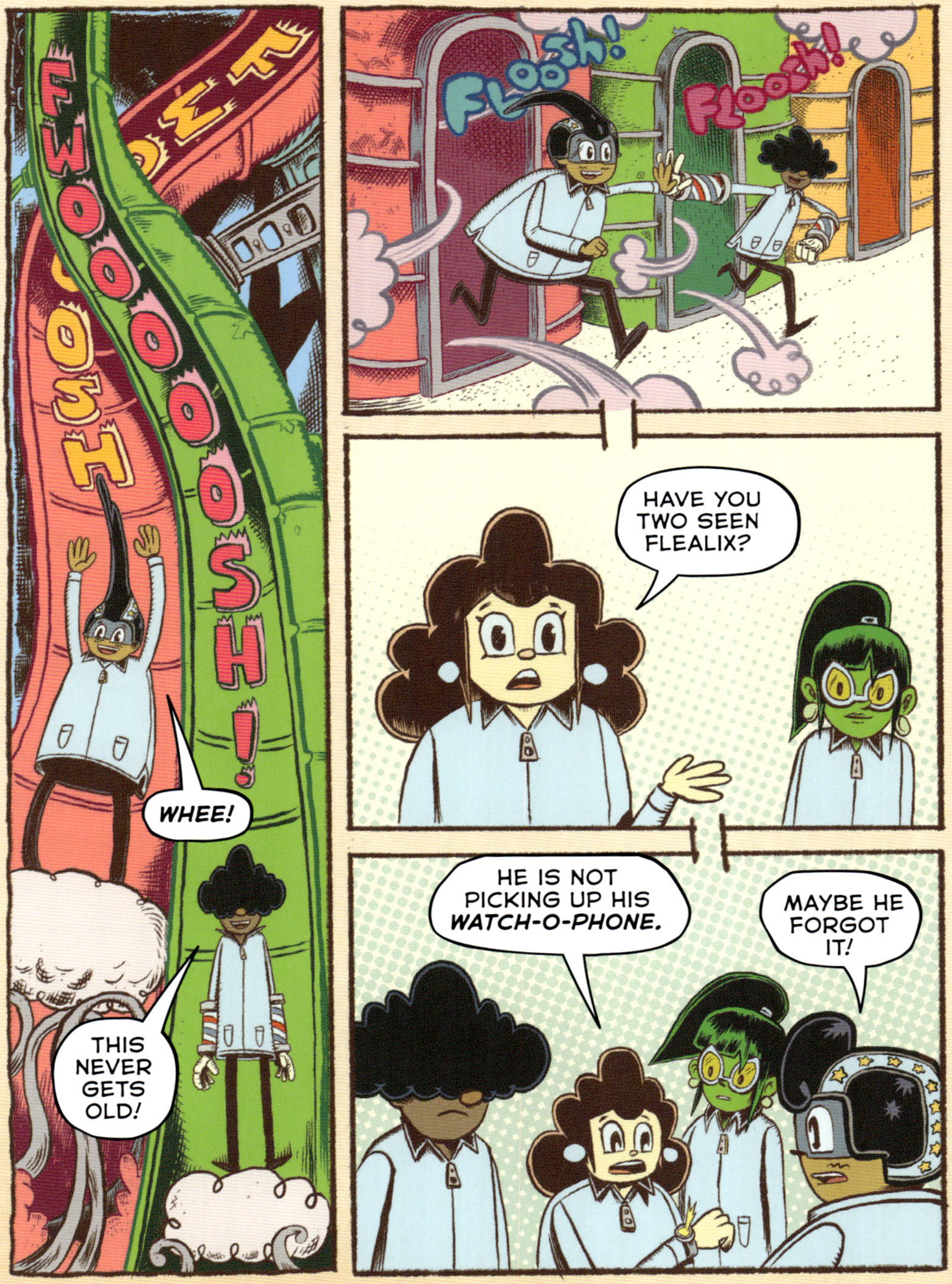
FWOOOOOOOSH!
WOOSH
WHEE!
THIS NEVER GETS OLD!
FLOOSH!
FLOOSH!
HAVE YOU TWO SEEN FLEALIX?
HE IS NOT PICKING UP HIS *WATCH-O-PHONE.*
MAYBE HE FORGOT IT!

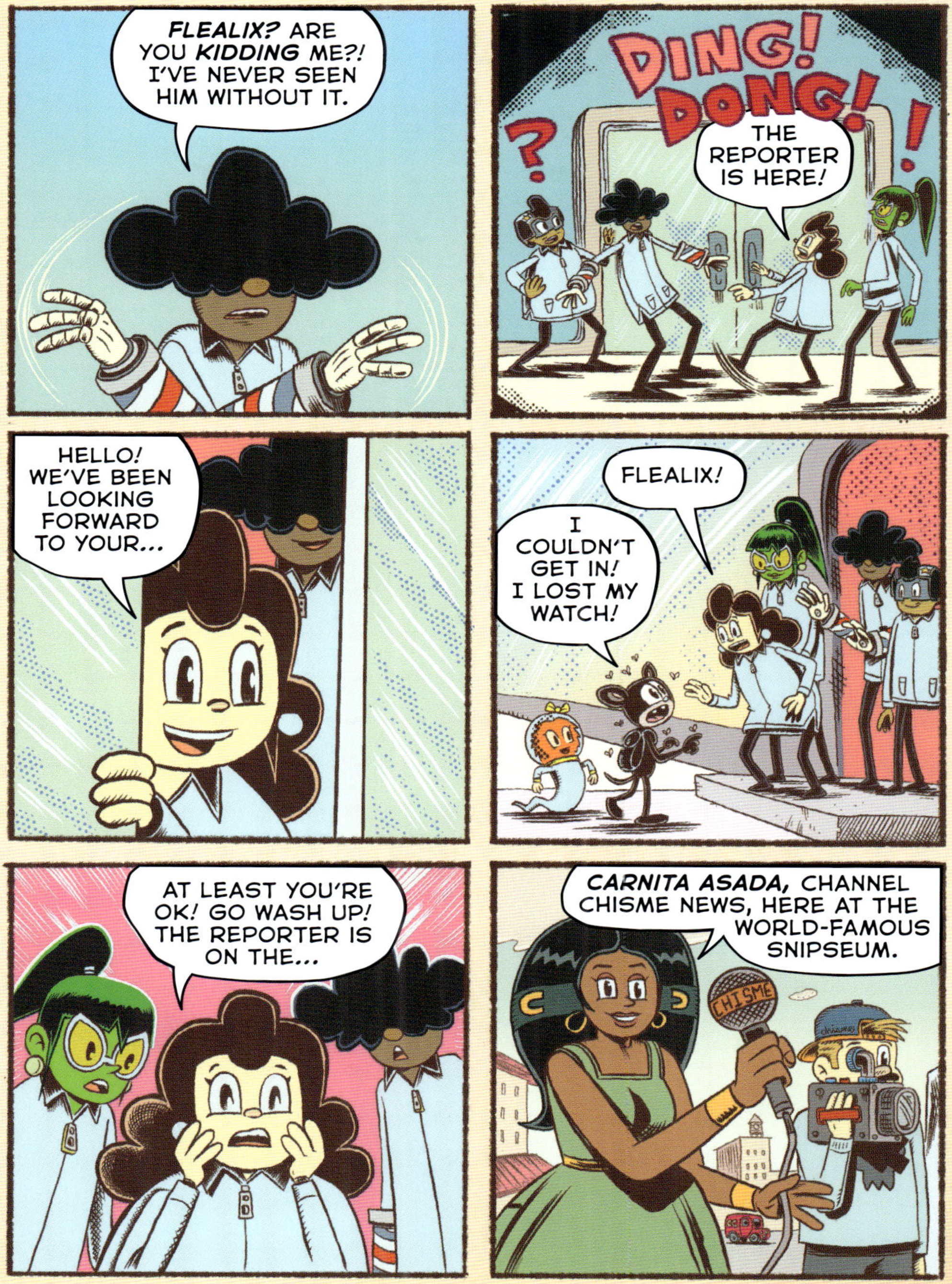

FLEALIX? ARE YOU *KIDDING* ME?! I'VE NEVER SEEN HIM WITHOUT IT.
DING! DONG!
?
!
THE REPORTER IS HERE!
HELLO! WE'VE BEEN LOOKING FORWARD TO YOUR...
FLEALIX!
I COULDN'T GET IN! I LOST MY WATCH!
AT LEAST YOU'RE OK! GO WASH UP! THE REPORTER IS ON THE...
CARNITA ASADA, CHANNEL CHISME NEWS, HERE AT THE WORLD-FAMOUS SNIPSEUM.
CHISME

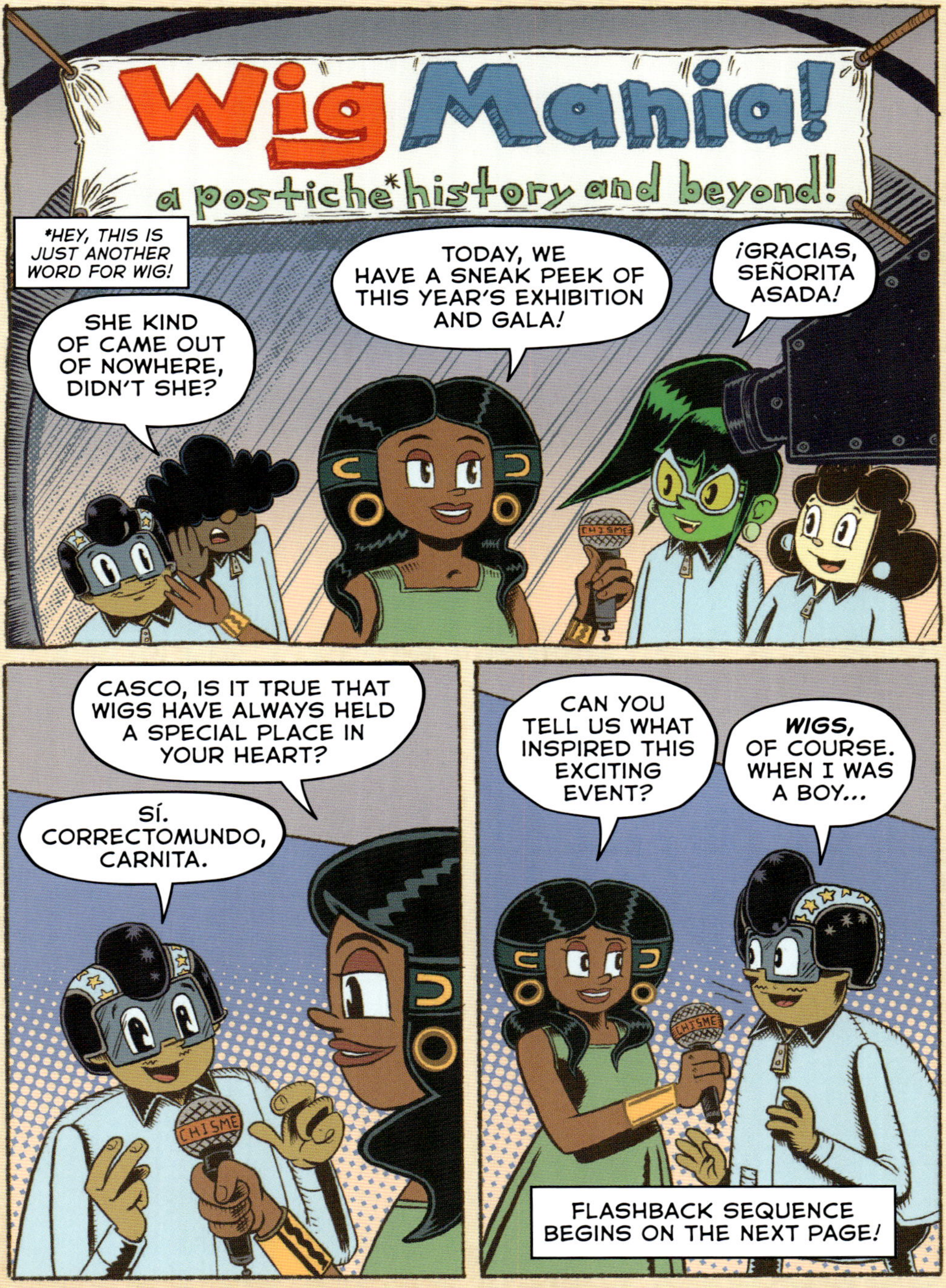
Wig Mania! a postiche* history and beyond!
*HEY, THIS IS JUST ANOTHER WORD FOR WIG!
SHE KIND OF CAME OUT OF NOWHERE, DIDN'T SHE?
TODAY, WE HAVE A SNEAK PEEK OF THIS YEAR'S EXHIBITION AND GALA!
¡GRACIAS, SEÑORITA ASADA!
CHISME
CASCO, IS IT TRUE THAT WIGS HAVE ALWAYS HELD A SPECIAL PLACE IN YOUR HEART?
SÍ. CORRECTOMUNDO, CARNITA.
CHISME
CAN YOU TELL US WHAT INSPIRED THIS EXCITING EVENT?
WIGS, OF COURSE. WHEN I WAS A BOY...
CHISME
FLASHBACK SEQUENCE BEGINS ON THE NEXT PAGE!

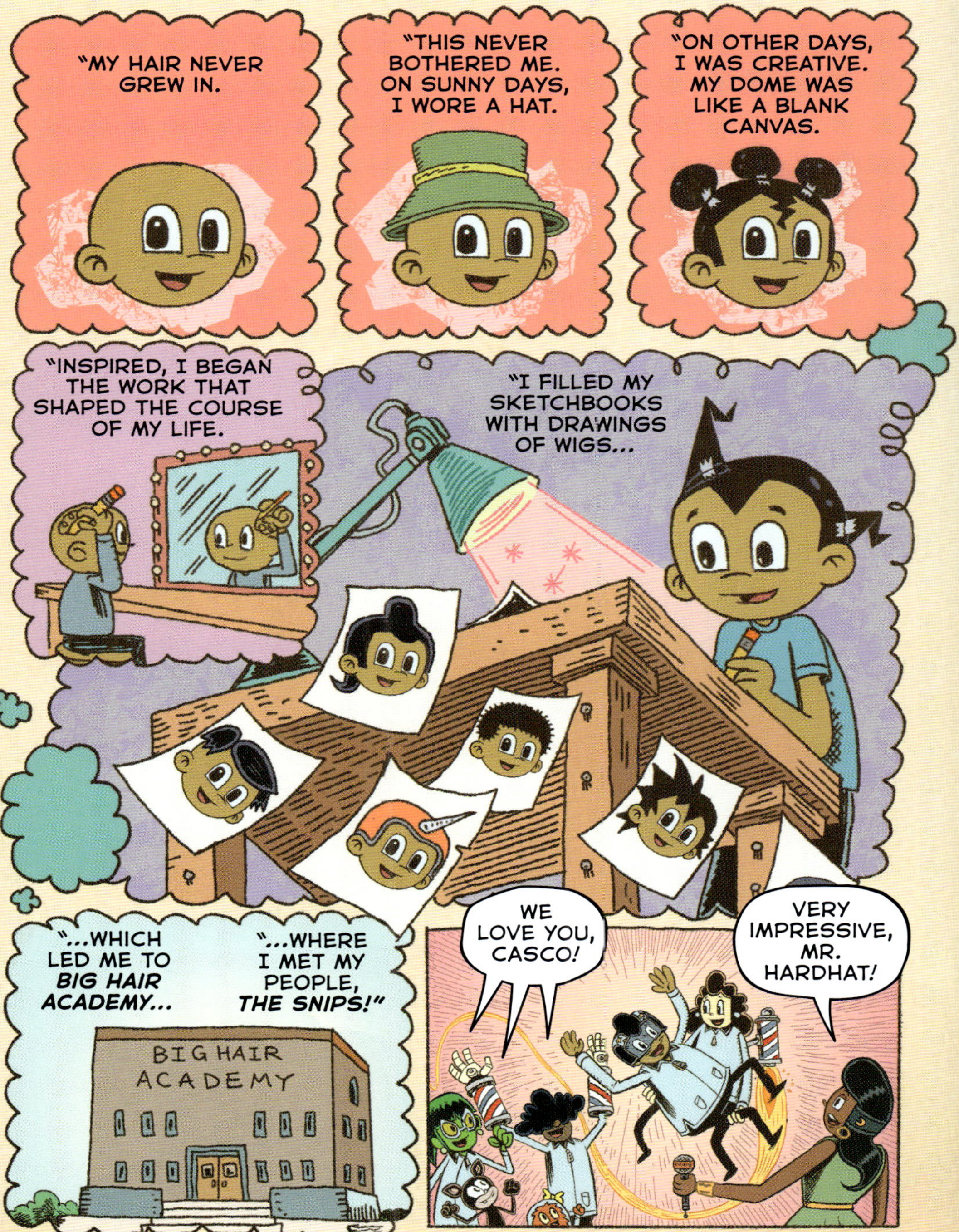
"MY HAIR NEVER GREW IN.
"THIS NEVER BOTHERED ME. ON SUNNY DAYS, I WORE A HAT.
"ON OTHER DAYS, I WAS CREATIVE. MY DOME WAS LIKE A BLANK CANVAS.
"INSPIRED, I BEGAN THE WORK THAT SHAPED THE COURSE OF MY LIFE.
"I FILLED MY SKETCHBOOKS WITH DRAWINGS OF WIGS...
"...WHICH LED ME TO BIG HAIR ACADEMY...
"...WHERE I MET MY PEOPLE, THE SNIPS!"
BIG HAIR ACADEMY
WE LOVE YOU, CASCO!
VERY IMPRESSIVE, MR. HARDHAT!

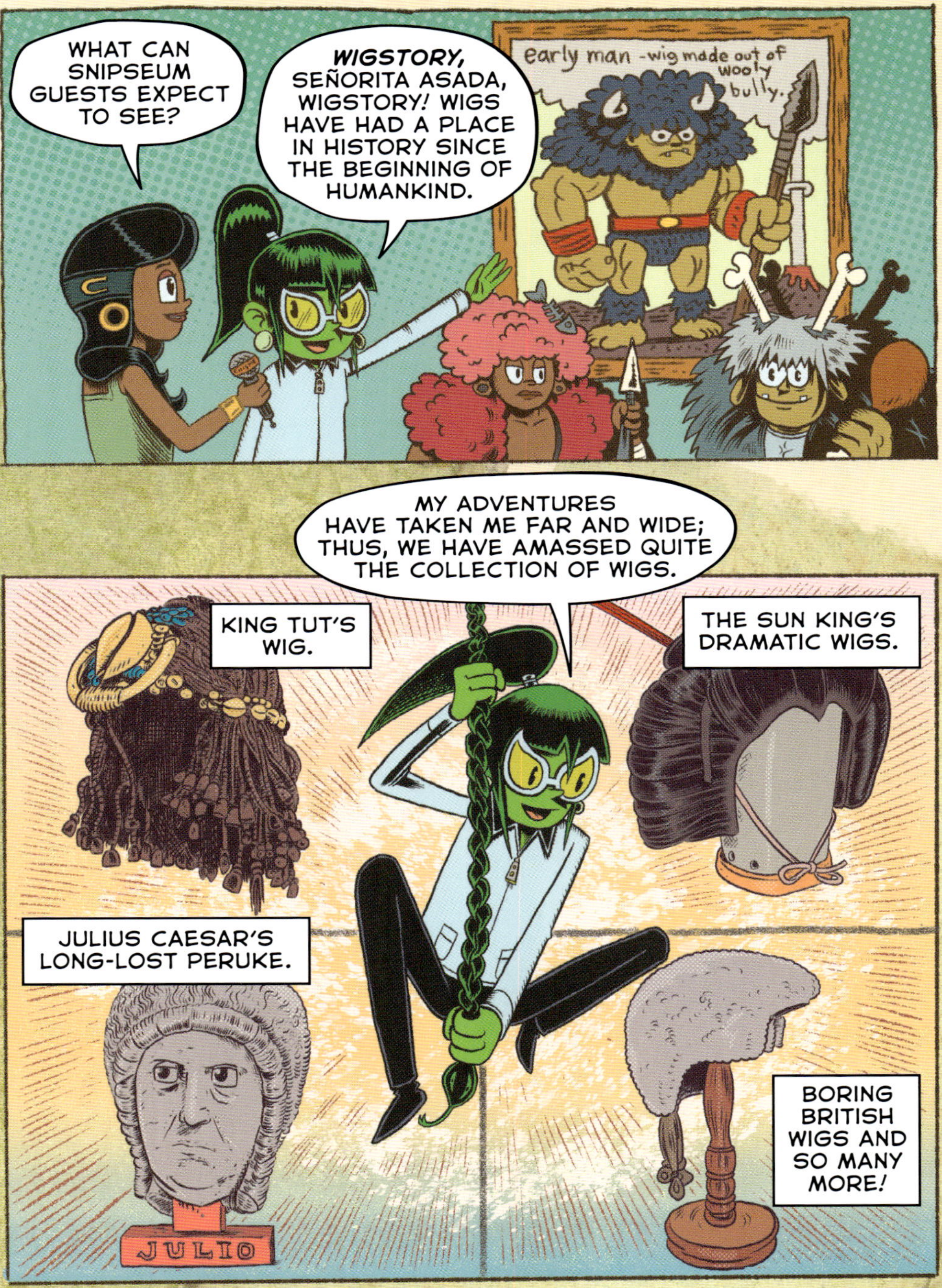
WHAT CAN SNIPSEUM GUESTS EXPECT TO SEE?
WIGSTORY, SEÑORITA ASADA, WIGSTORY! WIGS HAVE HAD A PLACE IN HISTORY SINCE THE BEGINNING OF HUMANKIND.
early man -wig made out of wooly bully.
MY ADVENTURES HAVE TAKEN ME FAR AND WIDE; THUS, WE HAVE AMASSED QUITE THE COLLECTION OF WIGS.
KING TUT'S WIG.
THE SUN KING'S DRAMATIC WIGS.
JULIUS CAESAR'S LONG-LOST PERUKE.
JULIO
BORING BRITISH WIGS AND SO MANY MORE!

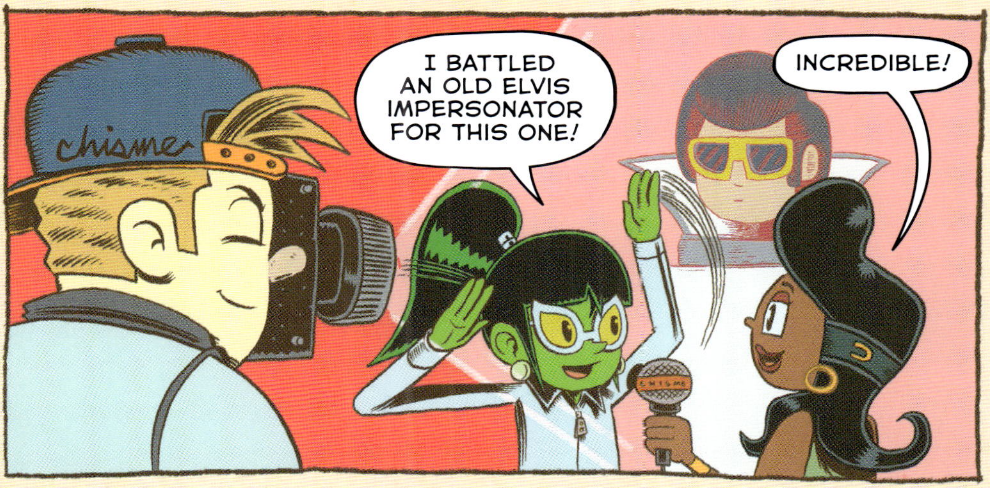
chisme
I BATTLED AN OLD ELVIS IMPERSONATOR FOR THIS ONE!
INCREDIBLE!

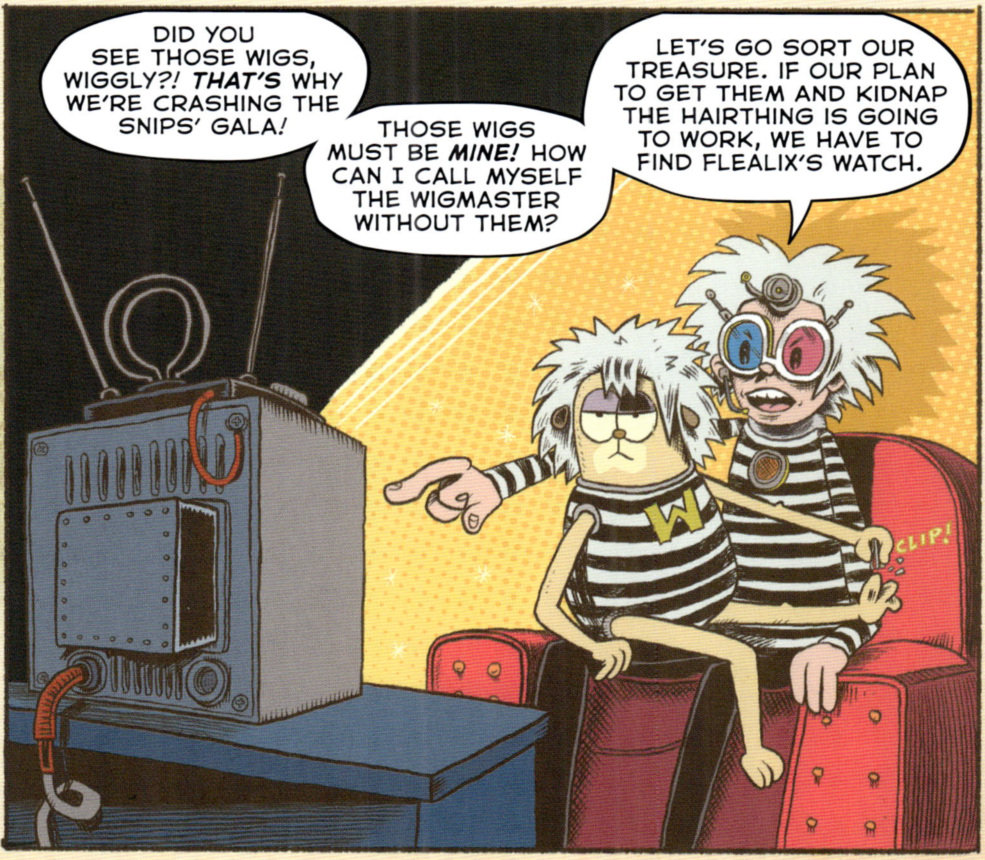
DID YOU SEE THOSE WIGS, WIGGLY?! *THAT'S* WHY WE'RE CRASHING THE SNIPS' GALA!
THOSE WIGS MUST BE *MINE!* HOW CAN I CALL MYSELF THE WIGMASTER WITHOUT THEM?
LET'S GO SORT OUR TREASURE. IF OUR PLAN TO GET THEM AND KIDNAP THE HAIRTHING IS GOING TO WORK, WE HAVE TO FIND FLEALIX'S WATCH.
CLIP!

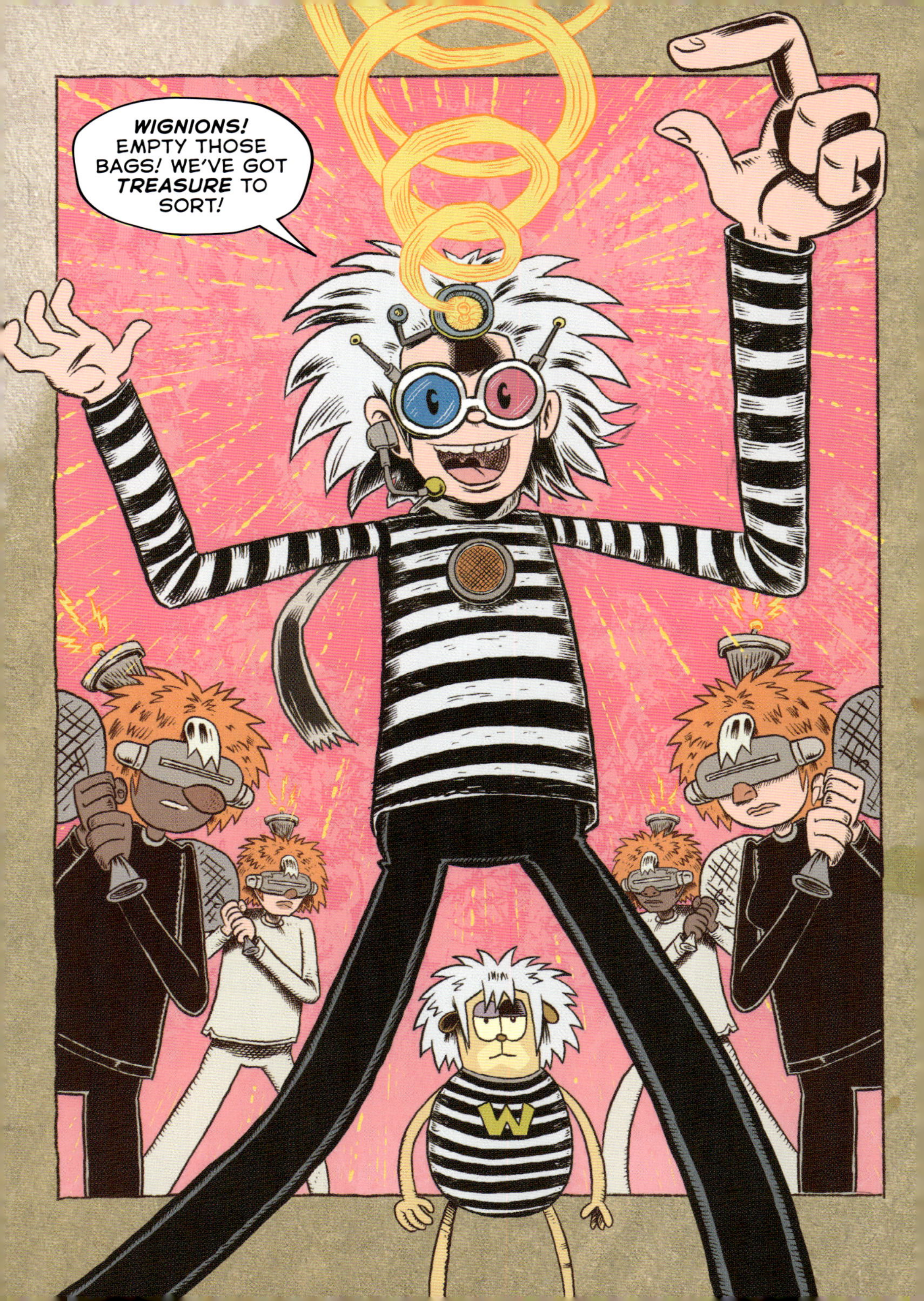

WIGNIONS! EMPTY THOSE BAGS! WE'VE GOT ***TREASURE*** TO SORT!

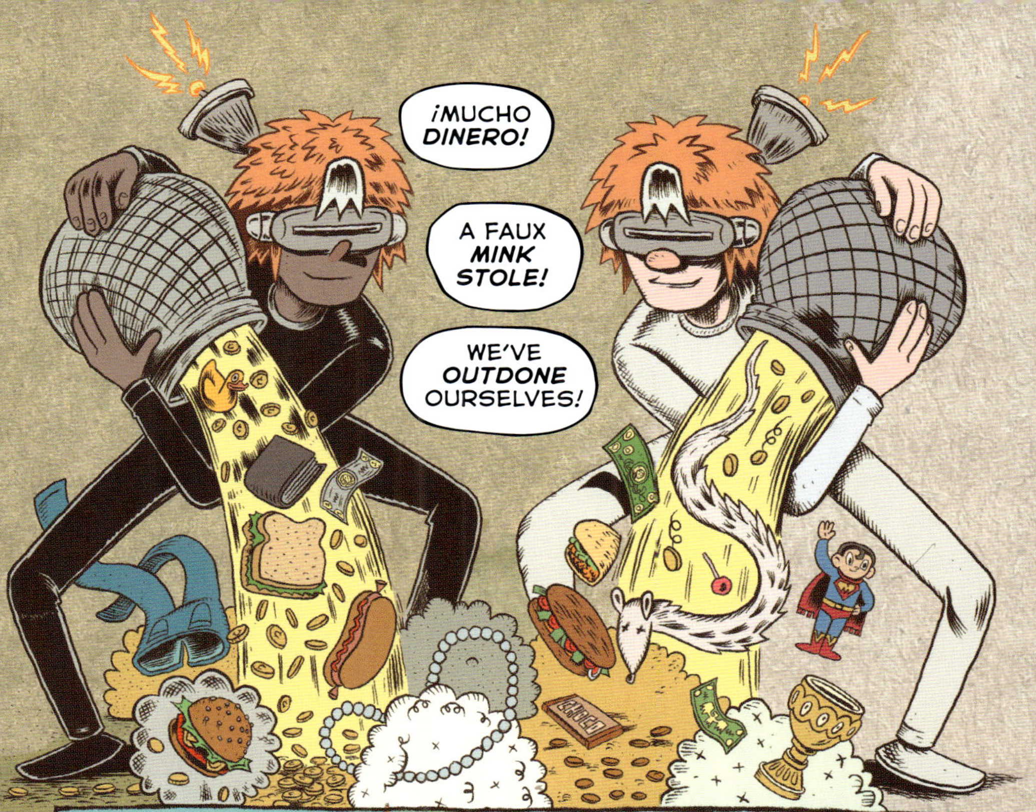
¡MUCHO *DINERO!*
A FAUX *MINK STOLE!*
WE'VE *OUTDONE* OURSELVES!

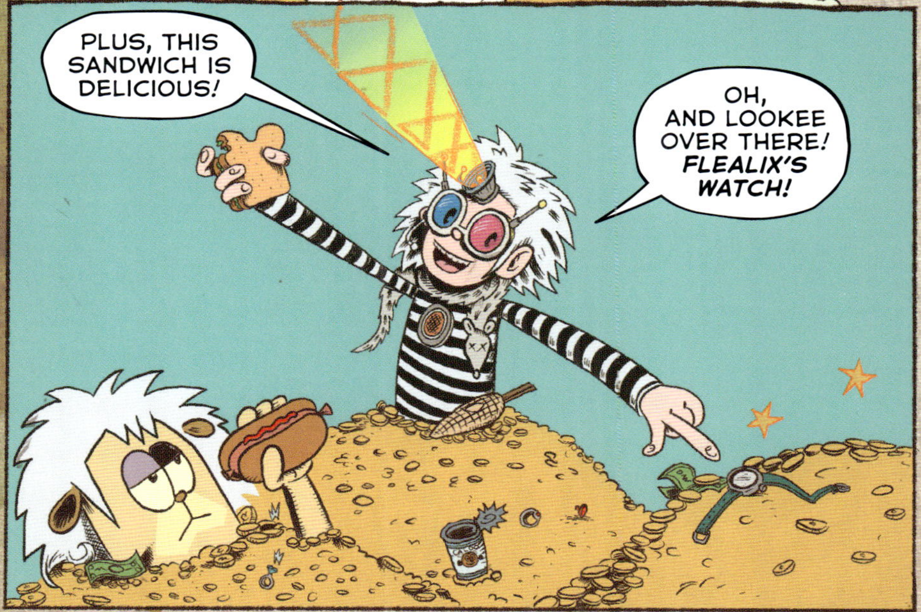
PLUS, THIS SANDWICH IS DELICIOUS!
OH, AND LOOKEE OVER THERE! *FLEALIX'S WATCH!*

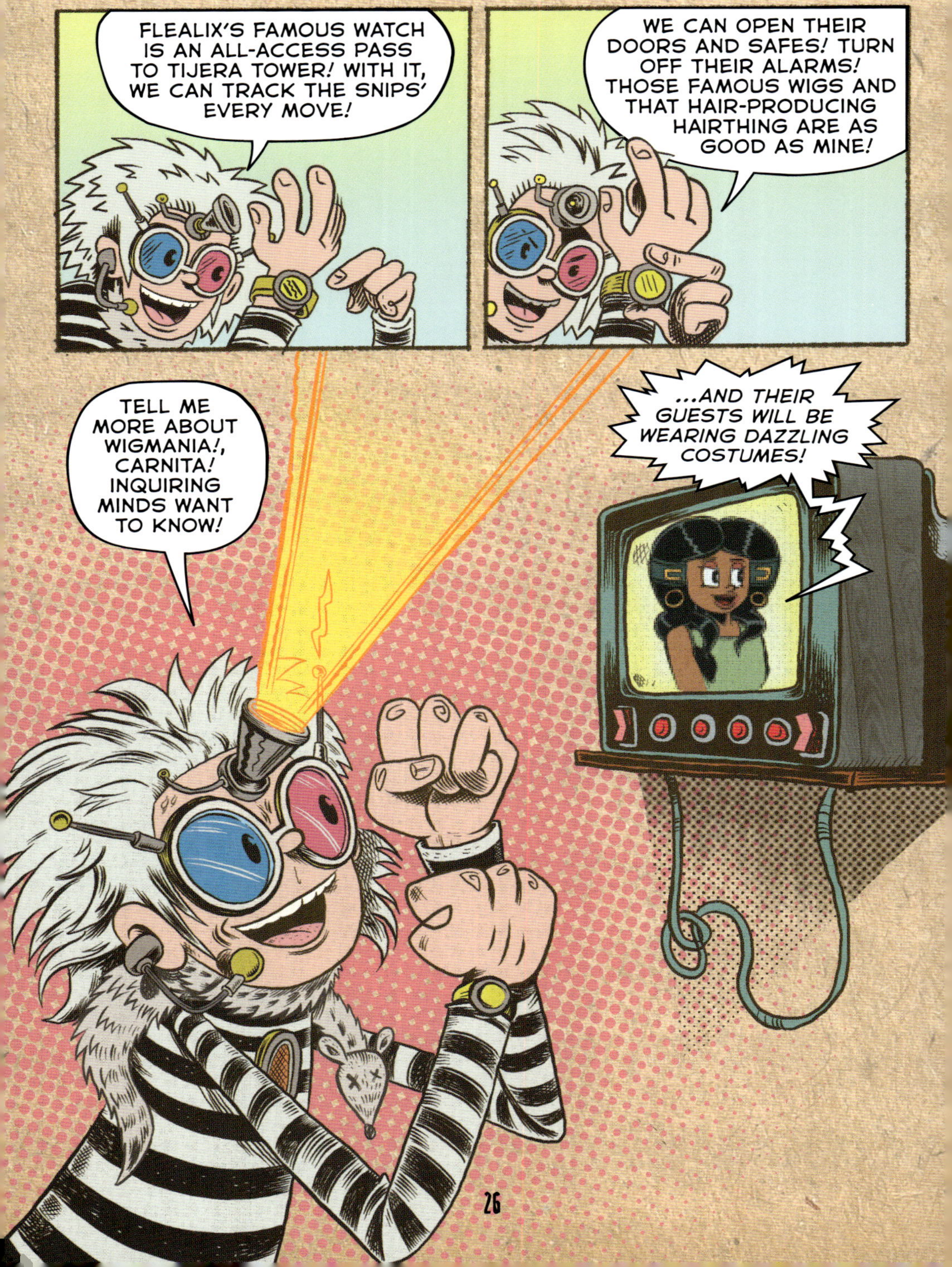
FLEALIX'S FAMOUS WATCH IS AN ALL-ACCESS PASS TO TIJERA TOWER! WITH IT, WE CAN TRACK THE SNIPS' EVERY MOVE!
WE CAN OPEN THEIR DOORS AND SAFES! TURN OFF THEIR ALARMS! THOSE FAMOUS WIGS AND THAT HAIR-PRODUCING HAIRTHING ARE AS GOOD AS MINE!
TELL ME MORE ABOUT WIGMANIA!, CARNITA! INQUIRING MINDS WANT TO KNOW!
...AND THEIR GUESTS WILL BE WEARING DAZZLING COSTUMES!

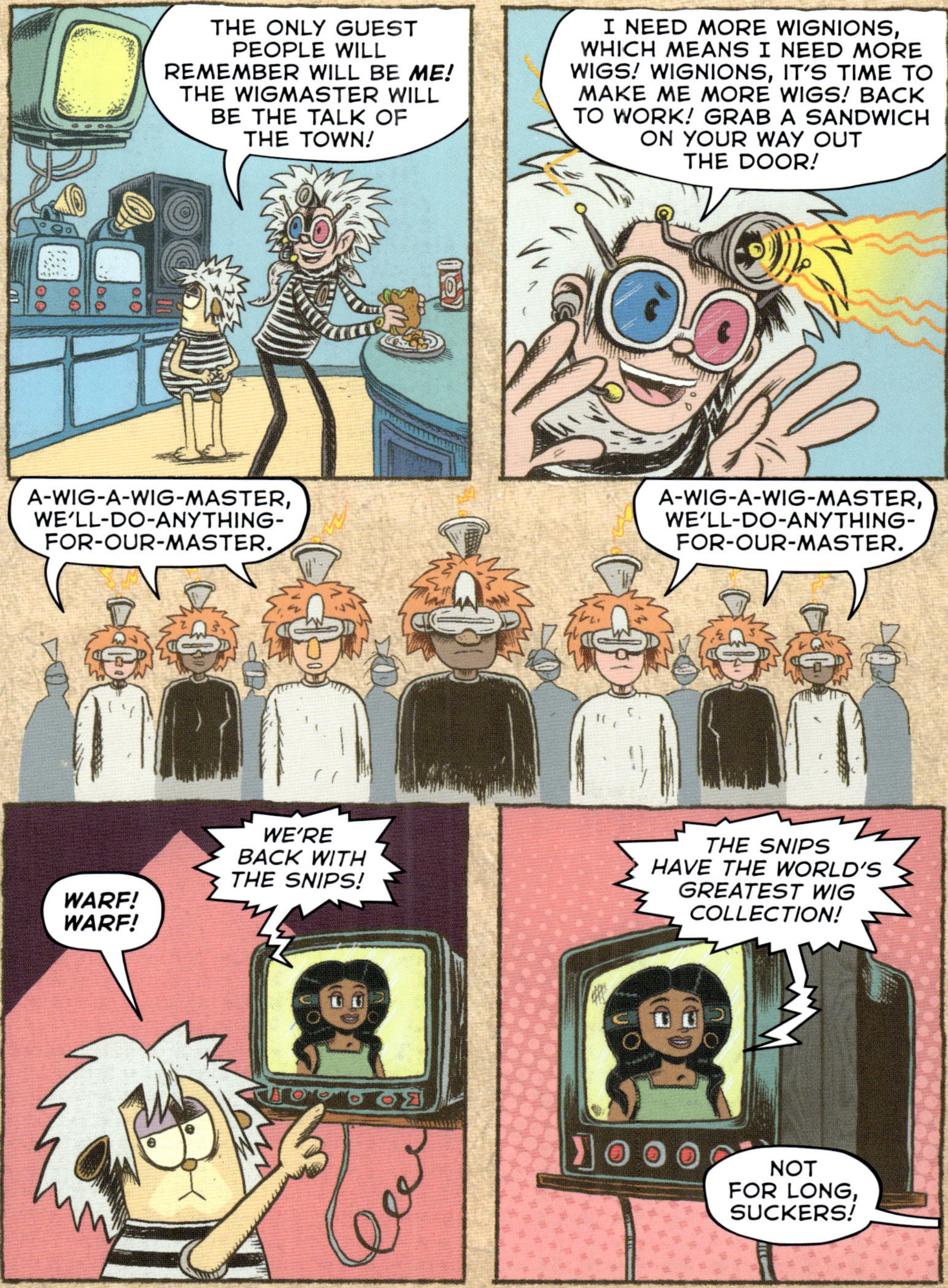
THE ONLY GUEST PEOPLE WILL REMEMBER WILL BE *ME!* THE WIGMASTER WILL BE THE TALK OF THE TOWN!
I NEED MORE WIGNIONS, WHICH MEANS I NEED MORE WIGS! WIGNIONS, IT'S TIME TO MAKE ME MORE WIGS! BACK TO WORK! GRAB A SANDWICH ON YOUR WAY OUT THE DOOR!
A-WIG-A-WIG-MASTER, WE'LL-DO-ANYTHING-FOR-OUR-MASTER.
A-WIG-A-WIG-MASTER, WE'LL-DO-ANYTHING-FOR-OUR-MASTER.
WARF! WARF!
WE'RE BACK WITH THE SNIPS!
THE SNIPS HAVE THE WORLD'S GREATEST WIG COLLECTION!
NOT FOR LONG, SUCKERS!

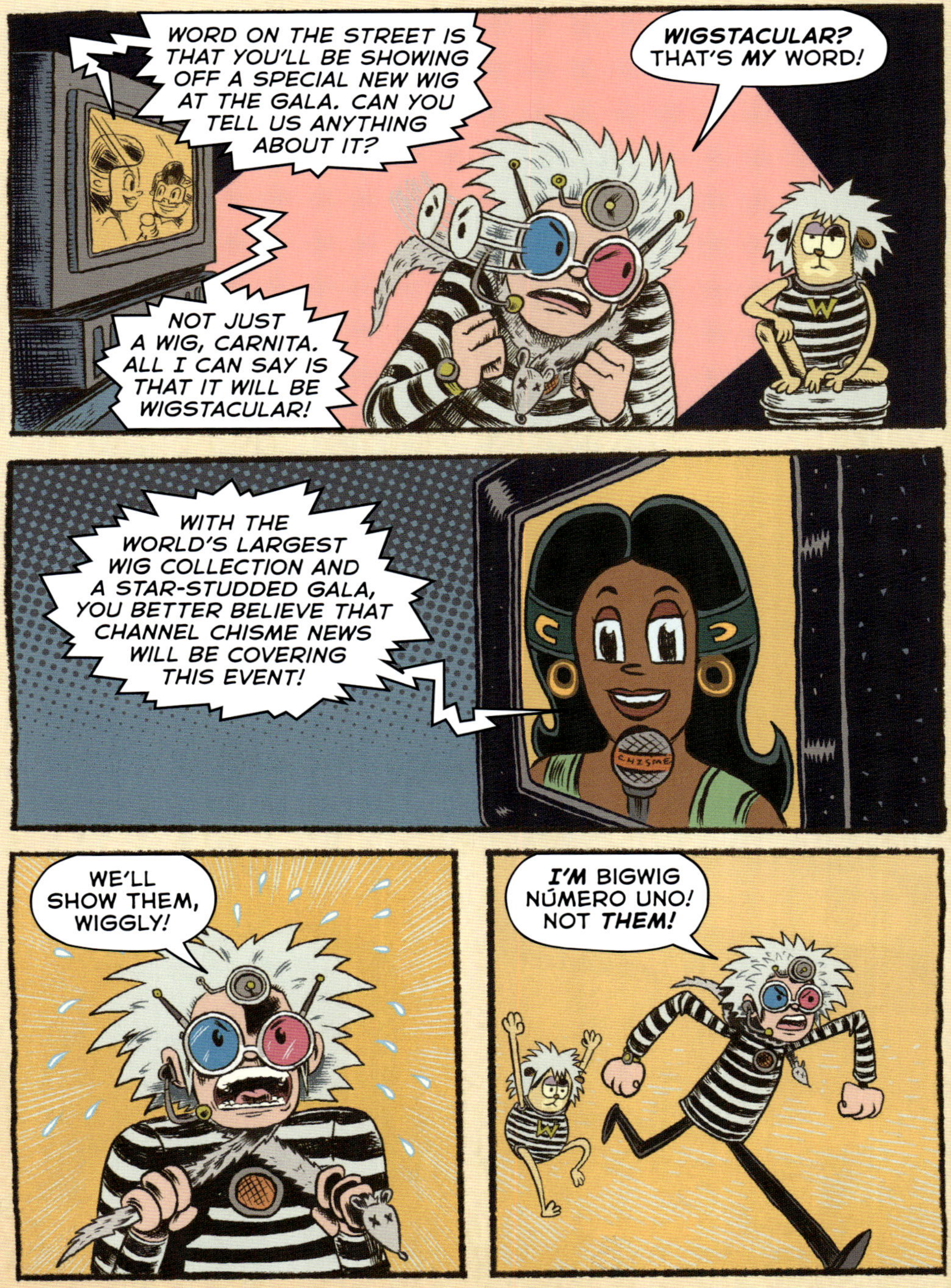
WORD ON THE STREET IS THAT YOU'LL BE SHOWING OFF A SPECIAL NEW WIG AT THE GALA. CAN YOU TELL US ANYTHING ABOUT IT?
NOT JUST A WIG, CARNITA. ALL I CAN SAY IS THAT IT WILL BE WIGSTACULAR!
WIGSTACULAR? THAT'S MY WORD!
WITH THE WORLD'S LARGEST WIG COLLECTION AND A STAR-STUDDED GALA, YOU BETTER BELIEVE THAT CHANNEL CHISME NEWS WILL BE COVERING THIS EVENT!
CHISME
WE'LL SHOW THEM, WIGGLY!
I'M BIGWIG NÚMERO UNO! NOT THEM!

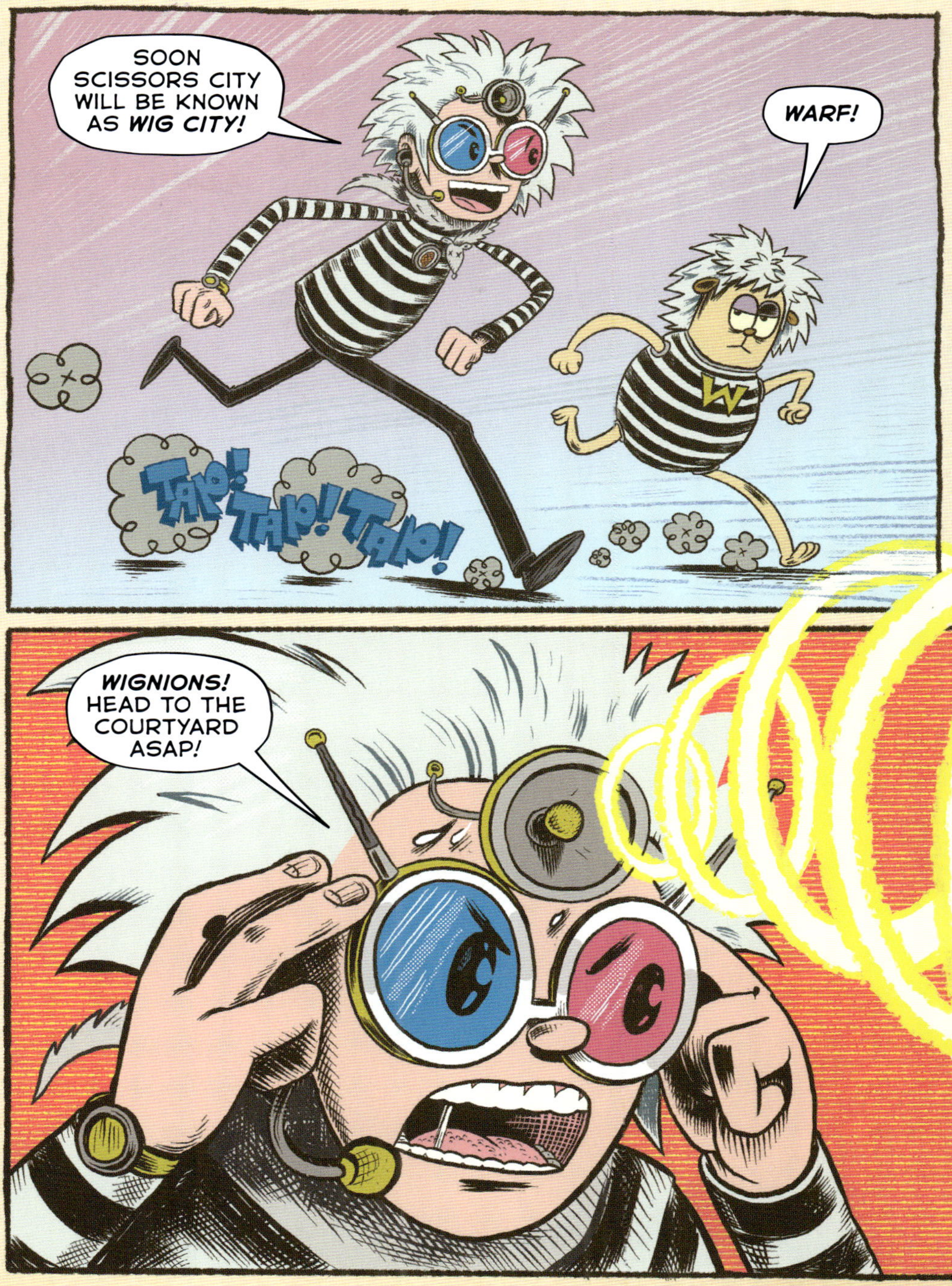
SOON SCISSORS CITY WILL BE KNOWN AS *WIG CITY!*
WARF!
TAP! TAP! TAP!
WIGNIONS! HEAD TO THE COURTYARD ASAP*!*

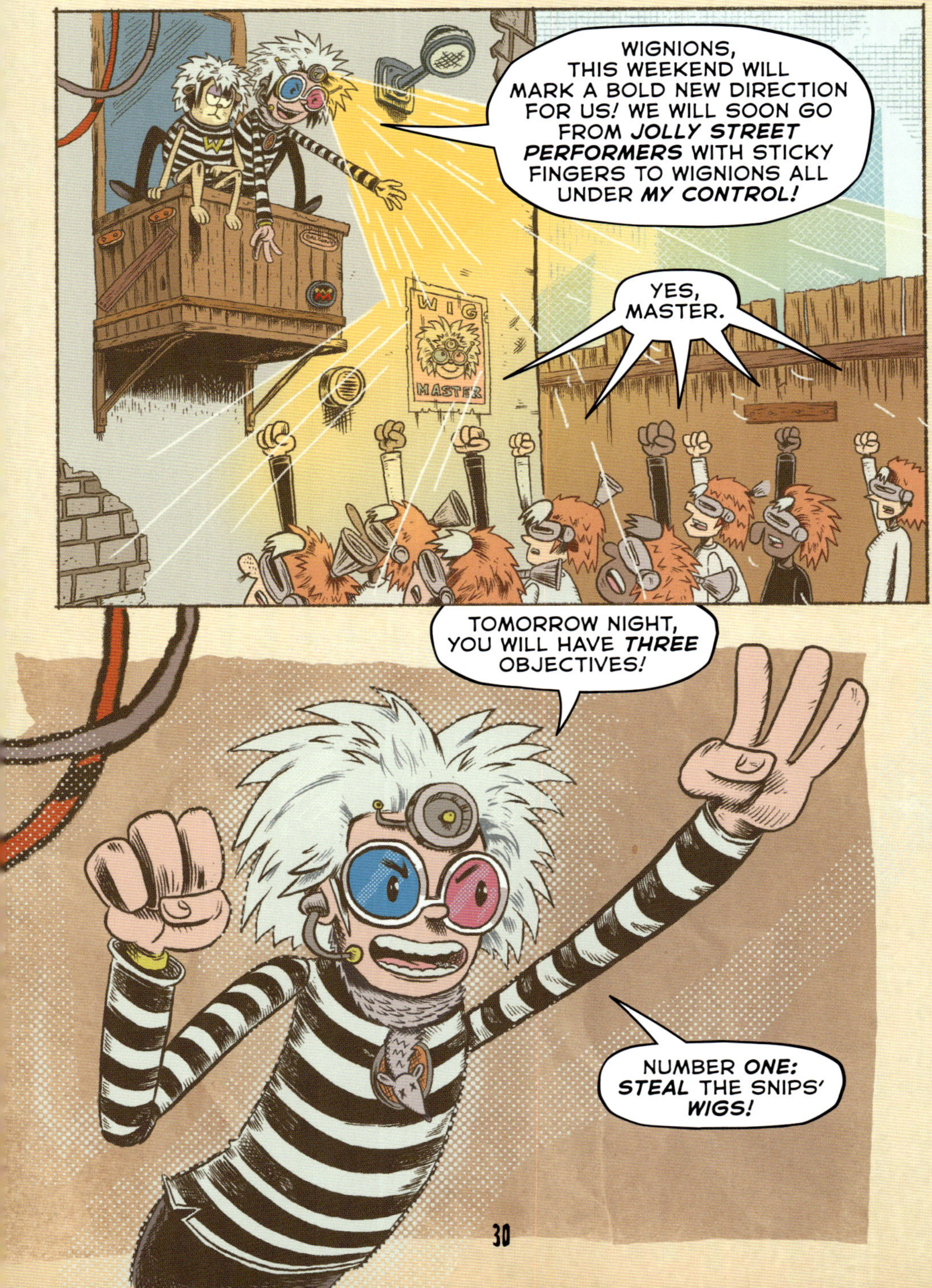
WIGNIONS, THIS WEEKEND WILL MARK A BOLD NEW DIRECTION FOR US! WE WILL SOON GO FROM JOLLY STREET PERFORMERS WITH STICKY FINGERS TO WIGNIONS ALL UNDER MY CONTROL!
WIG MASTER
YES, MASTER.
TOMORROW NIGHT, YOU WILL HAVE THREE OBJECTIVES!
NUMBER ONE: STEAL THE SNIPS' WIGS!

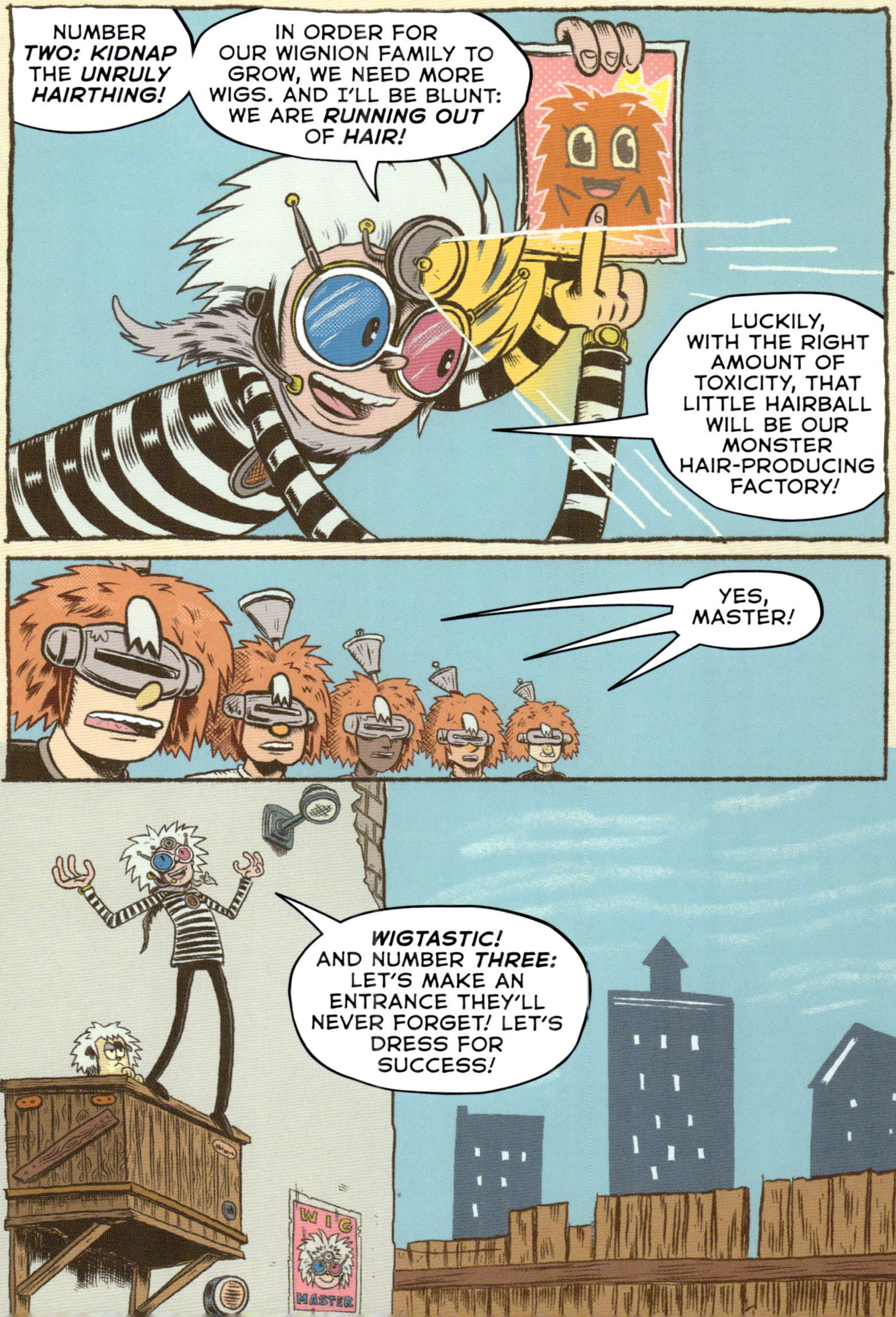
NUMBER TWO: KIDNAP THE UNRULY HAIRTHING!
IN ORDER FOR OUR WIGNION FAMILY TO GROW, WE NEED MORE WIGS. AND I'LL BE BLUNT: WE ARE RUNNING OUT OF HAIR!
LUCKILY, WITH THE RIGHT AMOUNT OF TOXICITY, THAT LITTLE HAIRBALL WILL BE OUR MONSTER HAIR-PRODUCING FACTORY!
YES, MASTER!
WIGTASTIC! AND NUMBER THREE: LET'S MAKE AN ENTRANCE THEY'LL NEVER FORGET! LET'S DRESS FOR SUCCESS!
WIG
MASTER

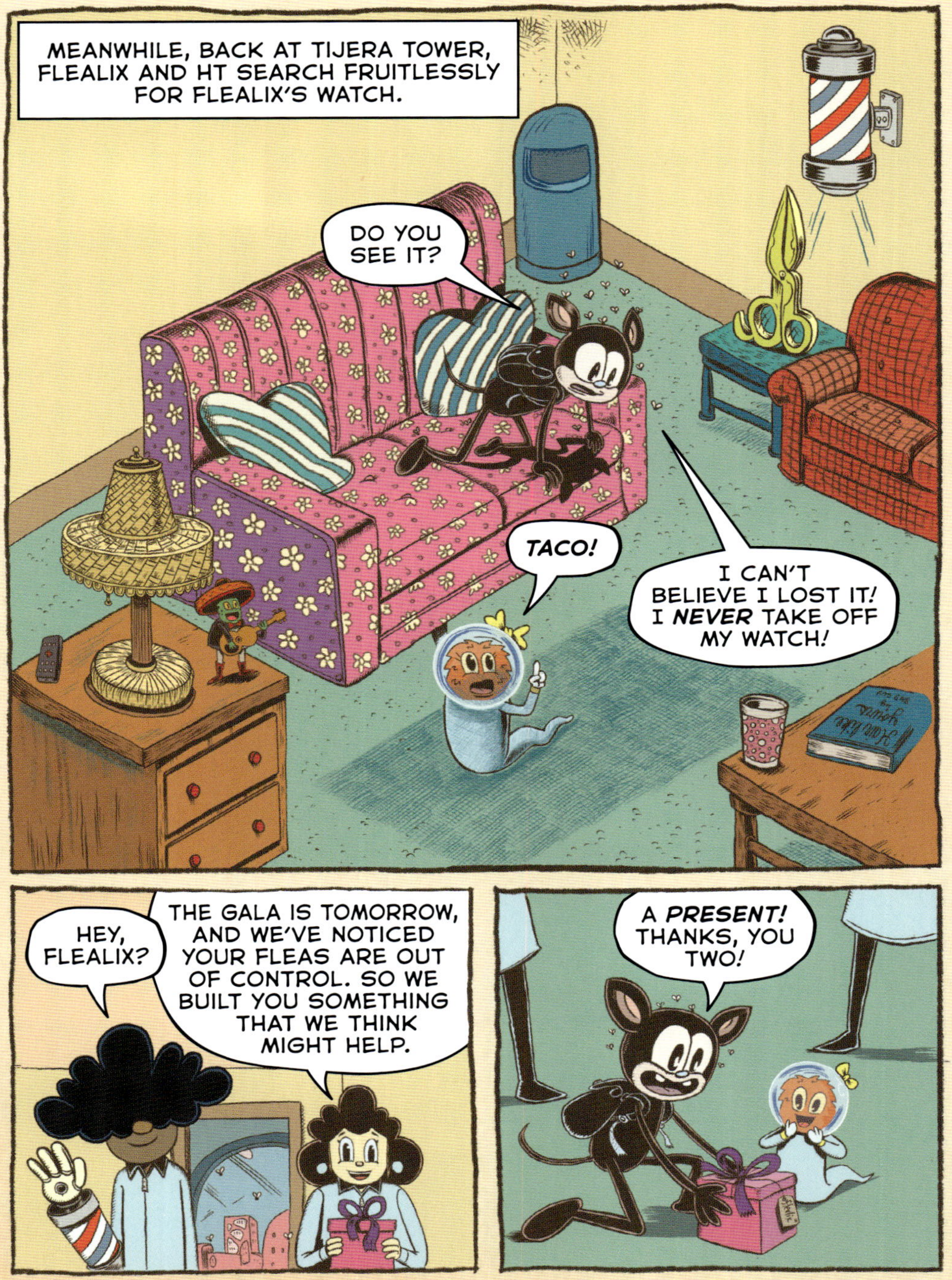
MEANWHILE, BACK AT TIJERA TOWER, FLEALIX AND HT SEARCH FRUITLESSLY FOR FLEALIX'S WATCH.
DO YOU SEE IT?
TACO!
I CAN'T BELIEVE I LOST IT! I *NEVER* TAKE OFF MY WATCH!
HEY, FLEALIX?
THE GALA IS TOMORROW, AND WE'VE NOTICED YOUR FLEAS ARE OUT OF CONTROL. SO WE BUILT YOU SOMETHING THAT WE THINK MIGHT HELP.
A *PRESENT!* THANKS, YOU TWO!

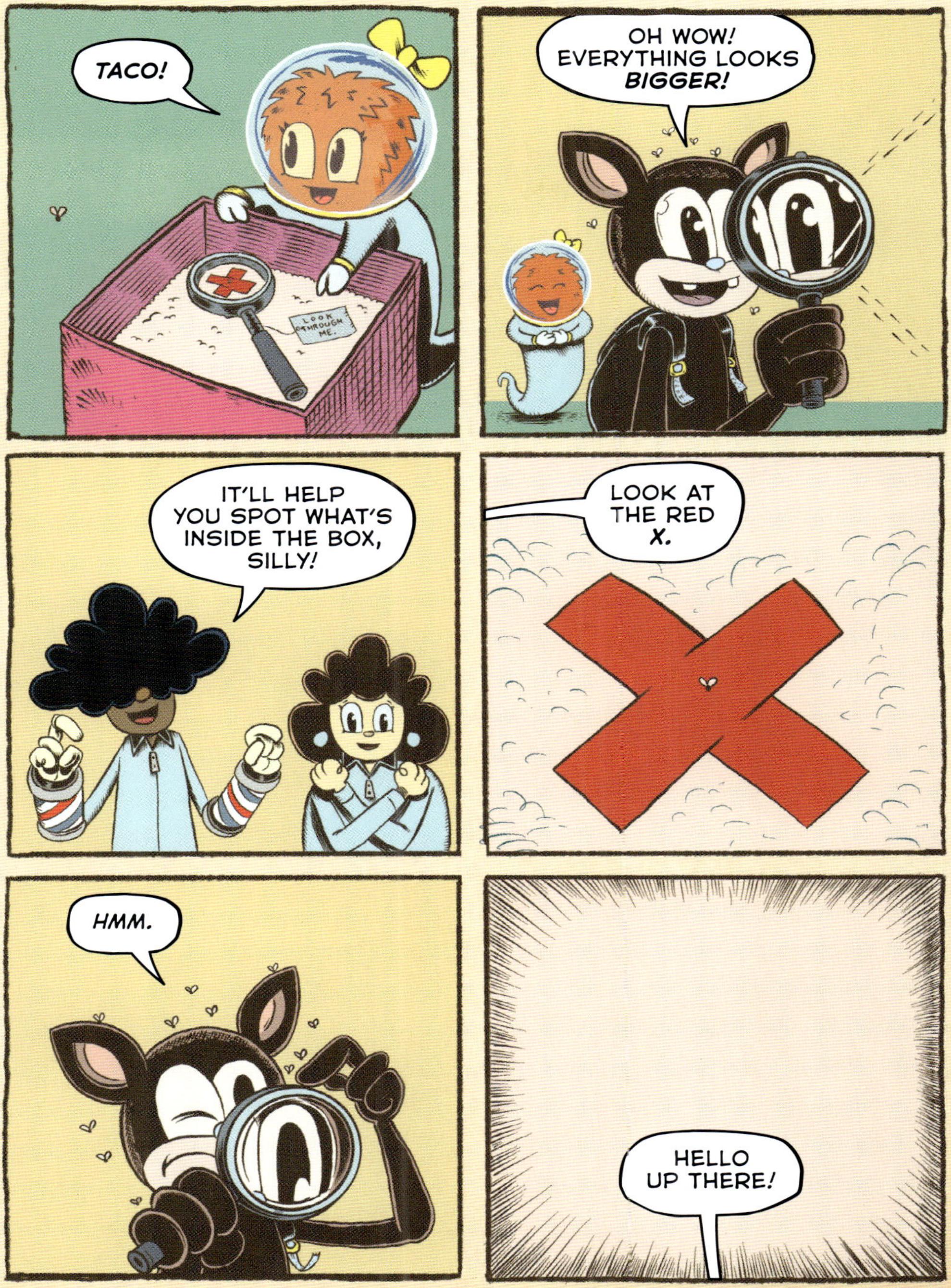
TACO!
OH WOW! EVERYTHING LOOKS BIGGER!
LOOK THROUGH ME.
IT'LL HELP YOU SPOT WHAT'S INSIDE THE BOX, SILLY!
LOOK AT THE RED X.
HMM.
HELLO UP THERE!

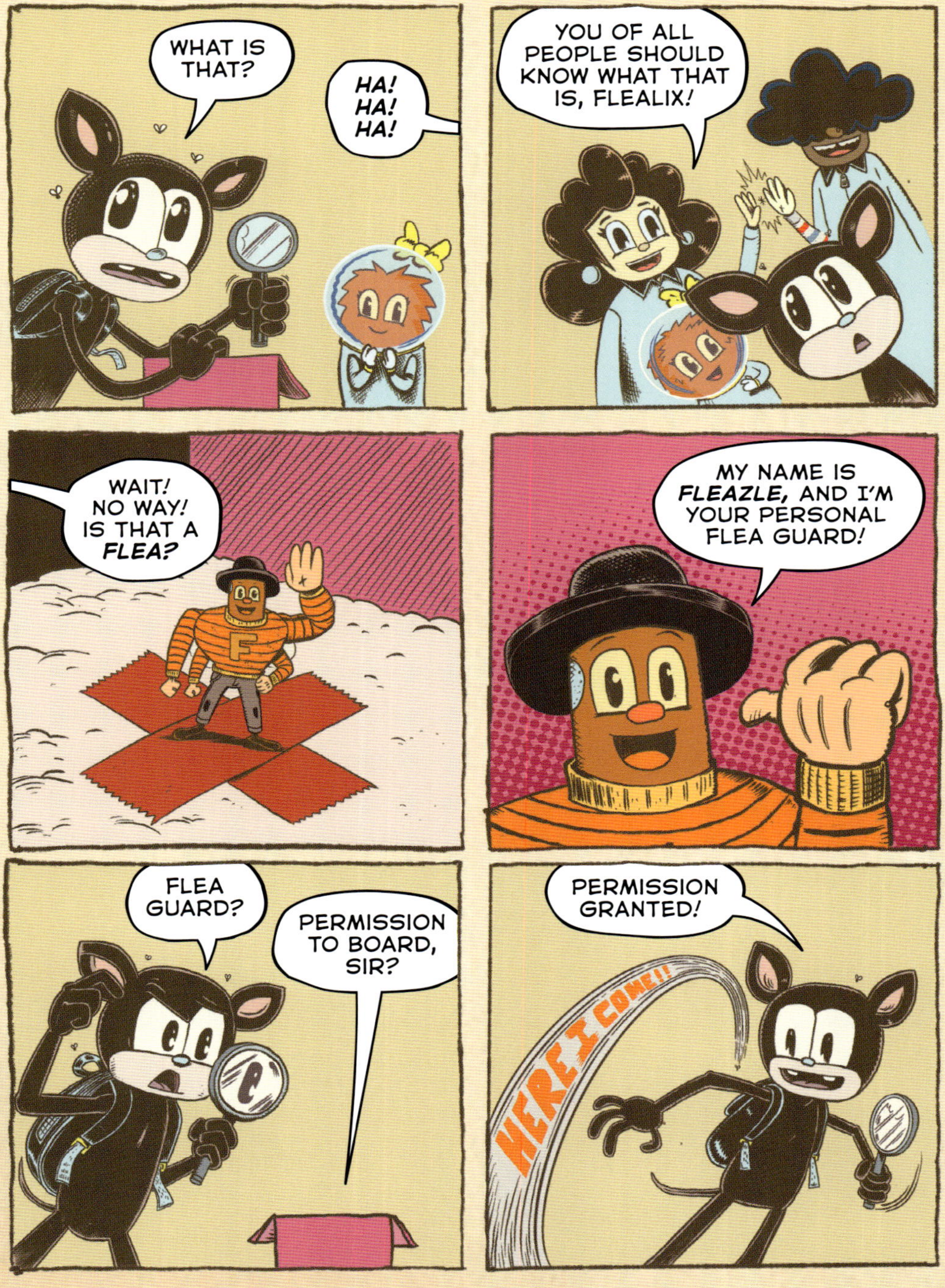
WHAT IS THAT?
HA! HA! HA!
YOU OF ALL PEOPLE SHOULD KNOW WHAT THAT IS, FLEALIX!
WAIT! NO WAY! IS THAT A *FLEA?*
MY NAME IS *FLEAZLE,* AND I'M YOUR PERSONAL FLEA GUARD!
FLEA GUARD?
PERMISSION TO BOARD, SIR?
PERMISSION GRANTED!
HERE I COME!!

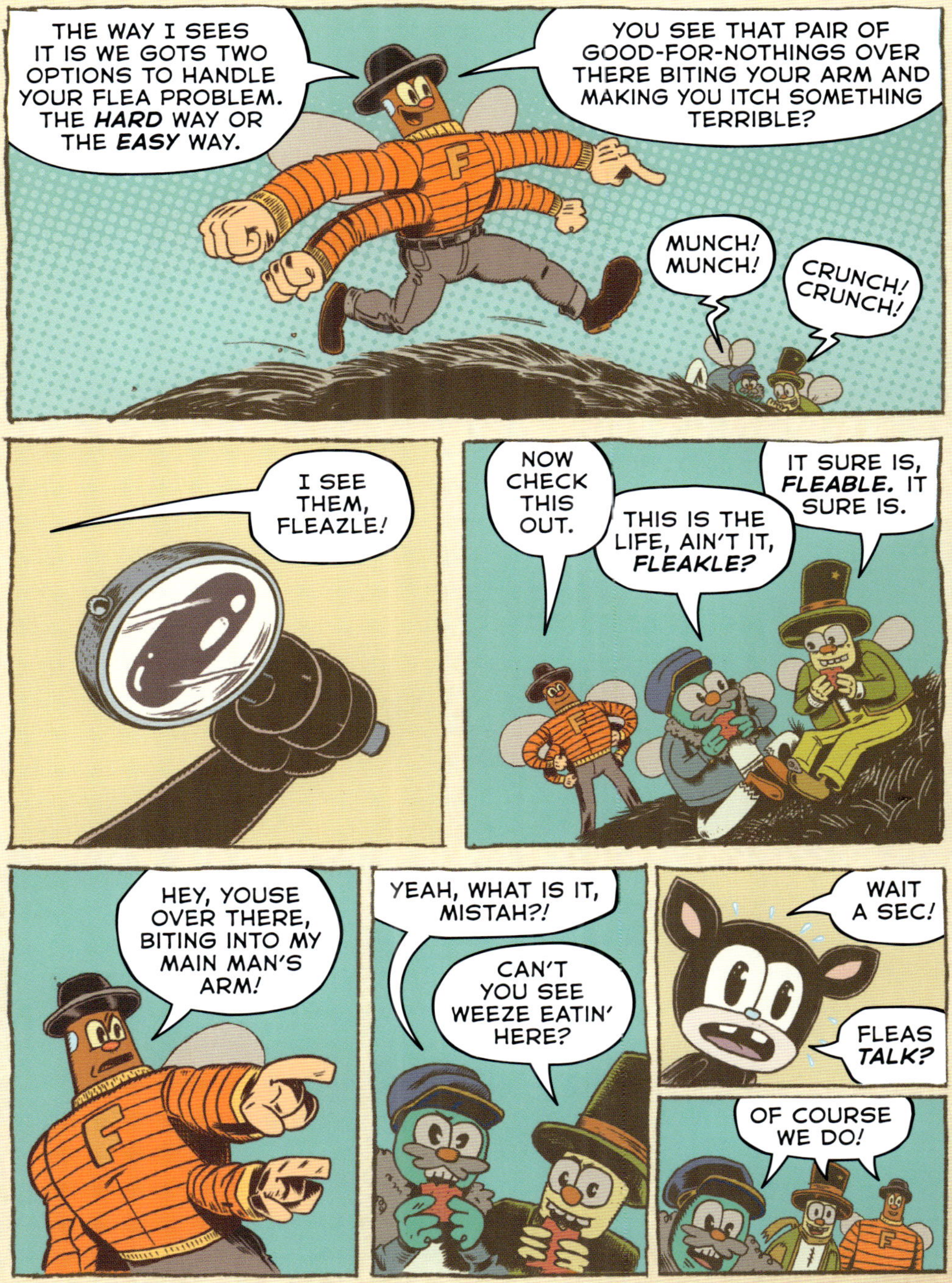
THE WAY I SEES IT IS WE GOTS TWO OPTIONS TO HANDLE YOUR FLEA PROBLEM. THE **HARD** WAY OR THE **EASY** WAY.
YOU SEE THAT PAIR OF GOOD-FOR-NOTHINGS OVER THERE BITING YOUR ARM AND MAKING YOU ITCH SOMETHING TERRIBLE?
MUNCH! MUNCH!
CRUNCH! CRUNCH!
I SEE THEM, FLEAZLE!
NOW CHECK THIS OUT.
THIS IS THE LIFE, AIN'T IT, **FLEAKLE?**
IT SURE IS, **FLEABLE.** IT SURE IS.
HEY, YOUSE OVER THERE, BITING INTO MY MAIN MAN'S ARM!
YEAH, WHAT IS IT, MISTAH?!
CAN'T YOU SEE WEEZE EATIN' HERE?
WAIT A SEC!
FLEAS **TALK?**
OF COURSE WE DO!

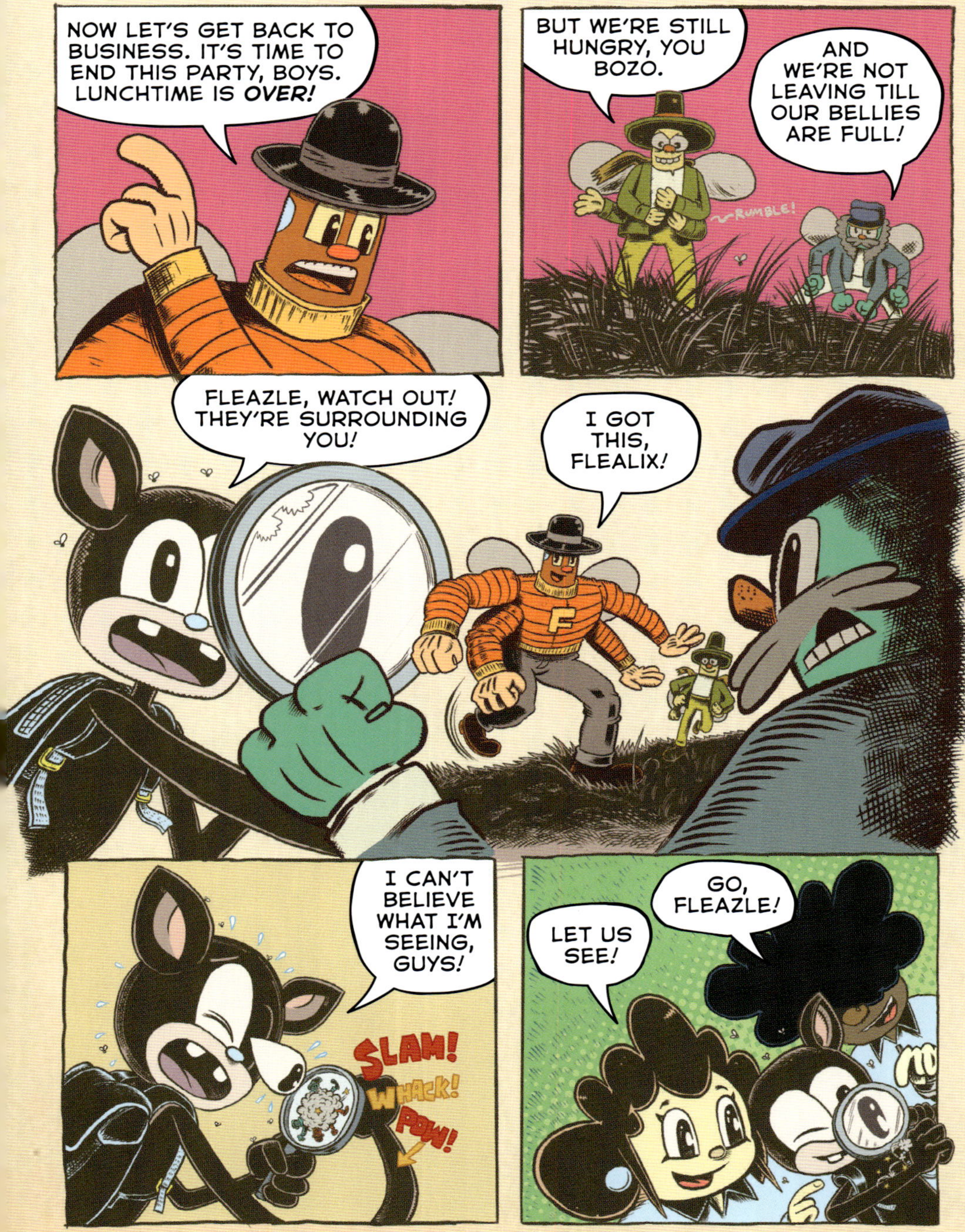
NOW LET'S GET BACK TO BUSINESS. IT'S TIME TO END THIS PARTY, BOYS. LUNCHTIME IS *OVER!*
BUT WE'RE STILL HUNGRY, YOU BOZO.
AND WE'RE NOT LEAVING TILL OUR BELLIES ARE FULL!
RUMBLE!
FLEAZLE, WATCH OUT! THEY'RE SURROUNDING YOU!
I GOT THIS, FLEALIX!
I CAN'T BELIEVE WHAT I'M SEEING, GUYS!
SLAM!
WHACK!
POW!
GO, FLEAZLE!
LET US SEE!

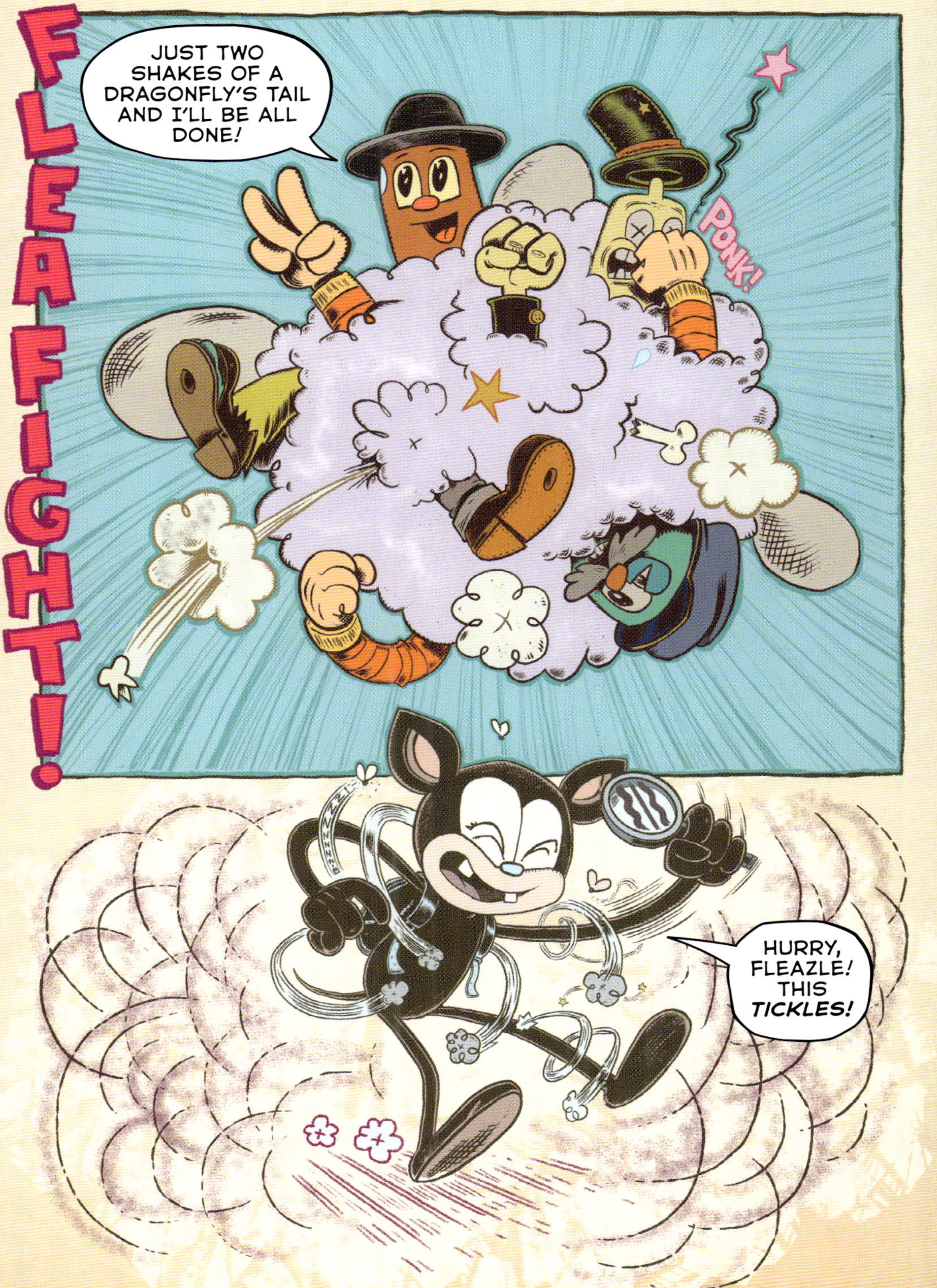
FLEA FIGHT!
JUST TWO SHAKES OF A DRAGONFLY'S TAIL AND I'LL BE ALL DONE!
PONK!
HURRY, FLEAZLE! THIS TICKLES!

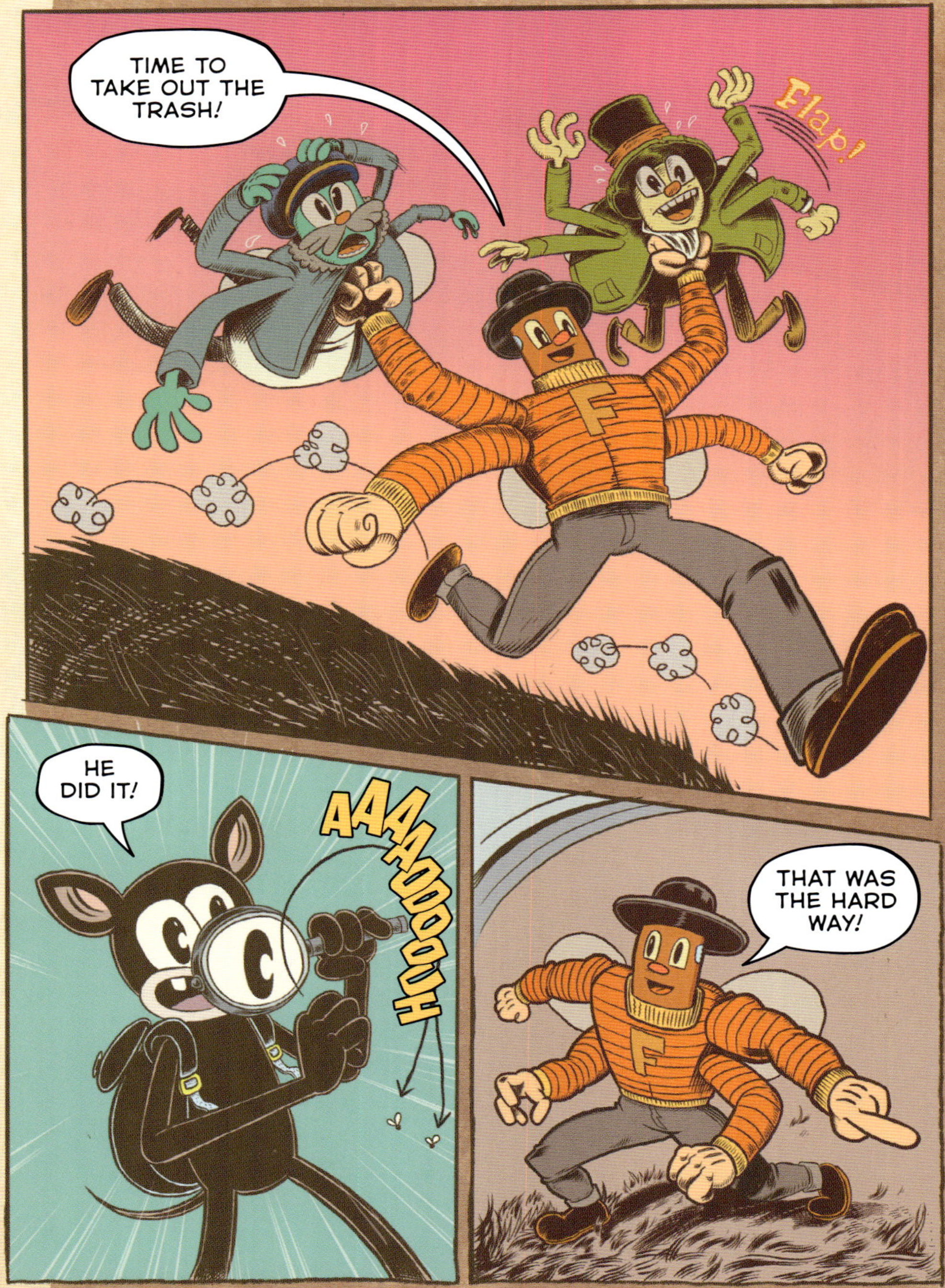
TIME TO TAKE OUT THE TRASH!
Flap!
HE DID IT!
AAAAAOOOOUH
THAT WAS THE HARD WAY!

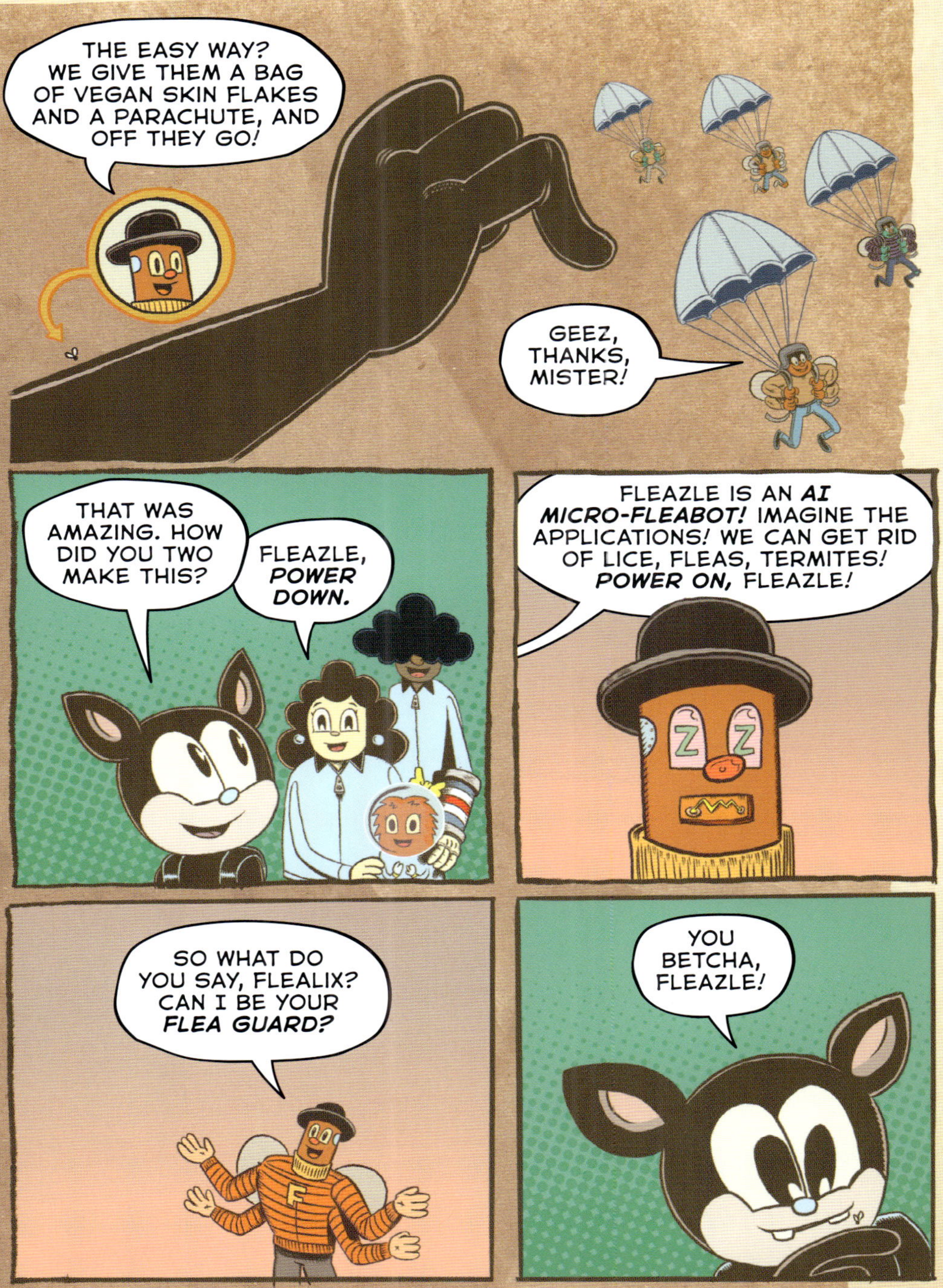
THE EASY WAY? WE GIVE THEM A BAG OF VEGAN SKIN FLAKES AND A PARACHUTE, AND OFF THEY GO!
GEEZ, THANKS, MISTER!
THAT WAS AMAZING. HOW DID YOU TWO MAKE THIS?
FLEAZLE, POWER DOWN.
FLEAZLE IS AN AI MICRO-FLEABOT! IMAGINE THE APPLICATIONS! WE CAN GET RID OF LICE, FLEAS, TERMITES! POWER ON, FLEAZLE!
SO WHAT DO YOU SAY, FLEALIX? CAN I BE YOUR FLEA GUARD?
YOU BETCHA, FLEAZLE!

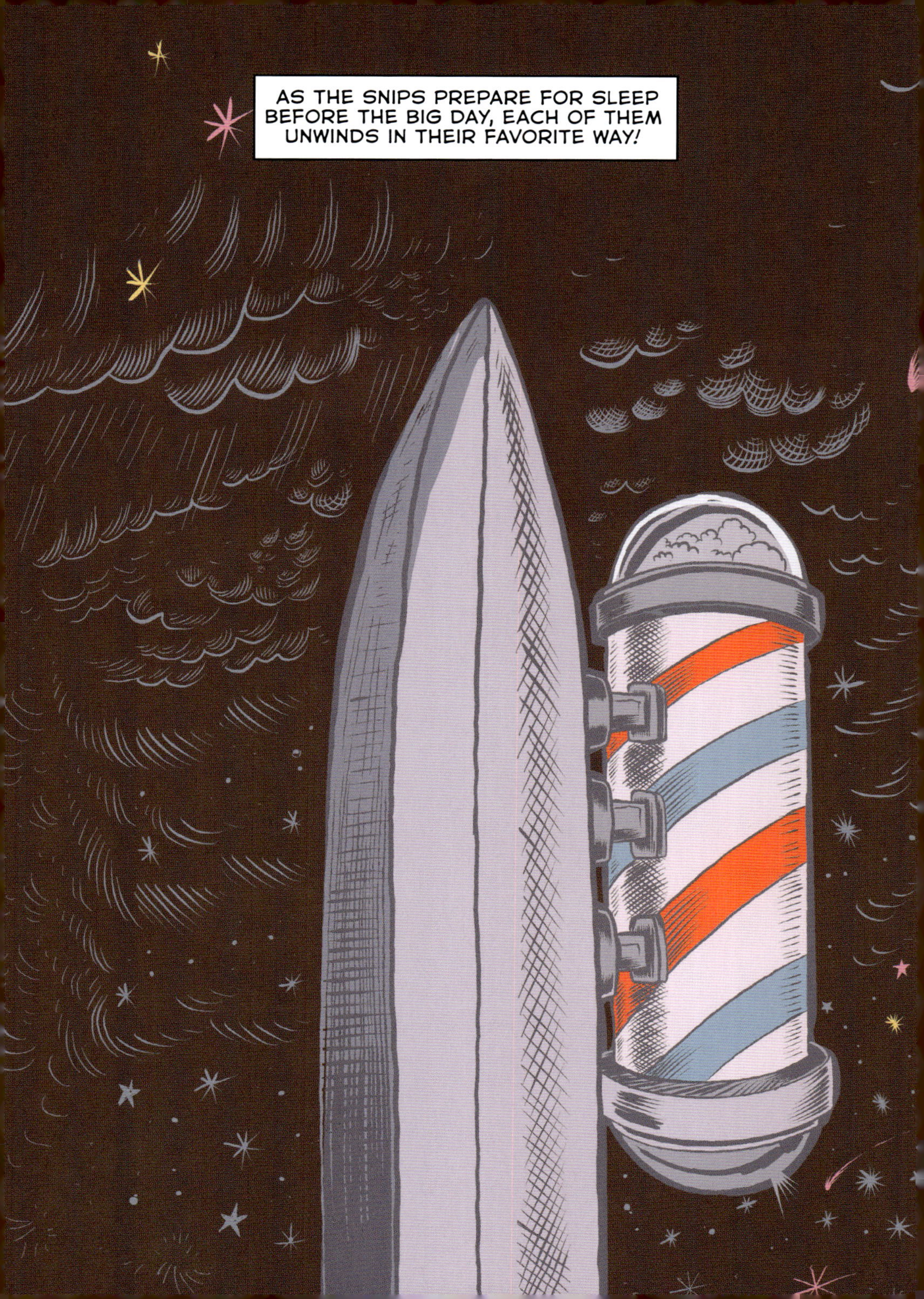
AS THE SNIPS PREPARE FOR SLEEP BEFORE THE BIG DAY, EACH OF THEM UNWINDS IN THEIR FAVORITE WAY!

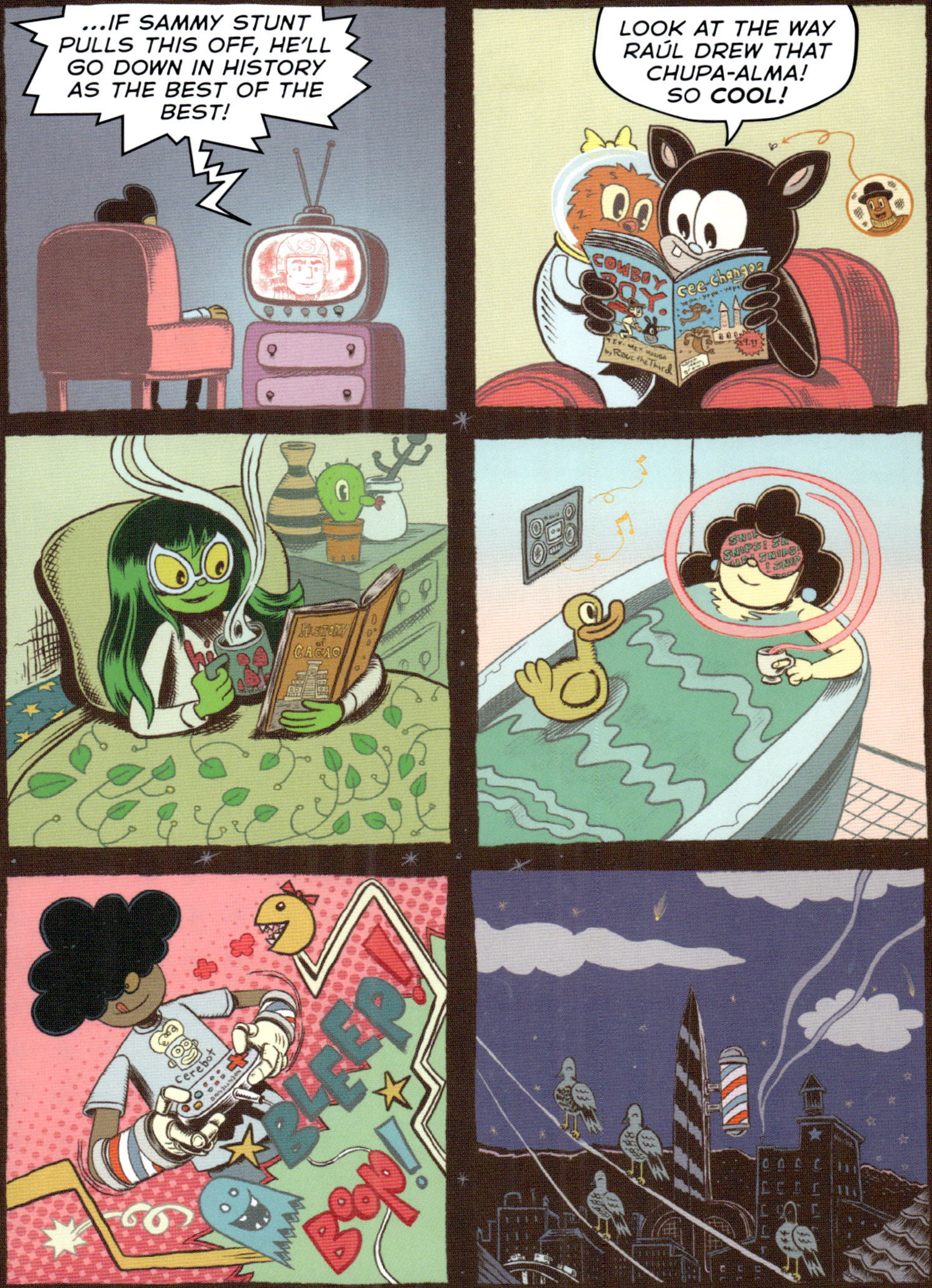
...IF SAMMY STUNT PULLS THIS OFF, HE'LL GO DOWN IN HISTORY AS THE BEST OF THE BEST!
LOOK AT THE WAY RAÚL DREW THAT CHUPA-ALMA! SO COOL!
COWBOY BOY
cee-changos
CACAO
cerebot
BLEEP!
BOOP!

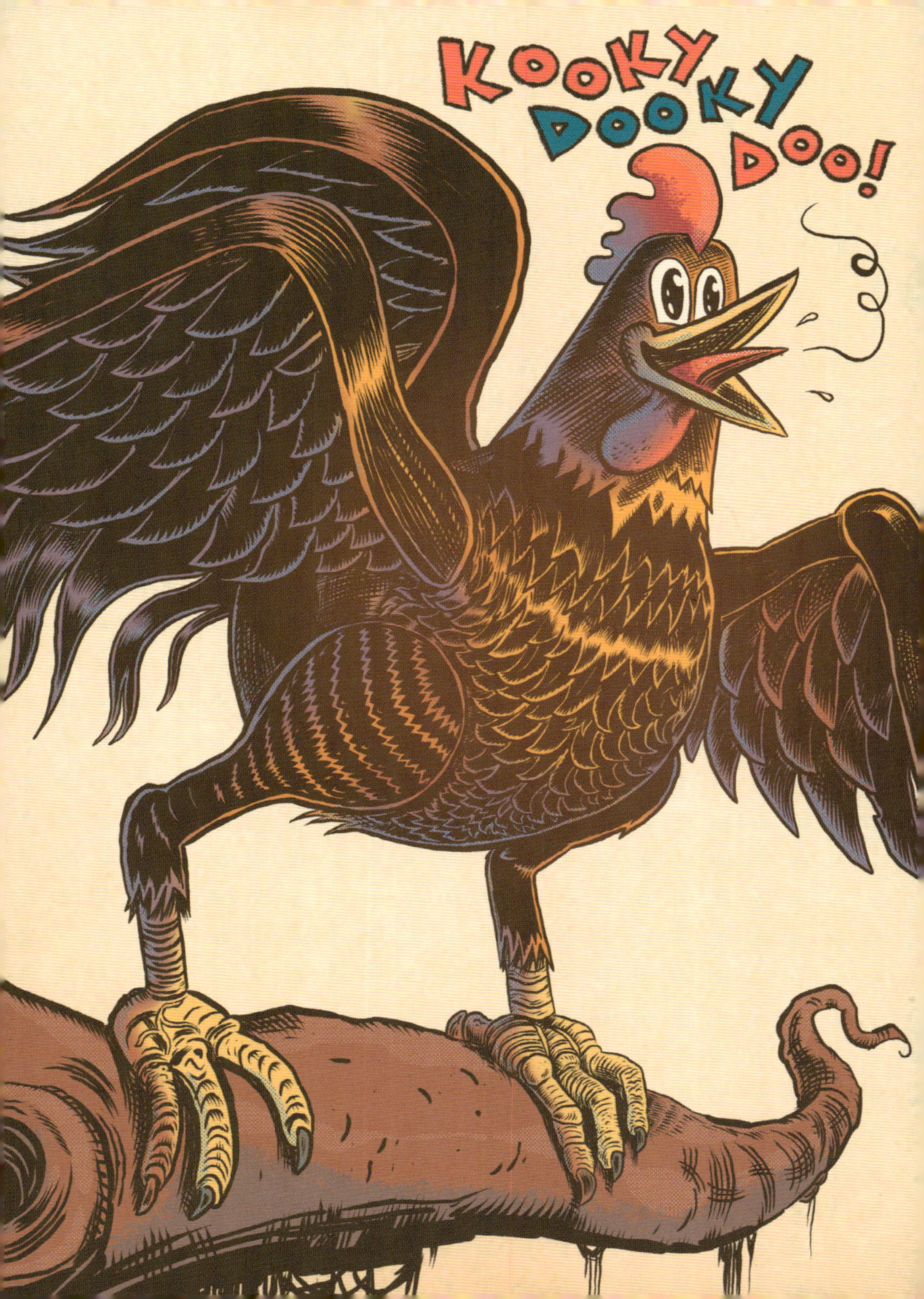
KOOKY DOOKY DOO!

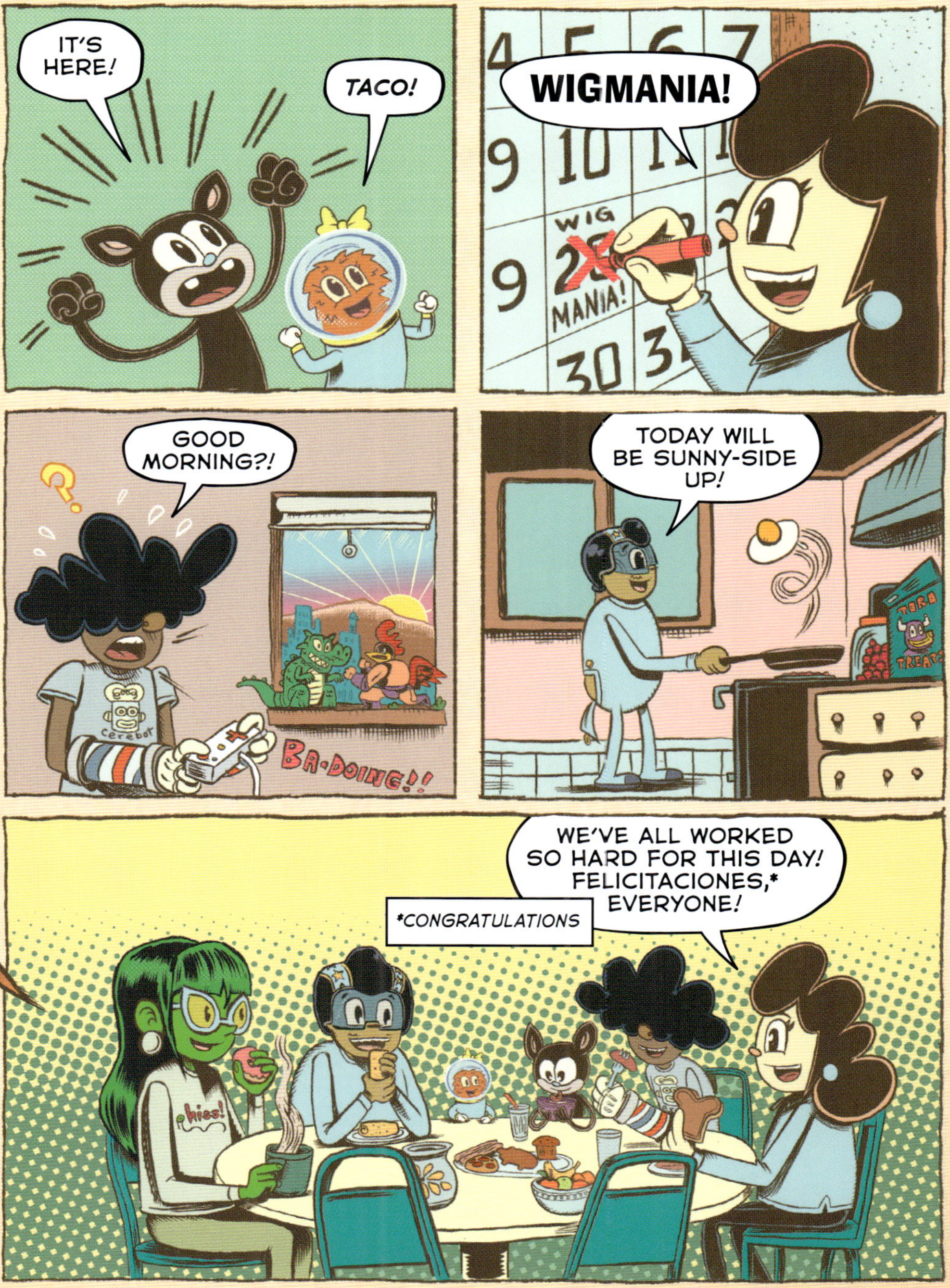
IT'S HERE!
TACO!
WIGMANIA!
WIG
MANIA!
GOOD MORNING?!
cerebot
BA-DOING!!
TODAY WILL BE SUNNY-SIDE UP!
WE'VE ALL WORKED SO HARD FOR THIS DAY! FELICITACIONES,* EVERYONE!
*CONGRATULATIONS

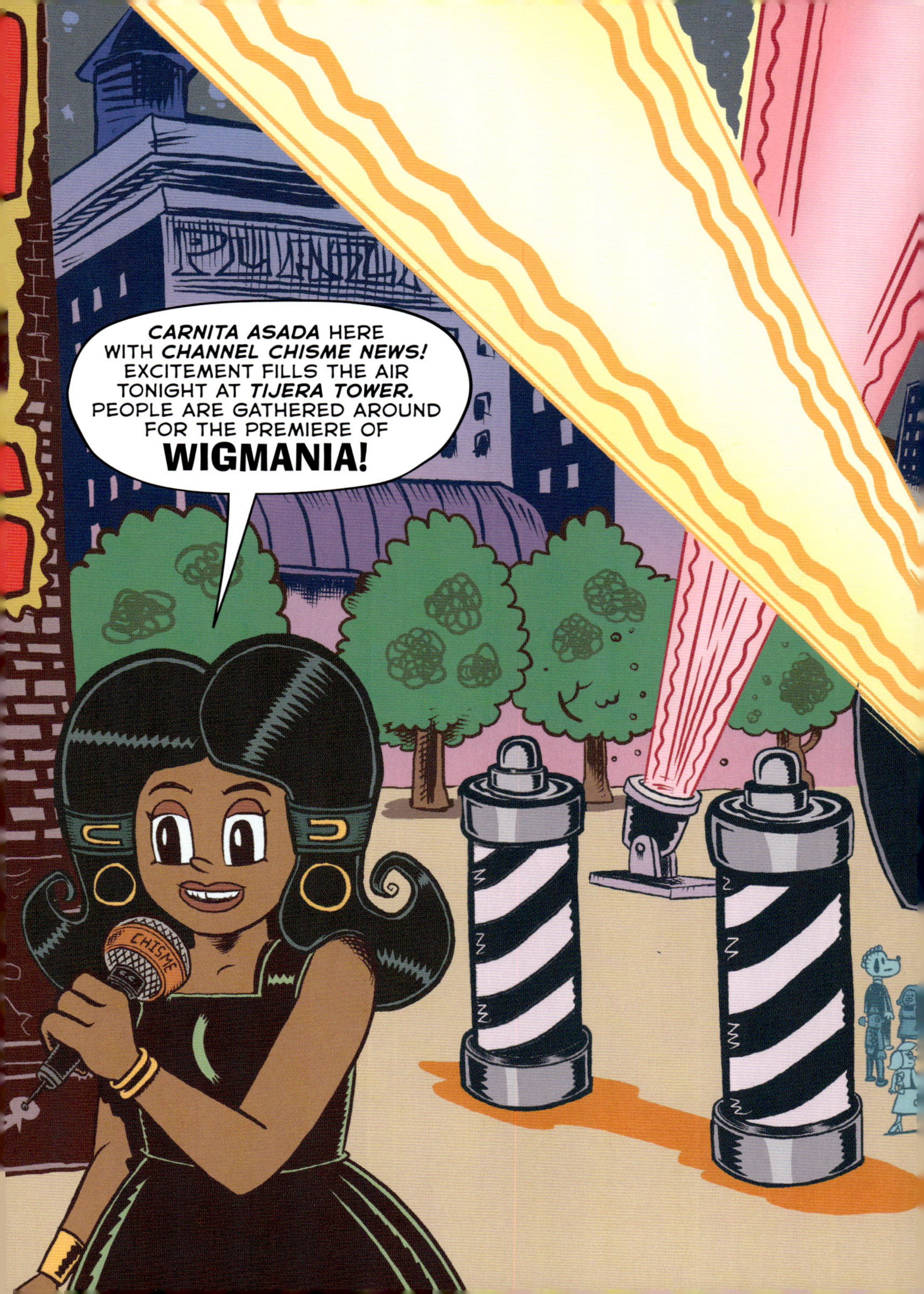
CARNITA ASADA HERE WITH CHANNEL CHISME NEWS! EXCITEMENT FILLS THE AIR TONIGHT AT TIJERA TOWER. PEOPLE ARE GATHERED AROUND FOR THE PREMIERE OF WIGMANIA!
CHISME

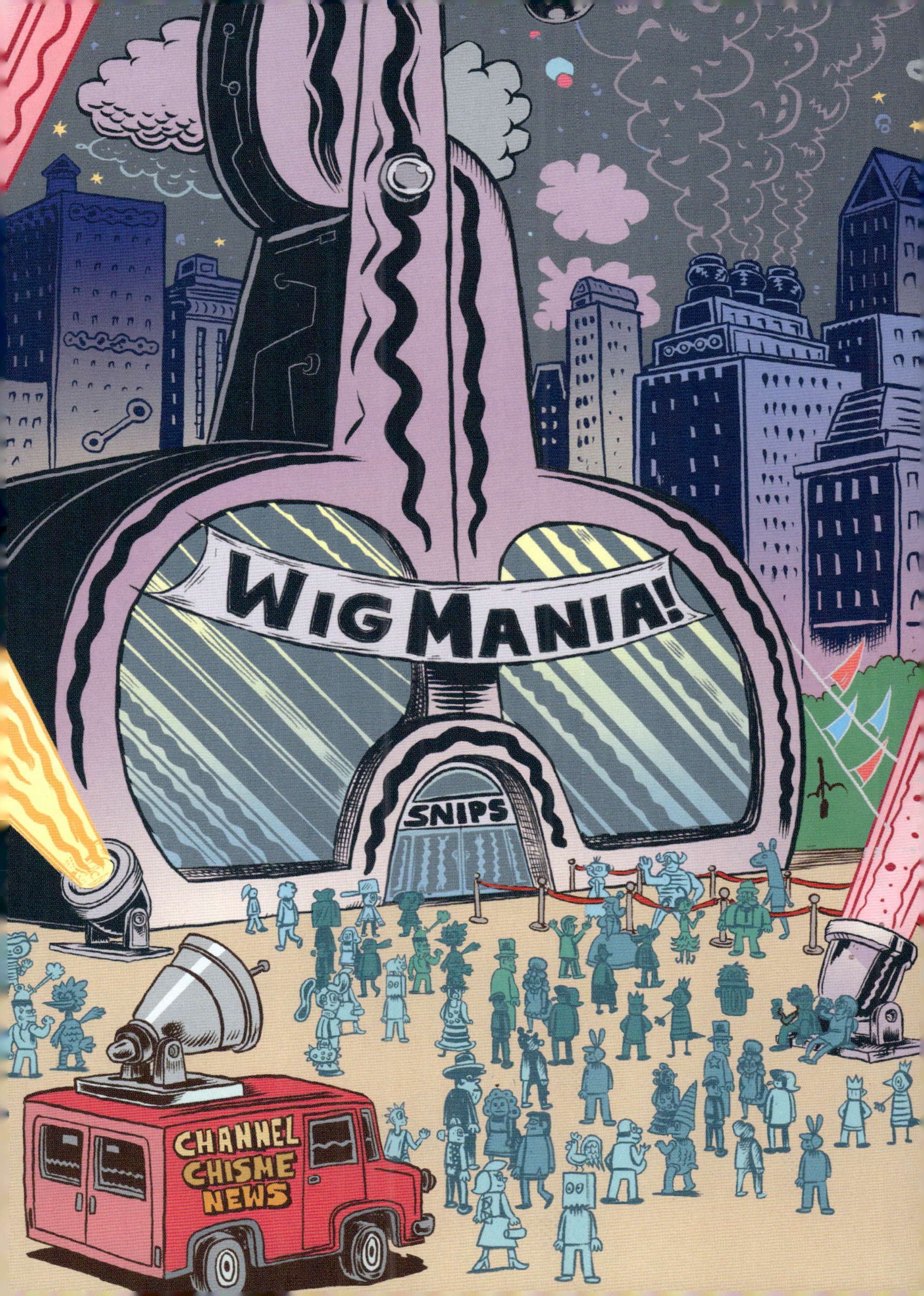
WIG MANIA!
SNIPS
CHANNEL
CHISME
NEWS

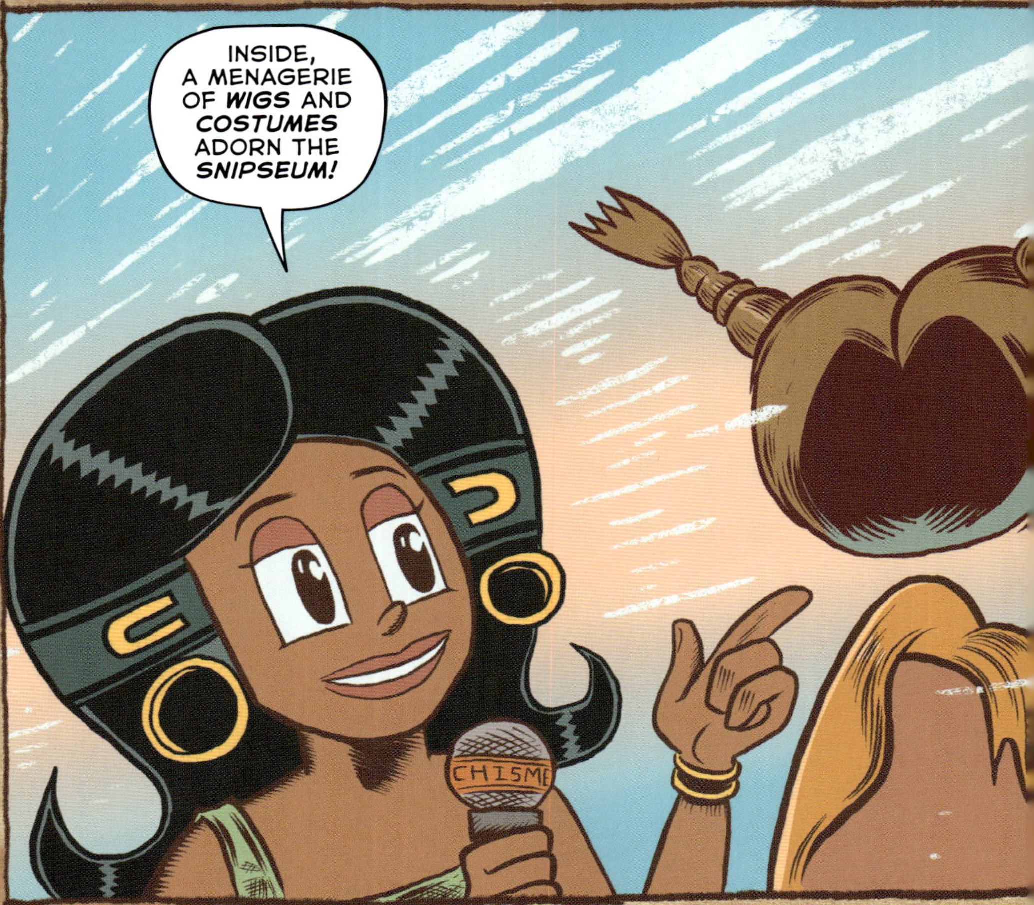
INSIDE, A MENAGERIE OF ***WIGS*** AND ***COSTUMES*** ADORN THE ***SNIPSEUM!***
CHISME

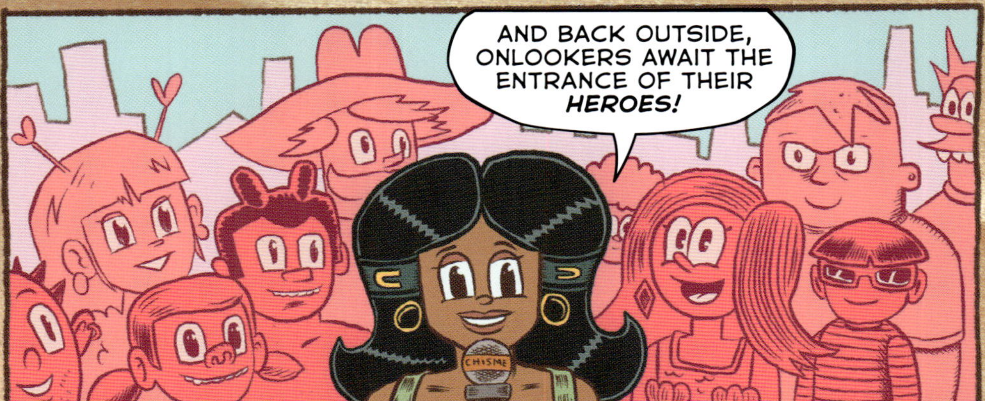
AND BACK OUTSIDE, ONLOOKERS AWAIT THE ENTRANCE OF THEIR ***HEROES!***
CHISME

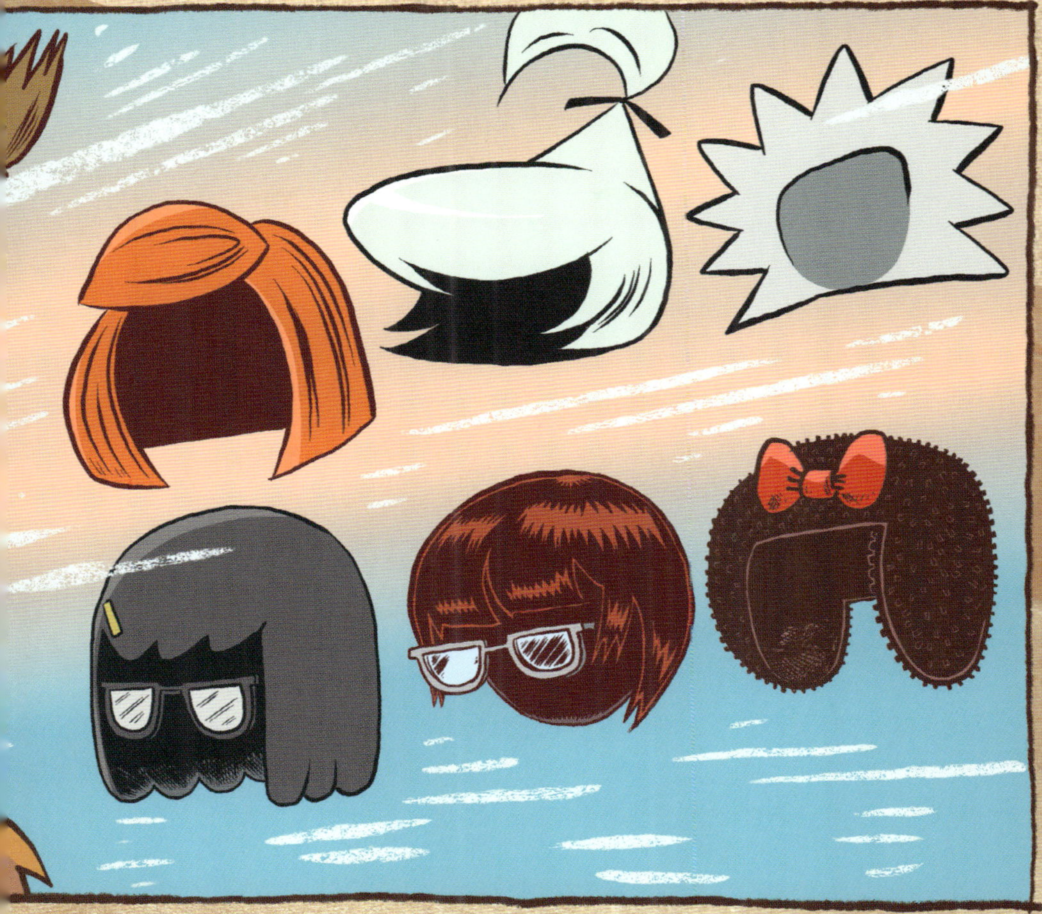

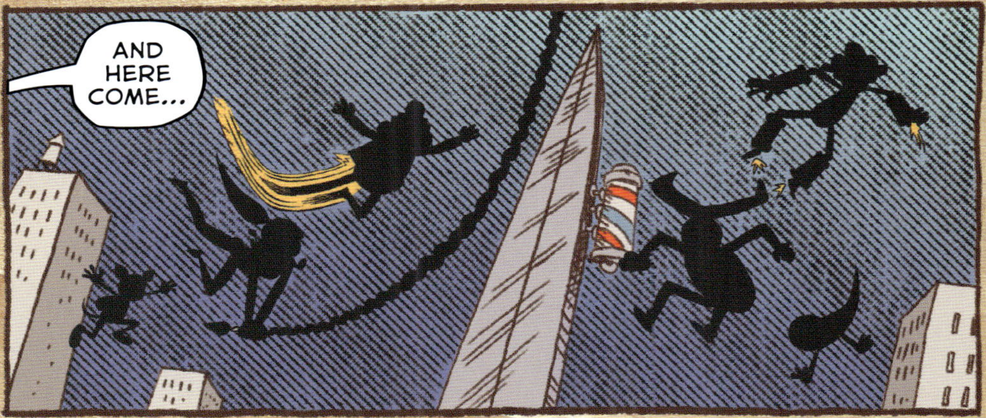
AND HERE COME...

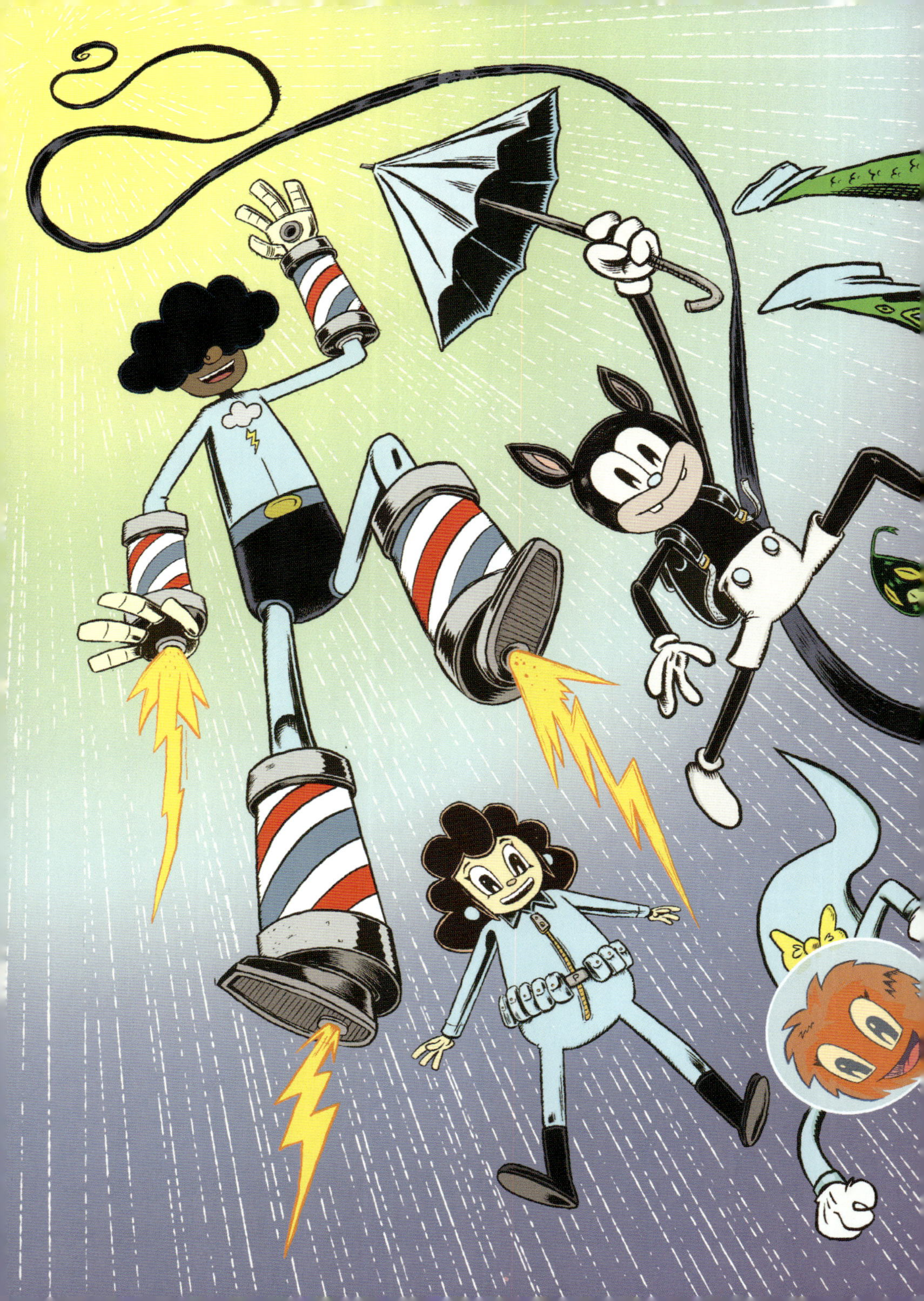

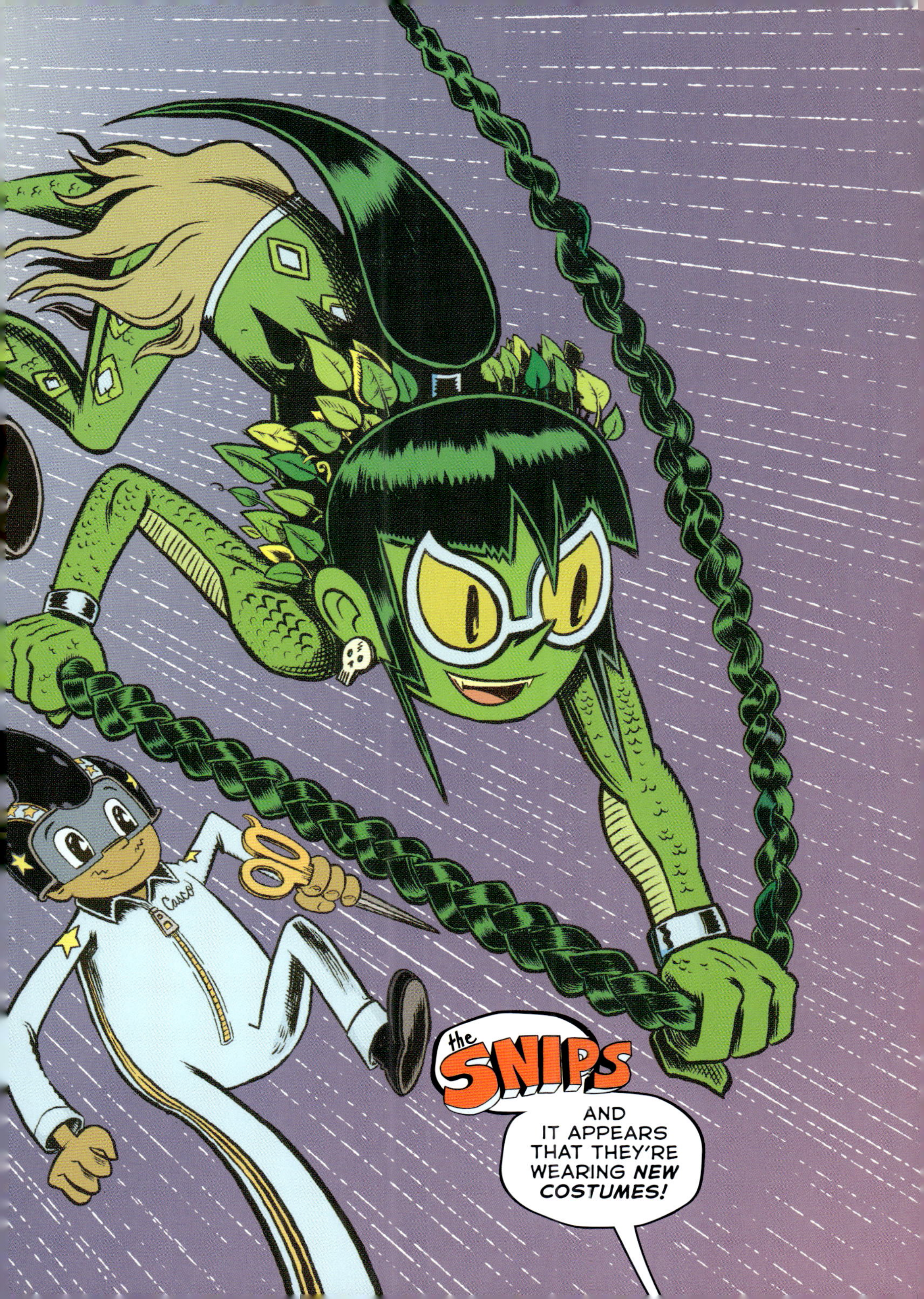
the SNIPS
AND IT APPEARS THAT THEY'RE WEARING *NEW COSTUMES!*

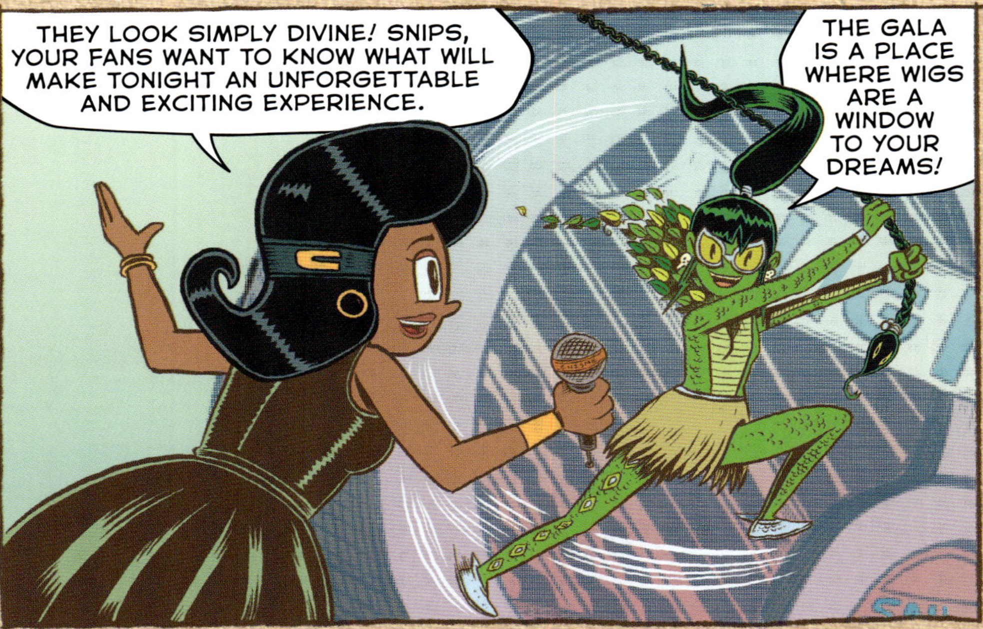
THEY LOOK SIMPLY DIVINE! SNIPS, YOUR FANS WANT TO KNOW WHAT WILL MAKE TONIGHT AN UNFORGETTABLE AND EXCITING EXPERIENCE.
THE GALA IS A PLACE WHERE WIGS ARE A WINDOW TO YOUR DREAMS!

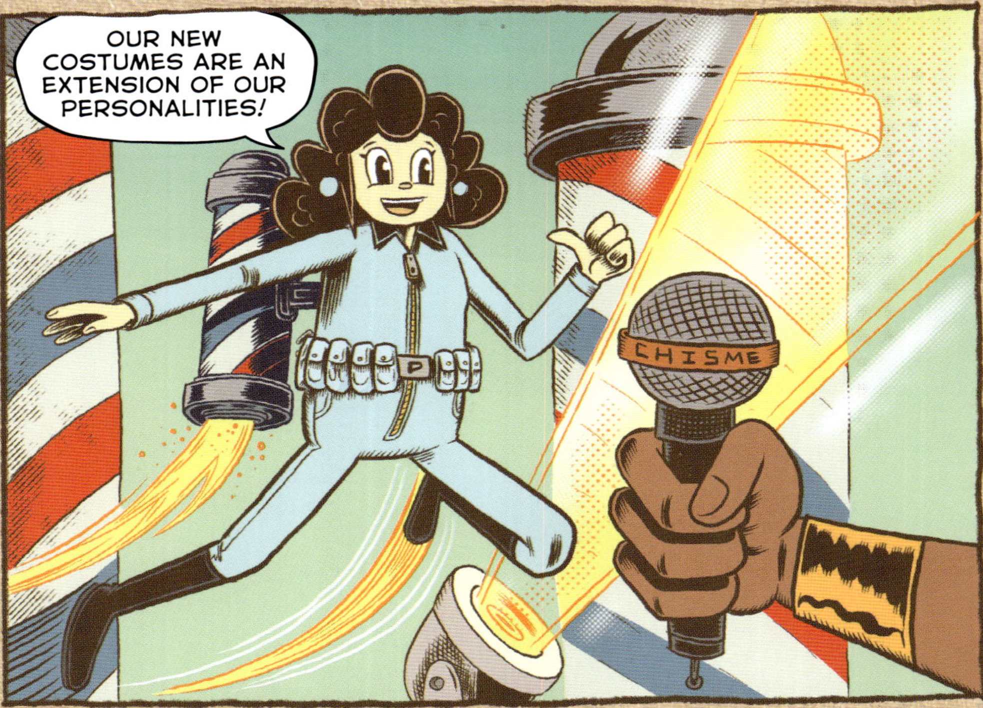
OUR NEW COSTUMES ARE AN EXTENSION OF OUR PERSONALITIES!
CHISME

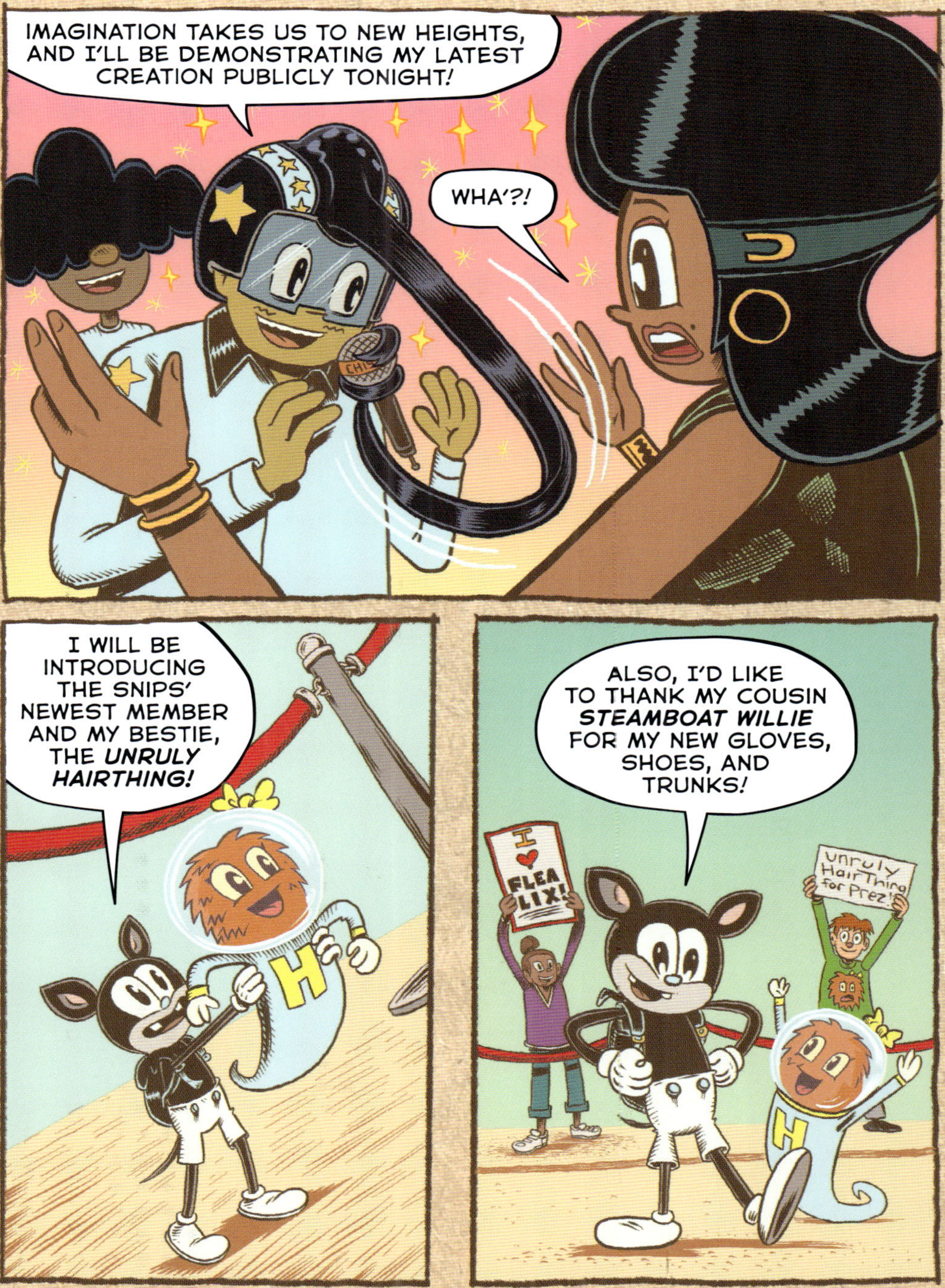
IMAGINATION TAKES US TO NEW HEIGHTS, AND I'LL BE DEMONSTRATING MY LATEST CREATION PUBLICLY TONIGHT!
WHA'?!
I WILL BE INTRODUCING THE SNIPS' NEWEST MEMBER AND MY BESTIE, THE *UNRULY HAIRTHING!*
ALSO, I'D LIKE TO THANK MY COUSIN ***STEAMBOAT WILLIE*** FOR MY NEW GLOVES, SHOES, AND TRUNKS!
I FLEA LIX!
Unruly HairThing for Prez!

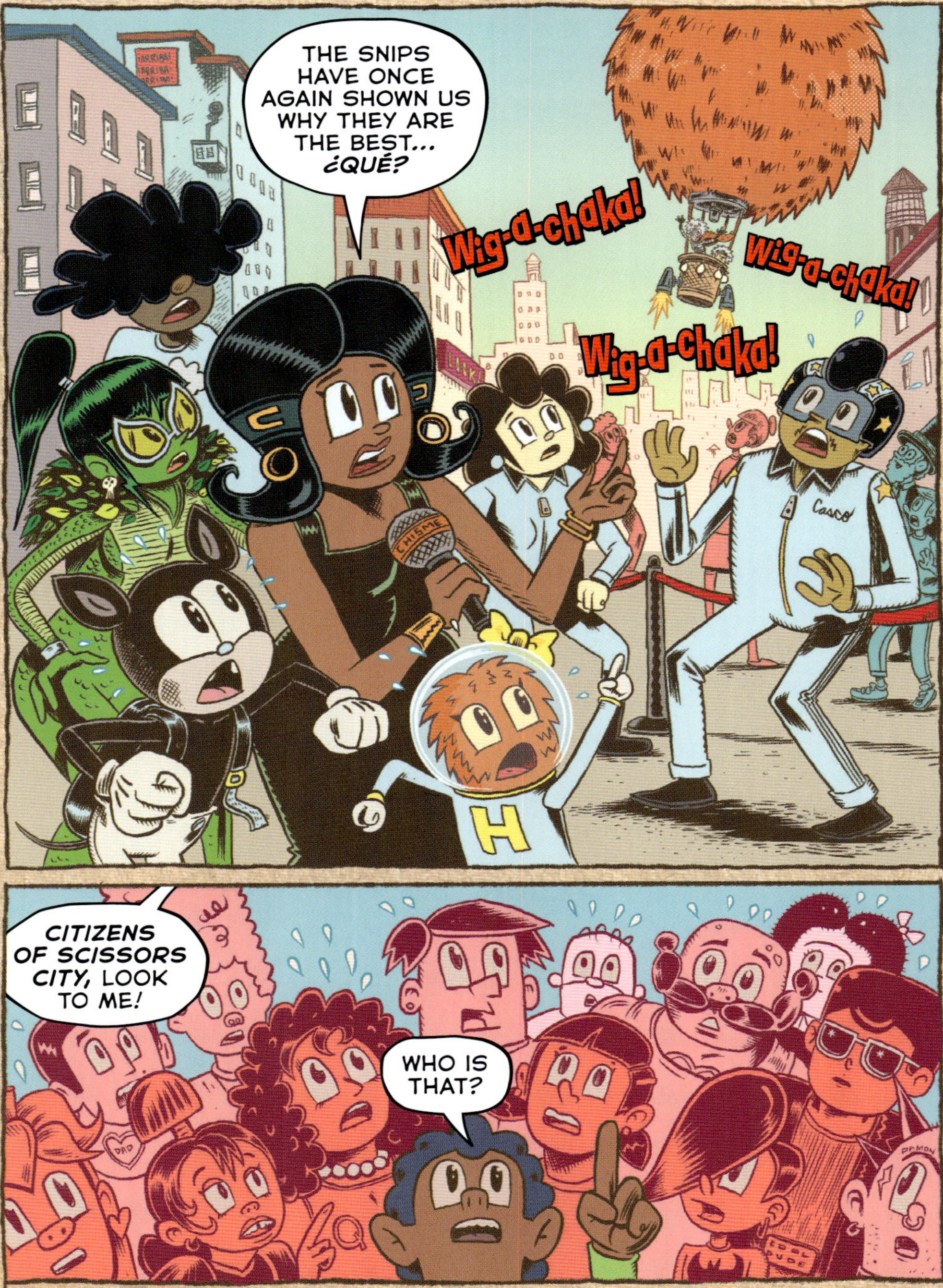
THE SNIPS HAVE ONCE AGAIN SHOWN US WHY THEY ARE THE BEST... ¿QUÉ?
Wig-a-chaka!
Wig-a-chaka!
Wig-a-chaka!
Casco
CHISME
H
CITIZENS OF SCISSORS CITY, LOOK TO ME!
WHO IS THAT?

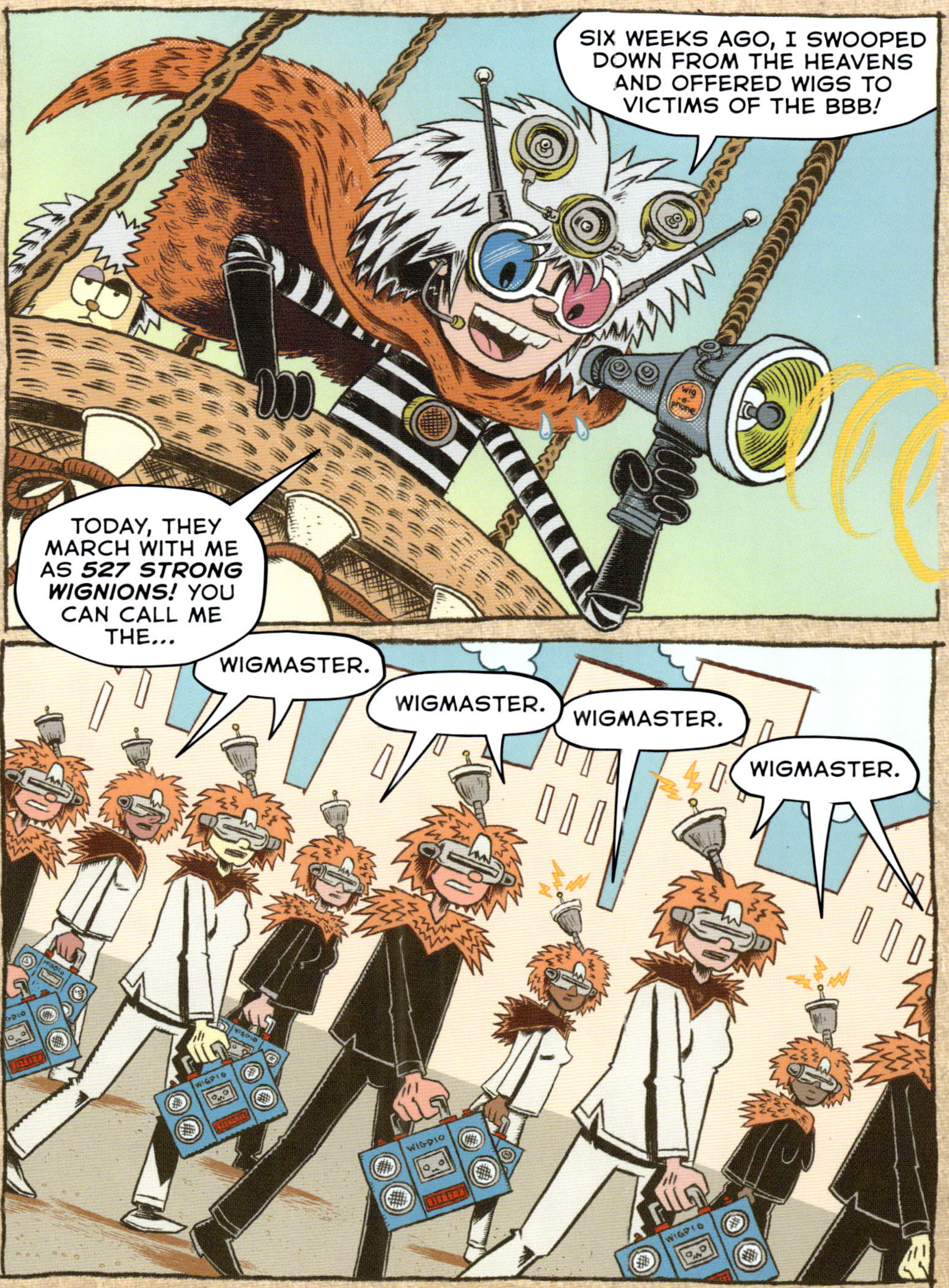
SIX WEEKS AGO, I SWOOPED DOWN FROM THE HEAVENS AND OFFERED WIGS TO VICTIMS OF THE BBB!
TODAY, THEY MARCH WITH ME AS ***527 STRONG WIGNIONS!*** YOU CAN CALL ME THE...
wig-o-phone
WIGMASTER.
WIGMASTER.
WIGMASTER.
WIGMASTER.
WIGDIO

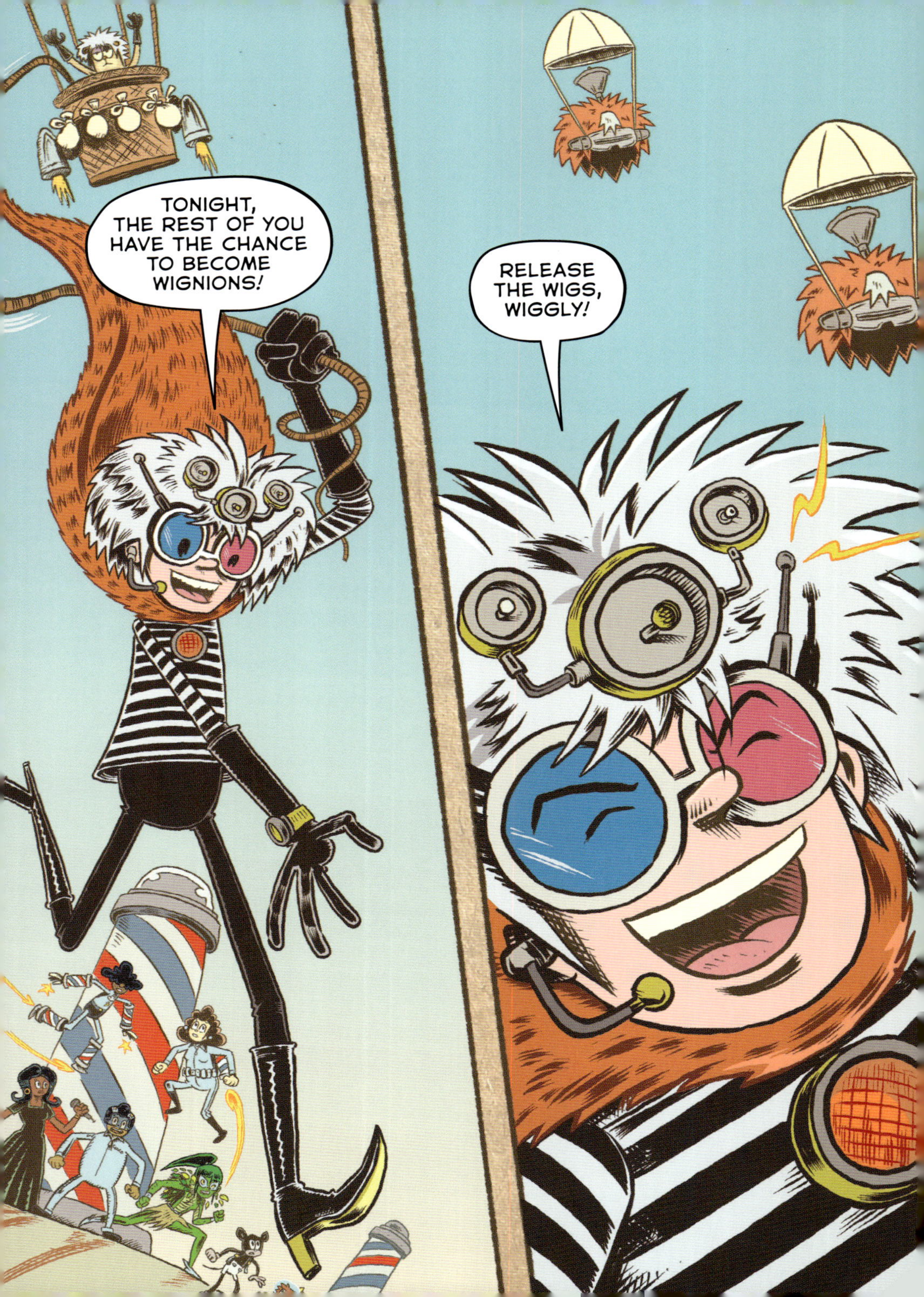
TONIGHT, THE REST OF YOU HAVE THE CHANCE TO BECOME WIGNIONS!
RELEASE THE WIGS, WIGGLY!

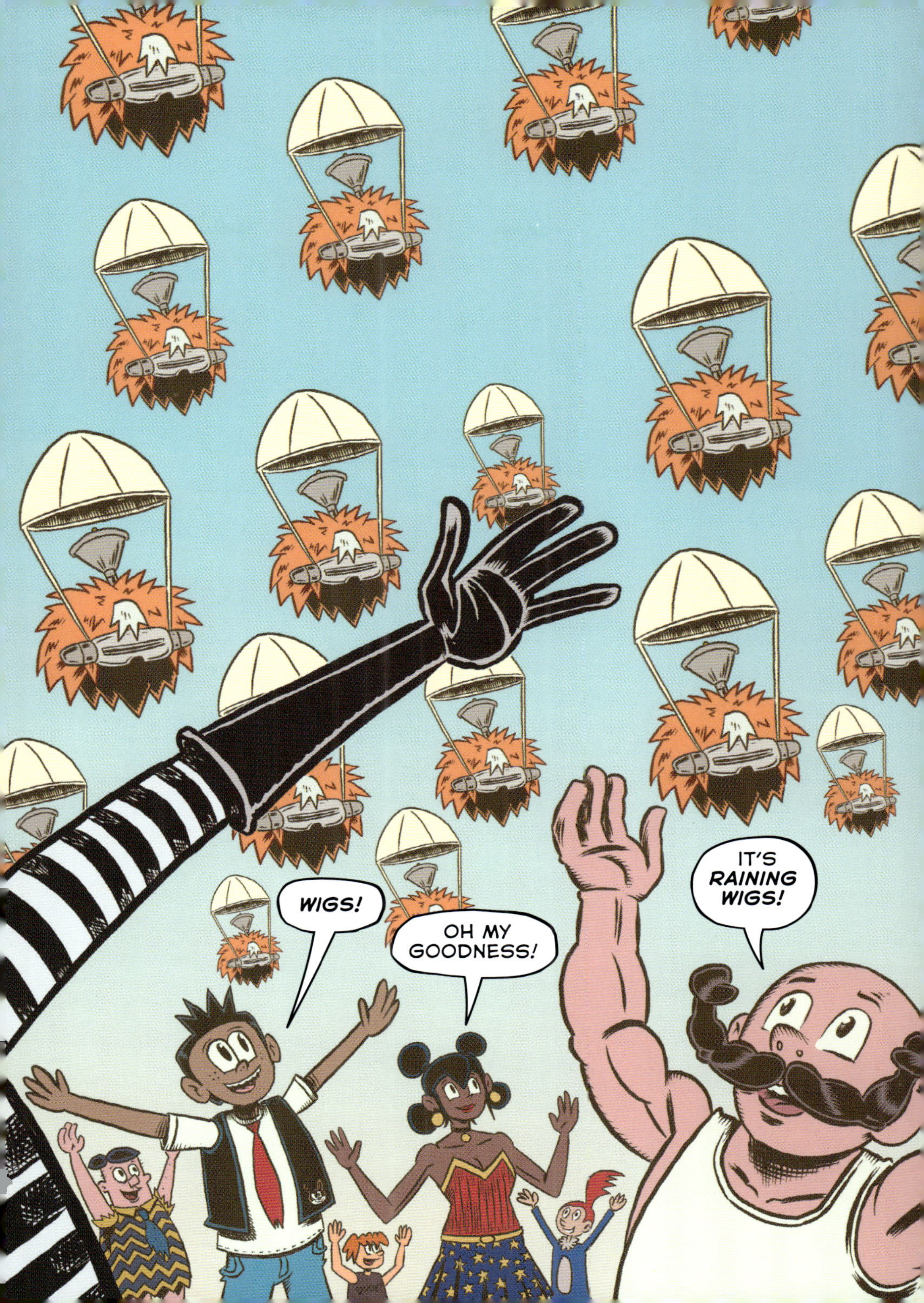
WIGS!
OH MY GOODNESS!
IT'S RAINING WIGS!

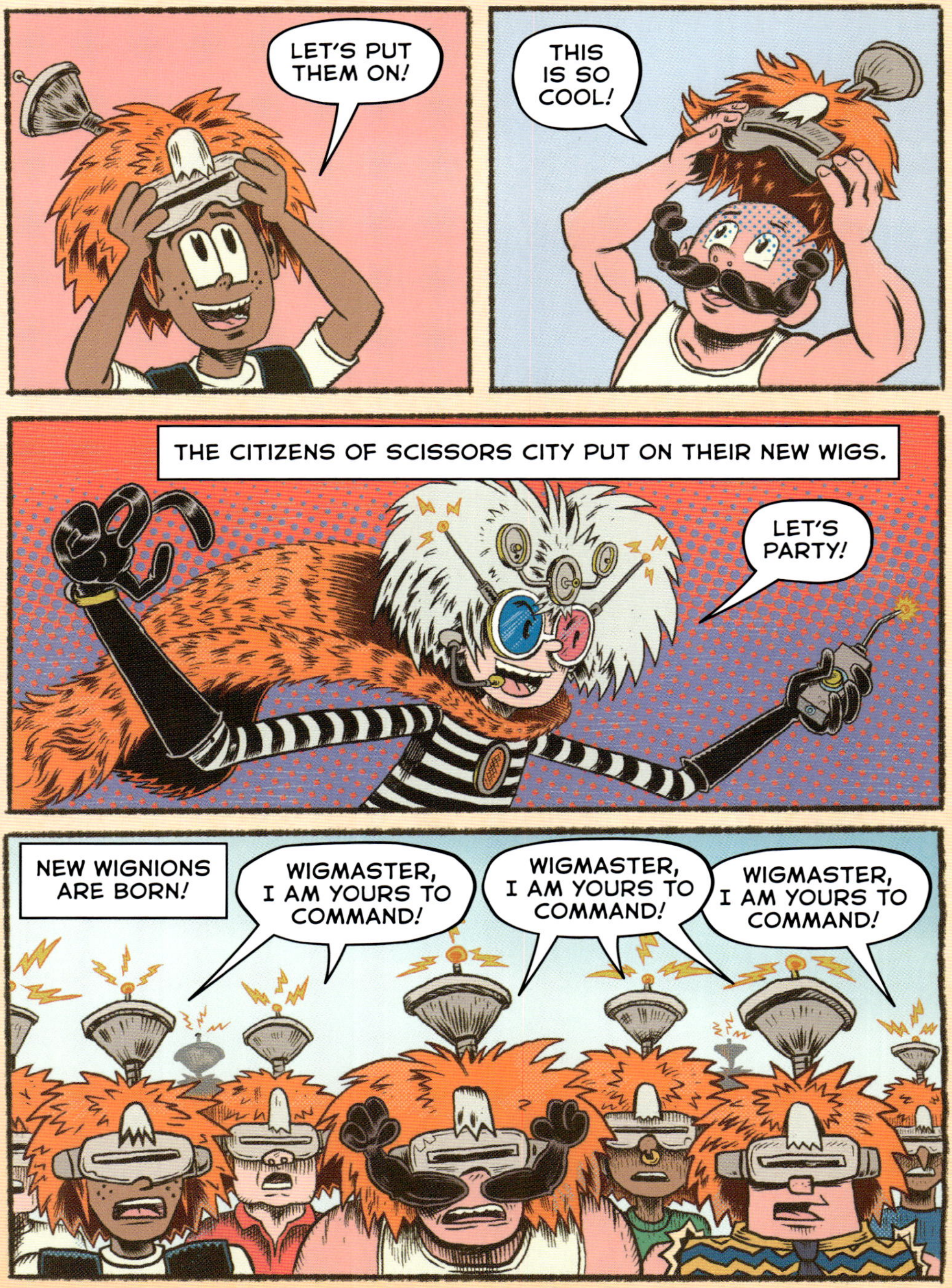
LET'S PUT THEM ON!
THIS IS SO COOL!
THE CITIZENS OF SCISSORS CITY PUT ON THEIR NEW WIGS.
LET'S PARTY!
NEW WIGNIONS ARE BORN!
WIGMASTER, I AM YOURS TO COMMAND!
WIGMASTER, I AM YOURS TO COMMAND!
WIGMASTER, I AM YOURS TO COMMAND!

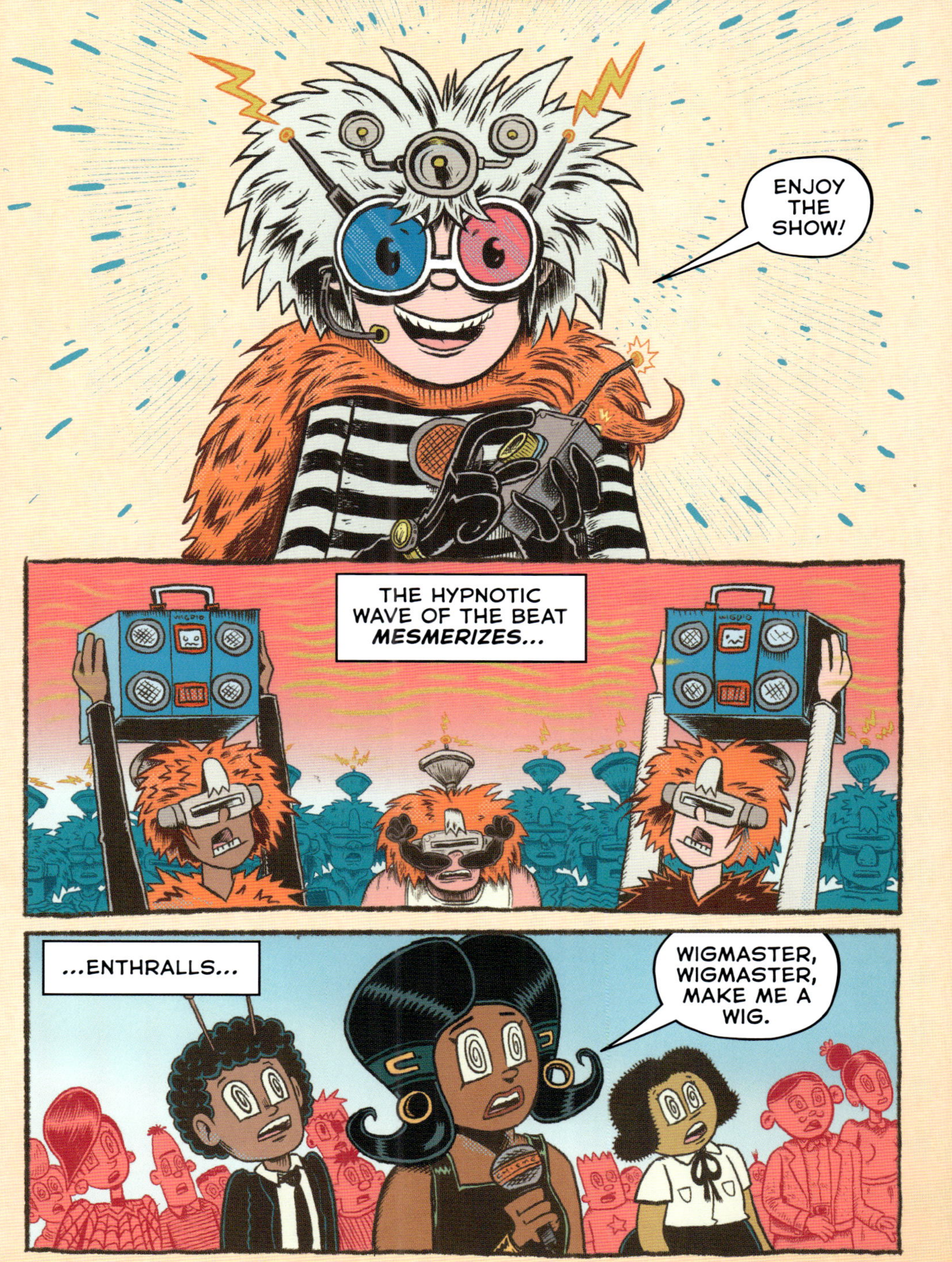
ENJOY THE SHOW!
THE HYPNOTIC WAVE OF THE BEAT *MESMERIZES...*
...ENTHRALLS...
WIGMASTER, WIGMASTER, MAKE ME A WIG.

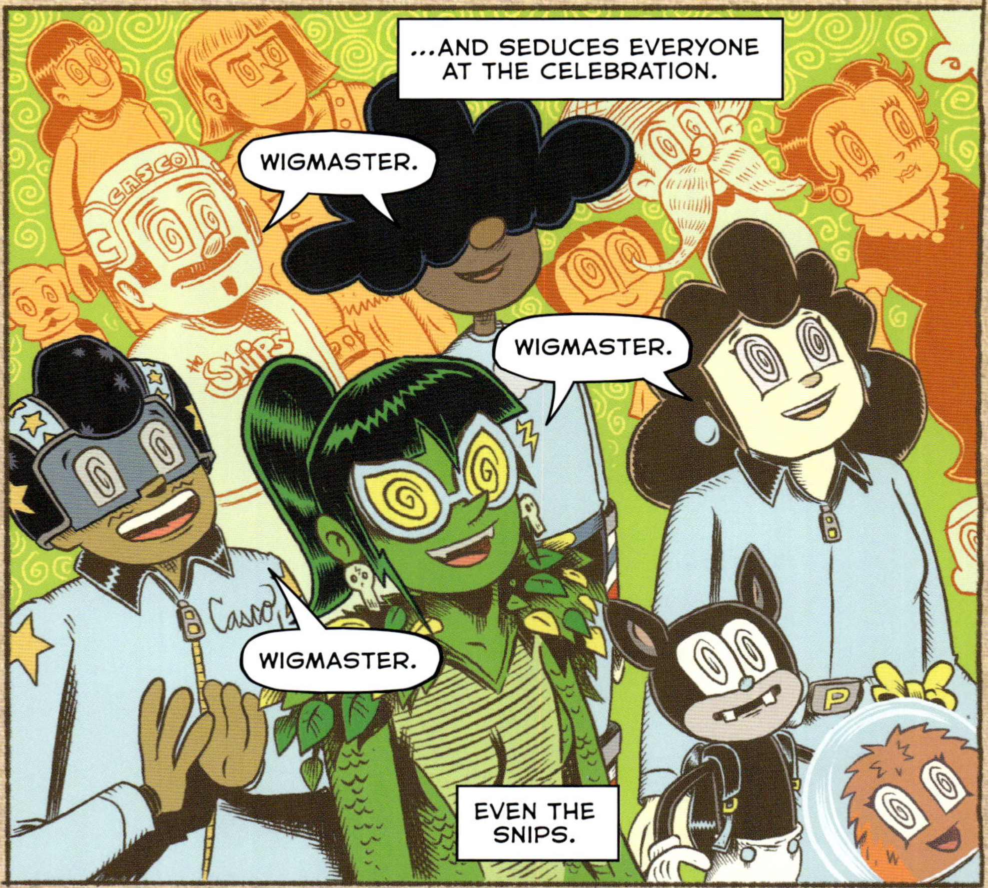
...AND SEDUCES EVERYONE AT THE CELEBRATION.
WIGMASTER.
WIGMASTER.
WIGMASTER.
EVEN THE SNIPS.

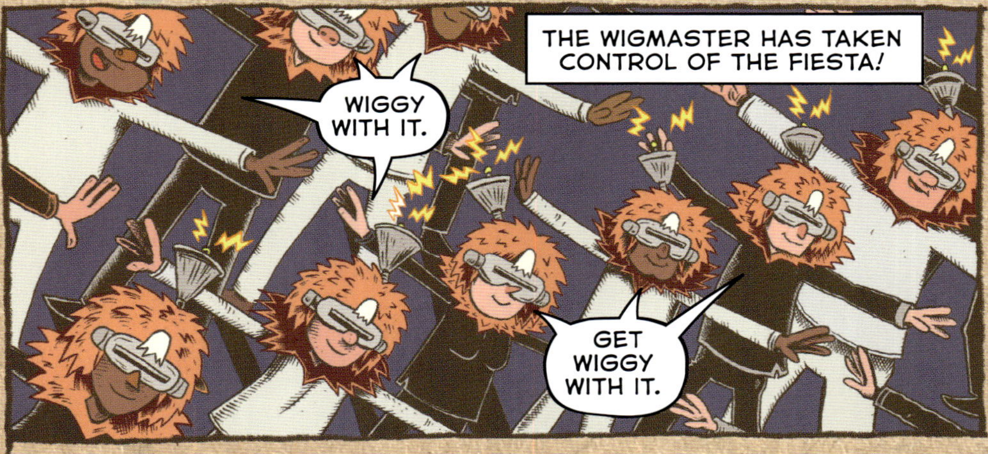
THE WIGMASTER HAS TAKEN CONTROL OF THE FIESTA!
WIGGY WITH IT.
GET WIGGY WITH IT.

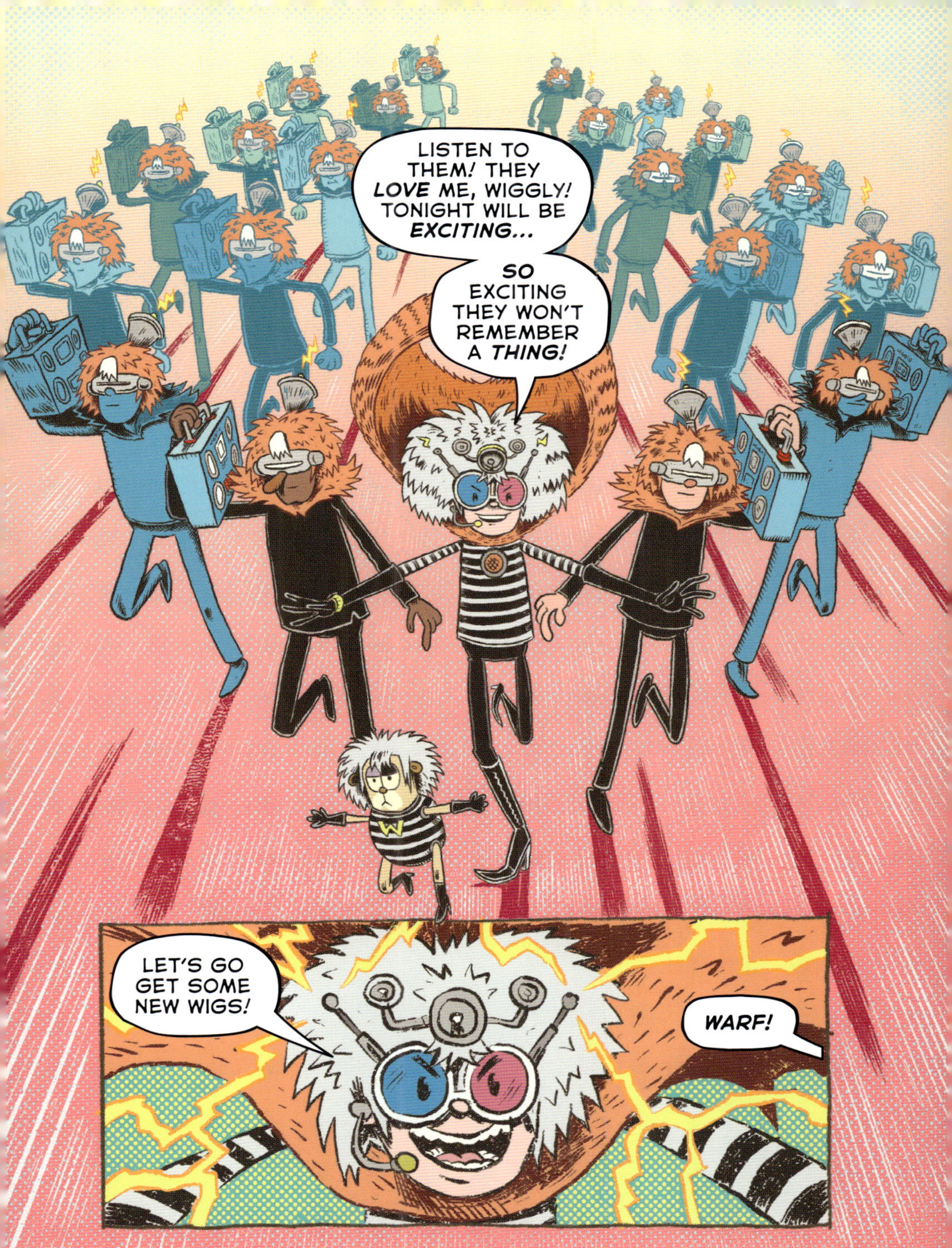

LISTEN TO THEM! THEY LOVE ME, WIGGLY! TONIGHT WILL BE EXCITING...
SO EXCITING THEY WON'T REMEMBER A THING!
LET'S GO GET SOME NEW WIGS!
WARF!

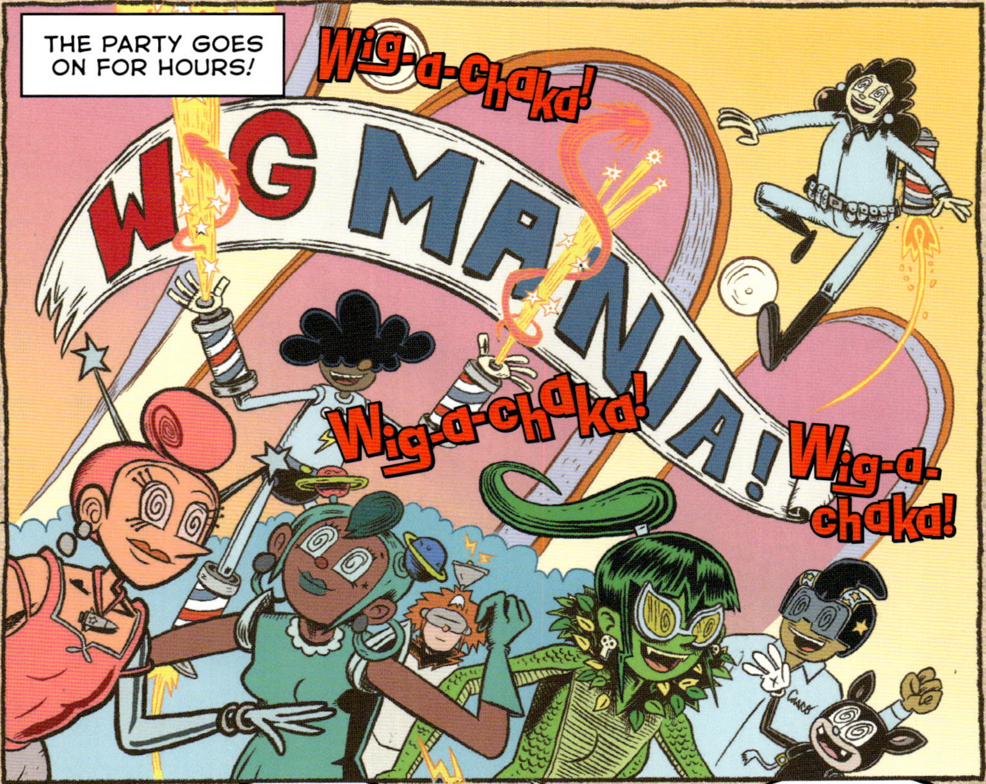
THE PARTY GOES ON FOR HOURS!
Wig-a-chaka!
WIG MANIA!
Wig-a-chaka!
Wig-a-chaka!

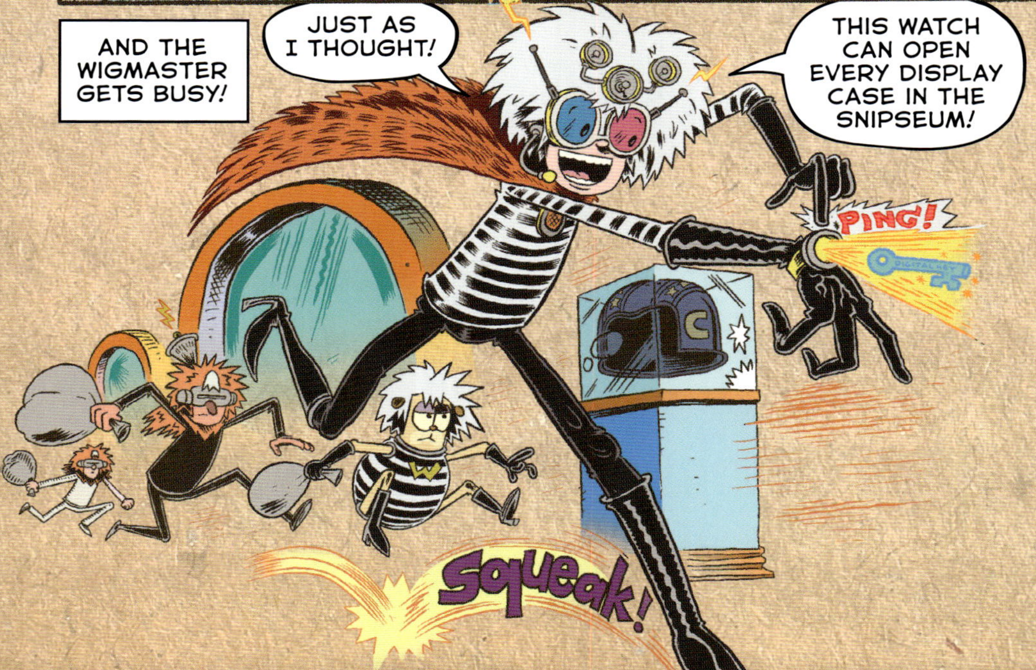
AND THE WIGMASTER GETS BUSY!
JUST AS I THOUGHT!
THIS WATCH CAN OPEN EVERY DISPLAY CASE IN THE SNIPSEUM!
PING!
Squeak!

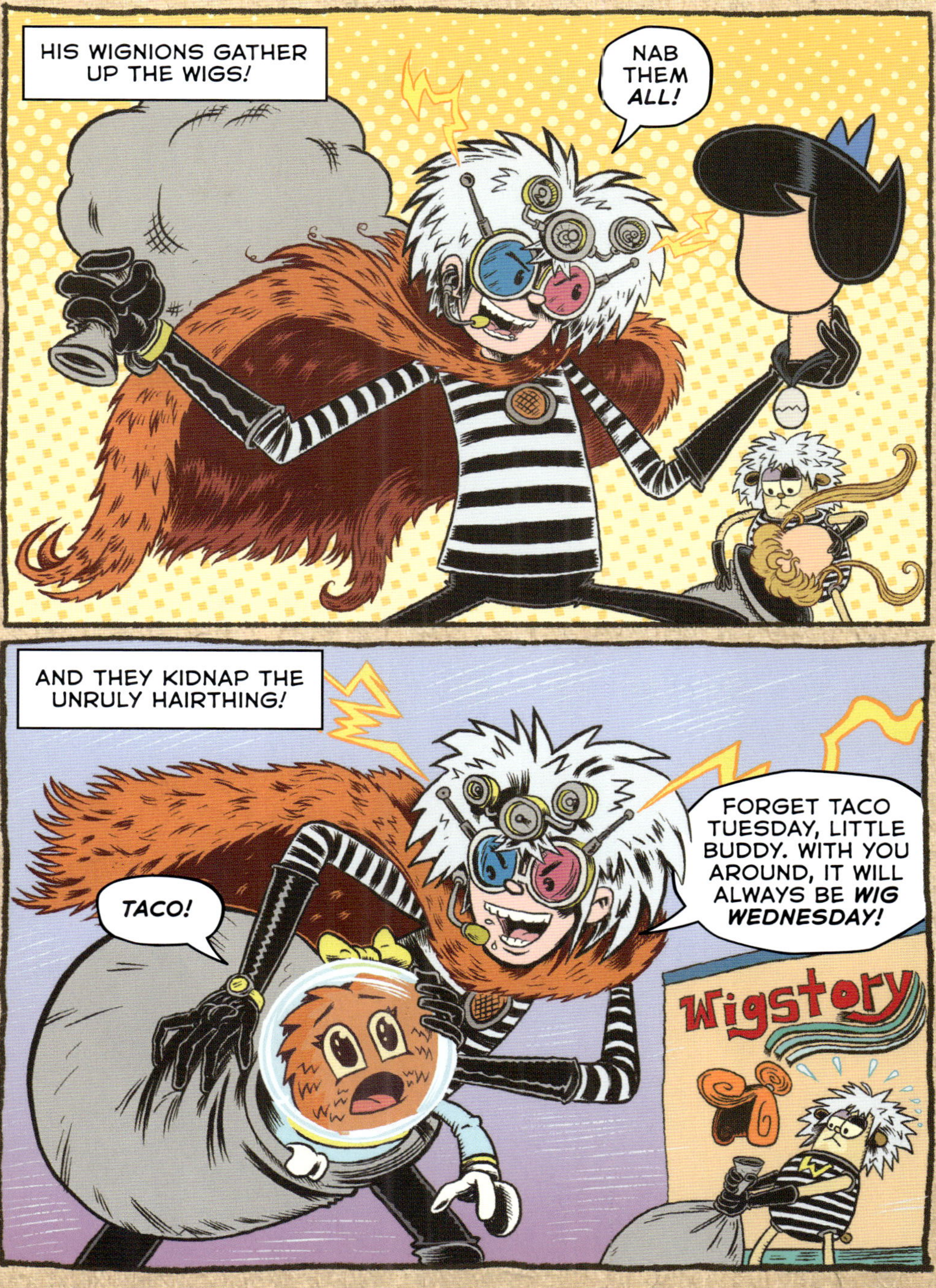
HIS WIGNIONS GATHER UP THE WIGS!
NAB THEM ALL!
AND THEY KIDNAP THE UNRULY HAIRTHING!
TACO!
FORGET TACO TUESDAY, LITTLE BUDDY. WITH YOU AROUND, IT WILL ALWAYS BE WIG WEDNESDAY!
Wigstory

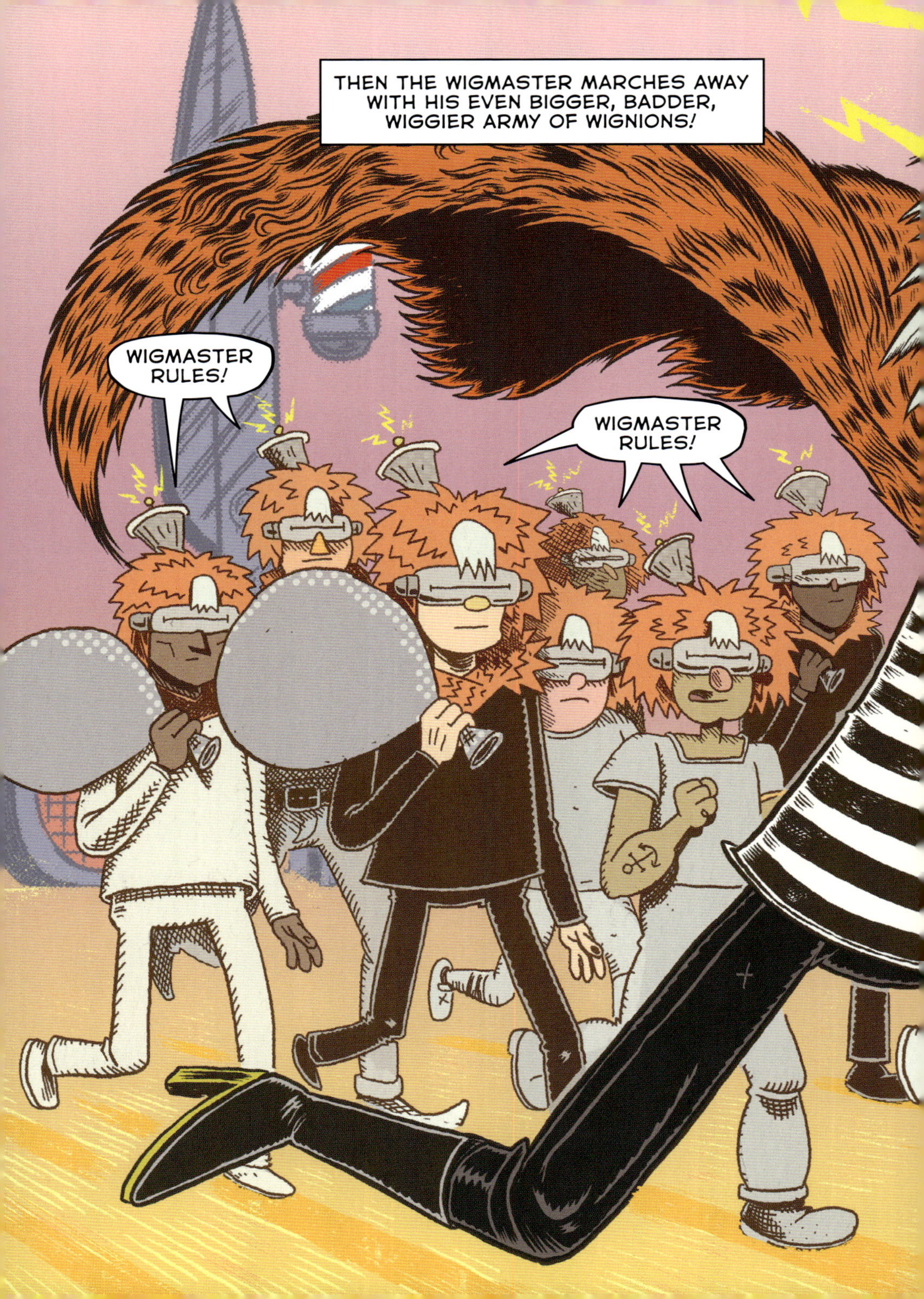
THEN THE WIGMASTER MARCHES AWAY WITH HIS EVEN BIGGER, BADDER, WIGGIER ARMY OF WIGNIONS!
WIGMASTER RULES!
WIGMASTER RULES!

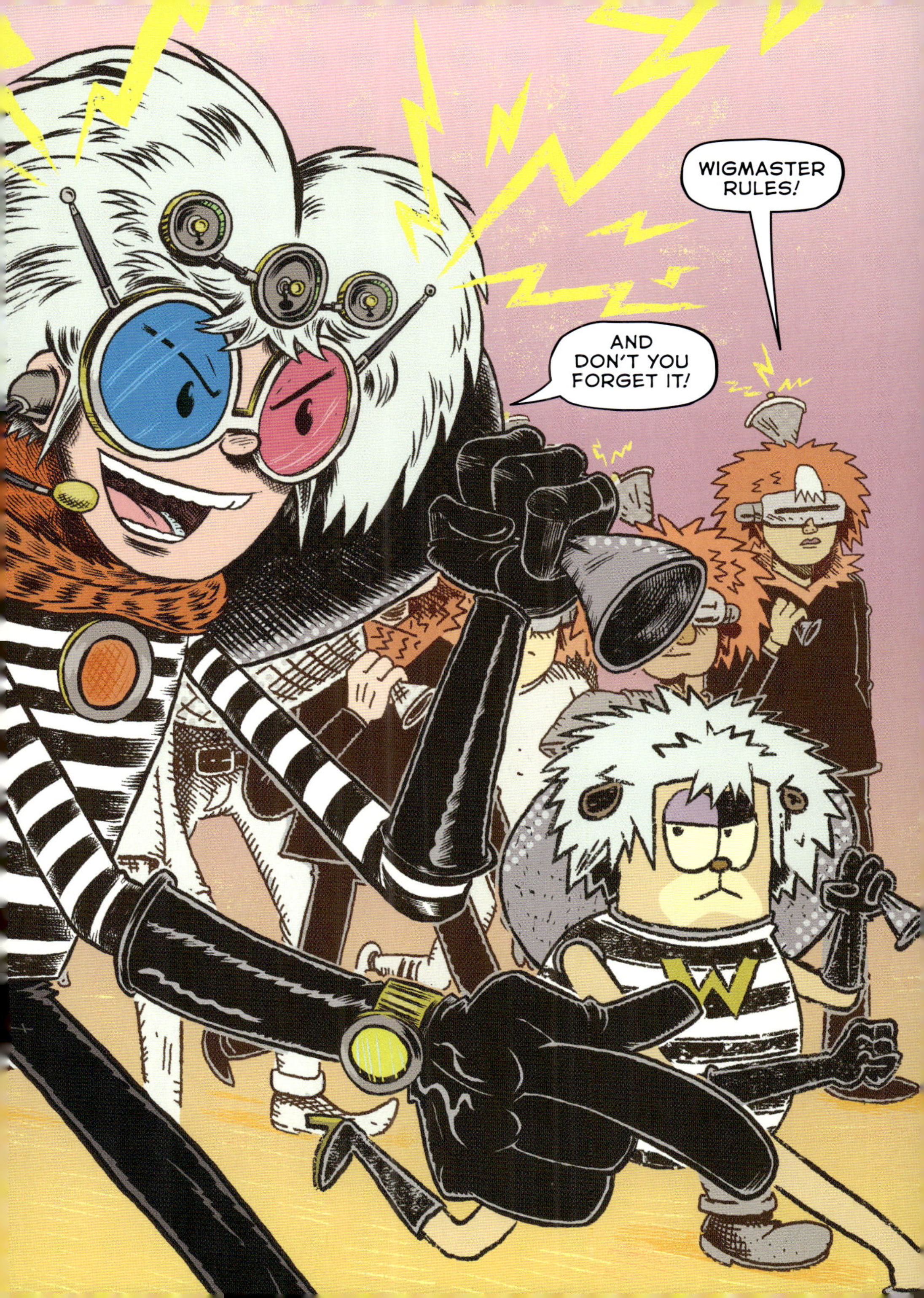
WIGMASTER RULES!
AND DON'T YOU FORGET IT!

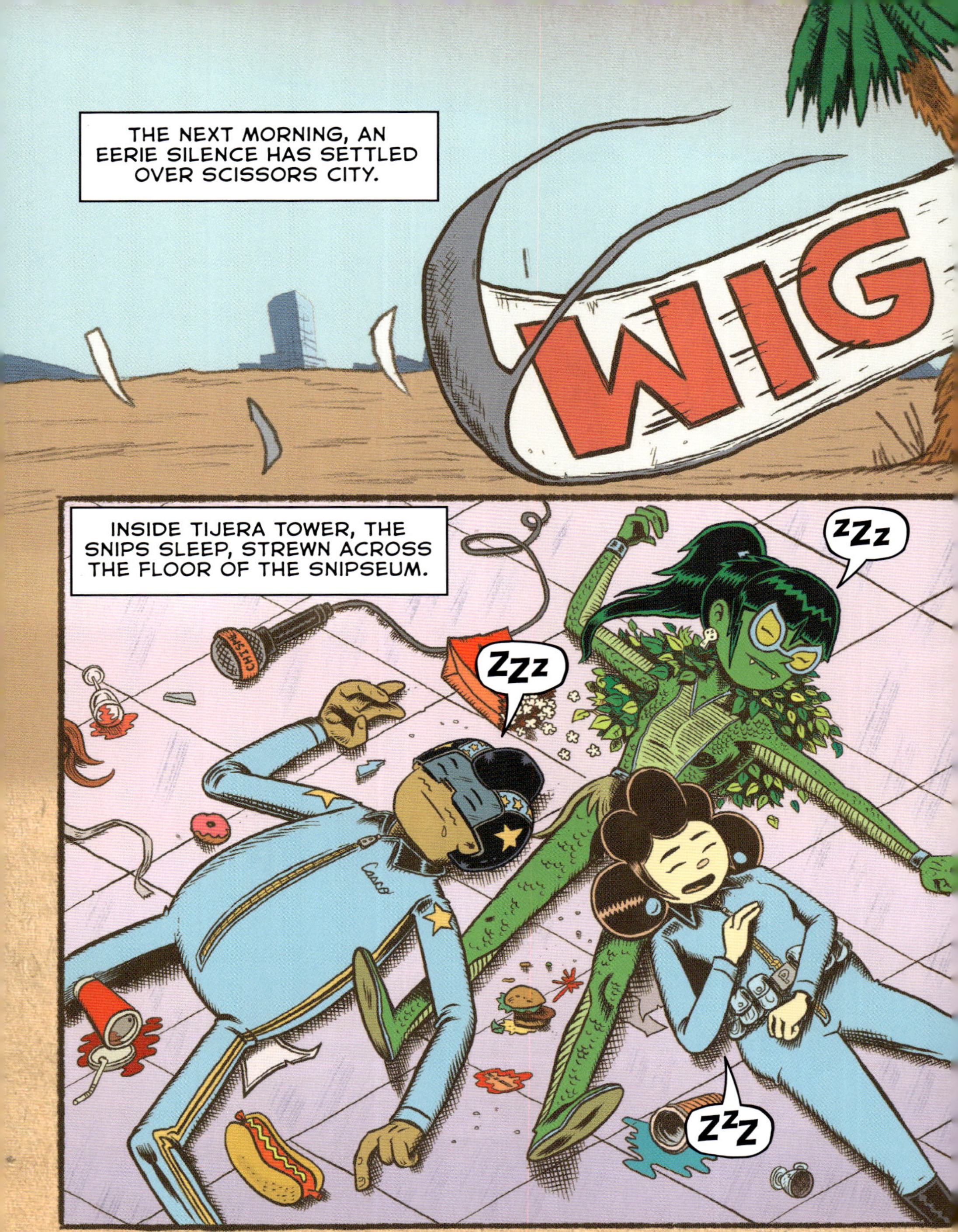
THE NEXT MORNING, AN EERIE SILENCE HAS SETTLED OVER SCISSORS CITY.
WIG
INSIDE TIJERA TOWER, THE SNIPS SLEEP, STREWN ACROSS THE FLOOR OF THE SNIPSEUM.
ZZZ
ZZZ
ZZZ

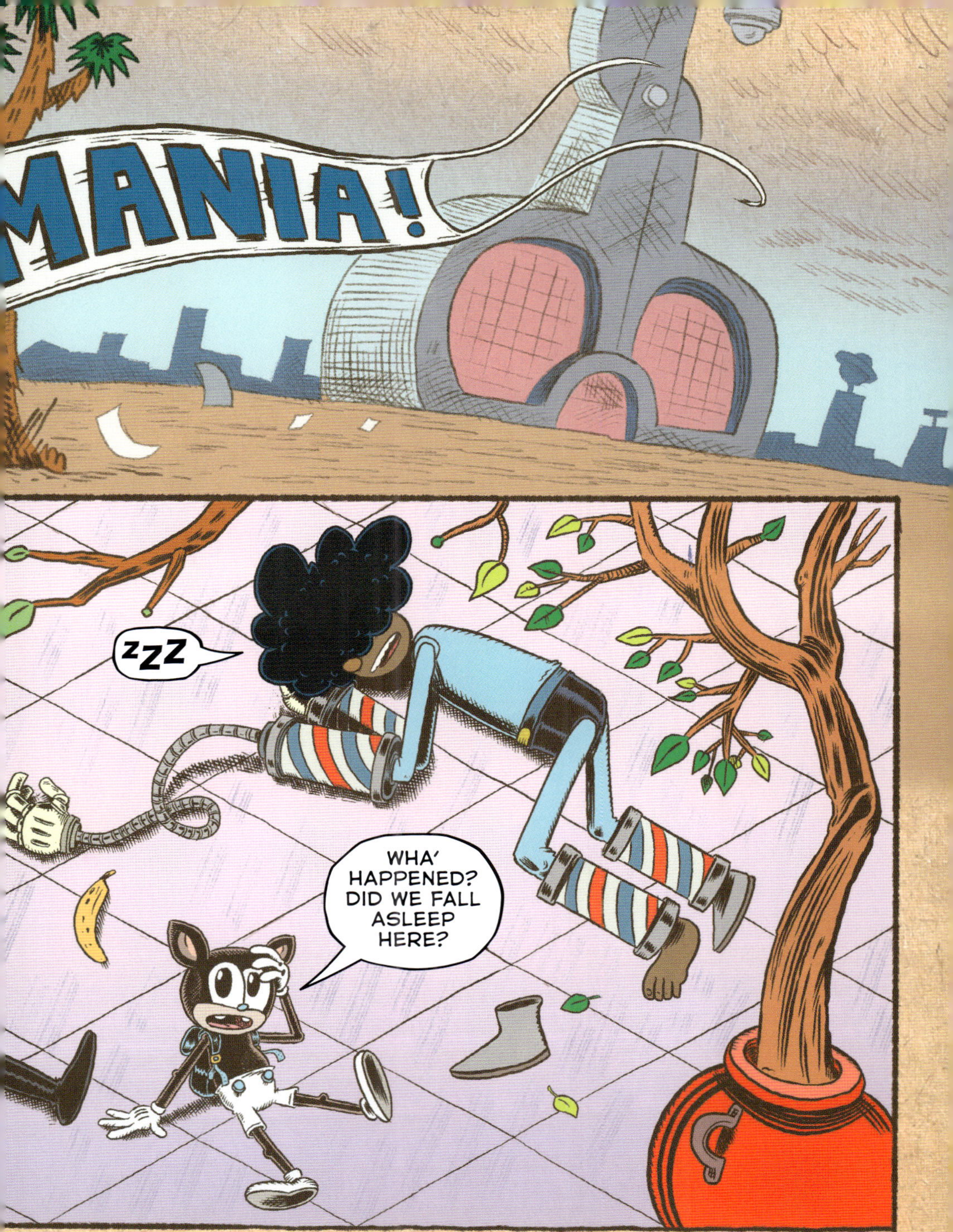
MANIA!
ZZZ
WHA' HAPPENED? DID WE FALL ASLEEP HERE?

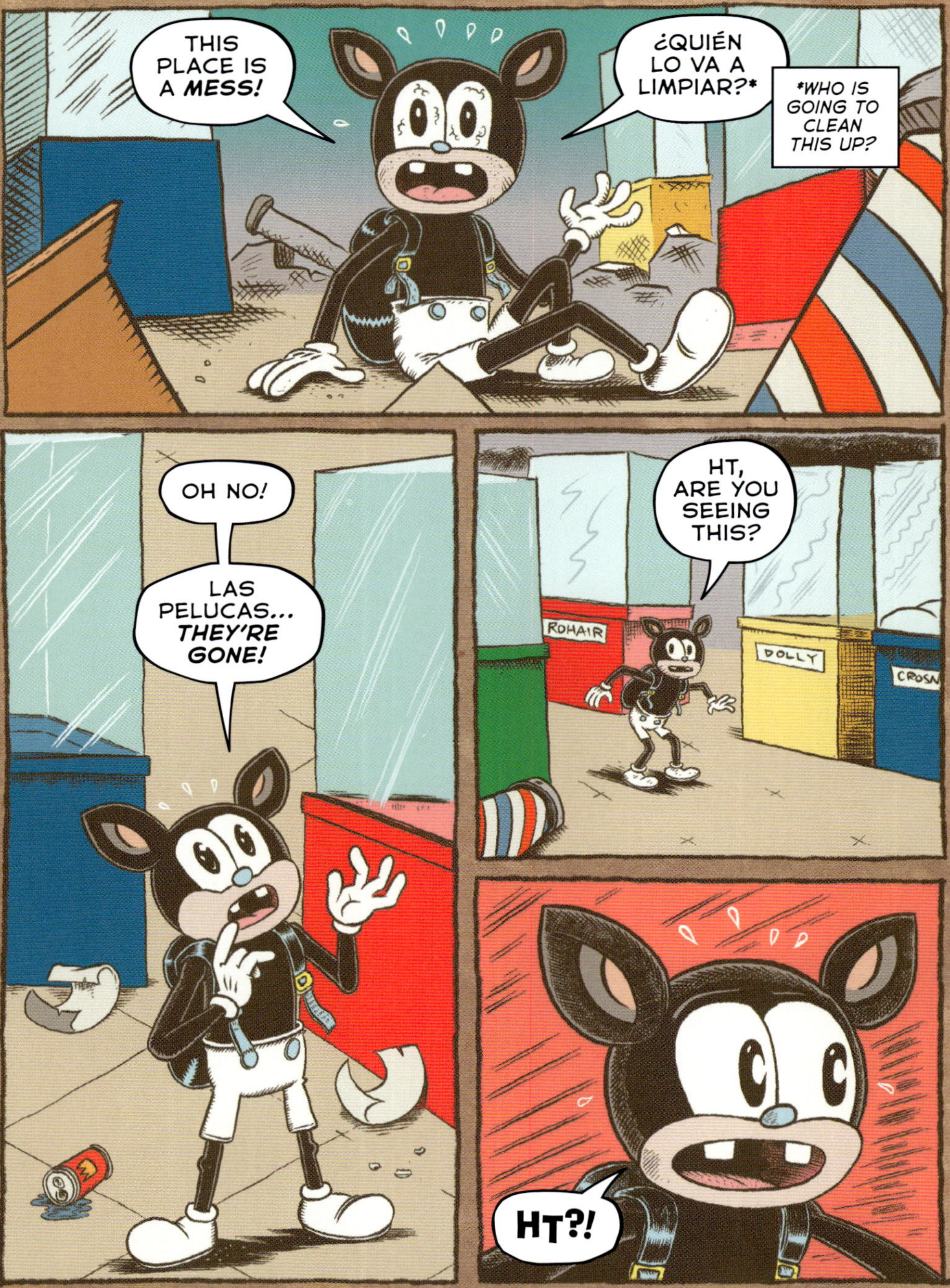

THIS PLACE IS A MESS!
¿QUIÉN LO VA A LIMPIAR?*
*WHO IS GOING TO CLEAN THIS UP?
OH NO!
LAS PELUCAS... THEY'RE GONE!
HT, ARE YOU SEEING THIS?
ROHAIR
DOLLY
HT?!

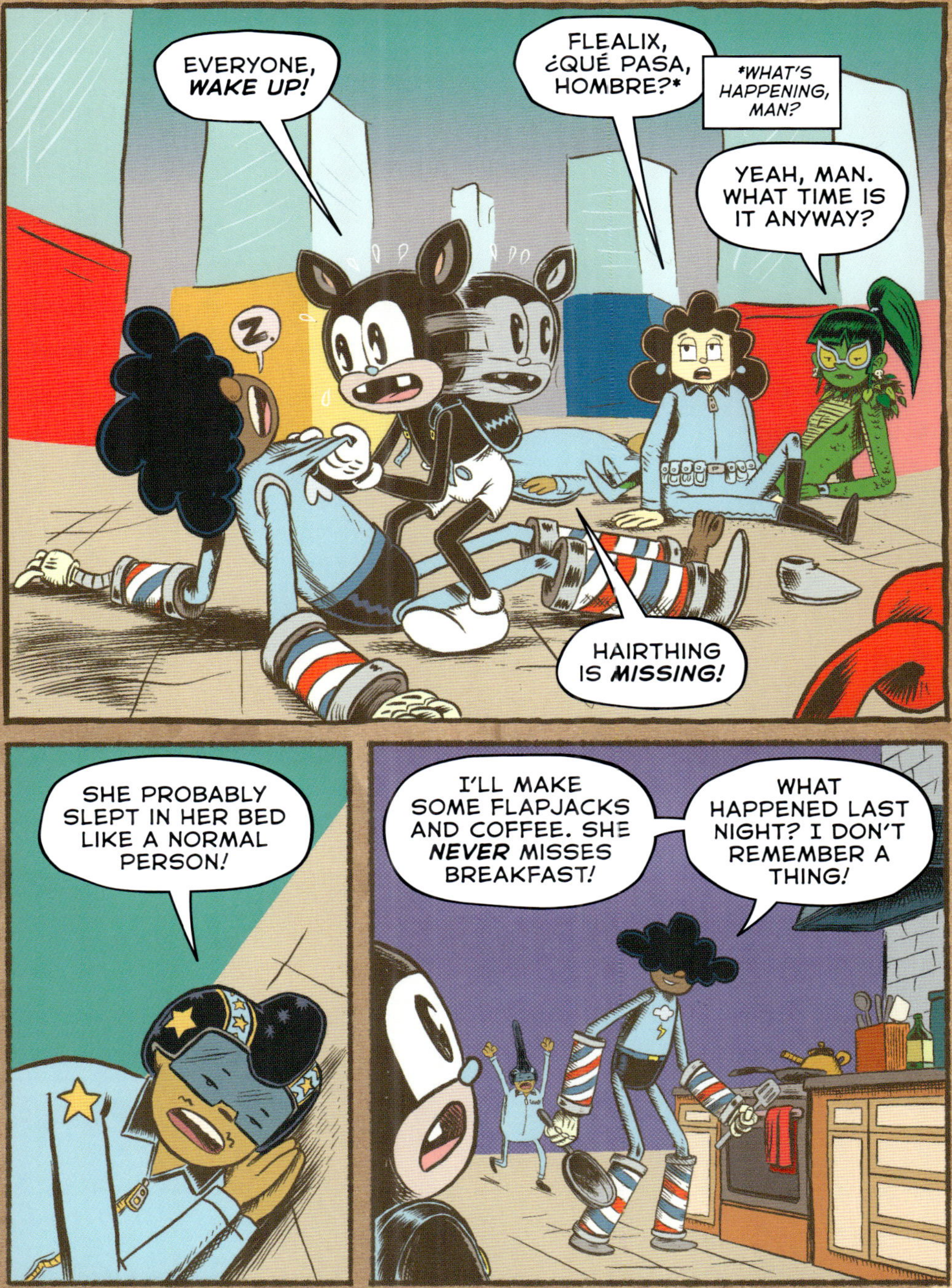
EVERYONE, *WAKE UP!*
FLEALIX, ¿QUÉ PASA, HOMBRE?*
*WHAT'S HAPPENING, MAN?
YEAH, MAN. WHAT TIME IS IT ANYWAY?
Z
HAIRTHING IS *MISSING!*
SHE PROBABLY SLEPT IN HER BED LIKE A NORMAL PERSON!
WHAT HAPPENED LAST NIGHT? I DON'T REMEMBER A THING!
I'LL MAKE SOME FLAPJACKS AND COFFEE. SHE *NEVER* MISSES BREAKFAST!

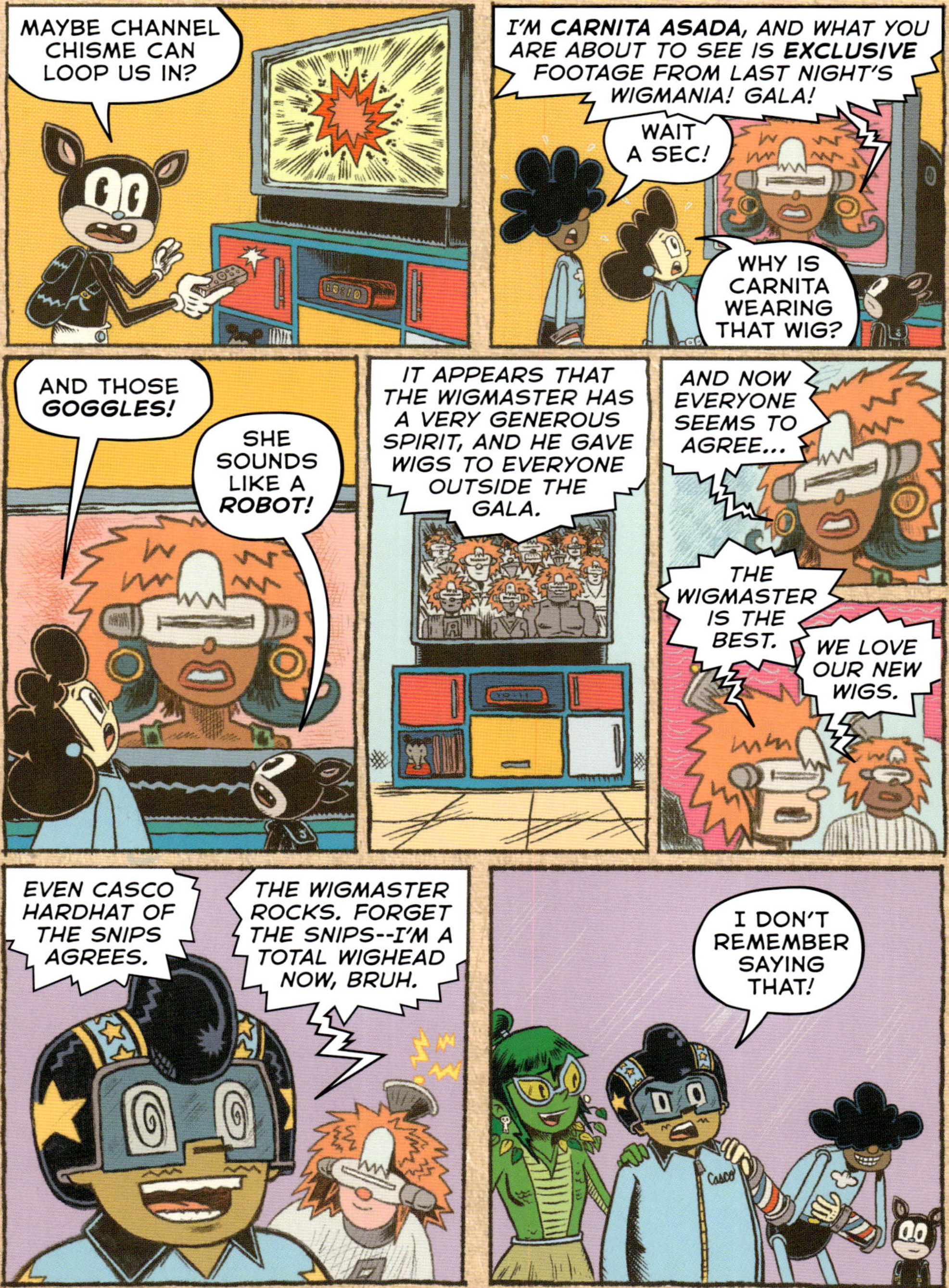
MAYBE CHANNEL CHISME CAN LOOP US IN?
I'M CARNITA ASADA, AND WHAT YOU ARE ABOUT TO SEE IS EXCLUSIVE FOOTAGE FROM LAST NIGHT'S WIGMANIA! GALA!
WAIT A SEC!
WHY IS CARNITA WEARING THAT WIG?
AND THOSE GOGGLES!
SHE SOUNDS LIKE A ROBOT!
IT APPEARS THAT THE WIGMASTER HAS A VERY GENEROUS SPIRIT, AND HE GAVE WIGS TO EVERYONE OUTSIDE THE GALA.
AND NOW EVERYONE SEEMS TO AGREE...
THE WIGMASTER IS THE BEST.
WE LOVE OUR NEW WIGS.
EVEN CASCO HARDHAT OF THE SNIPS AGREES.
THE WIGMASTER ROCKS. FORGET THE SNIPS--I'M A TOTAL WIGHEAD NOW, BRUH.
I DON'T REMEMBER SAYING THAT!

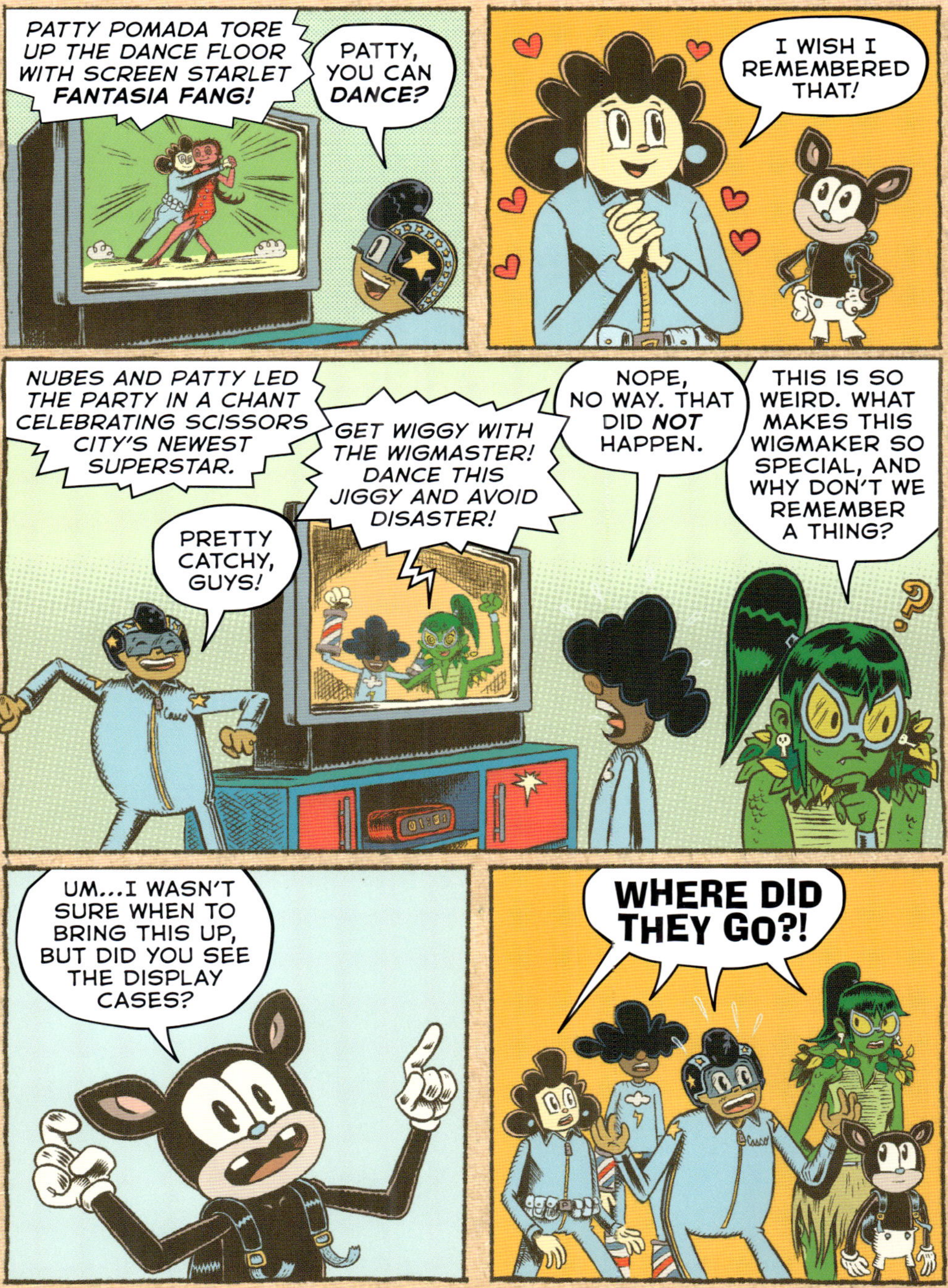
PATTY POMADA TORE UP THE DANCE FLOOR WITH SCREEN STARLET FANTASIA FANG!
PATTY, YOU CAN DANCE?
I WISH I REMEMBERED THAT!
NUBES AND PATTY LED THE PARTY IN A CHANT CELEBRATING SCISSORS CITY'S NEWEST SUPERSTAR.
GET WIGGY WITH THE WIGMASTER! DANCE THIS JIGGY AND AVOID DISASTER!
PRETTY CATCHY, GUYS!
NOPE, NO WAY. THAT DID NOT HAPPEN.
THIS IS SO WEIRD. WHAT MAKES THIS WIGMAKER SO SPECIAL, AND WHY DON'T WE REMEMBER A THING?
UM...I WASN'T SURE WHEN TO BRING THIS UP, BUT DID YOU SEE THE DISPLAY CASES?
WHERE DID THEY GO?!

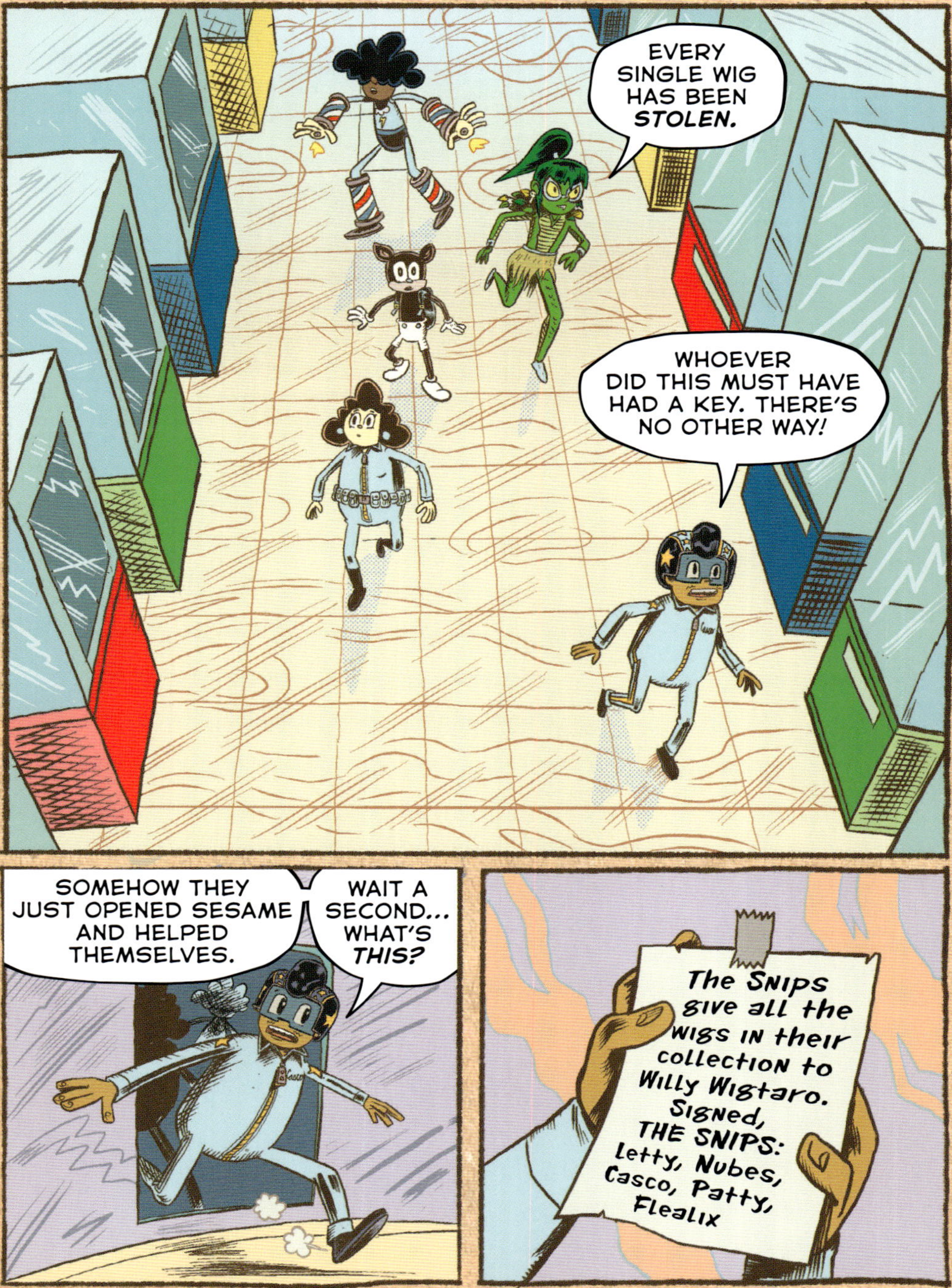
EVERY SINGLE WIG HAS BEEN *STOLEN.*
WHOEVER DID THIS MUST HAVE HAD A KEY. THERE'S NO OTHER WAY!
SOMEHOW THEY JUST OPENED SESAME AND HELPED THEMSELVES.
WAIT A SECOND... WHAT'S *THIS?*
The Snips give all the wigs in their collection to Willy Wigtaro. Signed, THE SNIPS: Letty, Nubes, Casco, Patty, Flealix

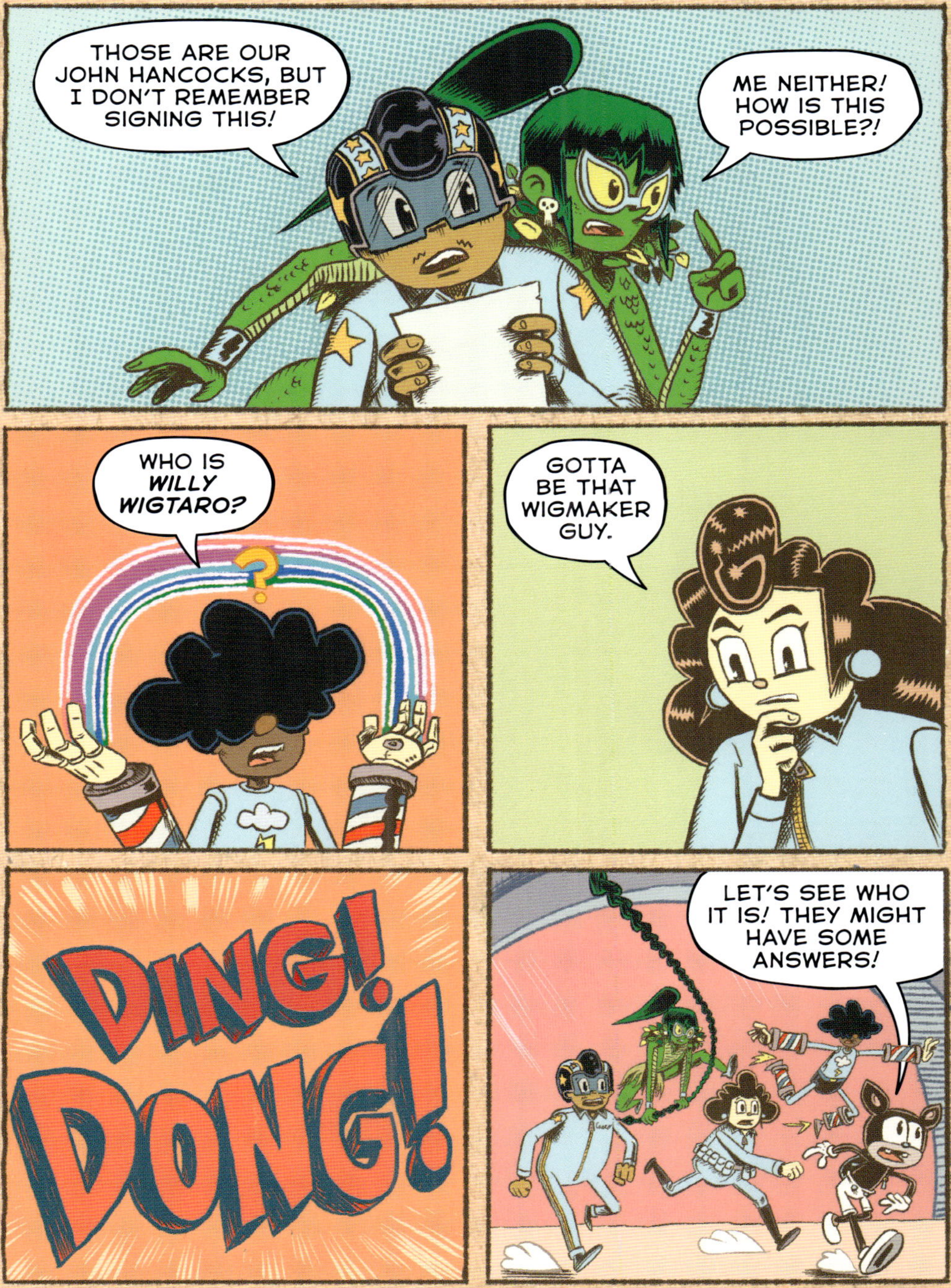
THOSE ARE OUR JOHN HANCOCKS, BUT I DON'T REMEMBER SIGNING THIS!
ME NEITHER! HOW IS THIS POSSIBLE?!
WHO IS *WILLY WIGTARO?*
GOTTA BE THAT WIGMAKER GUY.
DING! DONG!
LET'S SEE WHO IT IS! THEY MIGHT HAVE SOME ANSWERS!

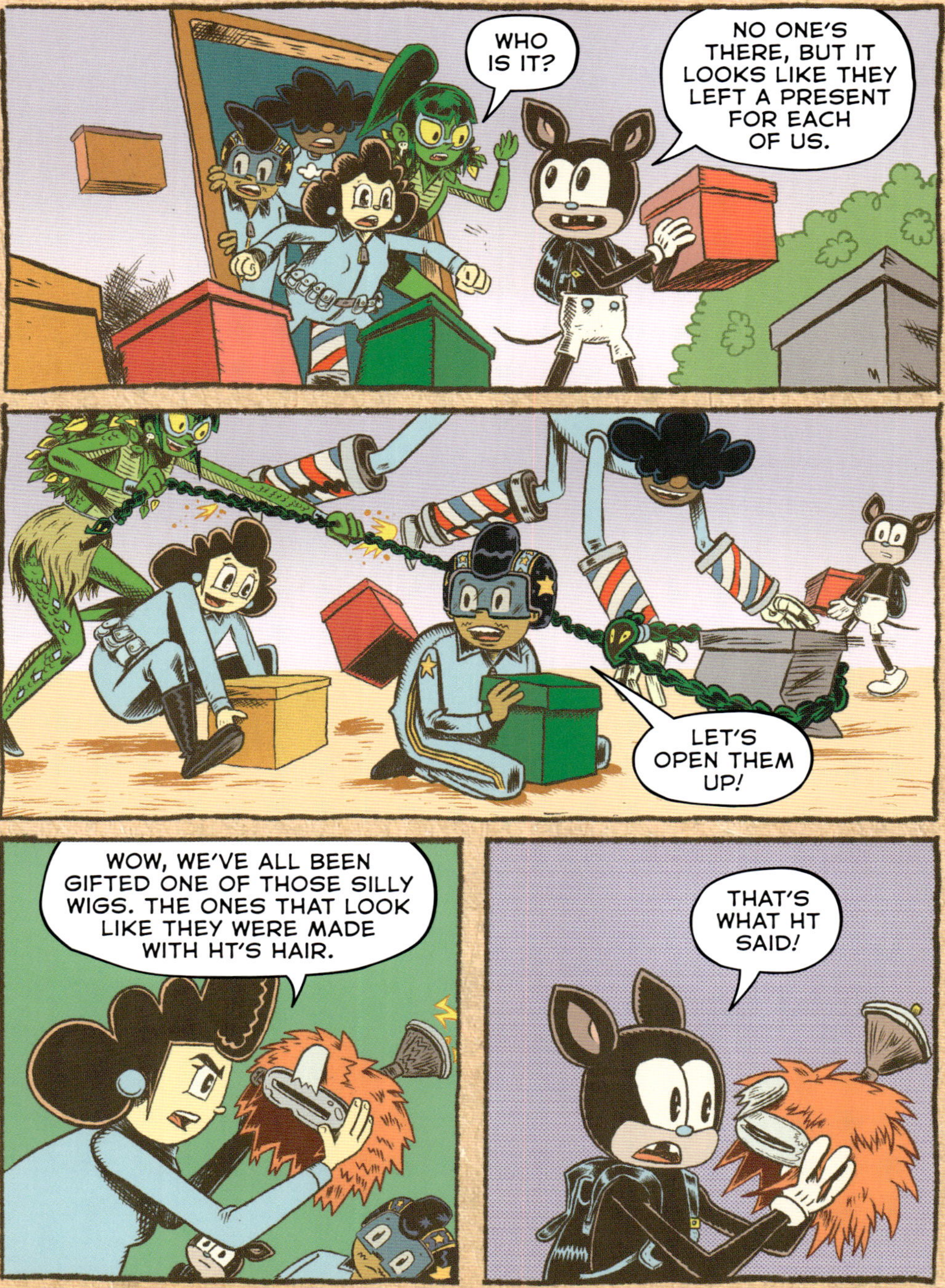
WHO IS IT?
NO ONE'S THERE, BUT IT LOOKS LIKE THEY LEFT A PRESENT FOR EACH OF US.
LET'S OPEN THEM UP!
WOW, WE'VE ALL BEEN GIFTED ONE OF THOSE SILLY WIGS. THE ONES THAT LOOK LIKE THEY WERE MADE WITH HT'S HAIR.
THAT'S WHAT HT SAID!

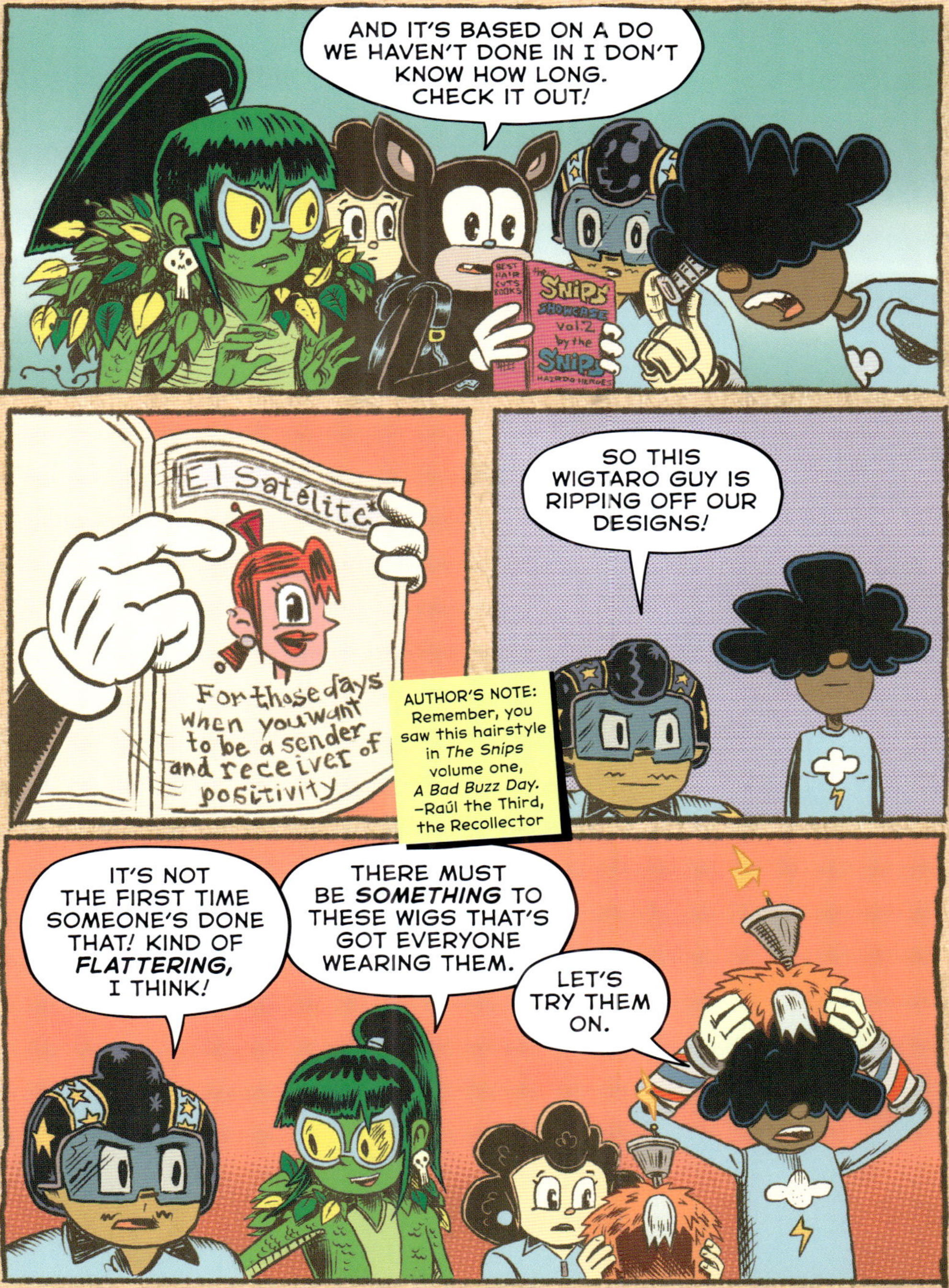
AND IT'S BASED ON A DO WE HAVEN'T DONE IN I DON'T KNOW HOW LONG. CHECK IT OUT!
BEST HAIR CUTS BOOKS
the SNIPS SHOWCASE vol.2 by the SNIPS
HAIRDO HEROES
El Satélite
For those days when you want to be a sender and receiver of positivity
SO THIS WIGTARO GUY IS RIPPING OFF OUR DESIGNS!
AUTHOR'S NOTE: Remember, you saw this hairstyle in *The Snips* volume one, *A Bad Buzz Day*. —Raúl the Third, the Recollector
IT'S NOT THE FIRST TIME SOMEONE'S DONE THAT! KIND OF ***FLATTERING,*** I THINK!
THERE MUST BE ***SOMETHING*** TO THESE WIGS THAT'S GOT EVERYONE WEARING THEM.
LET'S TRY THEM ON.

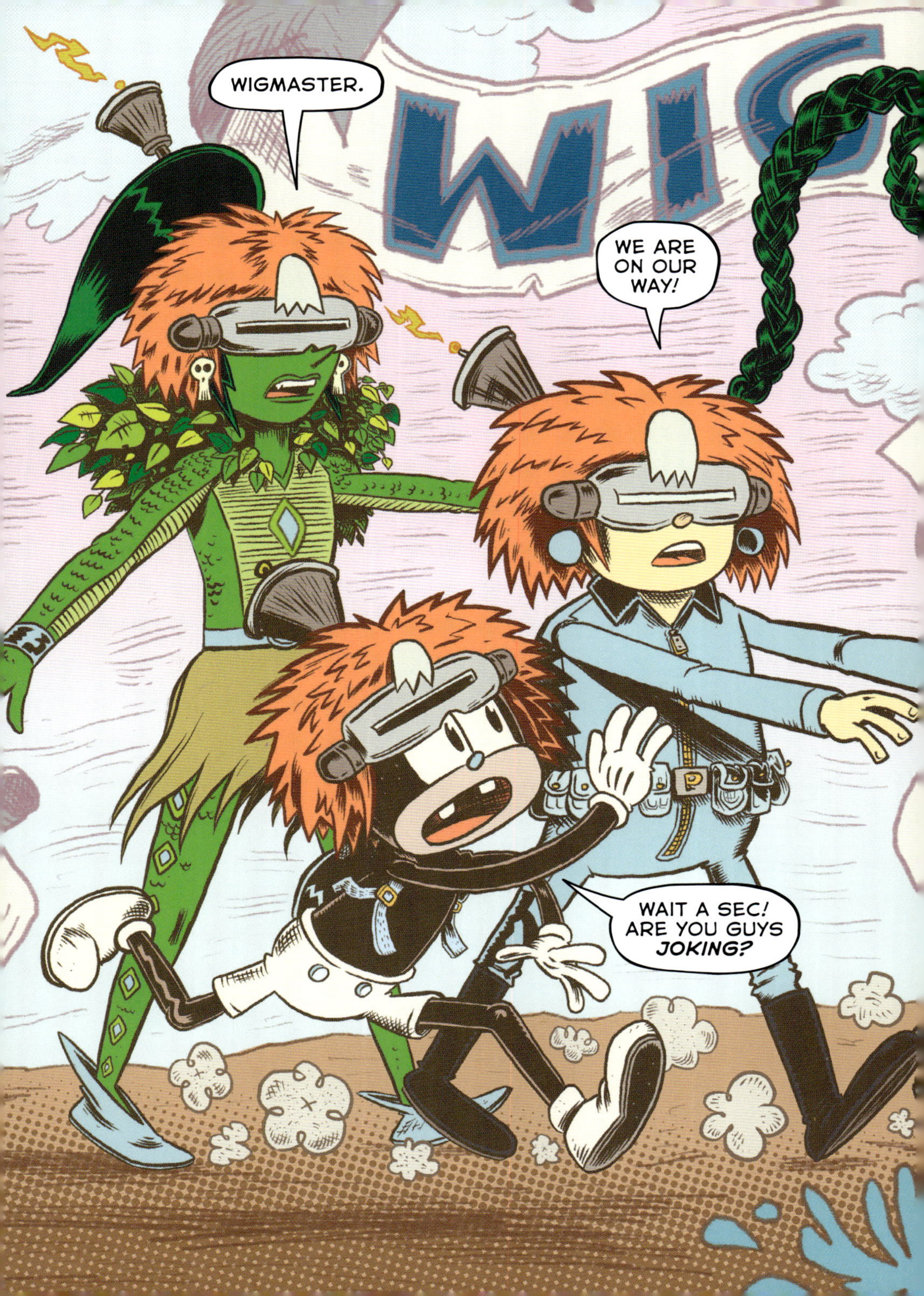
WIGMASTER.
WE ARE ON OUR WAY!
WAIT A SEC! ARE YOU GUYS *JOKING?*

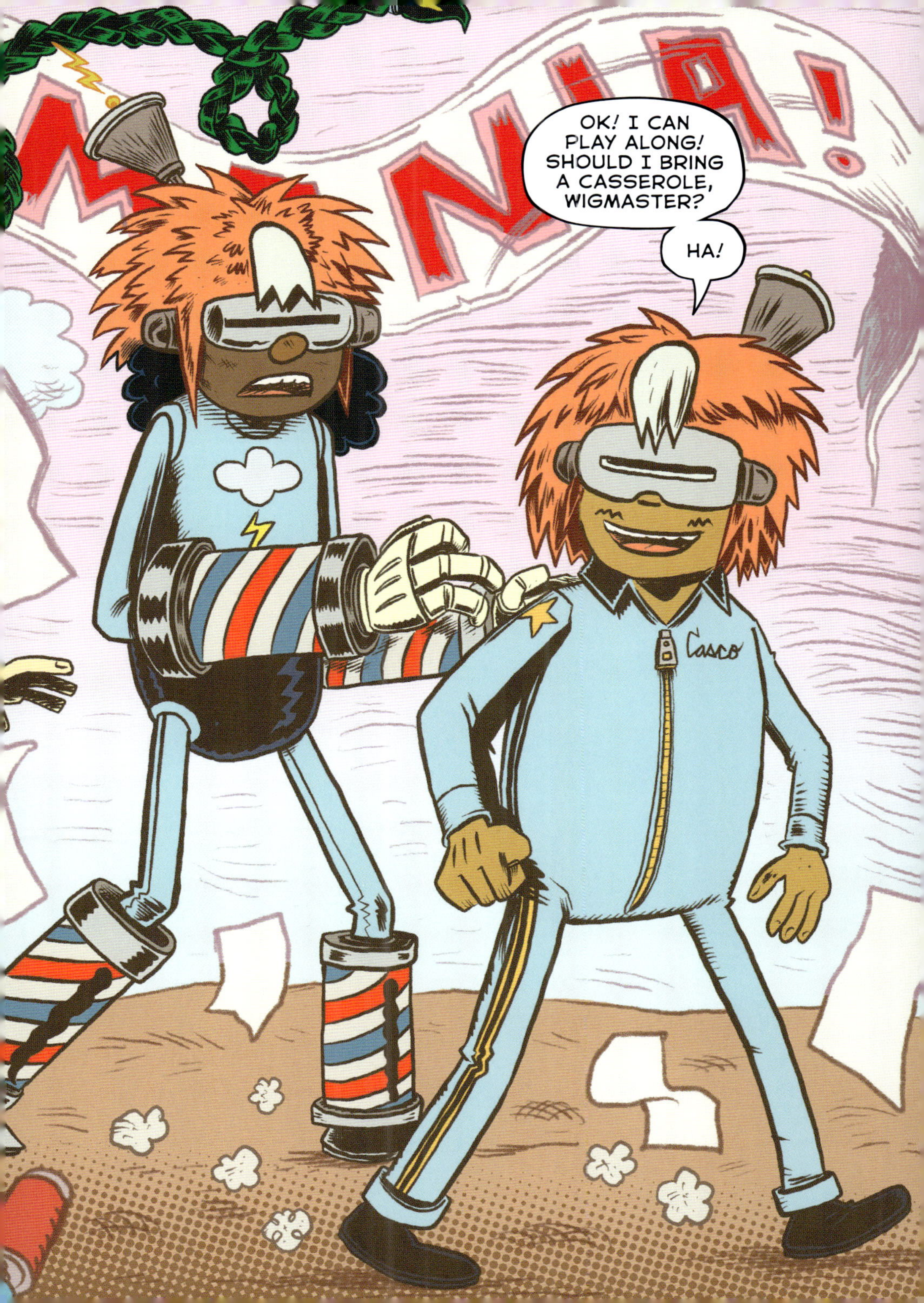
OK! I CAN PLAY ALONG! SHOULD I BRING A CASSEROLE, WIGMASTER?
HA!
Casco

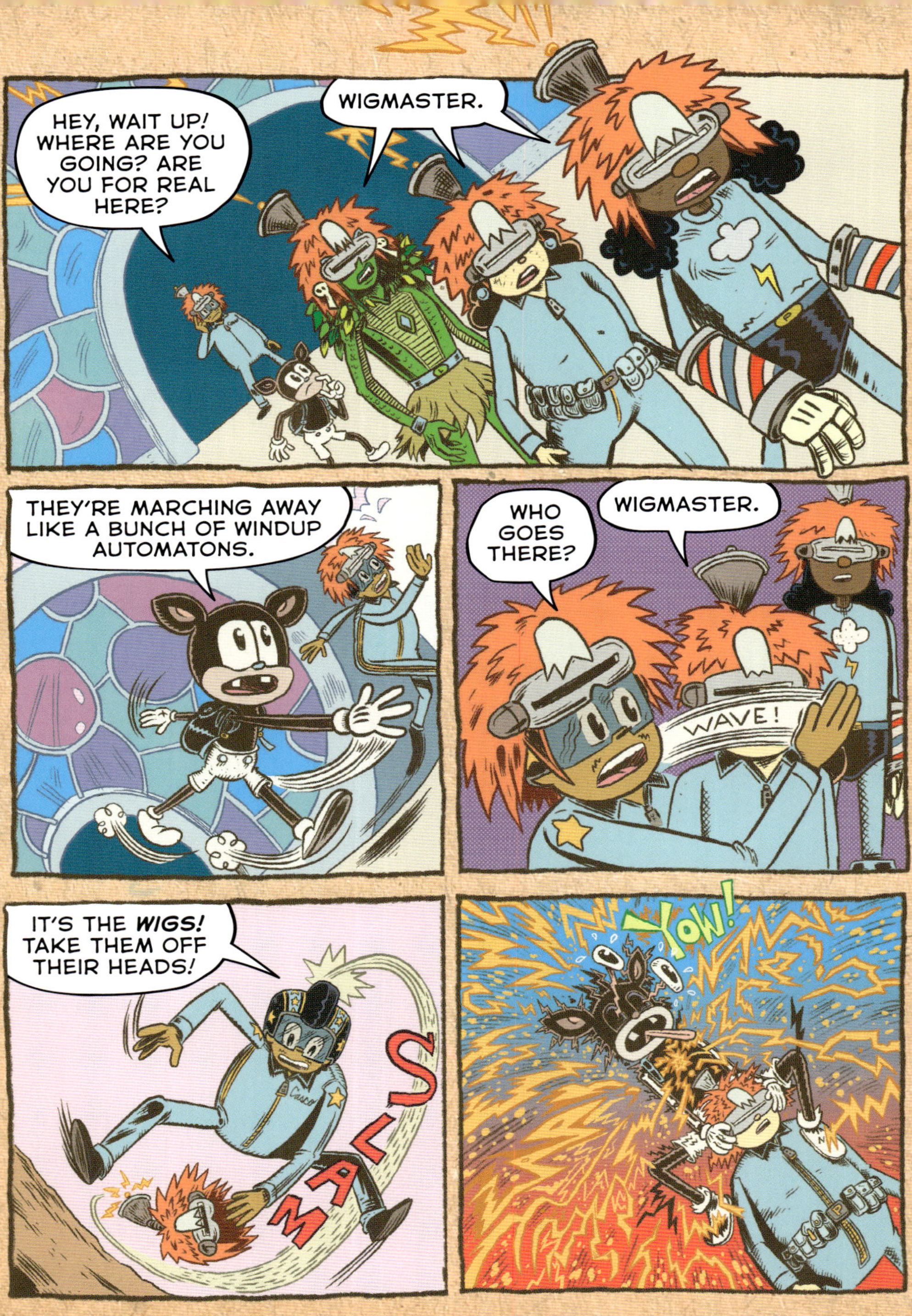
HEY, WAIT UP! WHERE ARE YOU GOING? ARE YOU FOR REAL HERE?
WIGMASTER.
THEY'RE MARCHING AWAY LIKE A BUNCH OF WINDUP AUTOMATONS.
WHO GOES THERE?
WIGMASTER.
WAVE!
IT'S THE WIGS! TAKE THEM OFF THEIR HEADS!
SLAM
YOW!

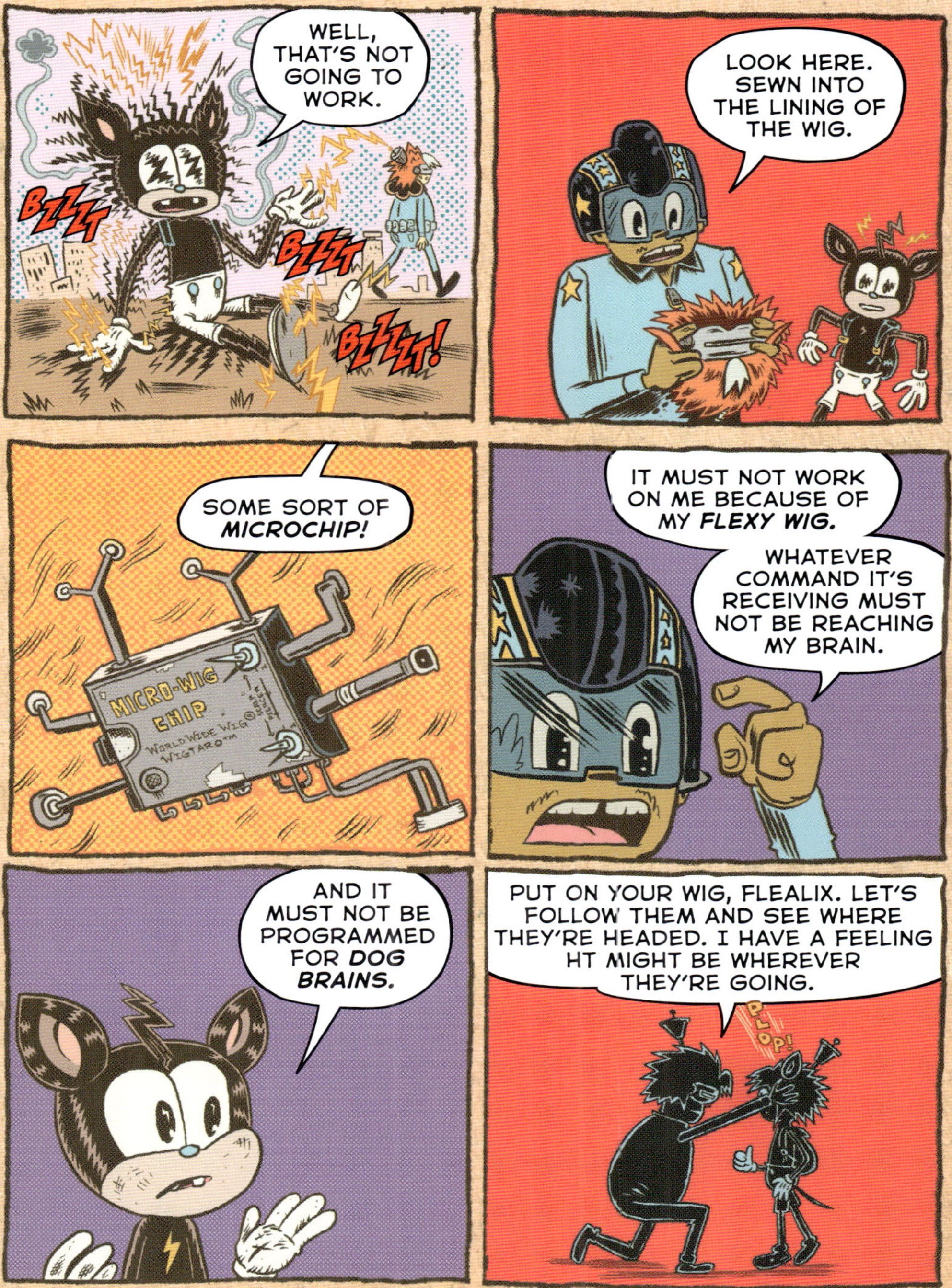
WELL, THAT'S NOT GOING TO WORK.
BZZZT
BZZZT
BZZZZT!
LOOK HERE. SEWN INTO THE LINING OF THE WIG.
SOME SORT OF ***MICROCHIP!***
MICRO-WIG CHIP
IT MUST NOT WORK ON ME BECAUSE OF MY ***FLEXY WIG.***
WHATEVER COMMAND IT'S RECEIVING MUST NOT BE REACHING MY BRAIN.
AND IT MUST NOT BE PROGRAMMED FOR ***DOG BRAINS.***
PUT ON YOUR WIG, FLEALIX. LET'S FOLLOW THEM AND SEE WHERE THEY'RE HEADED. I HAVE A FEELING HT MIGHT BE WHEREVER THEY'RE GOING.
PLOP!

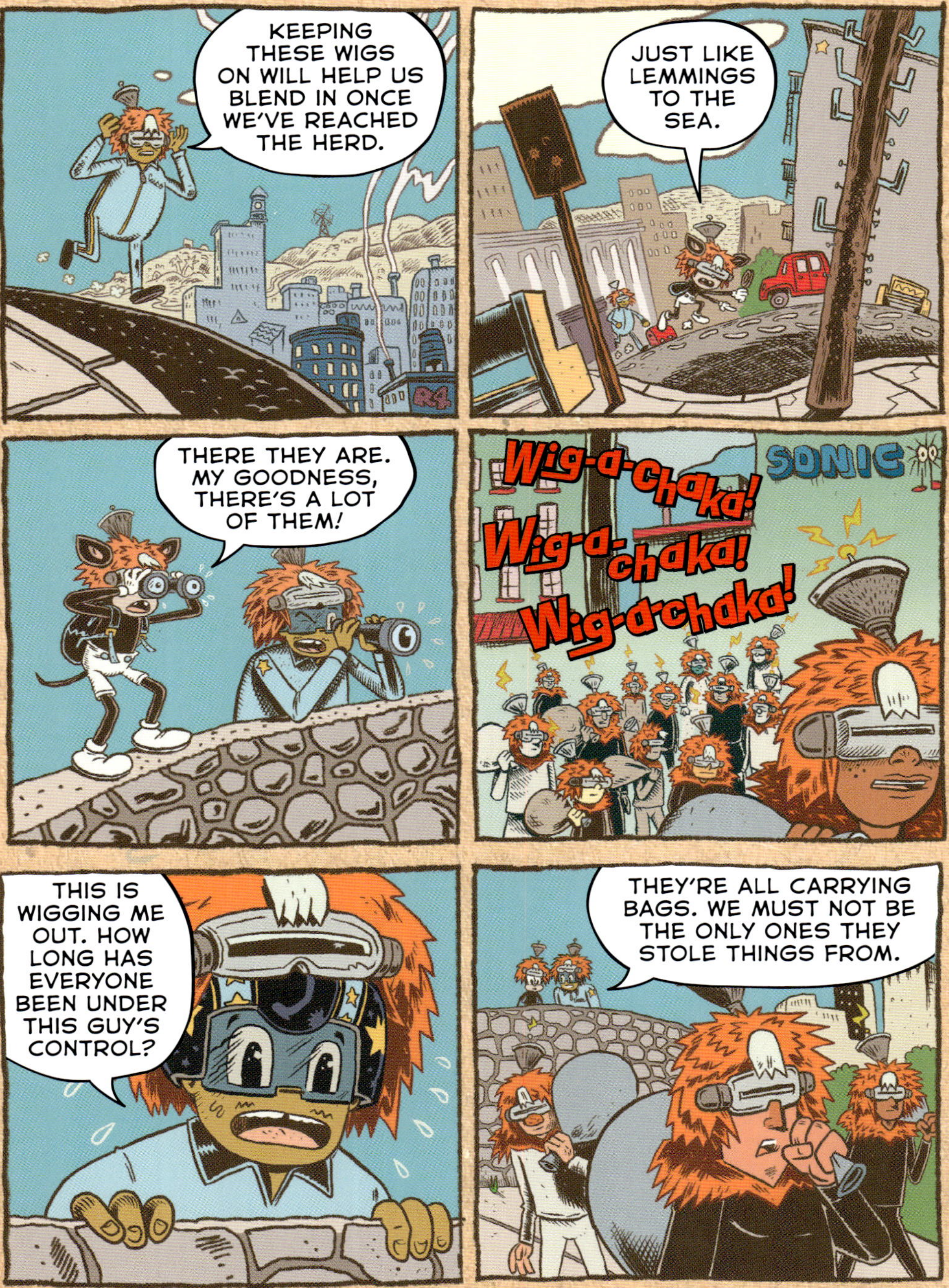
KEEPING THESE WIGS ON WILL HELP US BLEND IN ONCE WE'VE REACHED THE HERD.
JUST LIKE LEMMINGS TO THE SEA.
THERE THEY ARE. MY GOODNESS, THERE'S A LOT OF THEM!
Wig-a-chaka!
Wig-a-chaka!
Wig-a-chaka!
SONIC
THIS IS WIGGING ME OUT. HOW LONG HAS EVERYONE BEEN UNDER THIS GUY'S CONTROL?
THEY'RE ALL CARRYING BAGS. WE MUST NOT BE THE ONLY ONES THEY STOLE THINGS FROM.

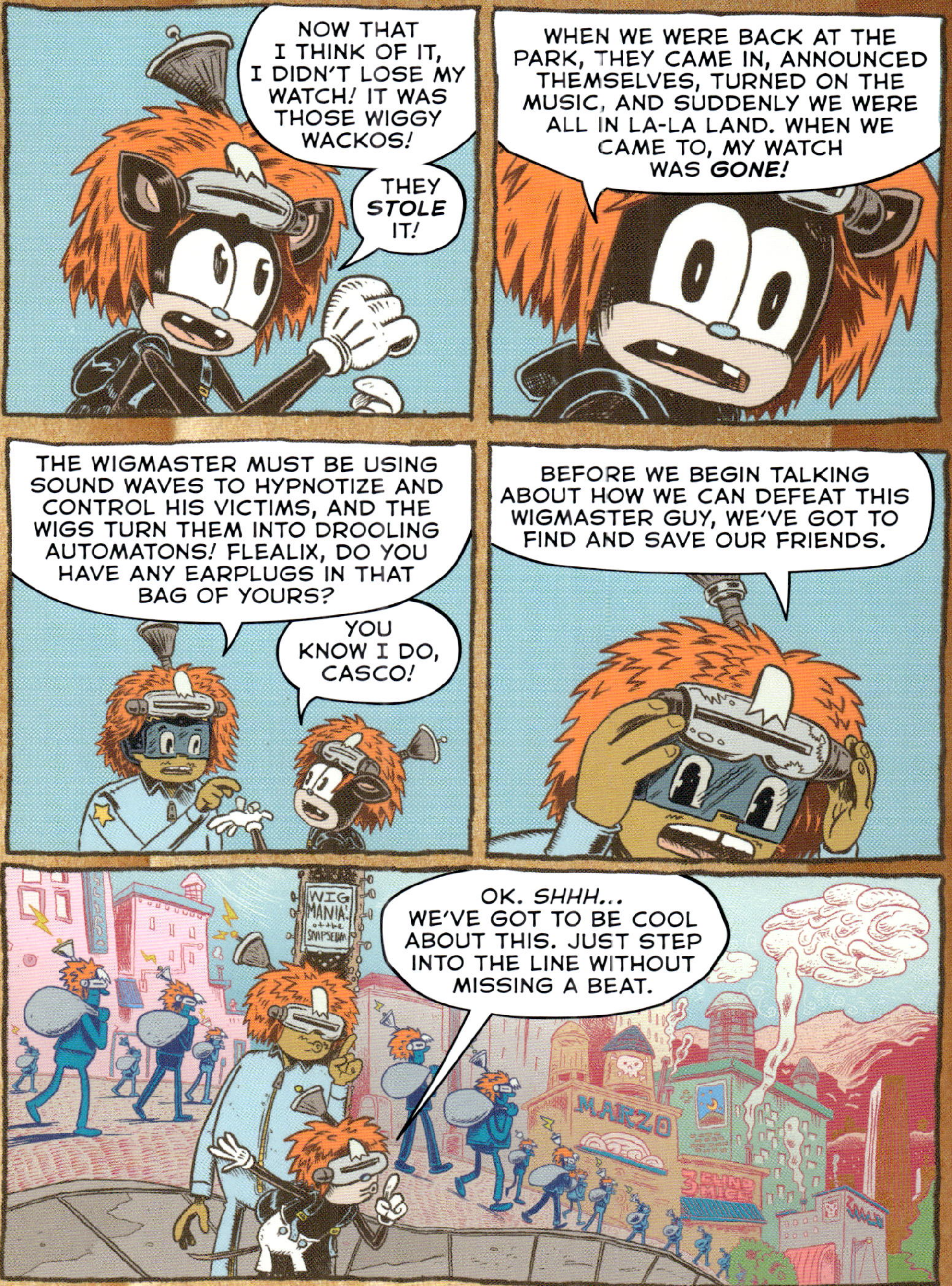
NOW THAT I THINK OF IT, I DIDN'T LOSE MY WATCH! IT WAS THOSE WIGGY WACKOS!
THEY *STOLE* IT!
WHEN WE WERE BACK AT THE PARK, THEY CAME IN, ANNOUNCED THEMSELVES, TURNED ON THE MUSIC, AND SUDDENLY WE WERE ALL IN LA-LA LAND. WHEN WE CAME TO, MY WATCH WAS ***GONE!***
THE WIGMASTER MUST BE USING SOUND WAVES TO HYPNOTIZE AND CONTROL HIS VICTIMS, AND THE WIGS TURN THEM INTO DROOLING AUTOMATONS! FLEALIX, DO YOU HAVE ANY EARPLUGS IN THAT BAG OF YOURS?
YOU KNOW I DO, CASCO!
BEFORE WE BEGIN TALKING ABOUT HOW WE CAN DEFEAT THIS WIGMASTER GUY, WE'VE GOT TO FIND AND SAVE OUR FRIENDS.
WIG MANIA!
OK. *SHHH...* WE'VE GOT TO BE COOL ABOUT THIS. JUST STEP INTO THE LINE WITHOUT MISSING A BEAT.
MARZO

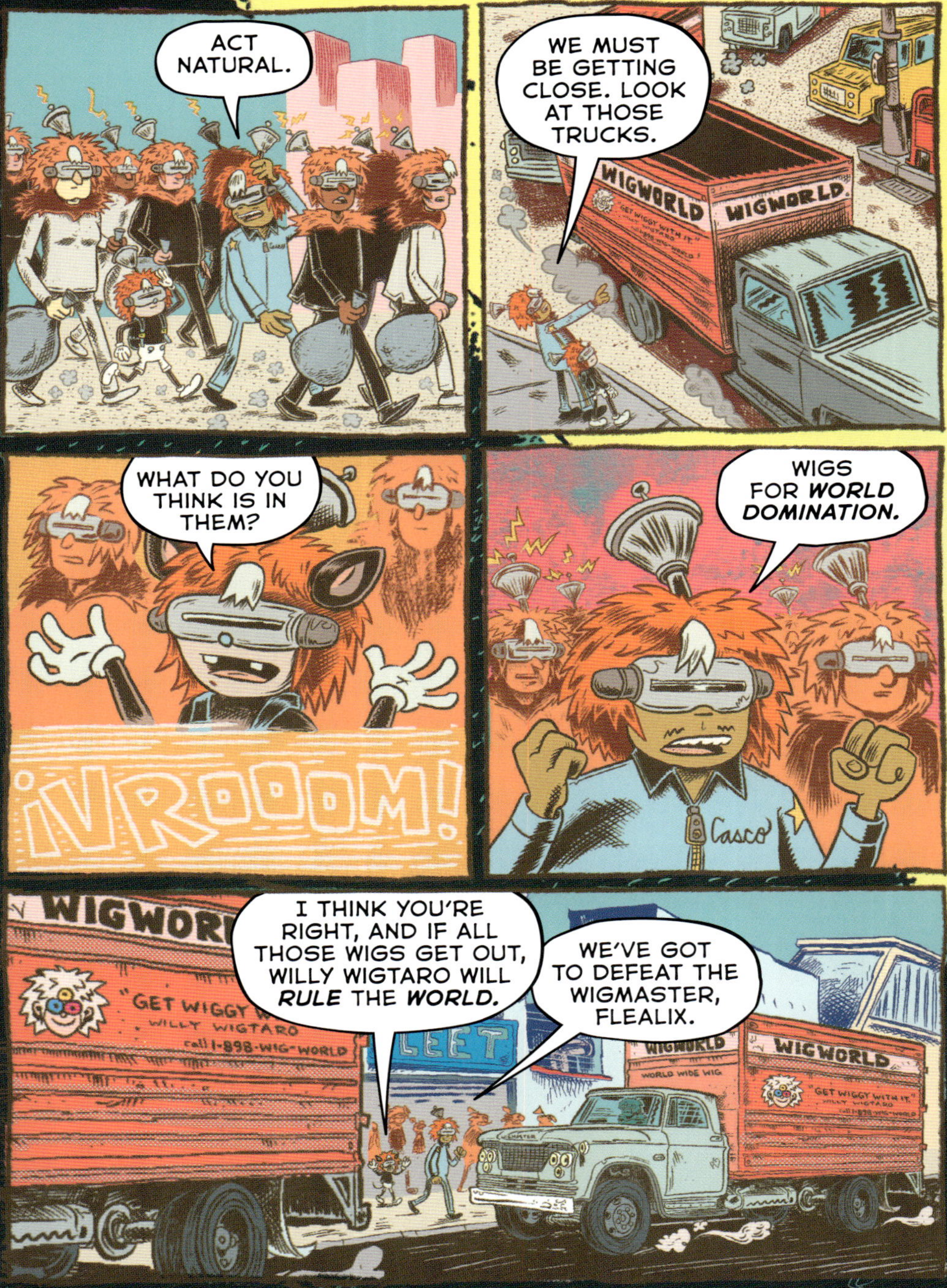
ACT NATURAL.
WE MUST BE GETTING CLOSE. LOOK AT THOSE TRUCKS.
WIGWORLD
WIGWORLD
WHAT DO YOU THINK IS IN THEM?
¡VROOOM!
WIGS FOR *WORLD DOMINATION.*
Casco
WIGWORL
"GET WIGGY W
WILLY WIGTARO
call 1-898-WIG-WORLD
I THINK YOU'RE RIGHT, AND IF ALL THOSE WIGS GET OUT, WILLY WIGTARO WILL *RULE* THE *WORLD.*
WE'VE GOT TO DEFEAT THE WIGMASTER, FLEALIX.
WIGWORLD
WIGWORLD
WORLD WIDE WIG

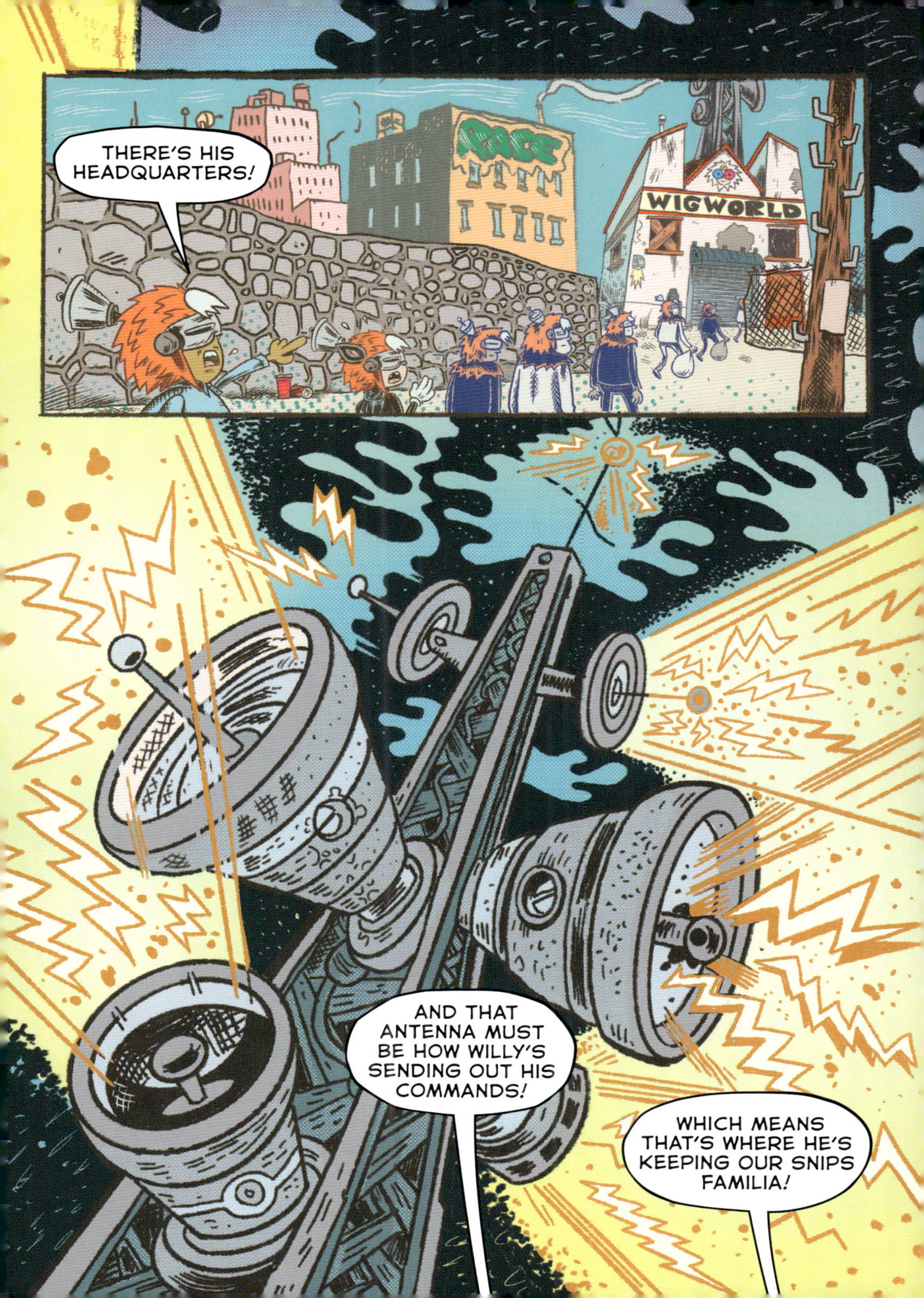
THERE'S HIS HEADQUARTERS!
RAGE
WIGWORLD
AND THAT ANTENNA MUST BE HOW WILLY'S SENDING OUT HIS COMMANDS!
WHICH MEANS THAT'S WHERE HE'S KEEPING OUR SNIPS FAMILIA!

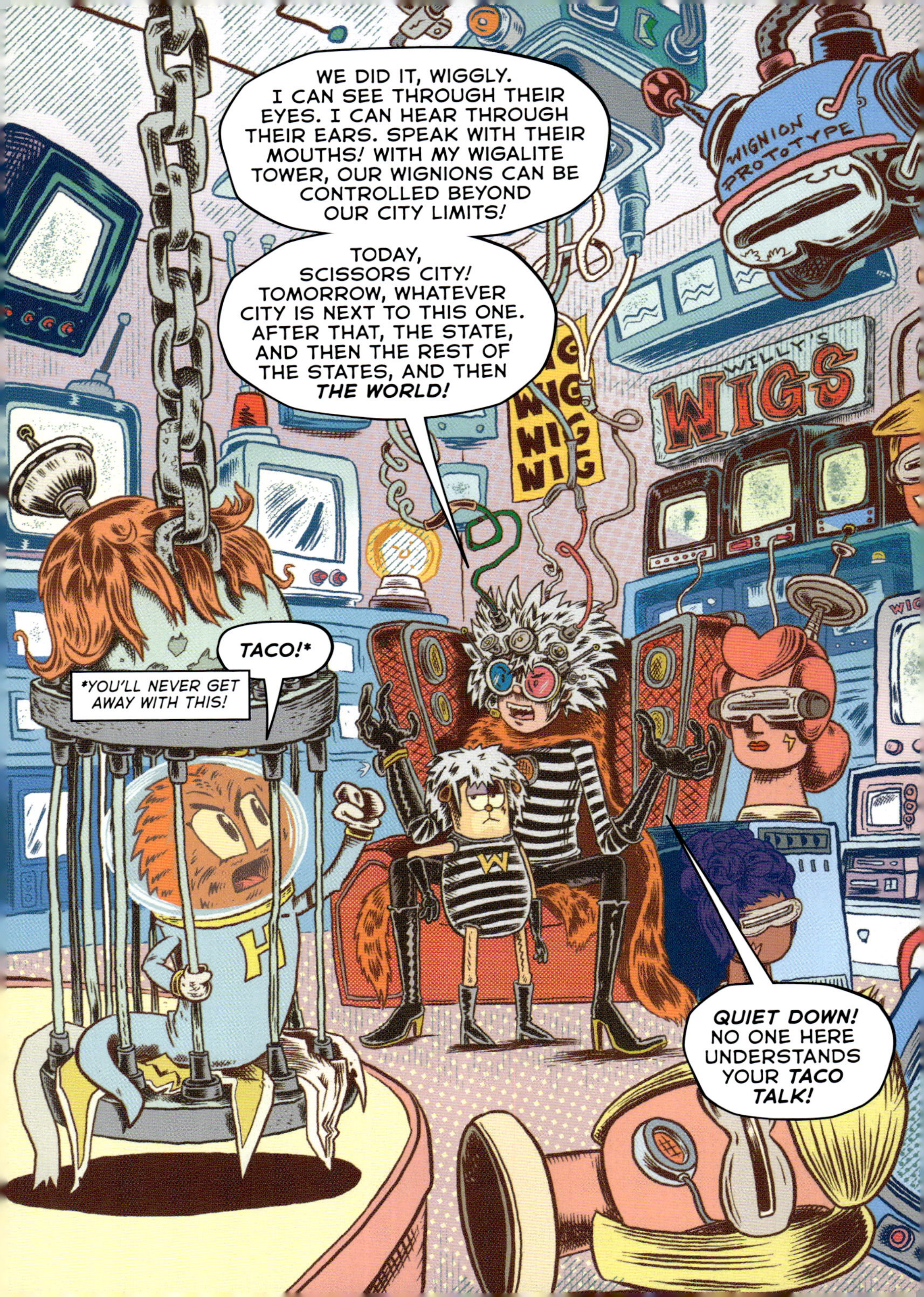
WE DID IT, WIGGLY. I CAN SEE THROUGH THEIR EYES. I CAN HEAR THROUGH THEIR EARS. SPEAK WITH THEIR MOUTHS! WITH MY WIGALITE TOWER, OUR WIGNIONS CAN BE CONTROLLED BEYOND OUR CITY LIMITS!
TODAY, SCISSORS CITY! TOMORROW, WHATEVER CITY IS NEXT TO THIS ONE. AFTER THAT, THE STATE, AND THEN THE REST OF THE STATES, AND THEN THE WORLD!
WIGNION PROTOTYPE
WILLY'S WIGS
TACO!*
*YOU'LL NEVER GET AWAY WITH THIS!
QUIET DOWN! NO ONE HERE UNDERSTANDS YOUR TACO TALK!

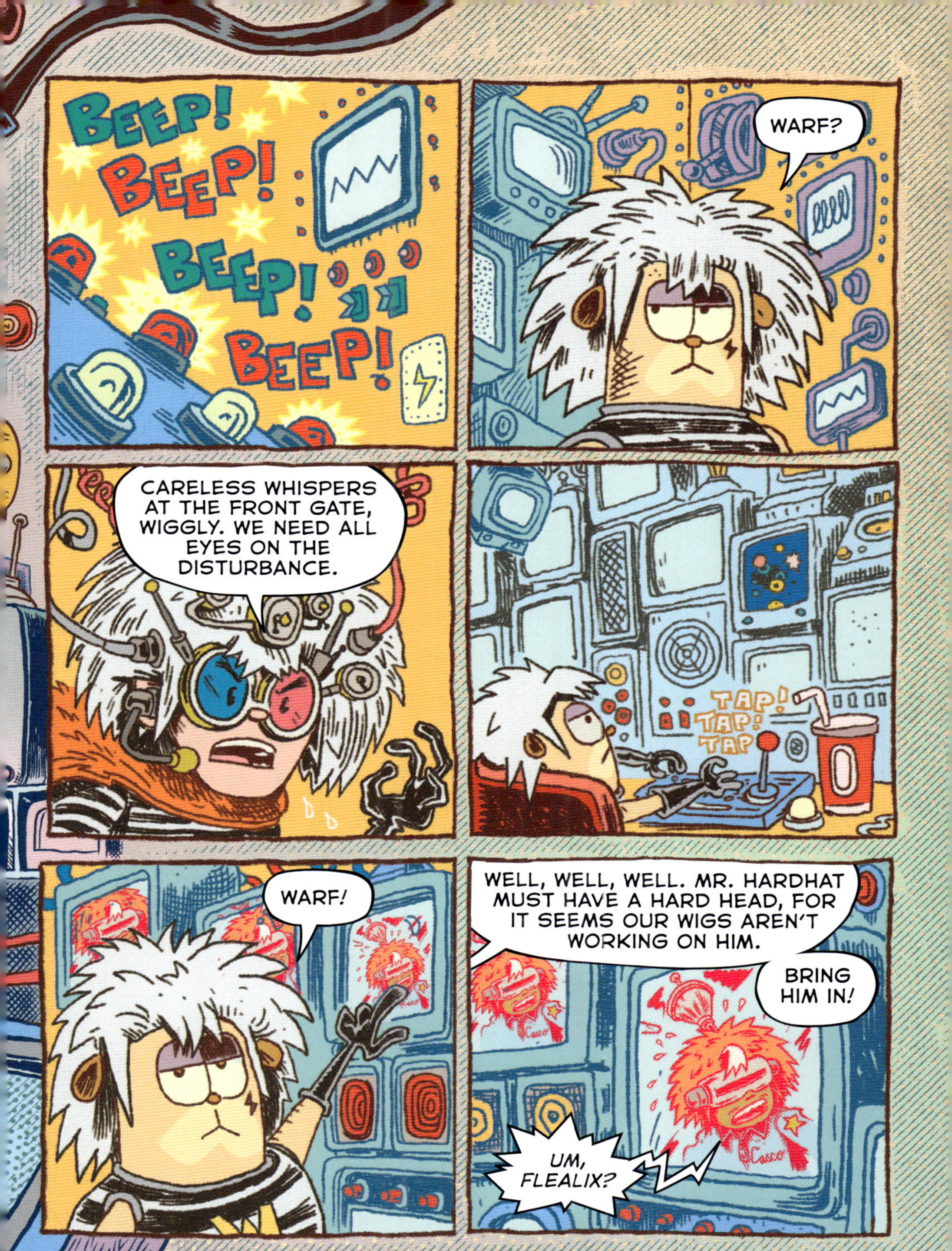
BEEP!
BEEP!
BEEP!
BEEP!
WARF?
CARELESS WHISPERS AT THE FRONT GATE, WIGGLY. WE NEED ALL EYES ON THE DISTURBANCE.
TAP! TAP! TAP
WARF!
WELL, WELL, WELL. MR. HARDHAT MUST HAVE A HARD HEAD, FOR IT SEEMS OUR WIGS AREN'T WORKING ON HIM.
BRING HIM IN!
UM, FLEALIX?

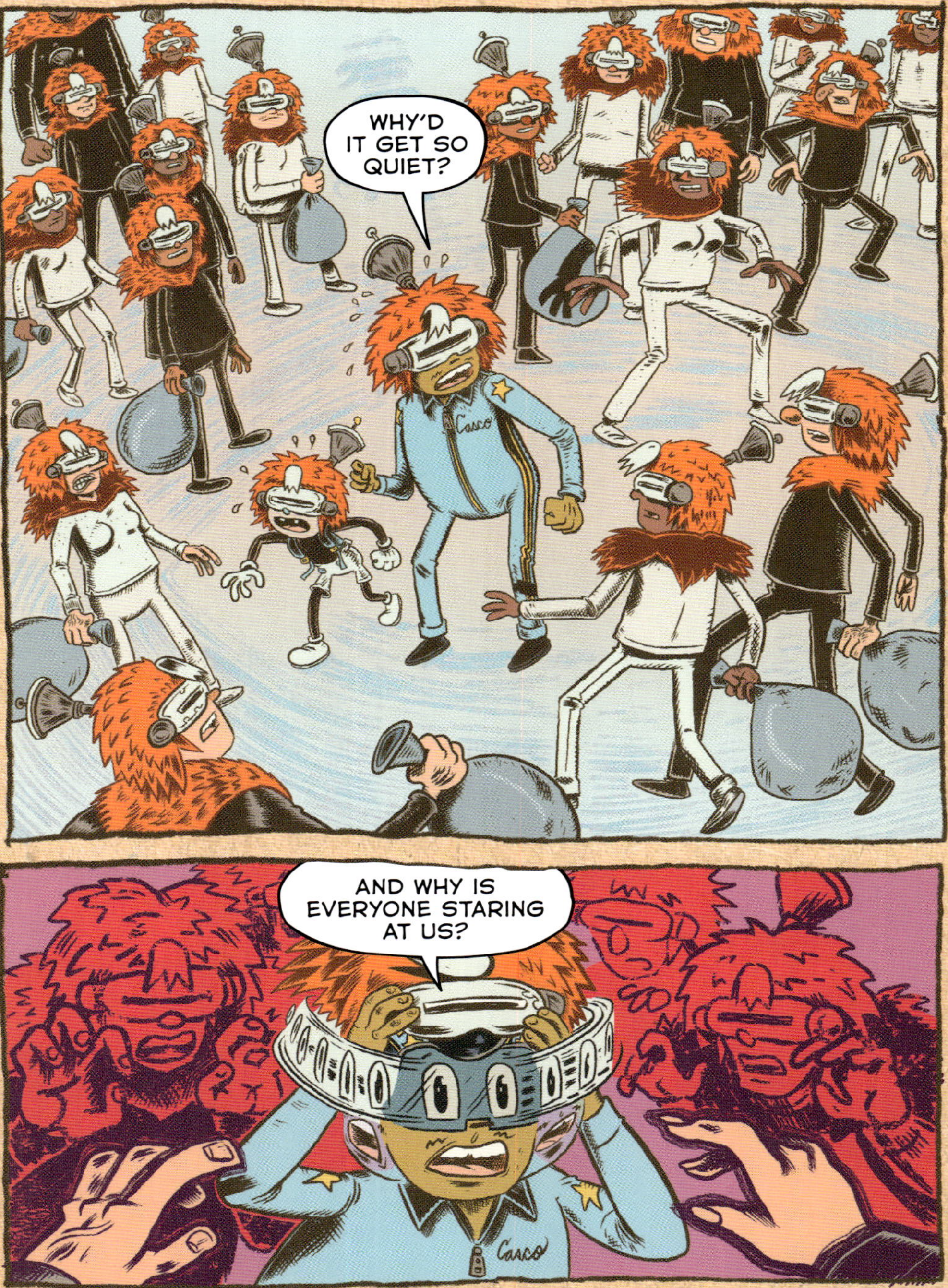
WHY'D IT GET SO QUIET?
AND WHY IS EVERYONE STARING AT US?

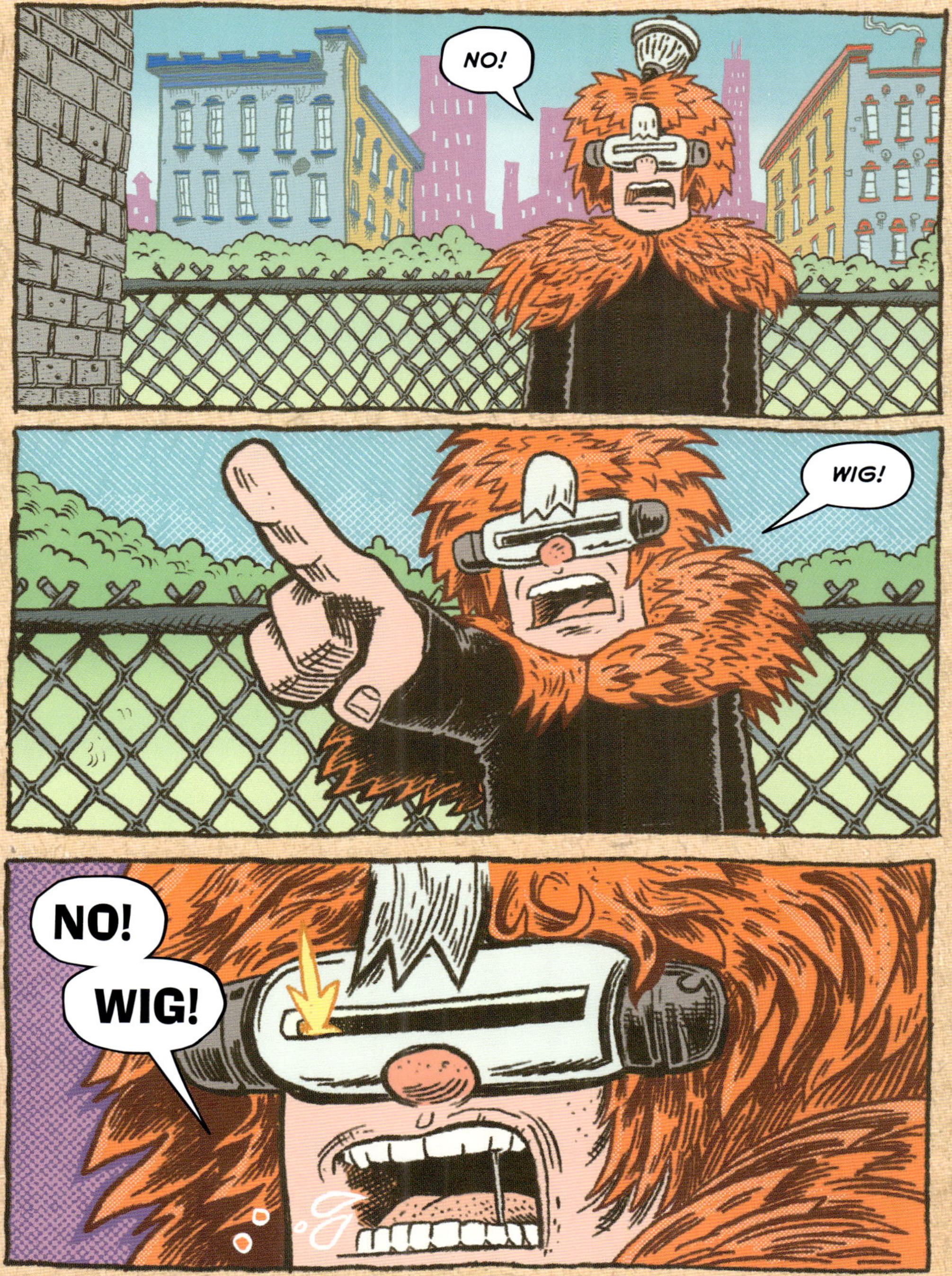
NO!
WIG!
NO!
WIG!

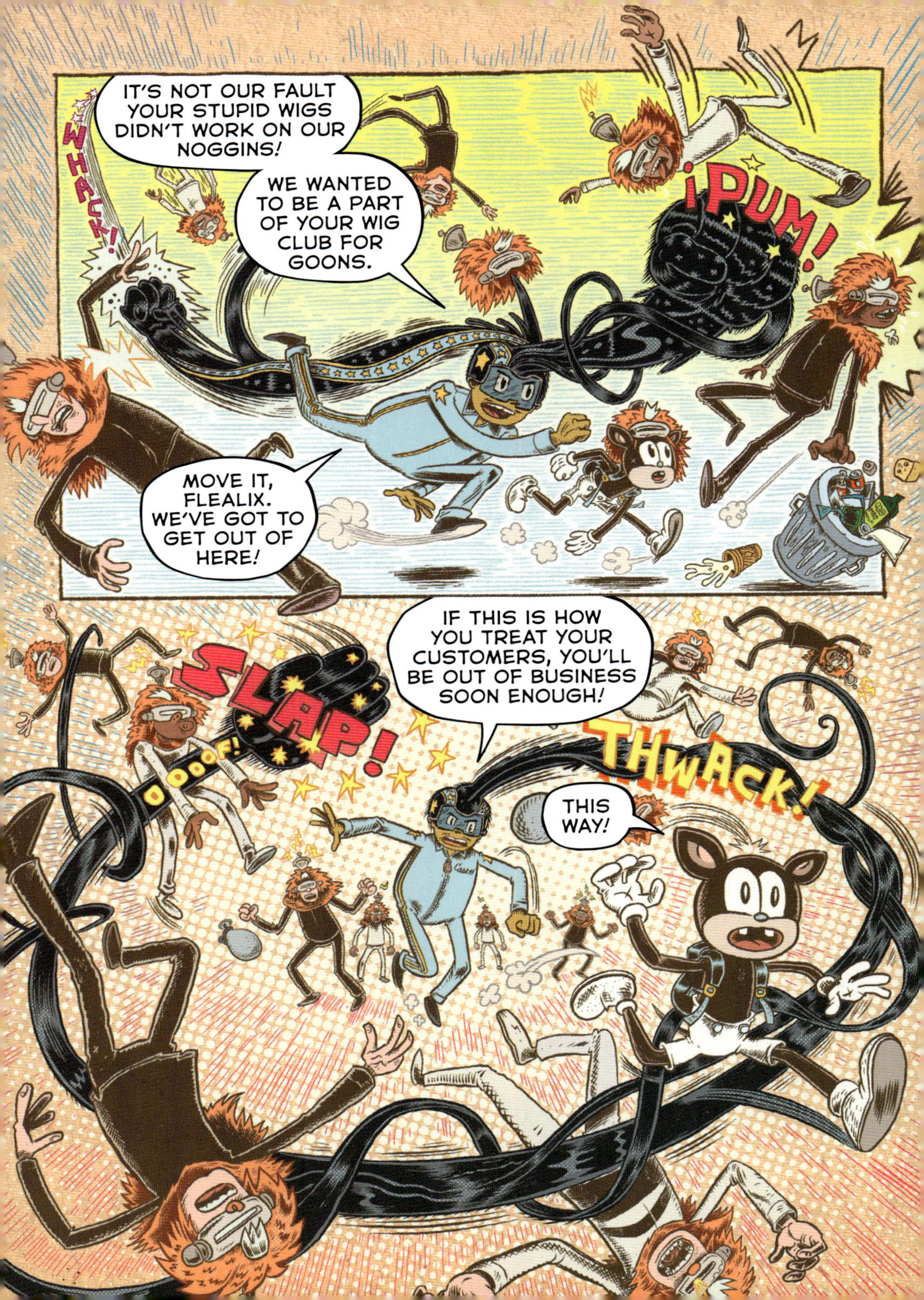
WHACK!
IT'S NOT OUR FAULT YOUR STUPID WIGS DIDN'T WORK ON OUR NOGGINS!
WE WANTED TO BE A PART OF YOUR WIG CLUB FOR GOONS.
¡PUM!
MOVE IT, FLEALIX. WE'VE GOT TO GET OUT OF HERE!
SLAP!
OOOOF!
IF THIS IS HOW YOU TREAT YOUR CUSTOMERS, YOU'LL BE OUT OF BUSINESS SOON ENOUGH!
THWACK!
THIS WAY!

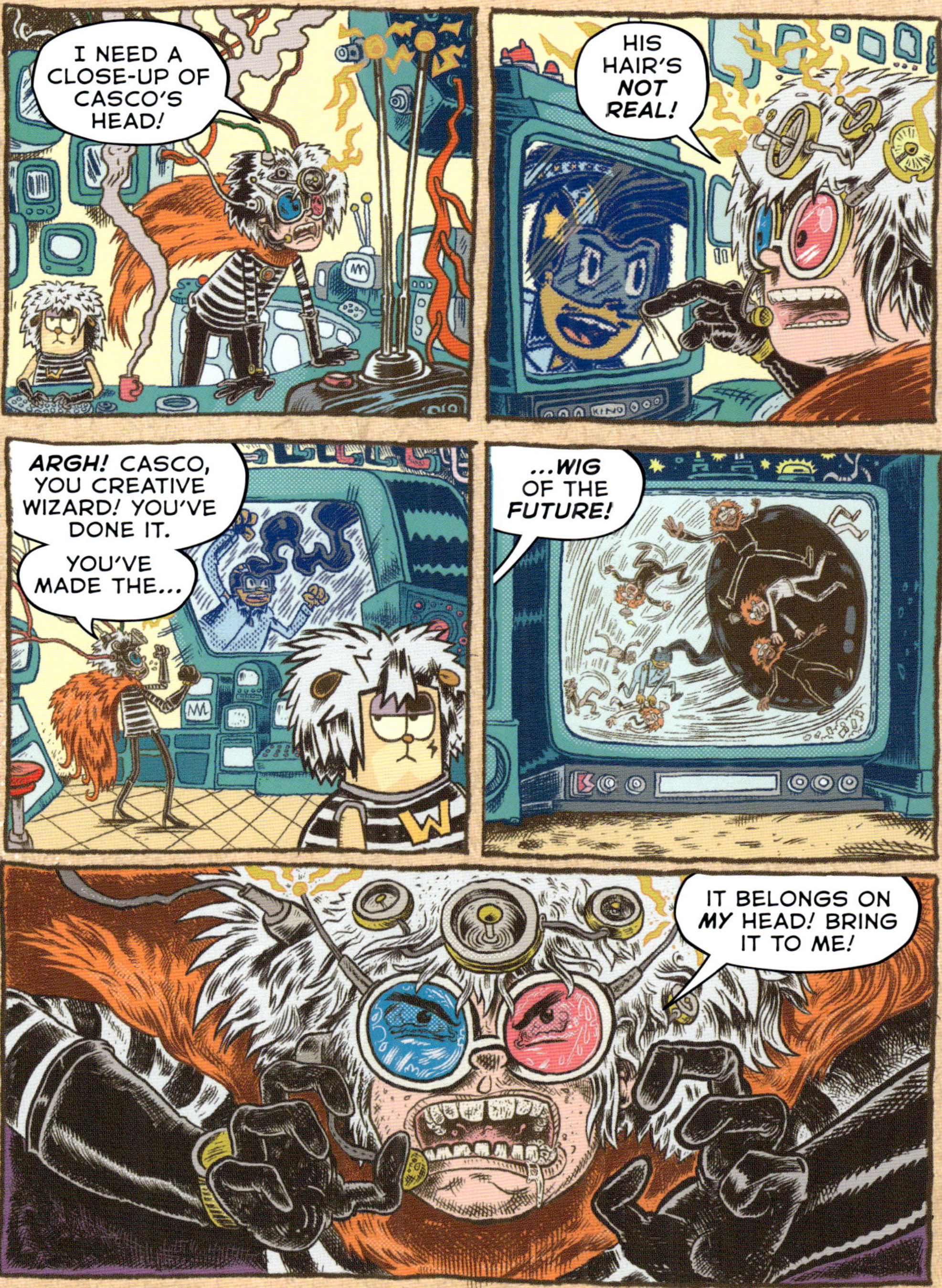
I NEED A CLOSE-UP OF CASCO'S HEAD!
HIS HAIR'S **NOT REAL!**
ARGH! CASCO, YOU CREATIVE WIZARD! YOU'VE DONE IT.
YOU'VE MADE THE...
...**WIG** OF THE **FUTURE!**
IT BELONGS ON **MY** HEAD! BRING IT TO ME!

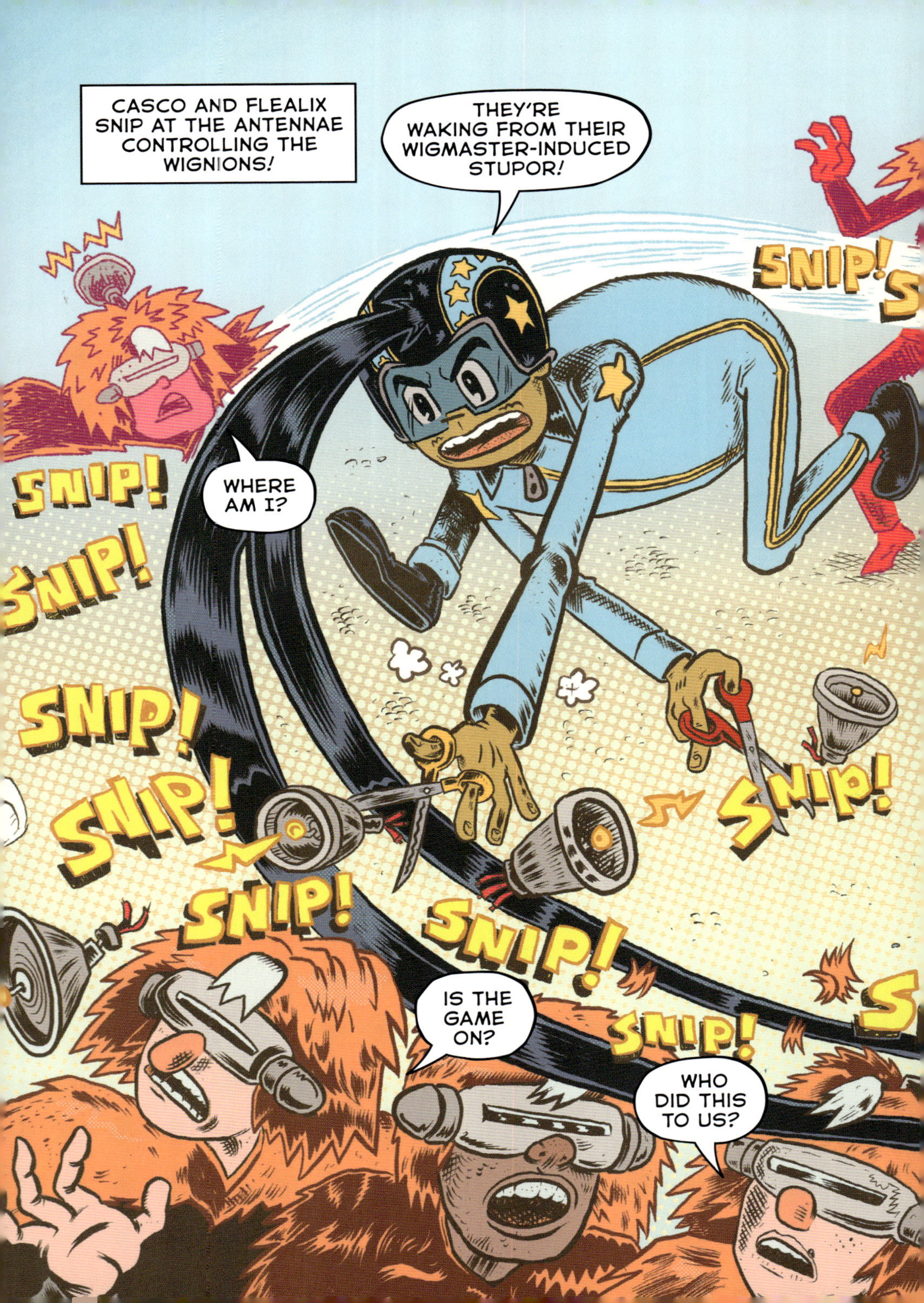
CASCO AND FLEALIX SNIP AT THE ANTENNAE CONTROLLING THE WIGNIONS!
THEY'RE WAKING FROM THEIR WIGMASTER-INDUCED STUPOR!
SNIP!
SNIP!
WHERE AM I?
SNIP!
SNIP!
SNIP!
SNIP!
SNIP!
SNIP!
SNIP!
IS THE GAME ON?
WHO DID THIS TO US?

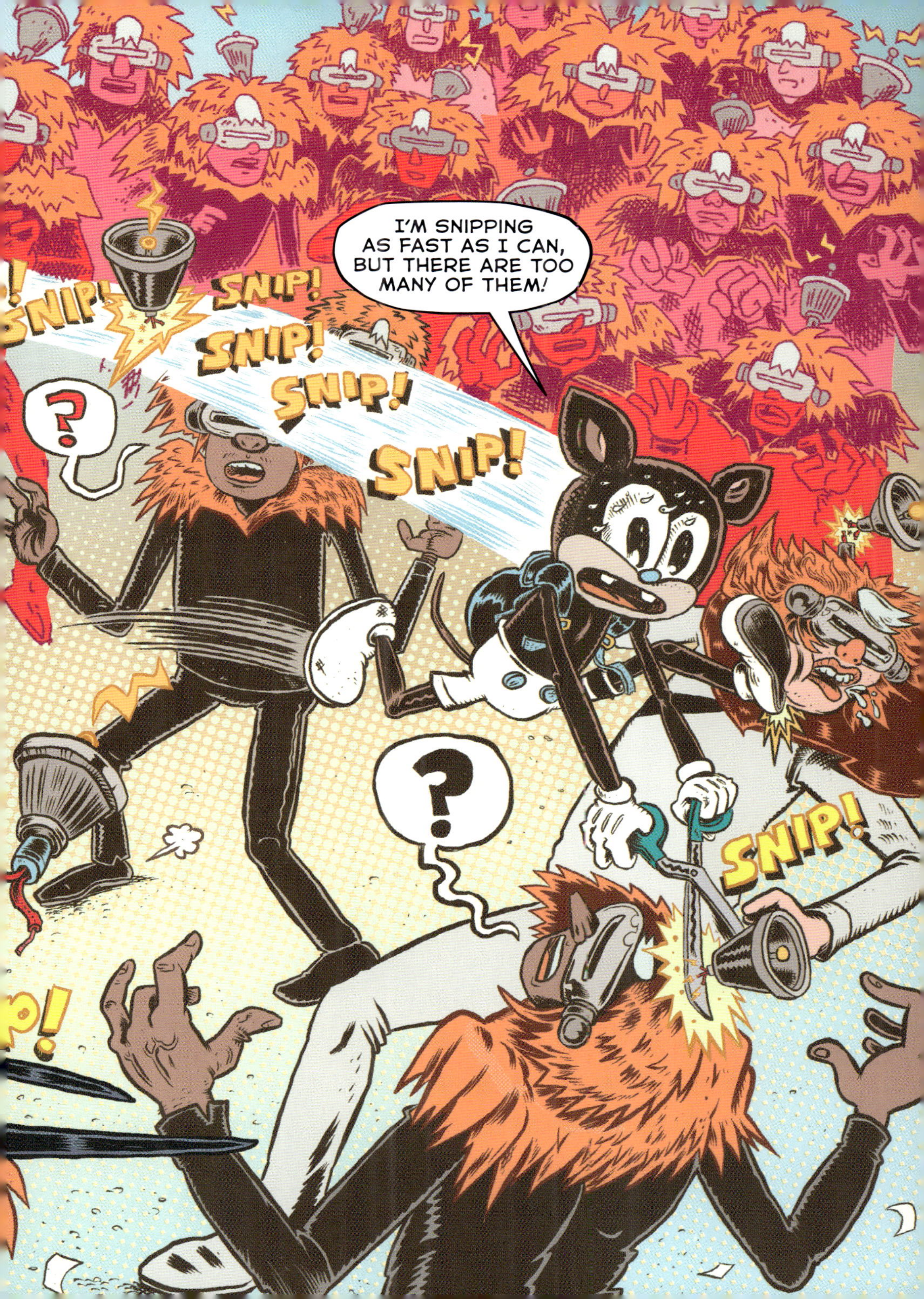

SNIP!
SNIP!
SNIP!
SNIP!
I'M SNIPPING AS FAST AS I CAN, BUT THERE ARE TOO MANY OF THEM!
SNIP!
?
?
SNIP!

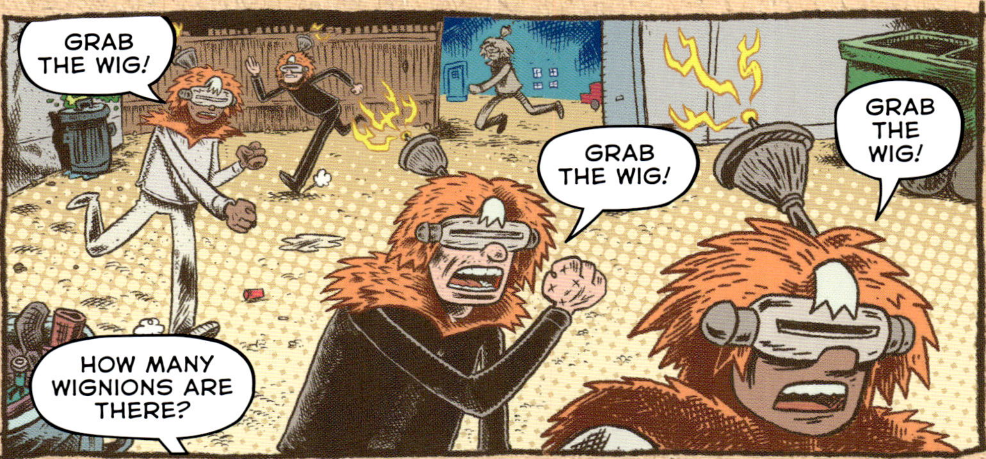
GRAB THE WIG!
GRAB THE WIG!
GRAB THE WIG!
HOW MANY WIGNIONS ARE THERE?

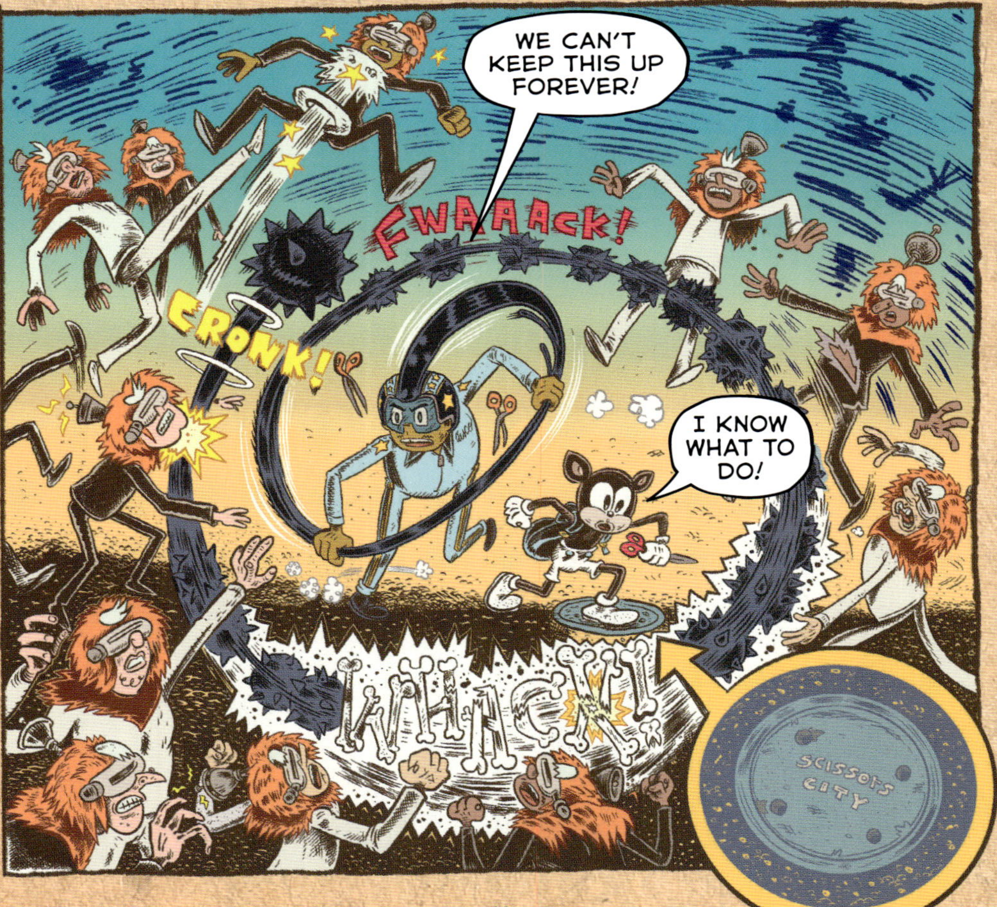
WE CAN'T KEEP THIS UP FOREVER!
FWAAAACK!
CRONK!
I KNOW WHAT TO DO!
WHACK!
SCISSORS CITY

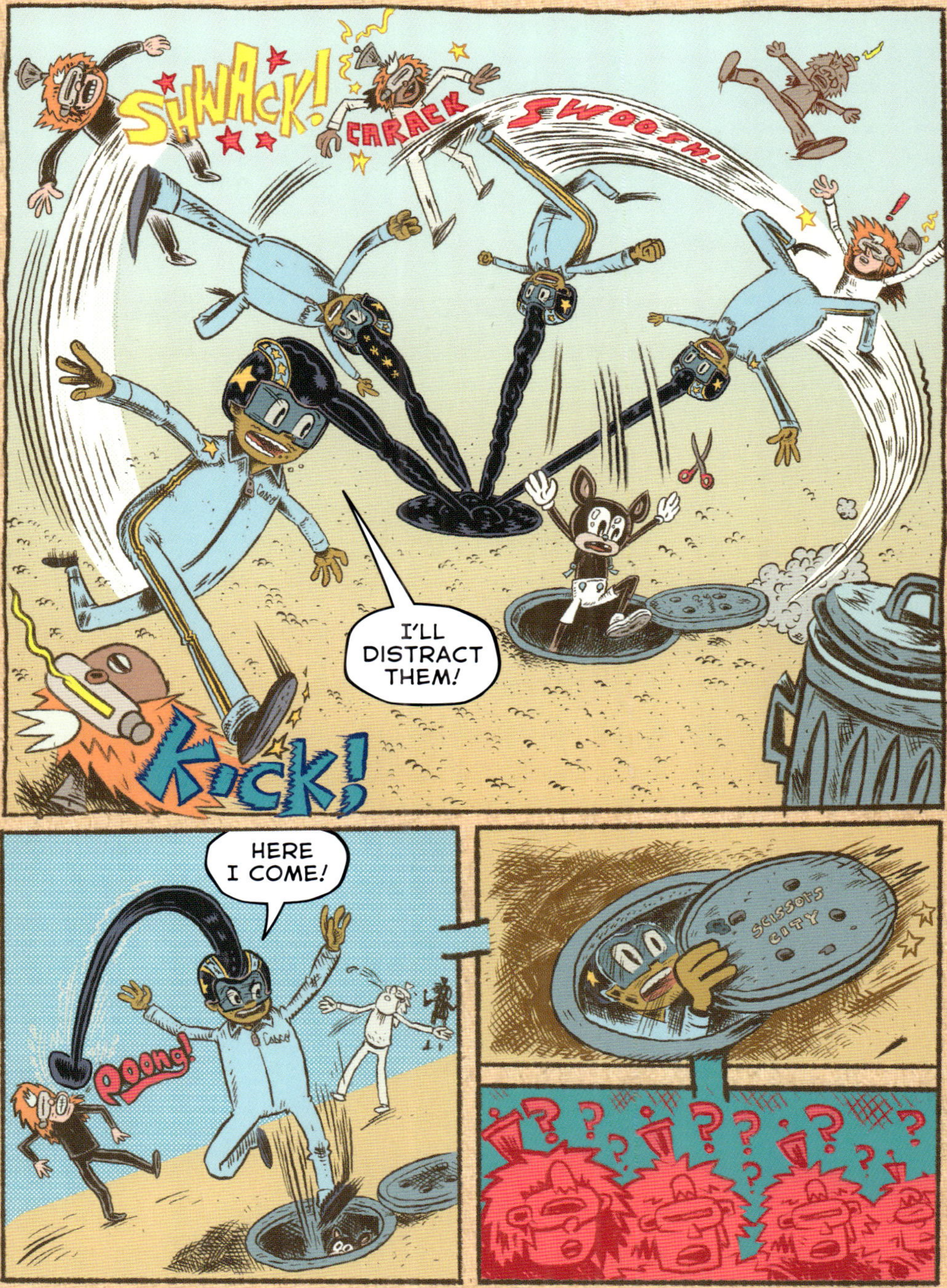
SHWACK!
CARACK
SWOOSH!
I'LL DISTRACT THEM!
KICK!
HERE I COME!
POONG!
SCISSORS CITY

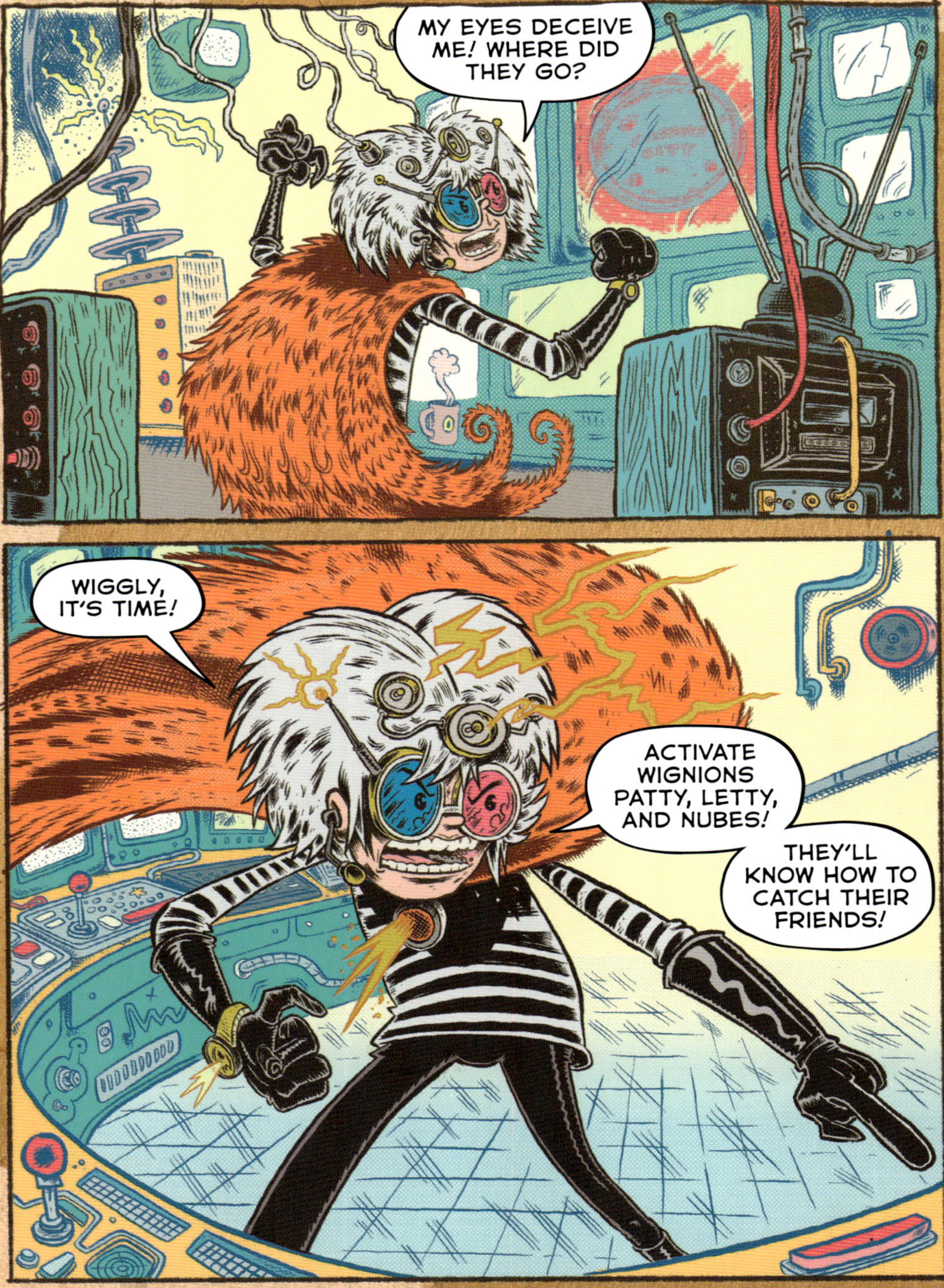
MY EYES DECEIVE ME! WHERE DID THEY GO?
WIGGLY, IT'S TIME!
ACTIVATE WIGNIONS PATTY, LETTY, AND NUBES!
THEY'LL KNOW HOW TO CATCH THEIR FRIENDS!

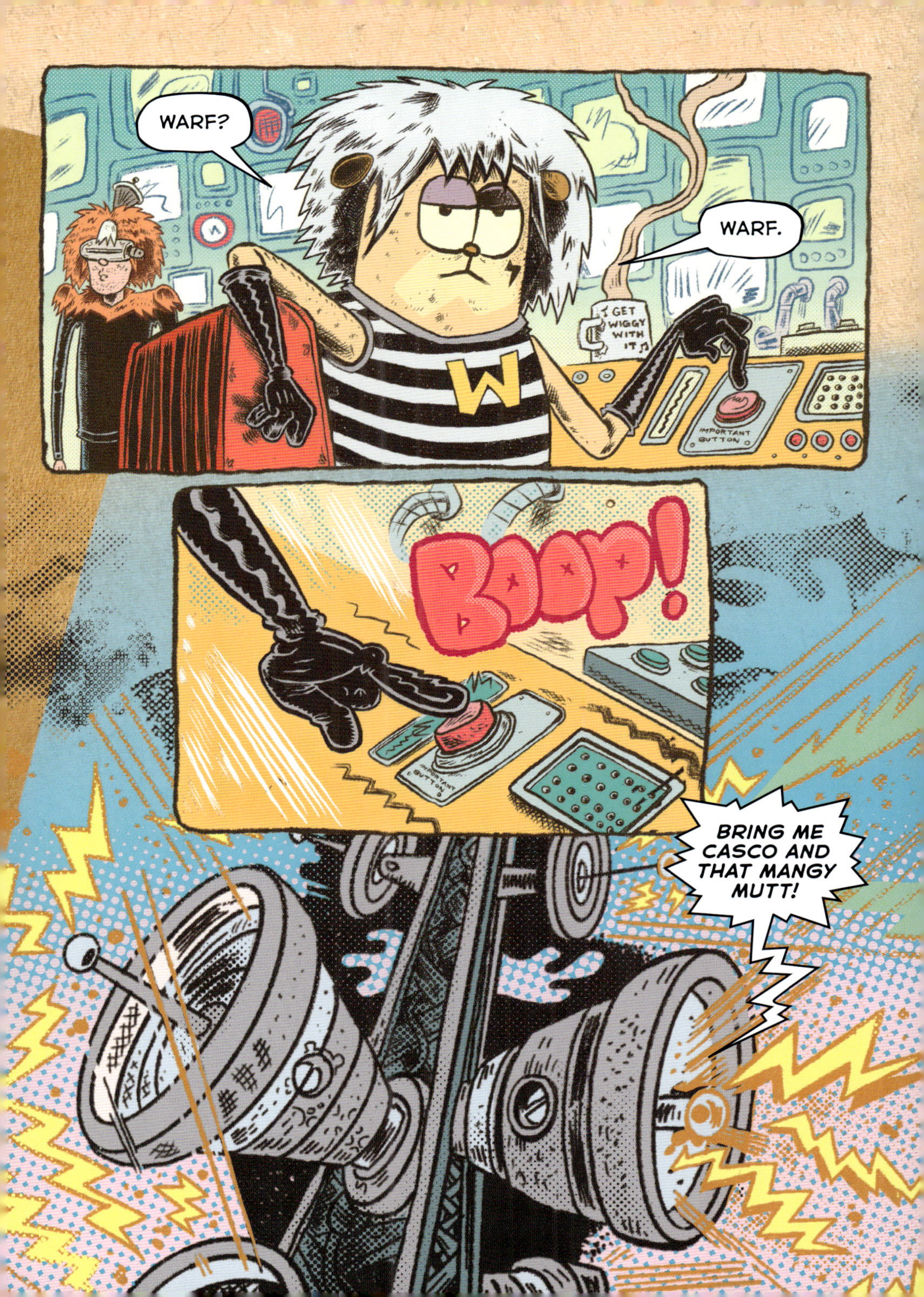
WARF?
WARF.
GET WIGGY WITH IT
IMPORTANT BUTTON
BOOP!
IMPORTANT BUTTON
BRING ME CASCO AND THAT MANGY MUTT!

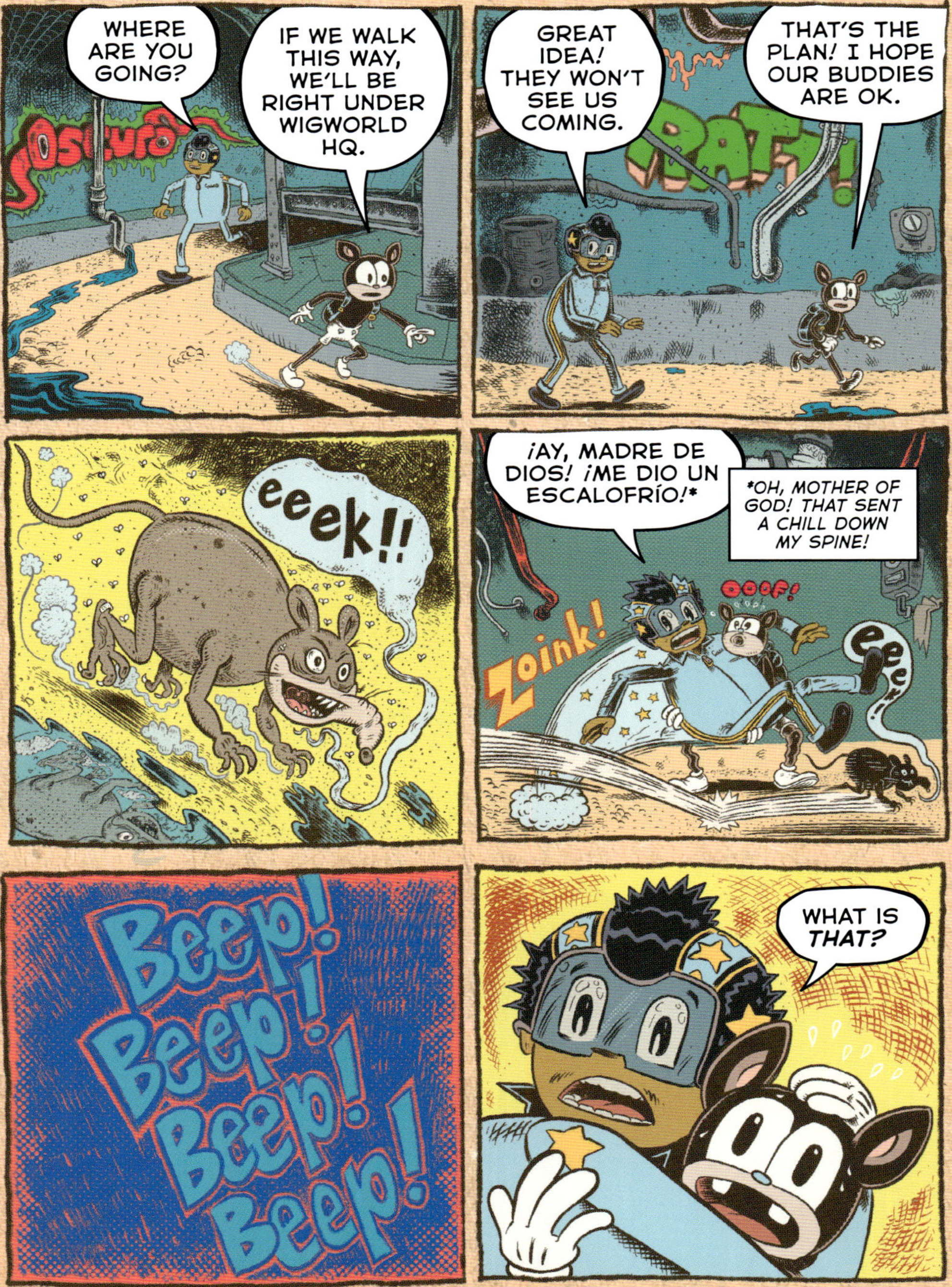
WHERE ARE YOU GOING?
IF WE WALK THIS WAY, WE'LL BE RIGHT UNDER WIGWORLD HQ.
OSCURO
GREAT IDEA! THEY WON'T SEE US COMING.
THAT'S THE PLAN! I HOPE OUR BUDDIES ARE OK.
eeek!!
¡AY, MADRE DE DIOS! ¡ME DIO UN ESCALOFRÍO!*
*OH, MOTHER OF GOD! THAT SENT A CHILL DOWN MY SPINE!
OOOF!
Zoink!
Beep! Beep! Beep! Beep!
WHAT IS *THAT?*

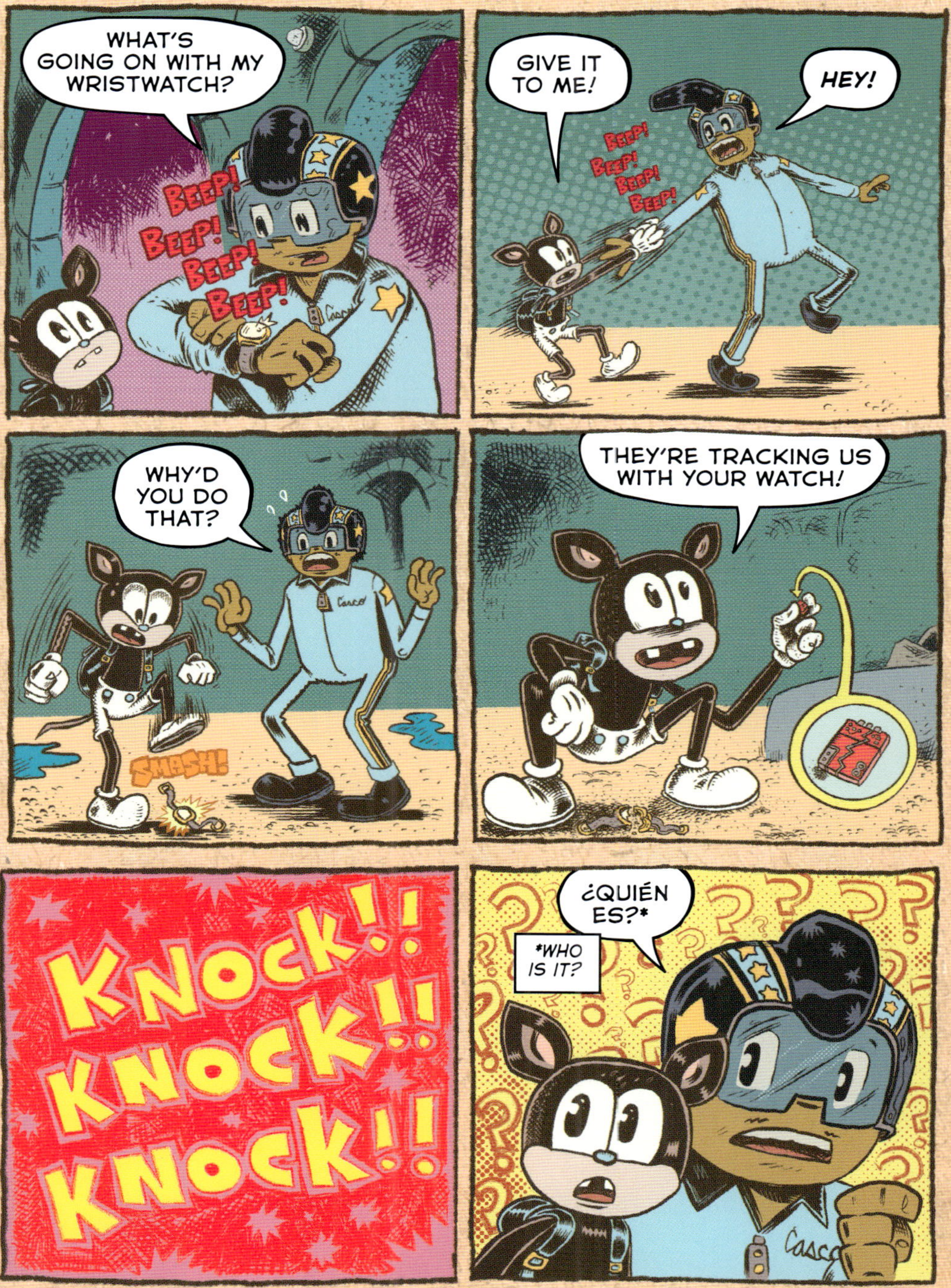
WHAT'S GOING ON WITH MY WRISTWATCH?
BEEP! BEEP! BEEP! BEEP!
GIVE IT TO ME!
HEY!
BEEP! BEEP! BEEP! BEEP!
WHY'D YOU DO THAT?
SMASH!
THEY'RE TRACKING US WITH YOUR WATCH!
KNOCK!! KNOCK!! KNOCK!!
¿QUIÉN ES?*
*WHO IS IT?

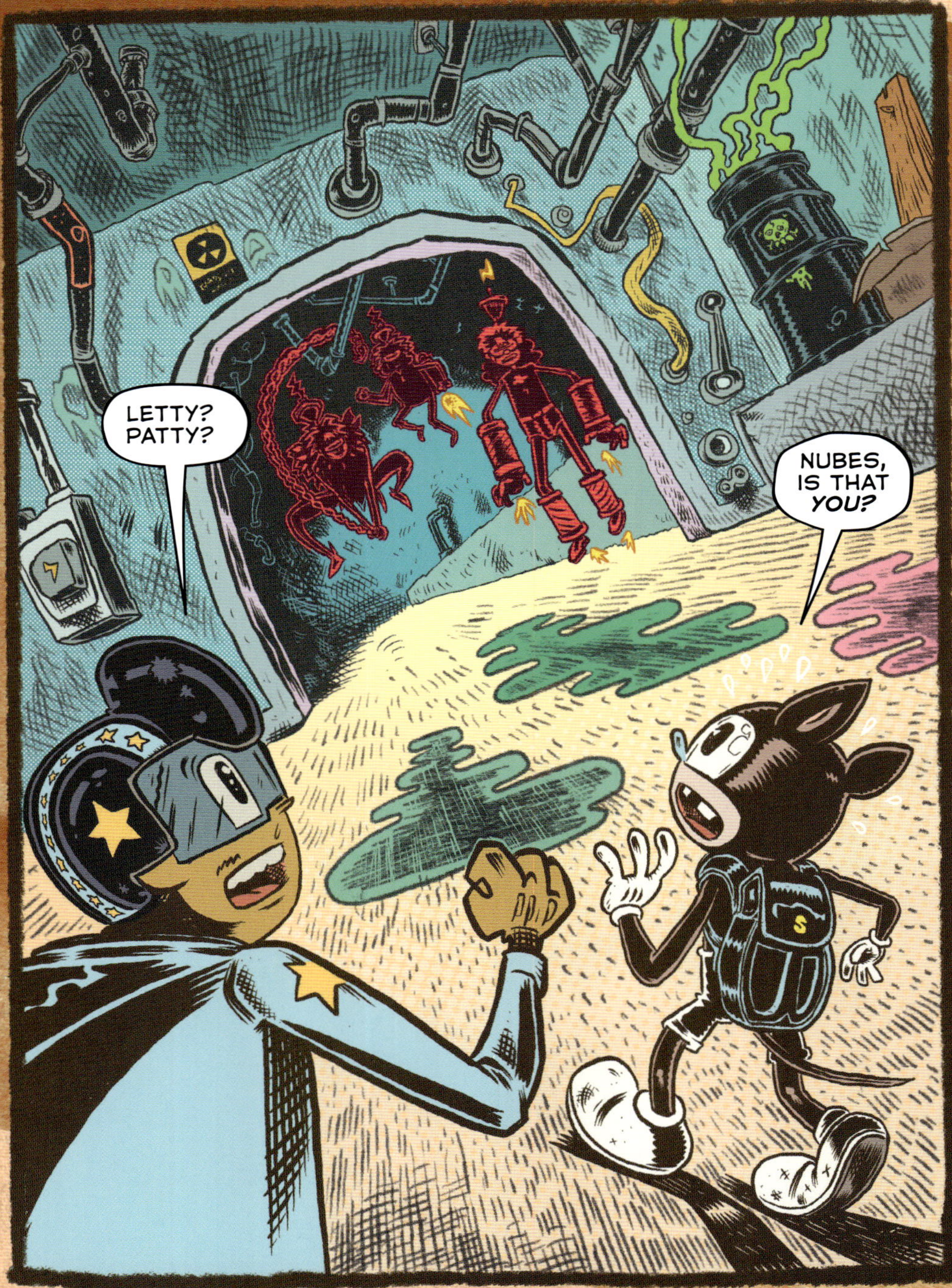
LETTY? PATTY?
NUBES, IS THAT *YOU?*

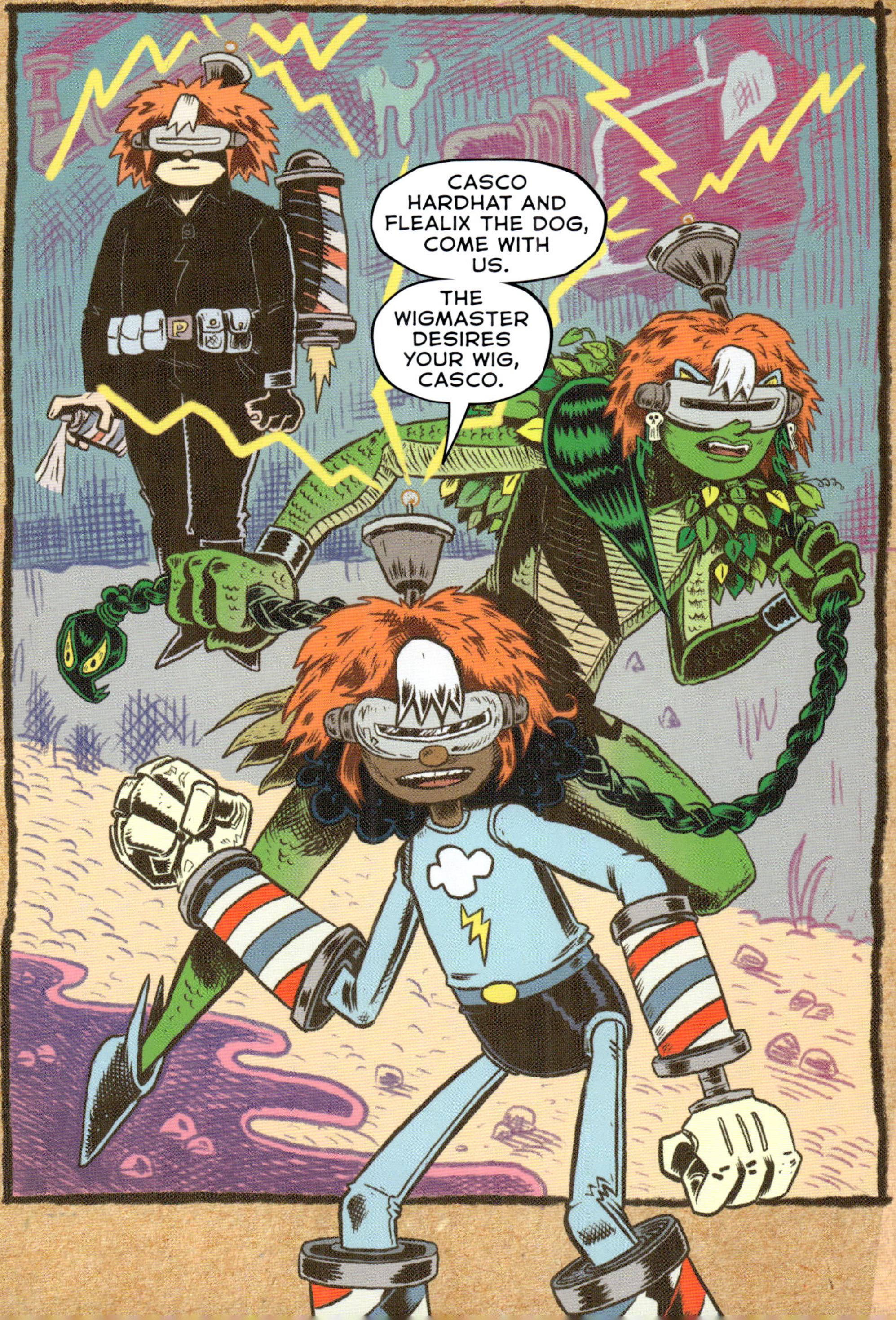
CASCO HARDHAT AND FLEALIX THE DOG, COME WITH US.
THE WIGMASTER DESIRES YOUR WIG, CASCO.

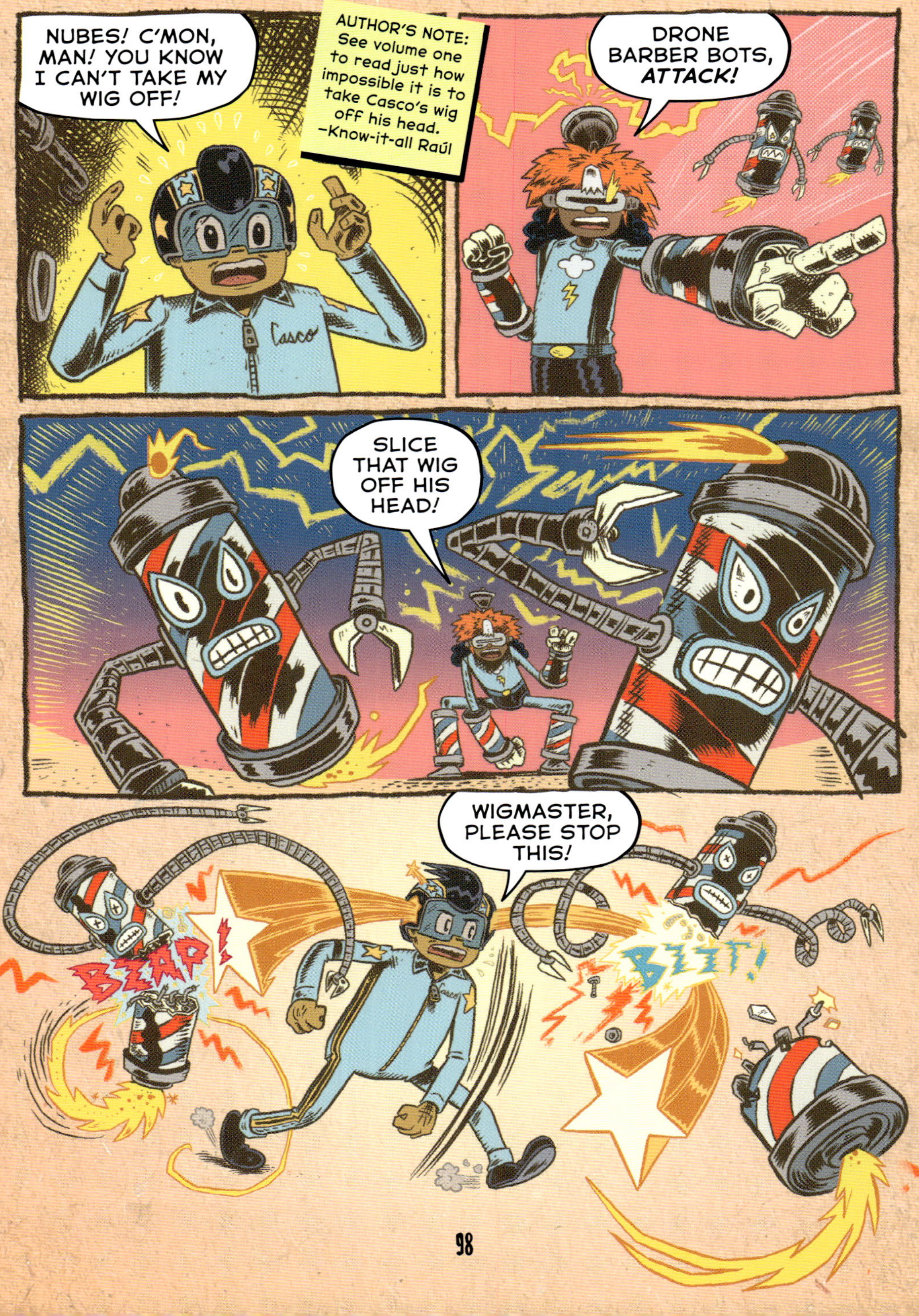
NUBES! C'MON, MAN! YOU KNOW I CAN'T TAKE MY WIG OFF!
AUTHOR'S NOTE: See volume one to read just how impossible it is to take Casco's wig off his head. –Know-it-all Raúl
Casco
DRONE BARBER BOTS, ATTACK!
SLICE THAT WIG OFF HIS HEAD!
WIGMASTER, PLEASE STOP THIS!
BZAP!
BZZT!

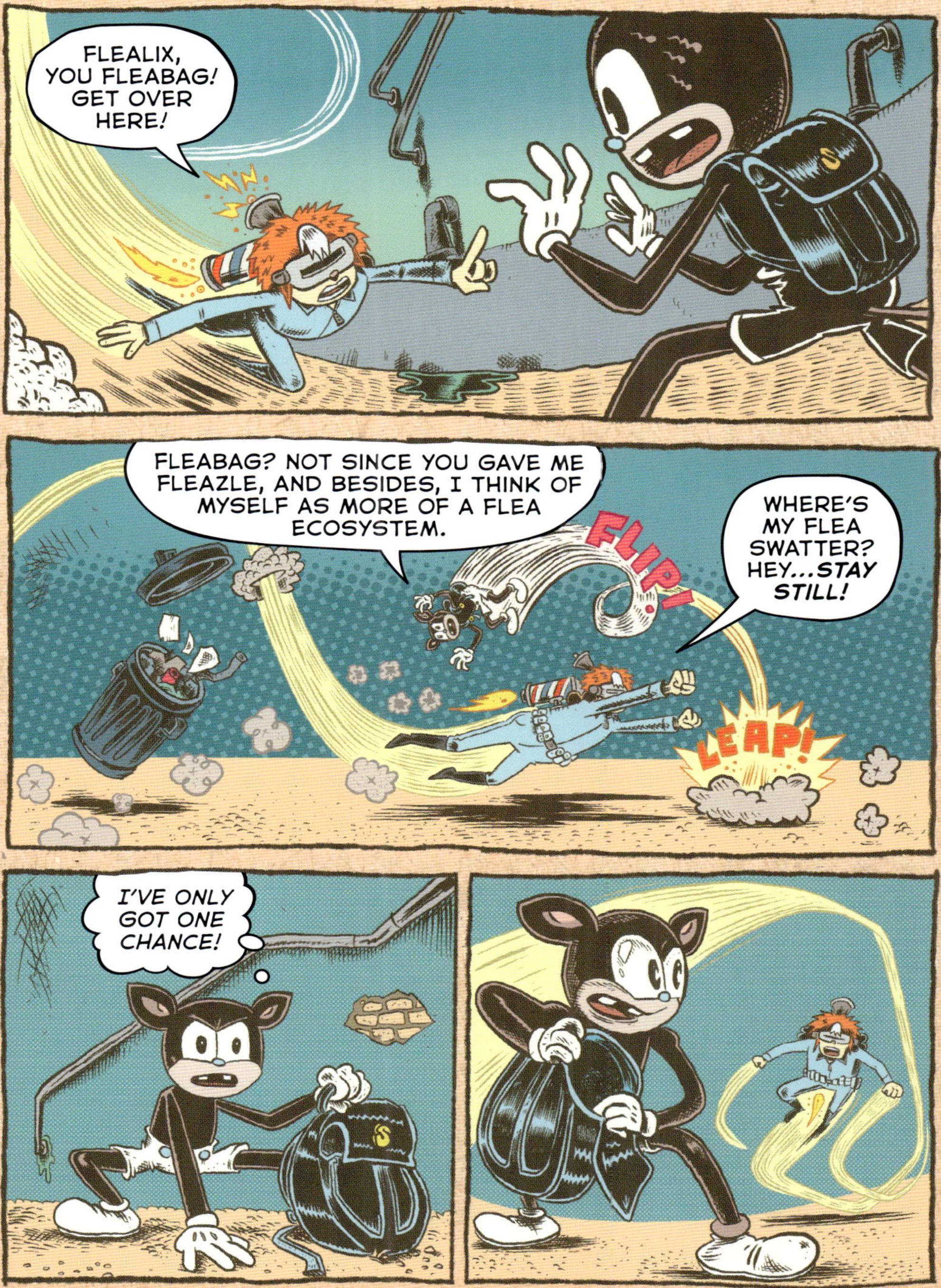
FLEALIX, YOU FLEABAG! GET OVER HERE!
FLEABAG? NOT SINCE YOU GAVE ME FLEAZLE, AND BESIDES, I THINK OF MYSELF AS MORE OF A FLEA ECOSYSTEM.
FLIP!
WHERE'S MY FLEA SWATTER? HEY...STAY STILL!
LEAP!
I'VE ONLY GOT ONE CHANCE!

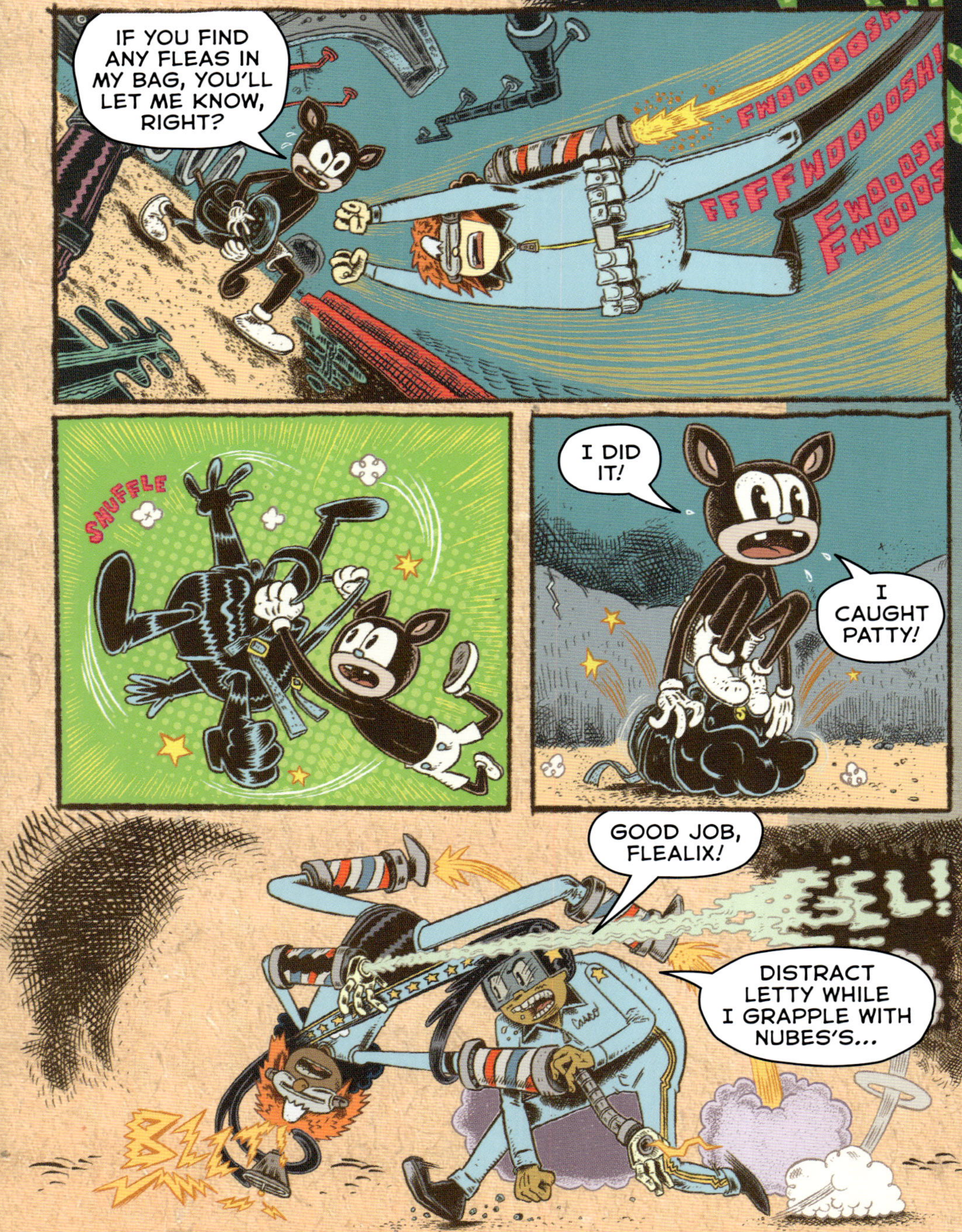
IF YOU FIND ANY FLEAS IN MY BAG, YOU'LL LET ME KNOW, RIGHT?
FWOOOOOSH!
SHUFFLE
I DID IT!
I CAUGHT PATTY!
GOOD JOB, FLEALIX!
DISTRACT LETTY WHILE I GRAPPLE WITH NUBES'S...

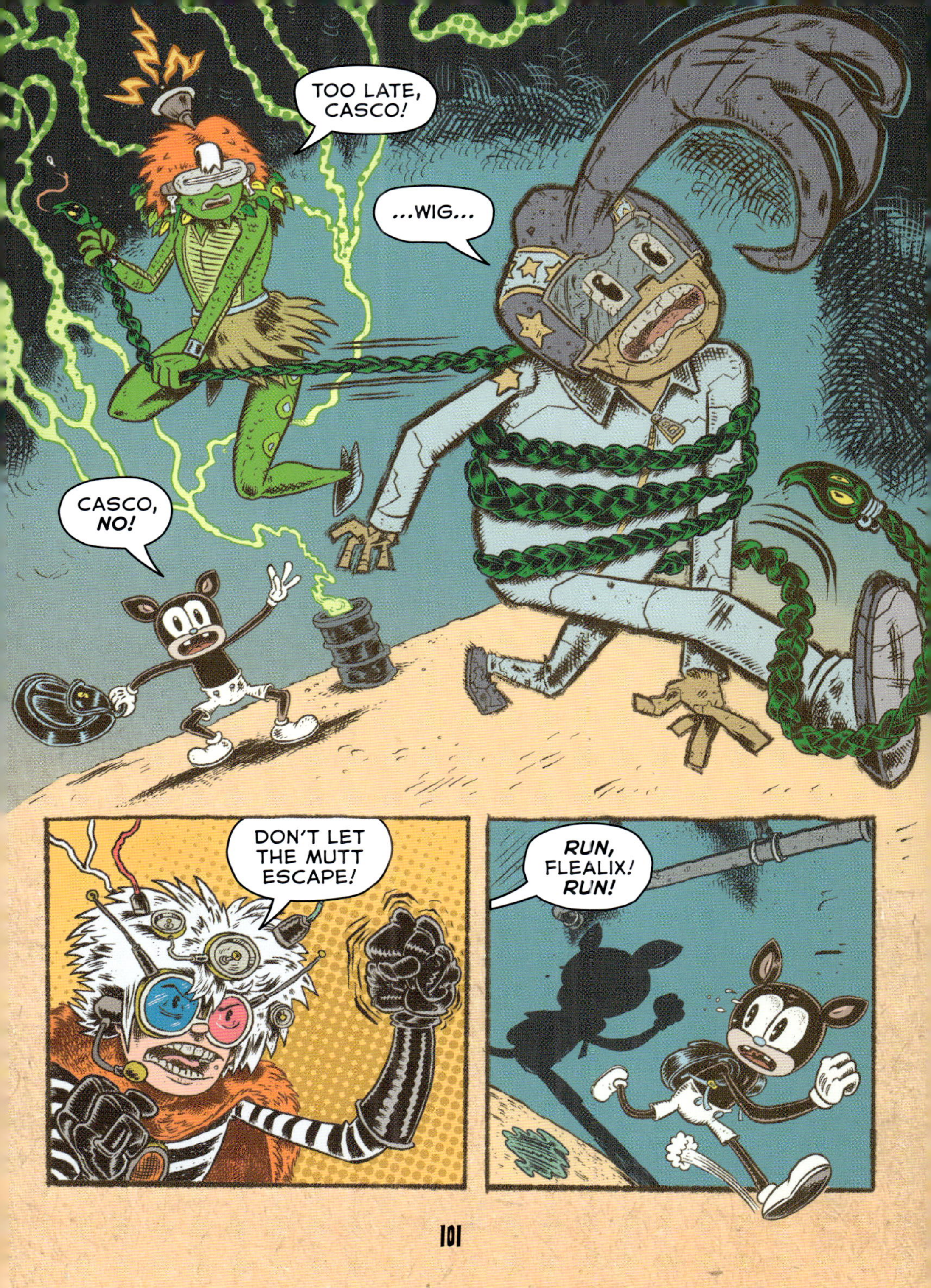
TOO LATE, CASCO!
...WIG...
CASCO, NO!
DON'T LET THE MUTT ESCAPE!
RUN, FLEALIX! RUN!

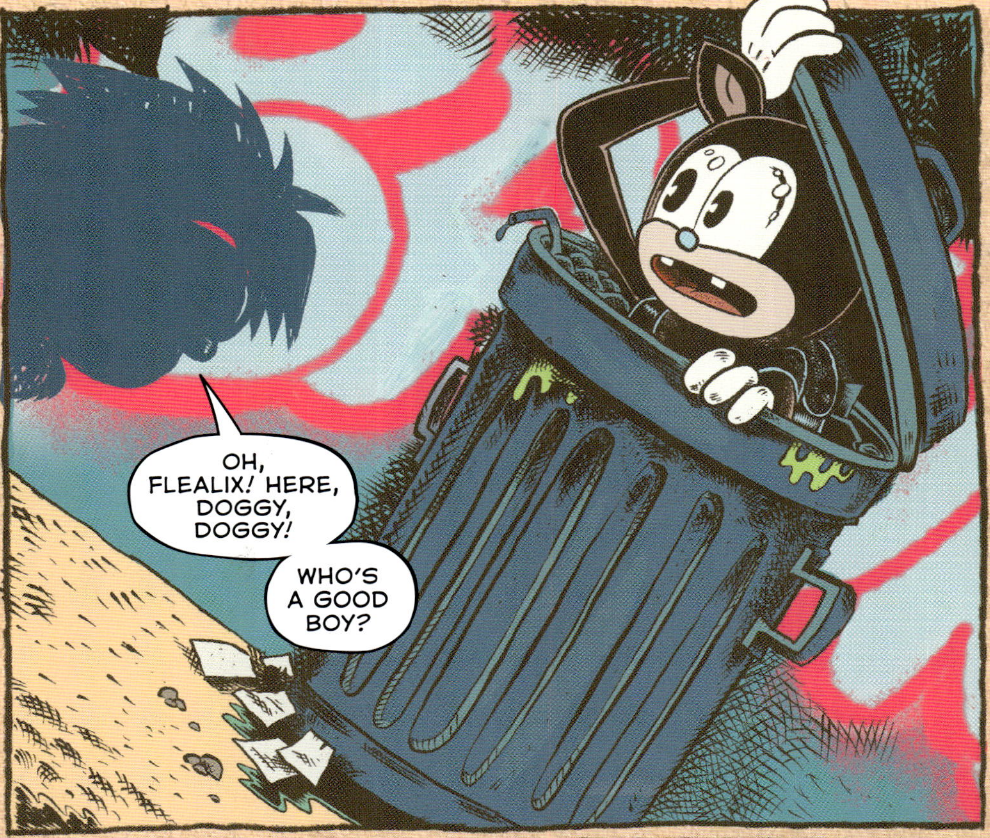
OH, FLEALIX! HERE, DOGGY, DOGGY!
WHO'S A GOOD BOY?

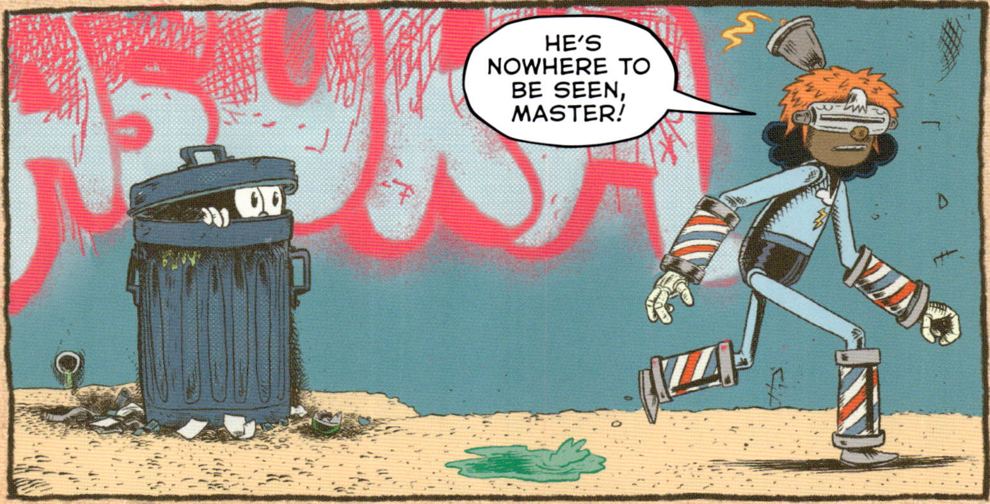
HE'S NOWHERE TO BE SEEN, MASTER!

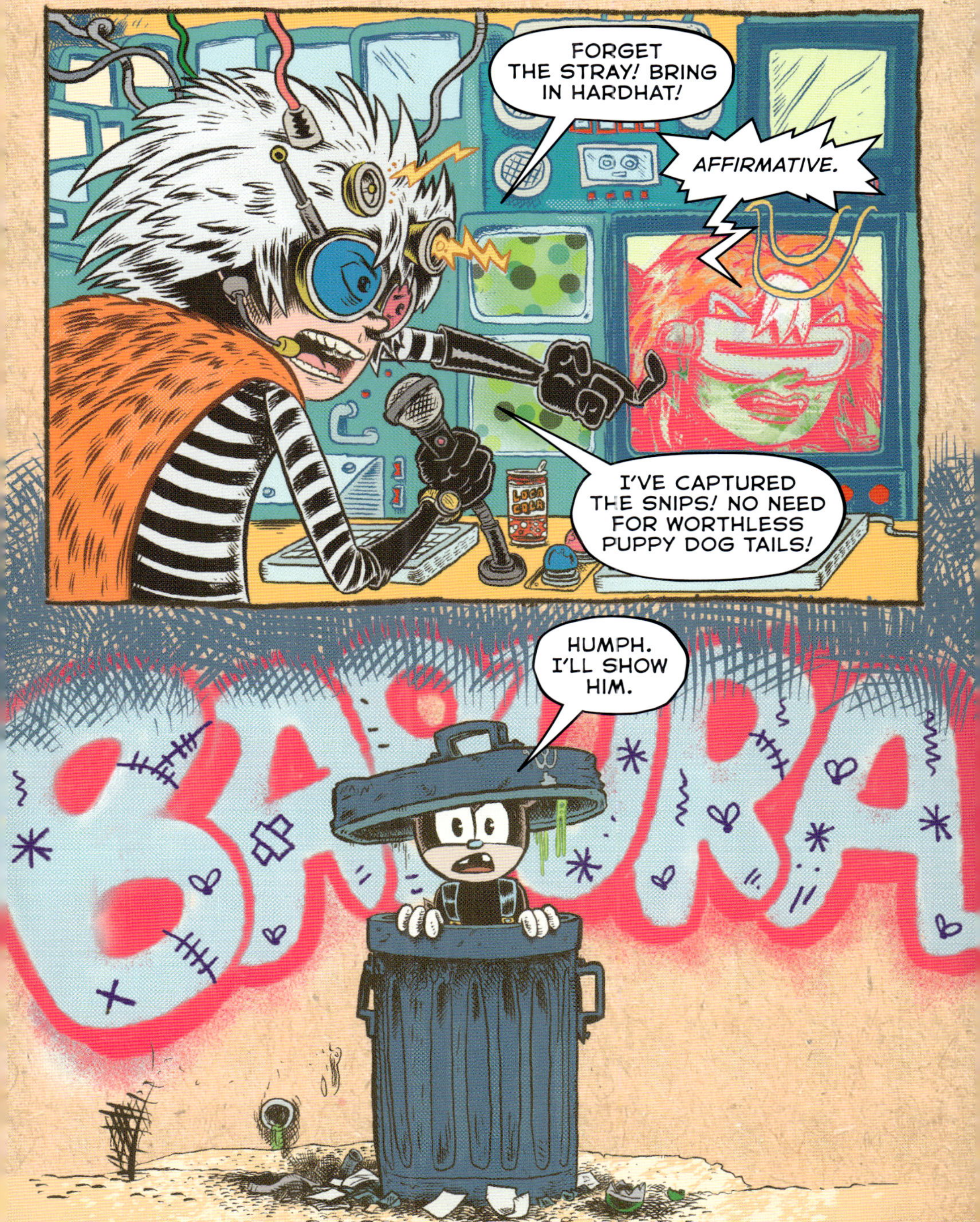
FORGET THE STRAY! BRING IN HARDHAT!
AFFIRMATIVE.
I'VE CAPTURED THE SNIPS! NO NEED FOR WORTHLESS PUPPY DOG TAILS!
HUMPH. I'LL SHOW HIM.

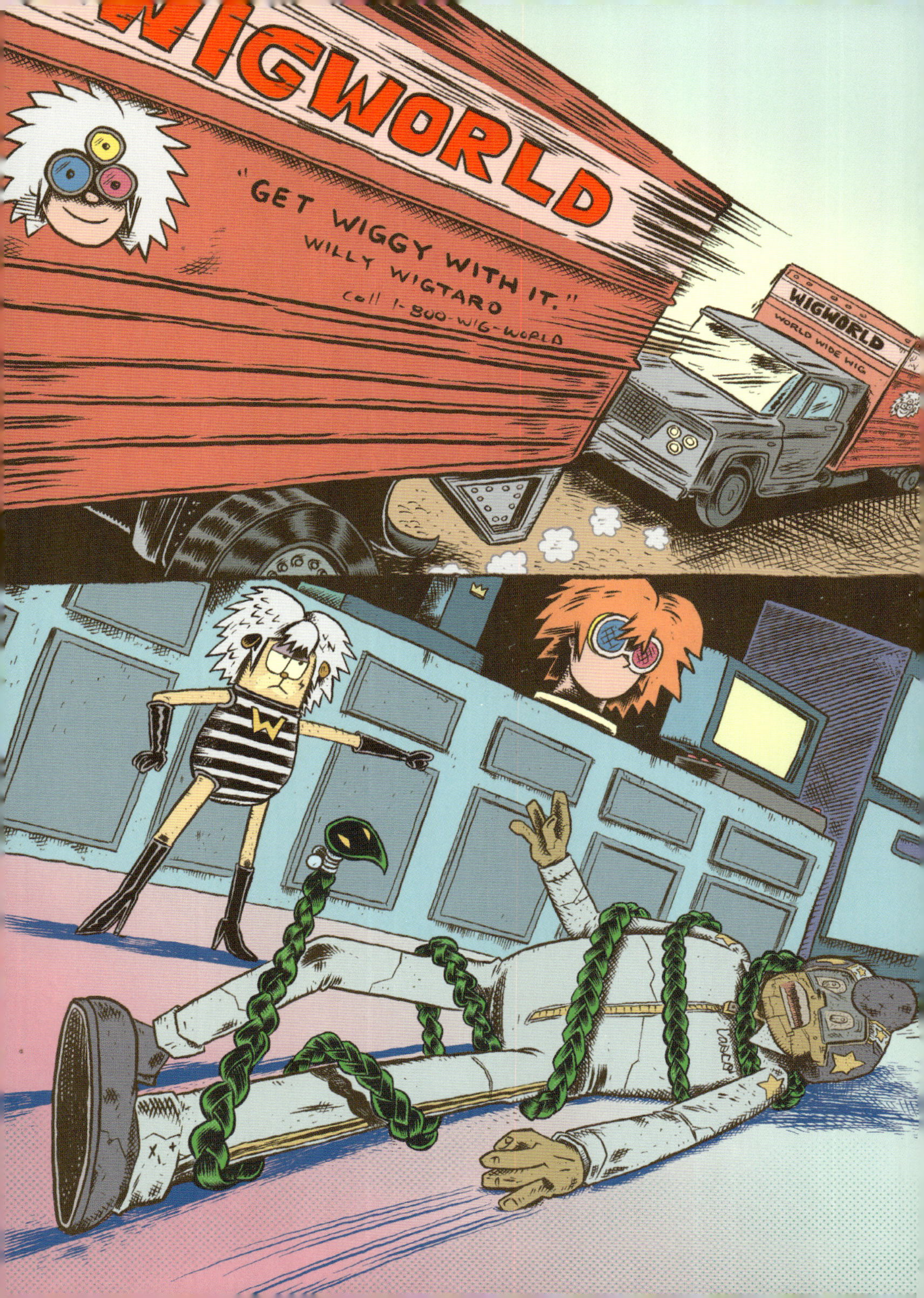
WIGWORLD
"GET WIGGY WITH IT."
WILLY WIGTARO
Call 1-800-WIG-WORLD
WIGWORLD
WORLD WIDE WIG

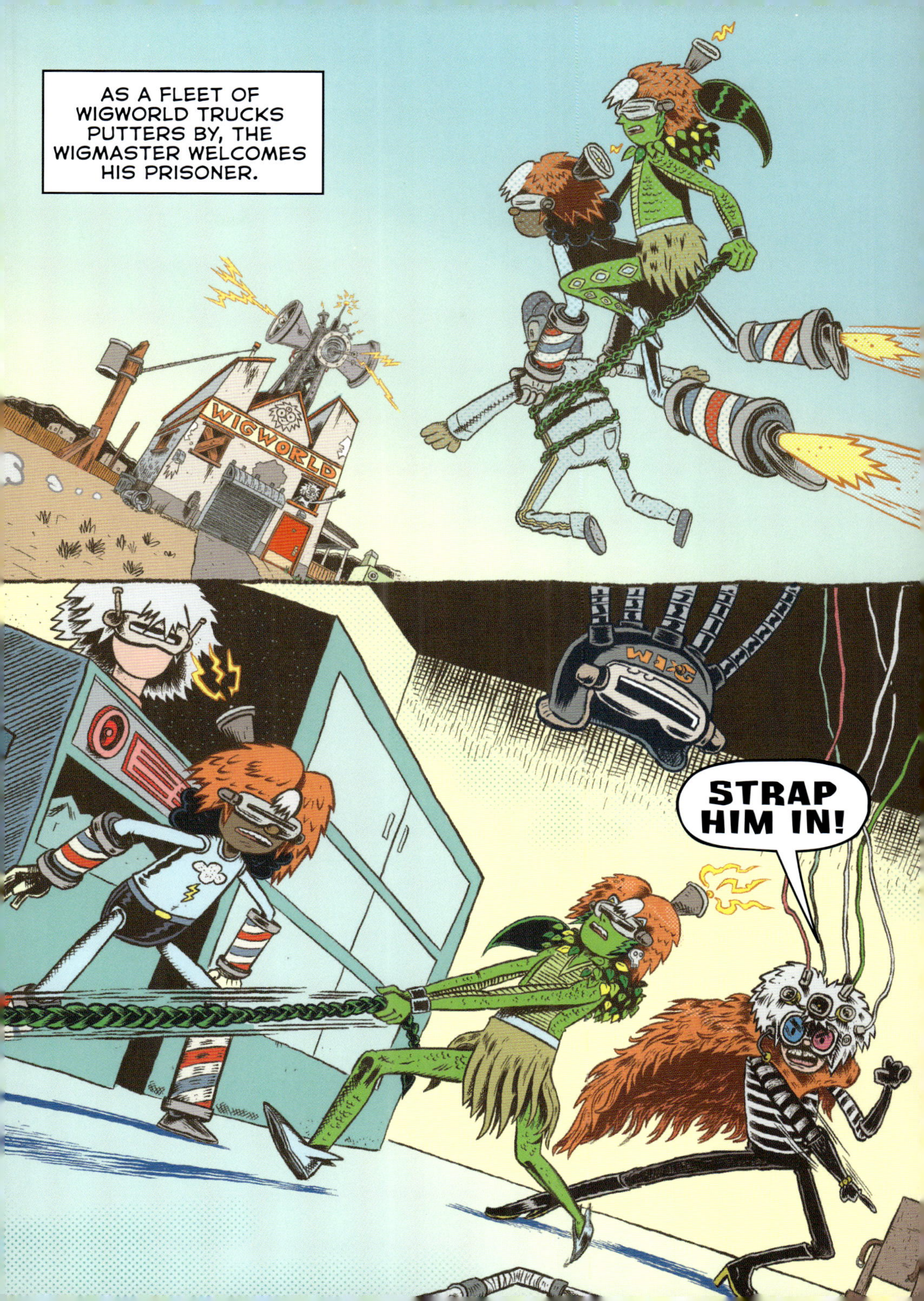
AS A FLEET OF WIGWORLD TRUCKS PUTTERS BY, THE WIGMASTER WELCOMES HIS PRISONER.
WIGWORLD
STRAP HIM IN!

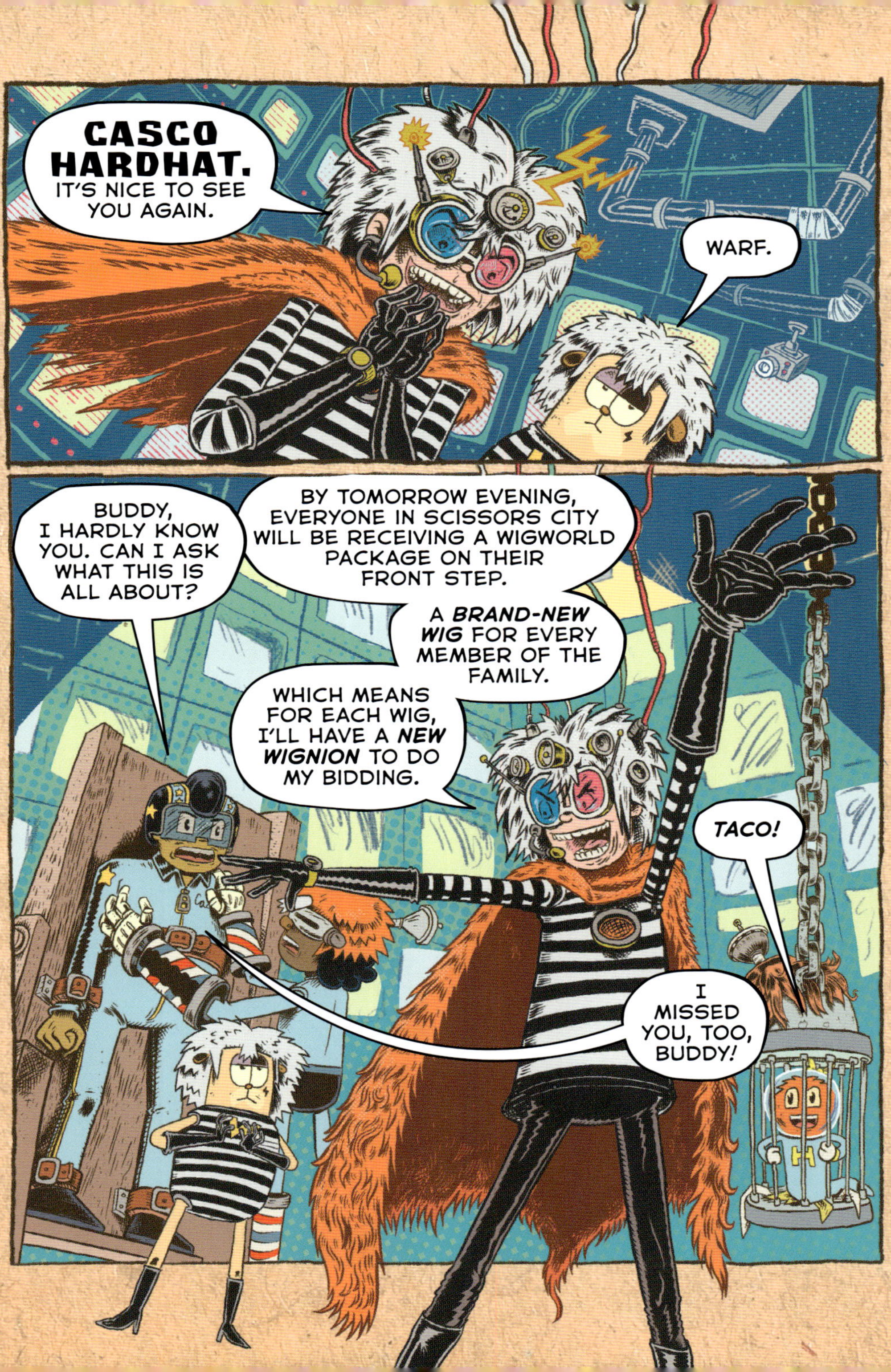
CASCO HARDHAT. IT'S NICE TO SEE YOU AGAIN.
WARF.
BUDDY, I HARDLY KNOW YOU. CAN I ASK WHAT THIS IS ALL ABOUT?
BY TOMORROW EVENING, EVERYONE IN SCISSORS CITY WILL BE RECEIVING A WIGWORLD PACKAGE ON THEIR FRONT STEP.
A **BRAND-NEW WIG** FOR EVERY MEMBER OF THE FAMILY.
WHICH MEANS FOR EACH WIG, I'LL HAVE A ***NEW WIGNION*** TO DO MY BIDDING.
TACO!
I MISSED YOU, TOO, BUDDY!

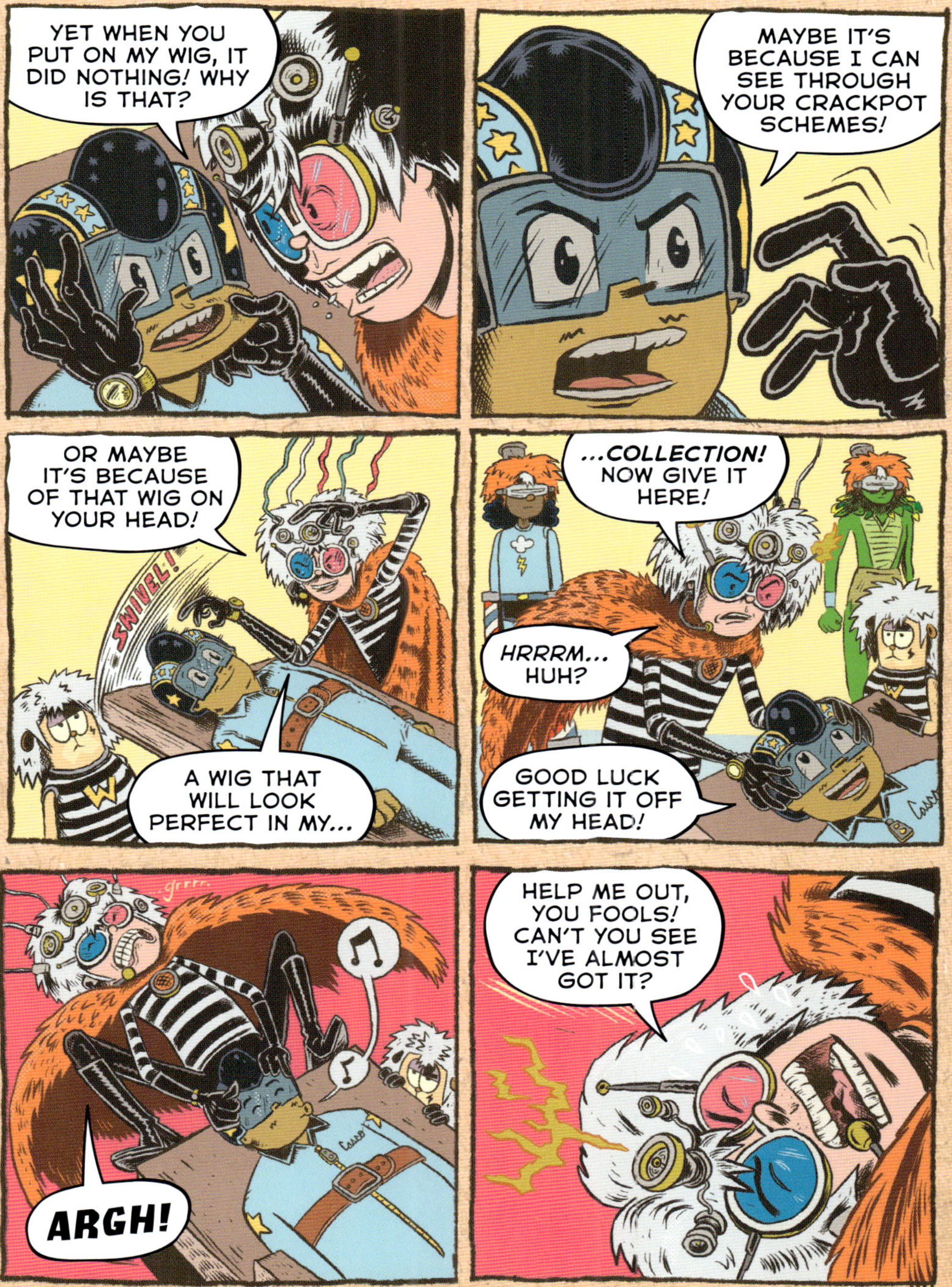
YET WHEN YOU PUT ON MY WIG, IT DID NOTHING! WHY IS THAT?
MAYBE IT'S BECAUSE I CAN SEE THROUGH YOUR CRACKPOT SCHEMES!
OR MAYBE IT'S BECAUSE OF THAT WIG ON YOUR HEAD!
SWIVEL!
A WIG THAT WILL LOOK PERFECT IN MY...
...COLLECTION! NOW GIVE IT HERE!
HRRRM... HUH?
GOOD LUCK GETTING IT OFF MY HEAD!
...grrrr.
ARGH!
HELP ME OUT, YOU FOOLS! CAN'T YOU SEE I'VE ALMOST GOT IT?

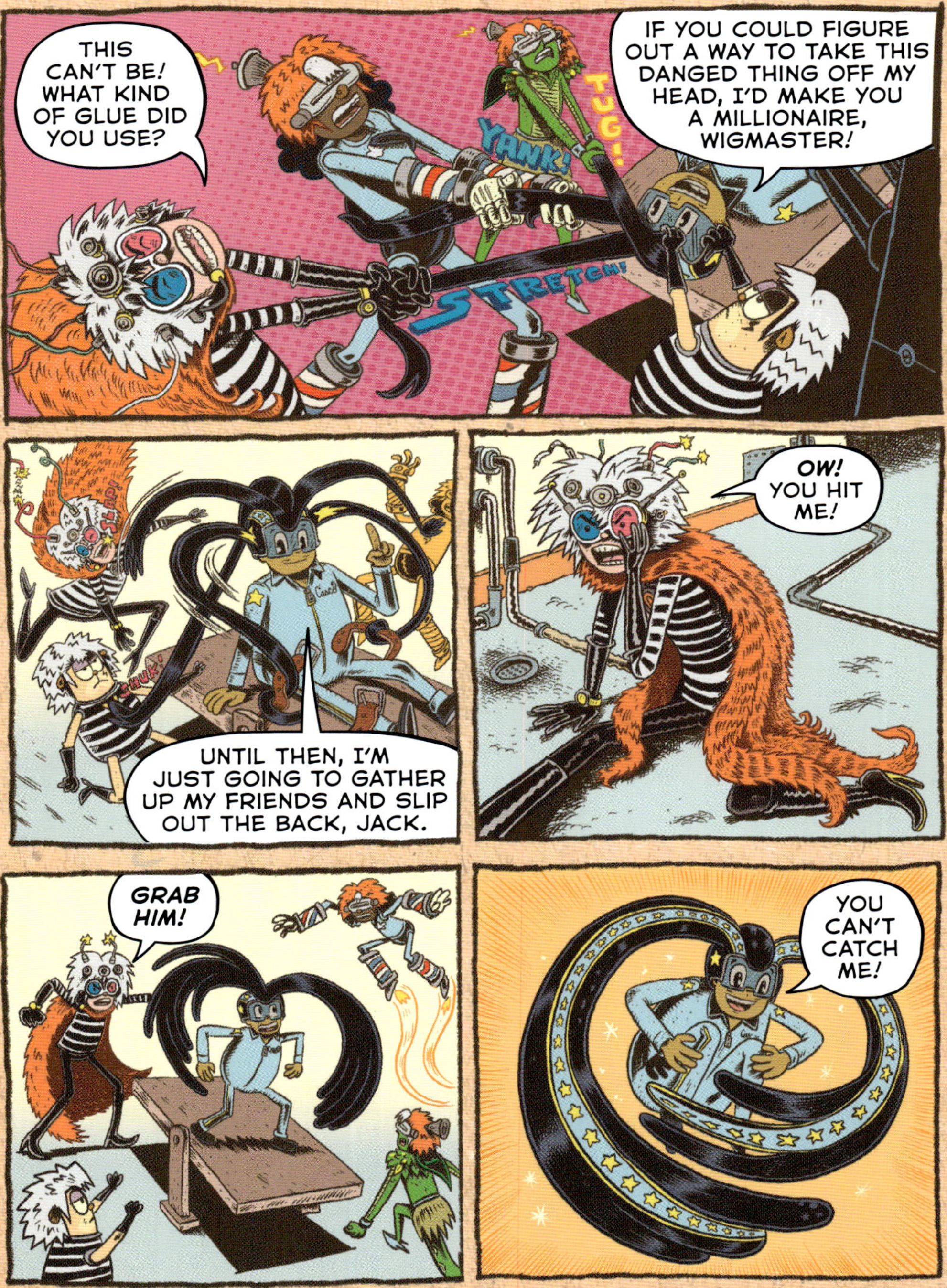
THIS CAN'T BE! WHAT KIND OF GLUE DID YOU USE?
TUG!
YANK!
IF YOU COULD FIGURE OUT A WAY TO TAKE THIS DANGED THING OFF MY HEAD, I'D MAKE YOU A MILLIONAIRE, WIGMASTER!
STRETCH!
UNTIL THEN, I'M JUST GOING TO GATHER UP MY FRIENDS AND SLIP OUT THE BACK, JACK.
OW! YOU HIT ME!
GRAB HIM!
YOU CAN'T CATCH ME!

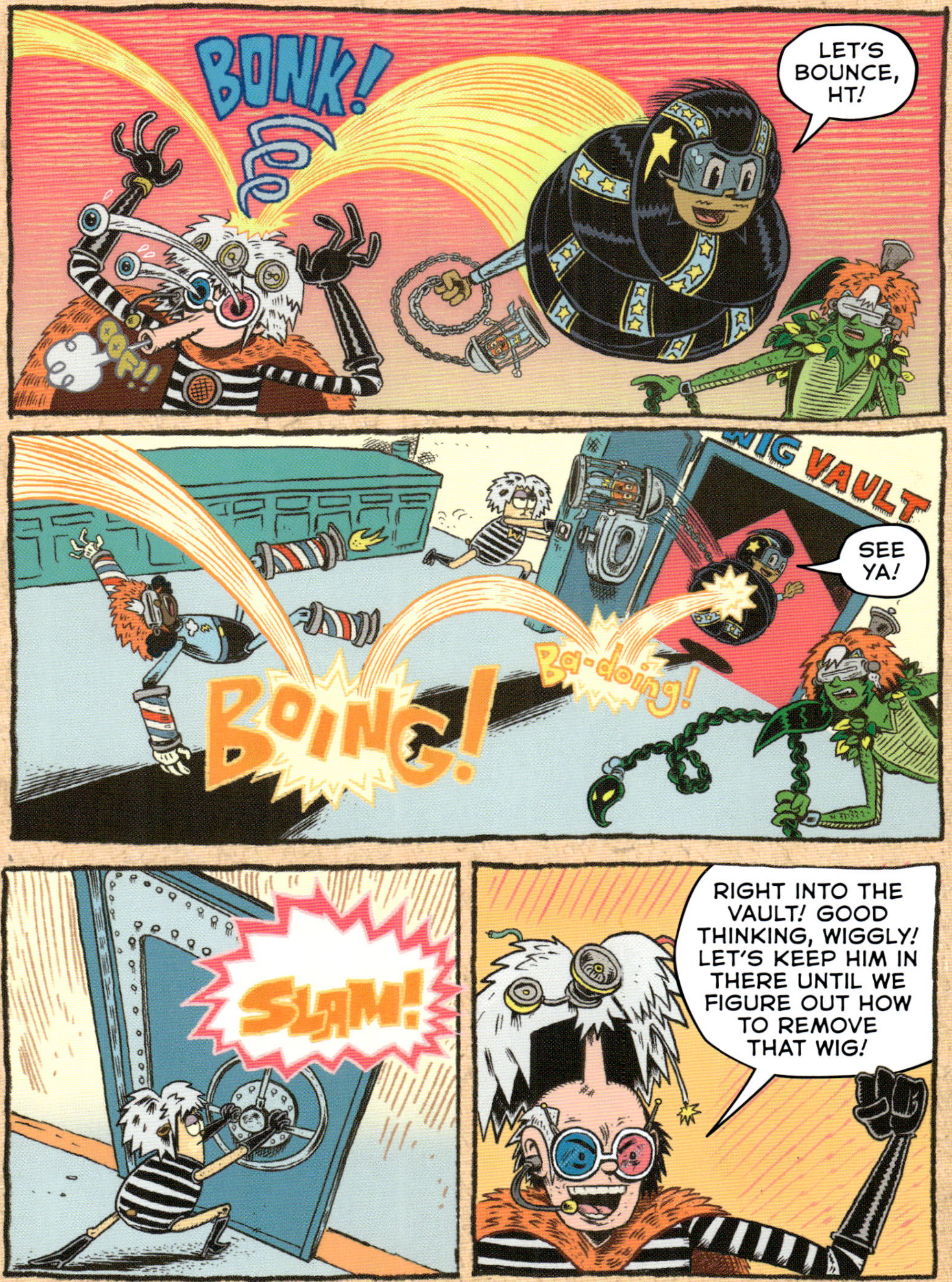
BONK!
OOF!!
LET'S BOUNCE, HT!
WIG VAULT
SEE YA!
BOING!
Ba-doing!
SLAM!
RIGHT INTO THE VAULT! GOOD THINKING, WIGGLY! LET'S KEEP HIM IN THERE UNTIL WE FIGURE OUT HOW TO REMOVE THAT WIG!

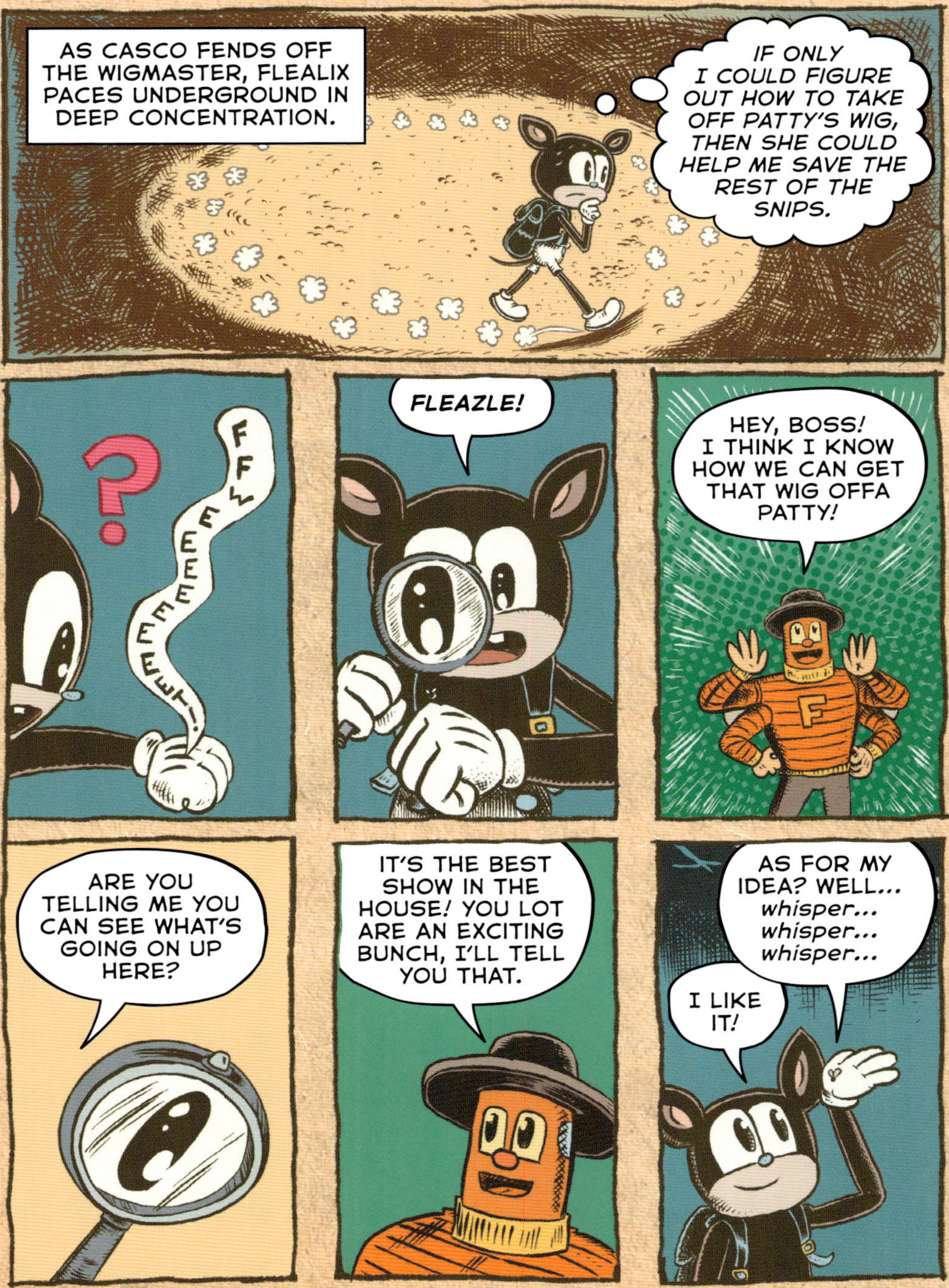
AS CASCO FENDS OFF THE WIGMASTER, FLEALIX PACES UNDERGROUND IN DEEP CONCENTRATION.
IF ONLY I COULD FIGURE OUT HOW TO TAKE OFF PATTY'S WIG, THEN SHE COULD HELP ME SAVE THE REST OF THE SNIPS.
FFWEEEEEEEEEET
FLEAZLE!
HEY, BOSS! I THINK I KNOW HOW WE CAN GET THAT WIG OFFA PATTY!
ARE YOU TELLING ME YOU CAN SEE WHAT'S GOING ON UP HERE?
IT'S THE BEST SHOW IN THE HOUSE! YOU LOT ARE AN EXCITING BUNCH, I'LL TELL YOU THAT.
AS FOR MY IDEA? WELL... *whisper... whisper... whisper...*
I LIKE IT!

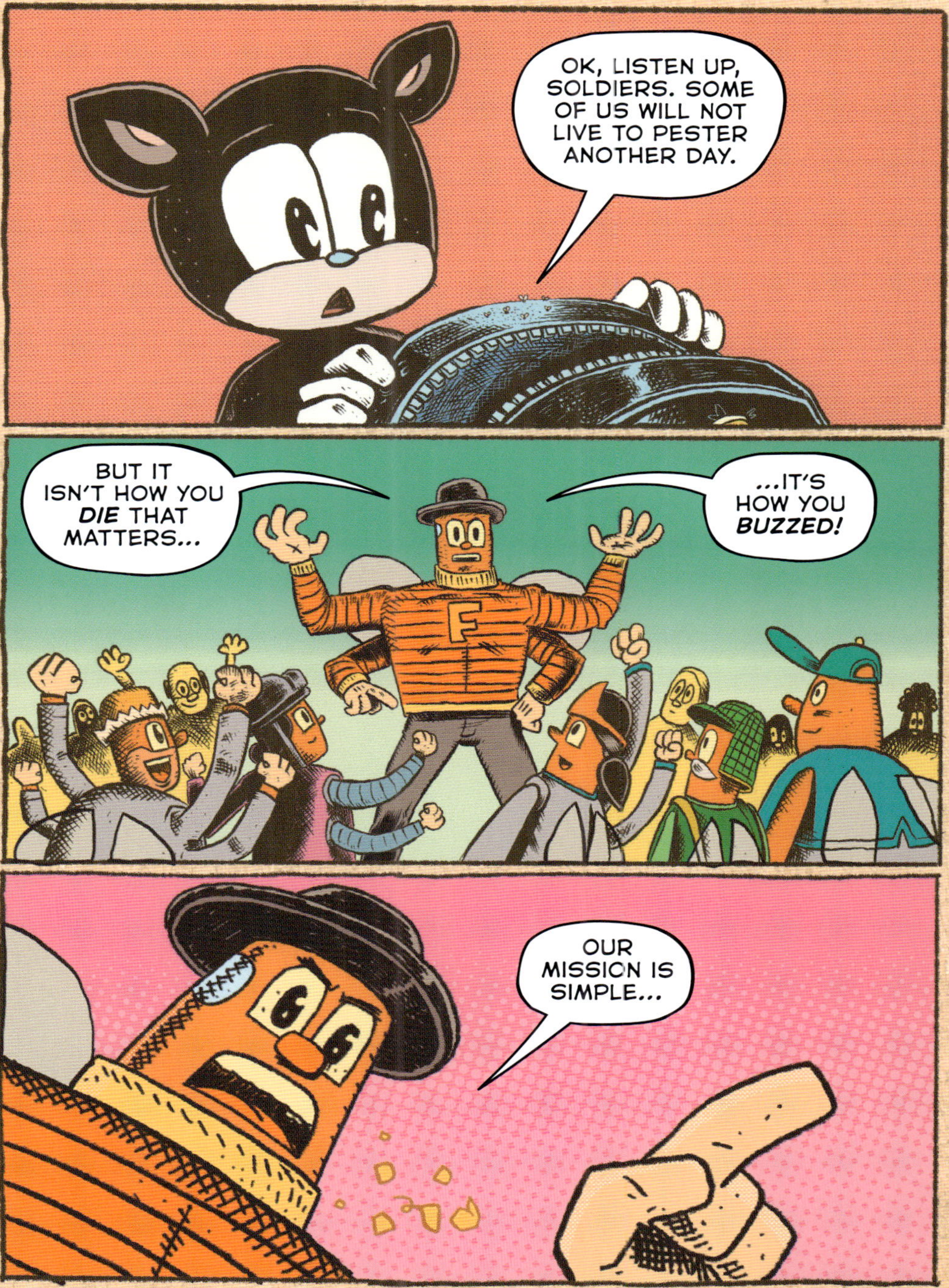
OK, LISTEN UP, SOLDIERS. SOME OF US WILL NOT LIVE TO PESTER ANOTHER DAY.
BUT IT ISN'T HOW YOU *DIE* THAT MATTERS...
...IT'S HOW YOU *BUZZED!*
OUR MISSION IS SIMPLE...

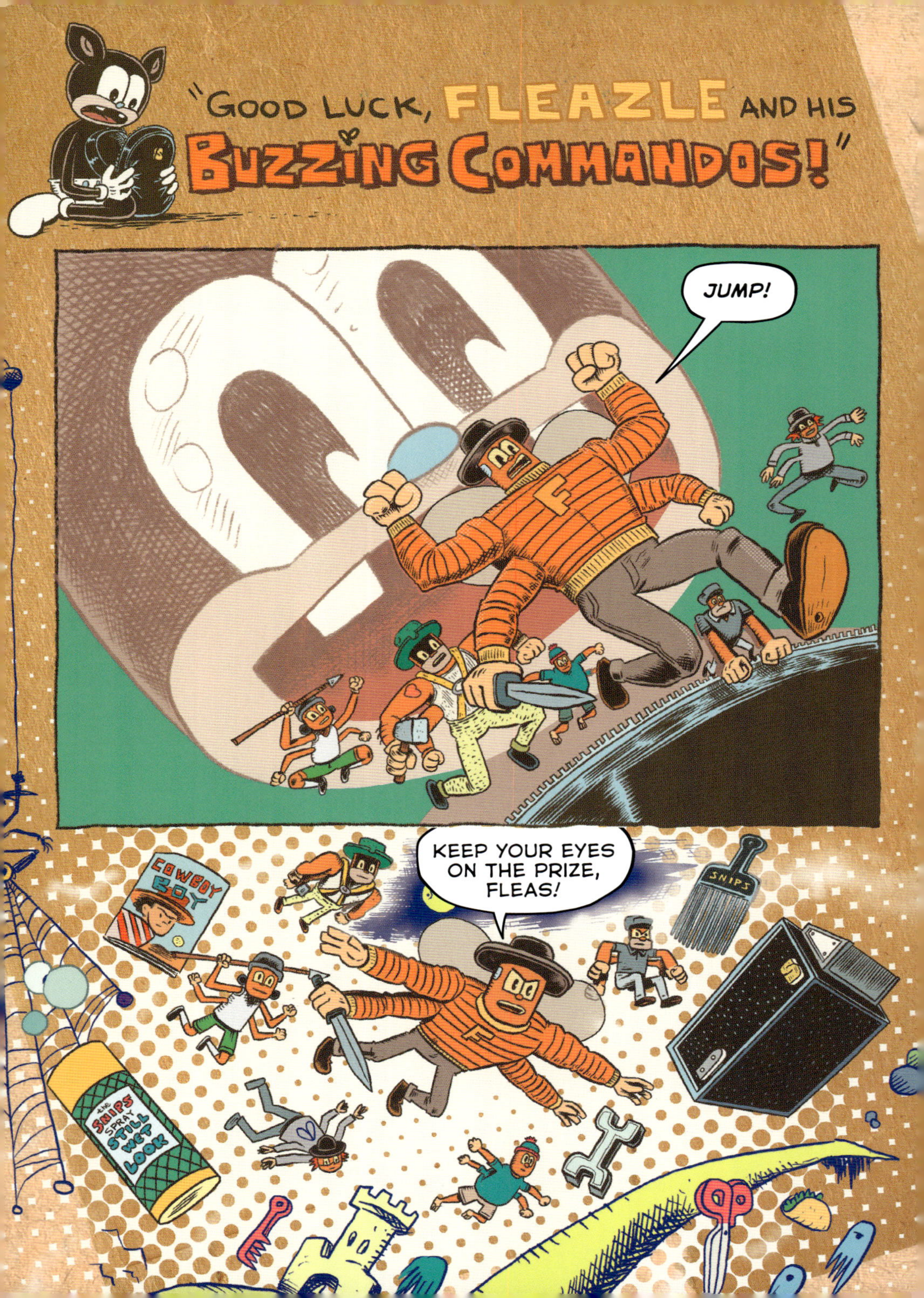
"GOOD LUCK, FLEAZLE AND HIS BUZZING COMMANDOS!"
JUMP!
KEEP YOUR EYES ON THE PRIZE, FLEAS!
COWBOY BOY
SNIPS
THE SNIPS SPRAY STILL WET LOOK

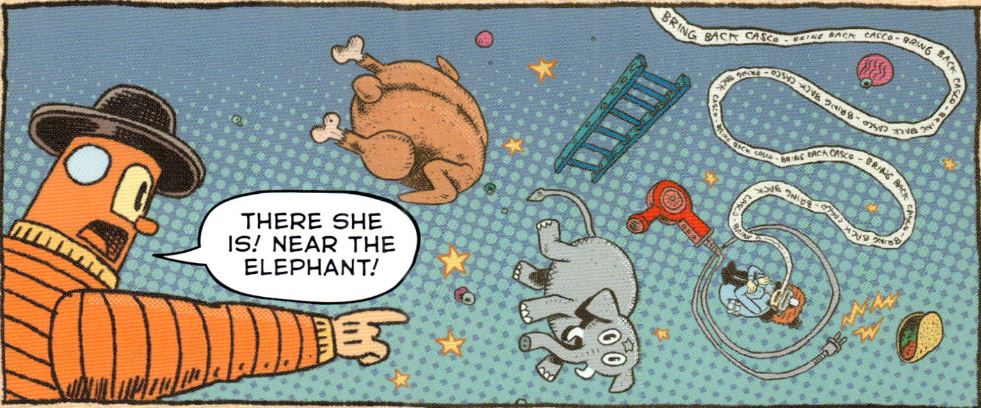
BRING BACK CASCO - BRING BACK CASCO - BRING BACK CASCO
THERE SHE IS! NEAR THE ELEPHANT!

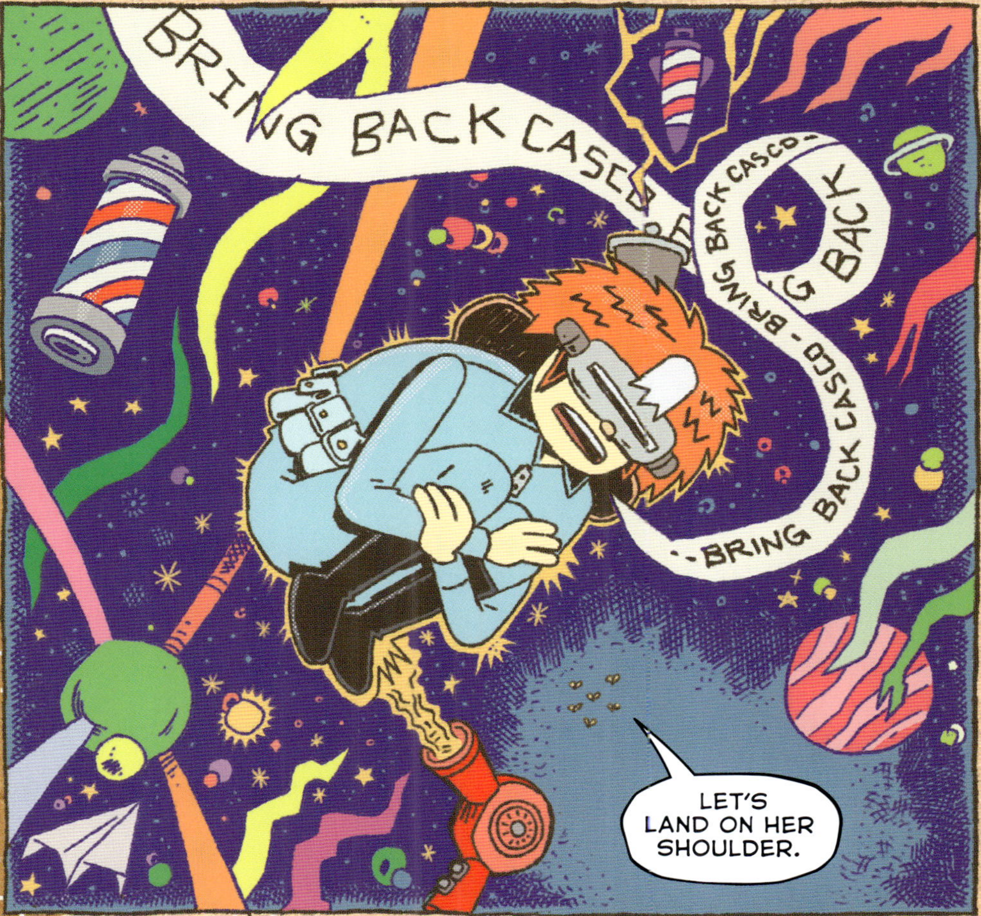
BRING BACK CASCO
BRING BACK CASCO-
BRING BACK CASCO
--BRING BACK CASCO
LET'S LAND ON HER SHOULDER.

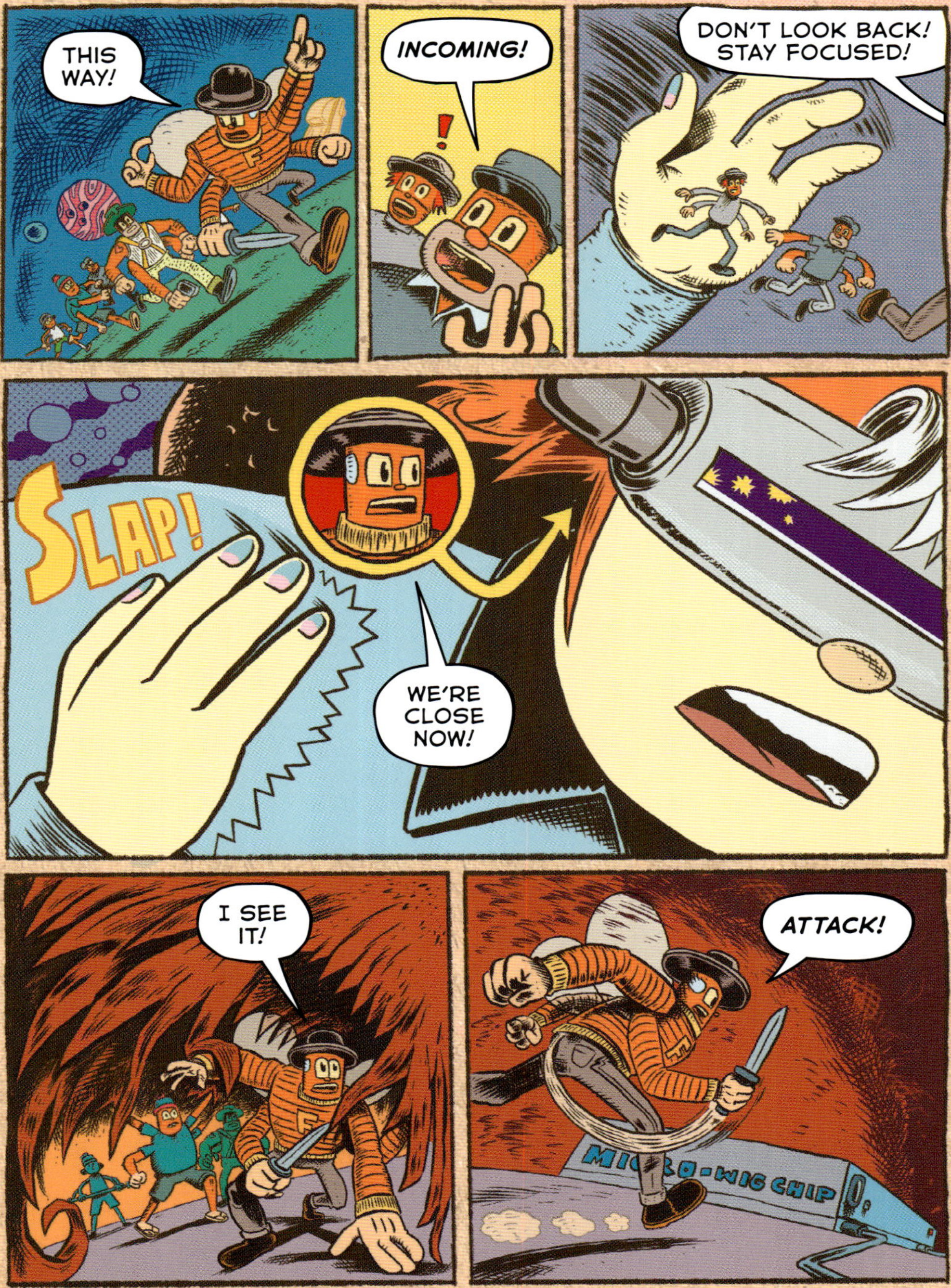
THIS WAY!
INCOMING!
!
DON'T LOOK BACK! STAY FOCUSED!
SLAP!
WE'RE CLOSE NOW!
I SEE IT!
ATTACK!
MICRO-WIG CHIP

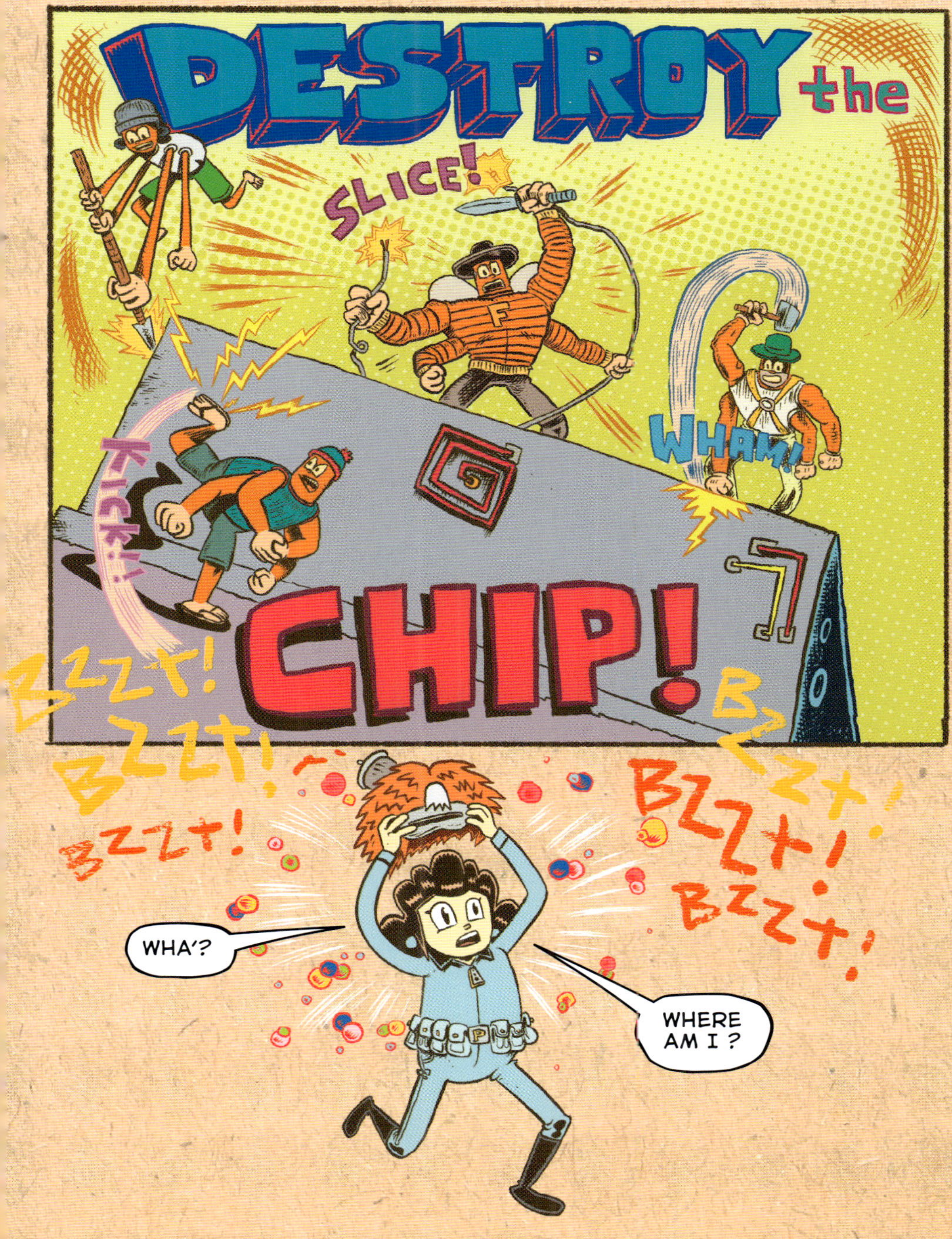
DESTROY the
SLICE!
WHAM!
KICK!!
CHIP!
BZZZT! BZZZT! BZZZT!
BZZZT! BZZZT! BZZZT!
WHA'?
WHERE AM I ?

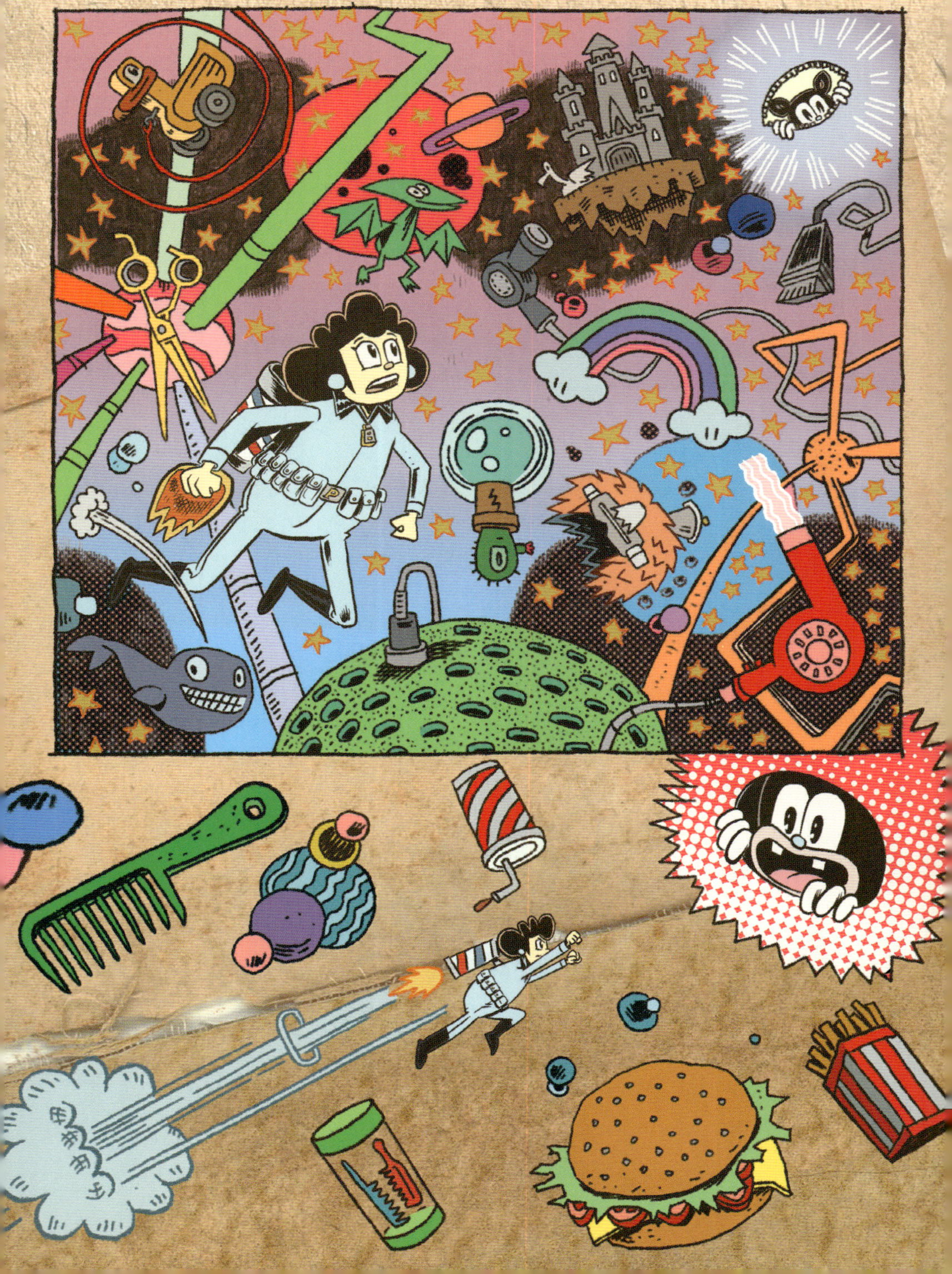

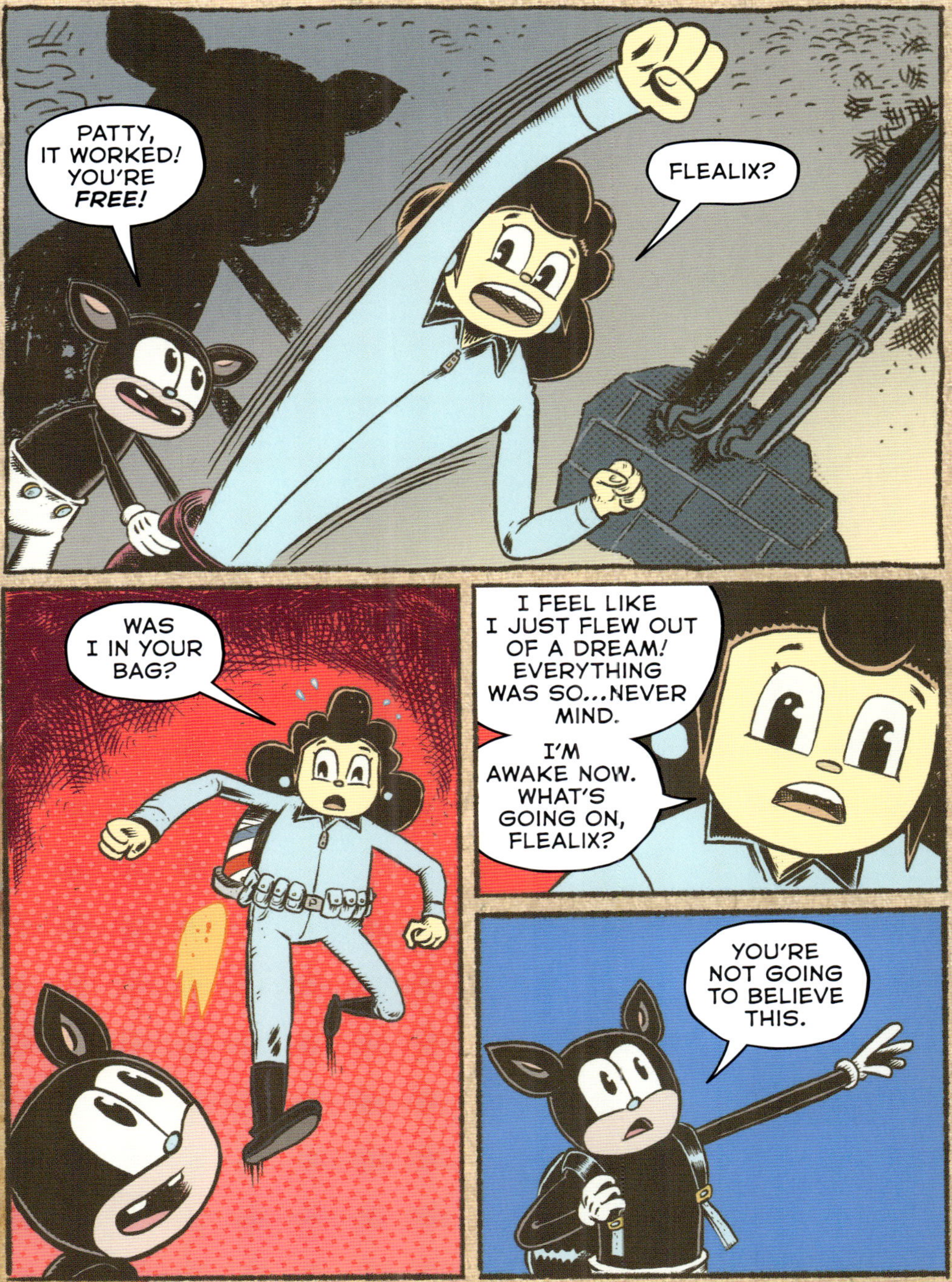

PATTY, IT WORKED! YOU'RE FREE!
FLEALIX?
WAS I IN YOUR BAG?
I FEEL LIKE I JUST FLEW OUT OF A DREAM! EVERYTHING WAS SO...NEVER MIND.
I'M AWAKE NOW. WHAT'S GOING ON, FLEALIX?
YOU'RE NOT GOING TO BELIEVE THIS.

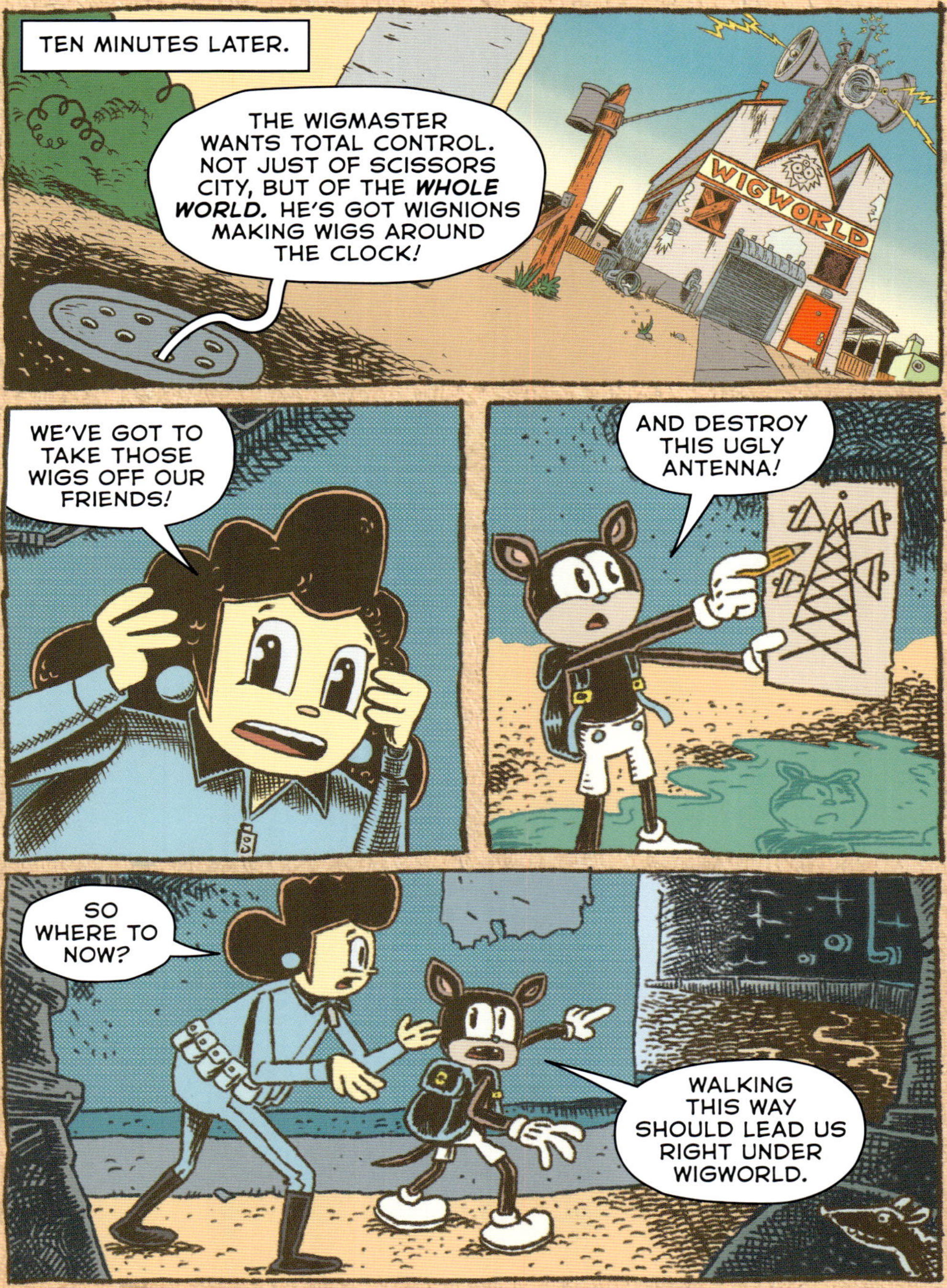
TEN MINUTES LATER.
THE WIGMASTER WANTS TOTAL CONTROL. NOT JUST OF SCISSORS CITY, BUT OF THE ***WHOLE WORLD.*** HE'S GOT WIGNIONS MAKING WIGS AROUND THE CLOCK!
WIGWORLD
WE'VE GOT TO TAKE THOSE WIGS OFF OUR FRIENDS!
AND DESTROY THIS UGLY ANTENNA!
SO WHERE TO NOW?
WALKING THIS WAY SHOULD LEAD US RIGHT UNDER WIGWORLD.

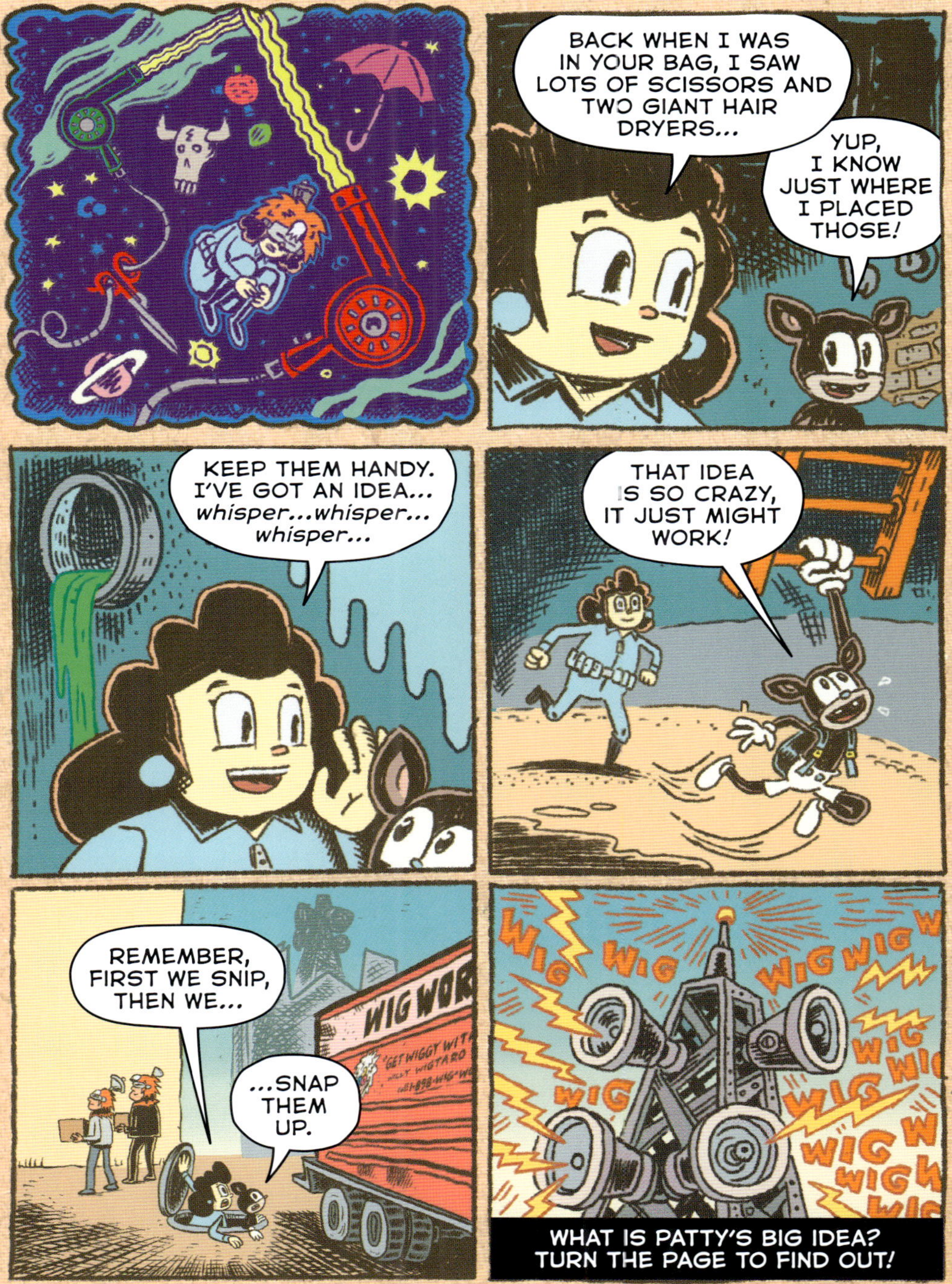
BACK WHEN I WAS IN YOUR BAG, I SAW LOTS OF SCISSORS AND TWO GIANT HAIR DRYERS...
YUP, I KNOW JUST WHERE I PLACED THOSE!
KEEP THEM HANDY. I'VE GOT AN IDEA... *whisper...whisper... whisper...*
THAT IDEA IS SO CRAZY, IT JUST MIGHT WORK!
REMEMBER, FIRST WE SNIP, THEN WE...
...SNAP THEM UP.
WIG WIG WIG WIG WIG WIG WIG WIG
WHAT IS PATTY'S BIG IDEA? TURN THE PAGE TO FIND OUT!

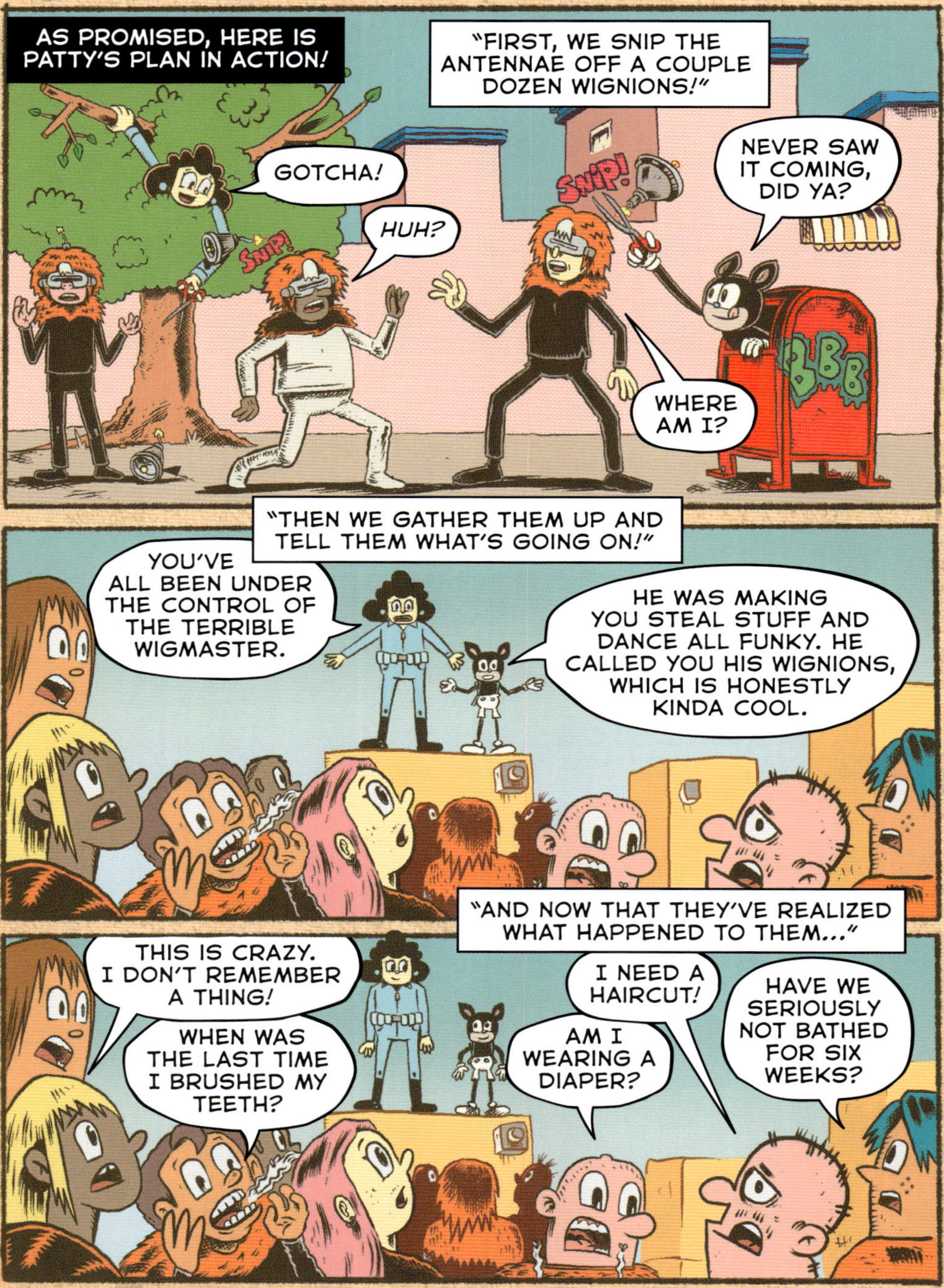
AS PROMISED, HERE IS PATTY'S PLAN IN ACTION!
"FIRST, WE SNIP THE ANTENNAE OFF A COUPLE DOZEN WIGNIONS!"
GOTCHA!
SNIP!
HUH?
SNIP!
NEVER SAW IT COMING, DID YA?
WHERE AM I?
BBB
"THEN WE GATHER THEM UP AND TELL THEM WHAT'S GOING ON!"
YOU'VE ALL BEEN UNDER THE CONTROL OF THE TERRIBLE WIGMASTER.
HE WAS MAKING YOU STEAL STUFF AND DANCE ALL FUNKY. HE CALLED YOU HIS WIGNIONS, WHICH IS HONESTLY KINDA COOL.
"AND NOW THAT THEY'VE REALIZED WHAT HAPPENED TO THEM..."
THIS IS CRAZY. I DON'T REMEMBER A THING!
WHEN WAS THE LAST TIME I BRUSHED MY TEETH?
I NEED A HAIRCUT!
AM I WEARING A DIAPER?
HAVE WE SERIOUSLY NOT BATHED FOR SIX WEEKS?

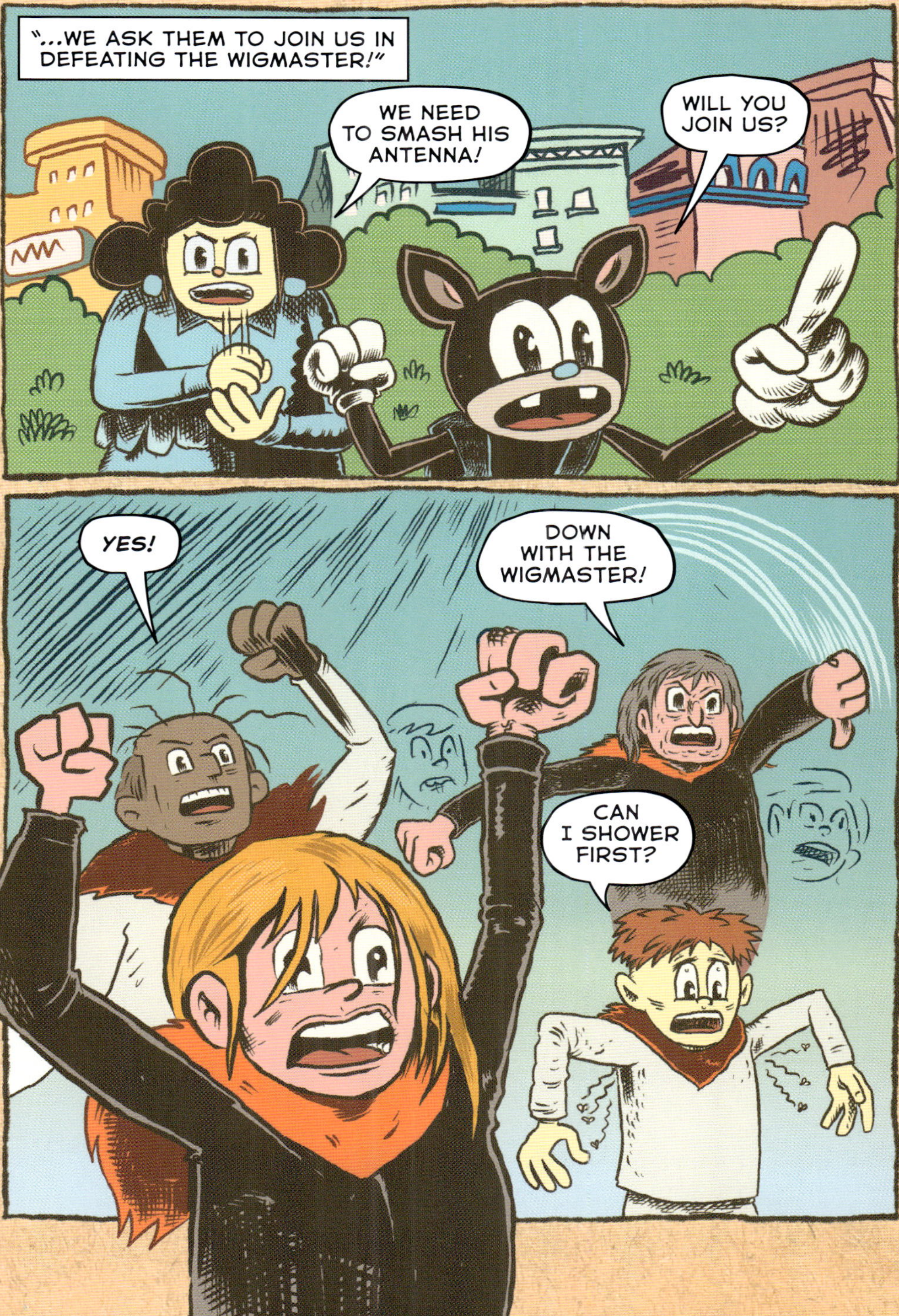
"...WE ASK THEM TO JOIN US IN DEFEATING THE WIGMASTER!"
WE NEED TO SMASH HIS ANTENNA!
WILL YOU JOIN US?
YES!
DOWN WITH THE WIGMASTER!
CAN I SHOWER FIRST?

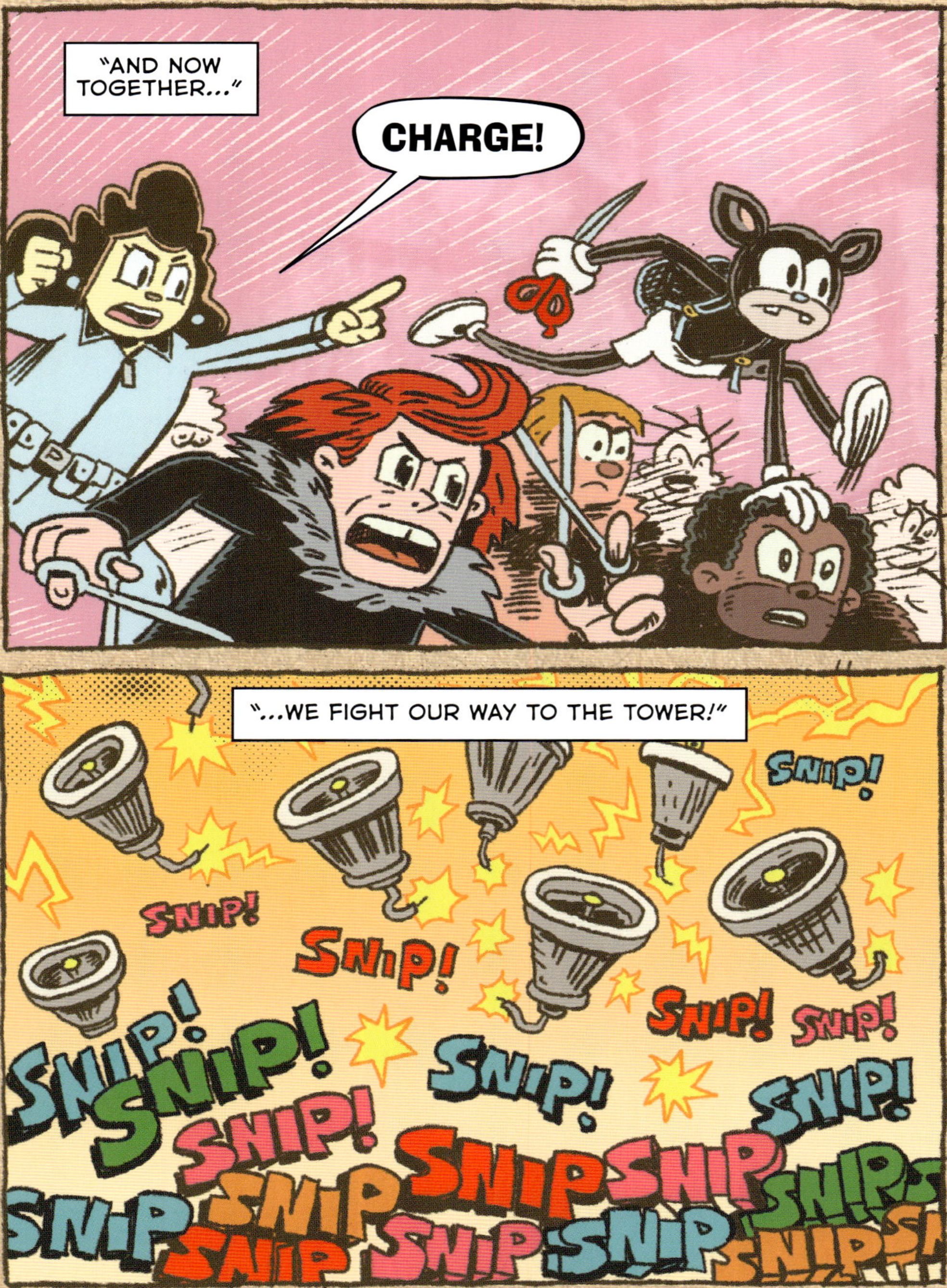
"AND NOW TOGETHER..."
CHARGE!
"...WE FIGHT OUR WAY TO THE TOWER!"
SNIP!
SNIP!
SNIP!
SNIP!
SNIP!
SNIP!
SNIP!
SNIP!
SNIP!
SNIP!
SNIP!
SNIP
SNIP
SNIP
SNIP
SNIP
SNIP
SNIP
SNIP

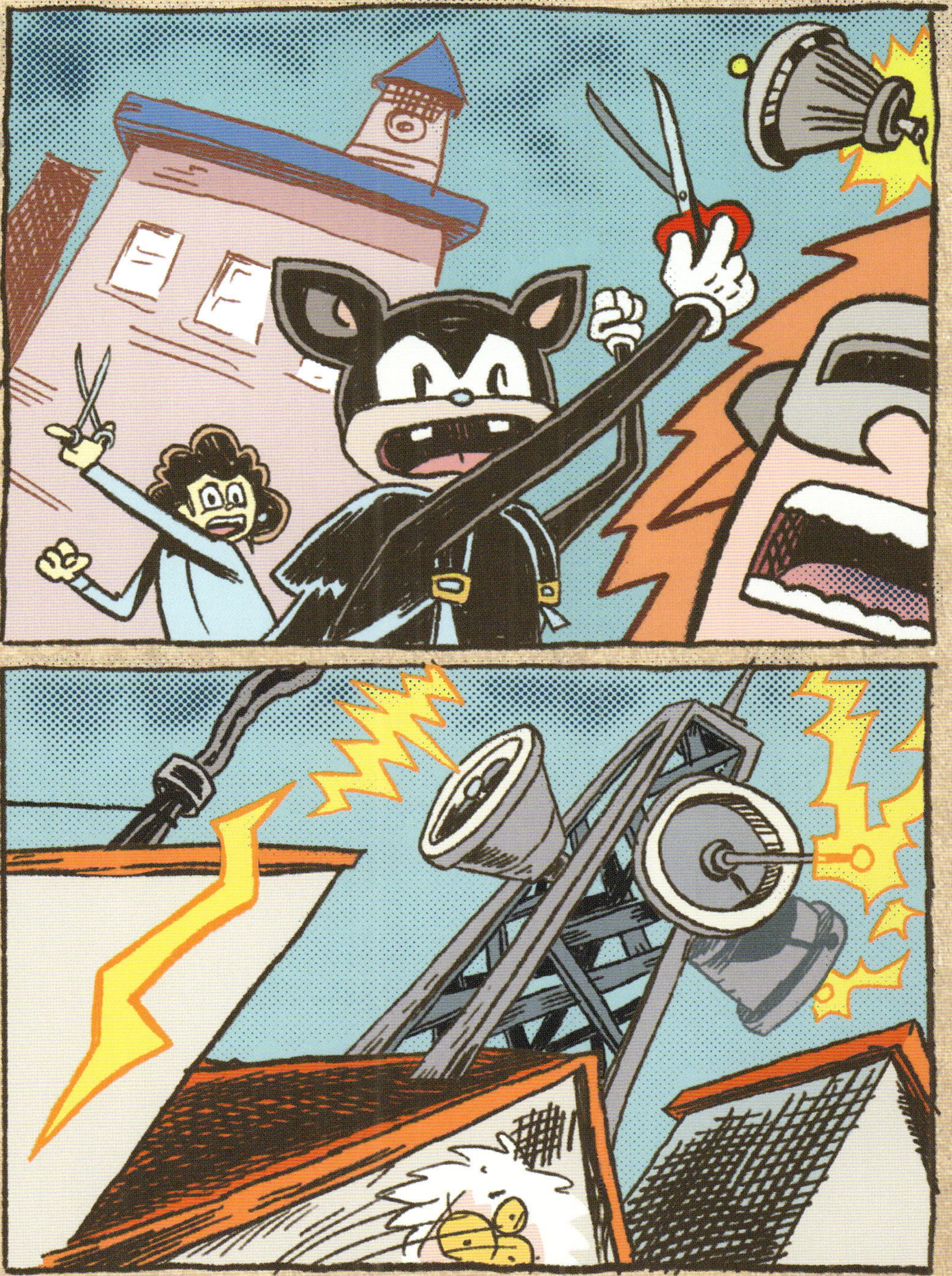

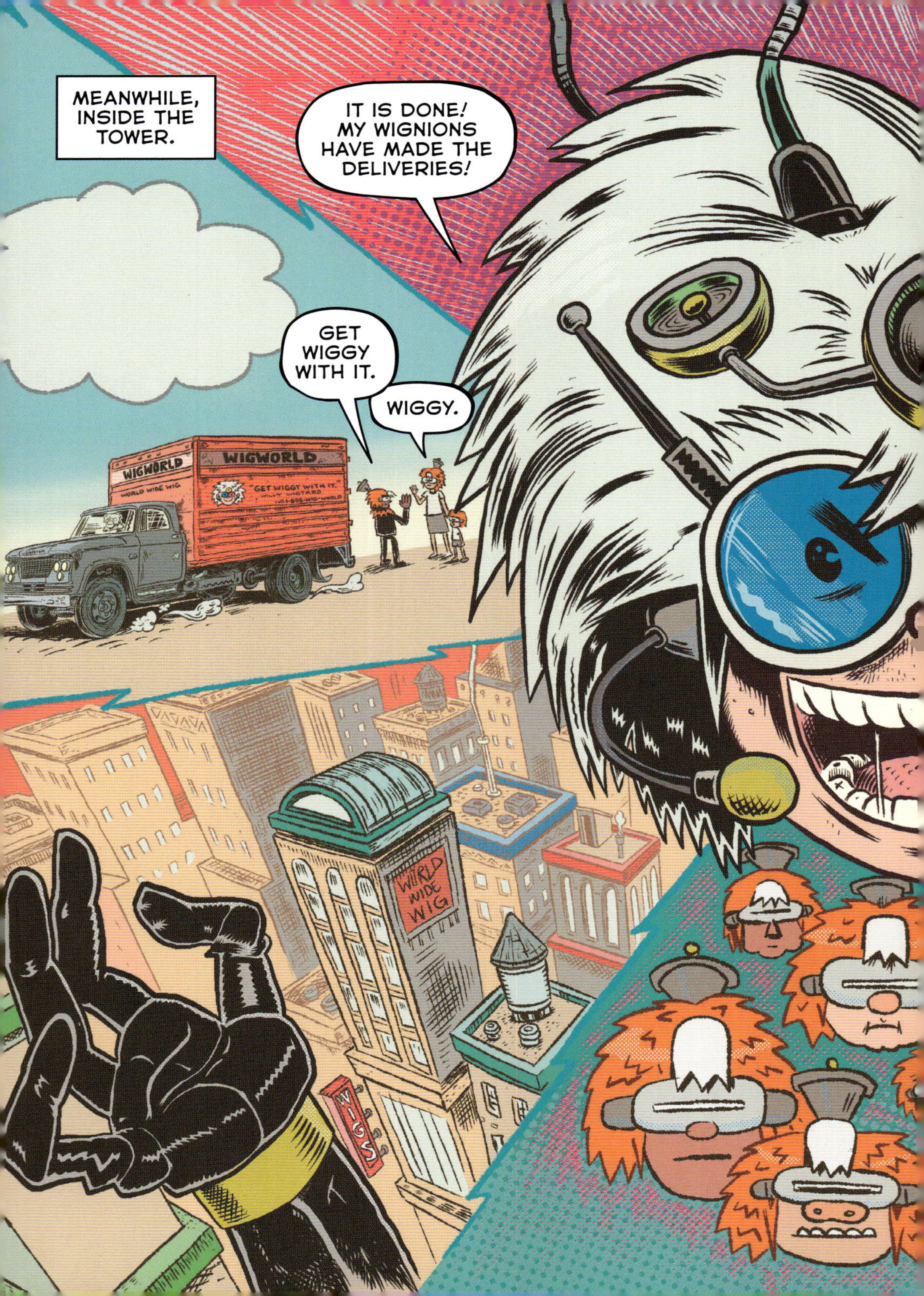
MEANWHILE, INSIDE THE TOWER.
IT IS DONE! MY WIGNIONS HAVE MADE THE DELIVERIES!
GET WIGGY WITH IT.
WIGGY.
WIGWORLD
WIGWORLD
WORLD WIDE WIG
GET WIGGY WITH IT.
WIGS

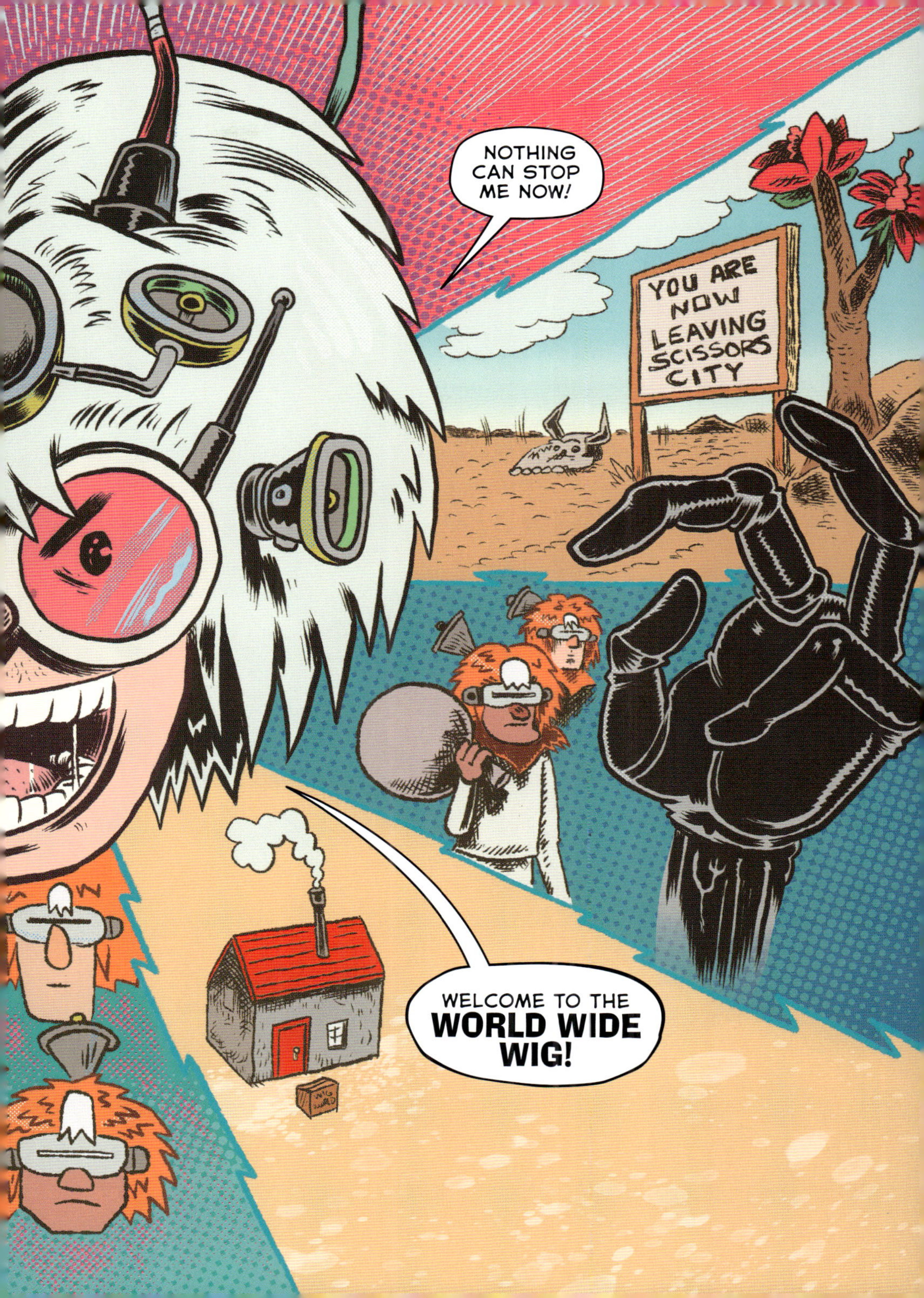
NOTHING CAN STOP ME NOW!
YOU ARE NOW LEAVING SCISSORS CITY
WELCOME TO THE WORLD WIDE WIG!

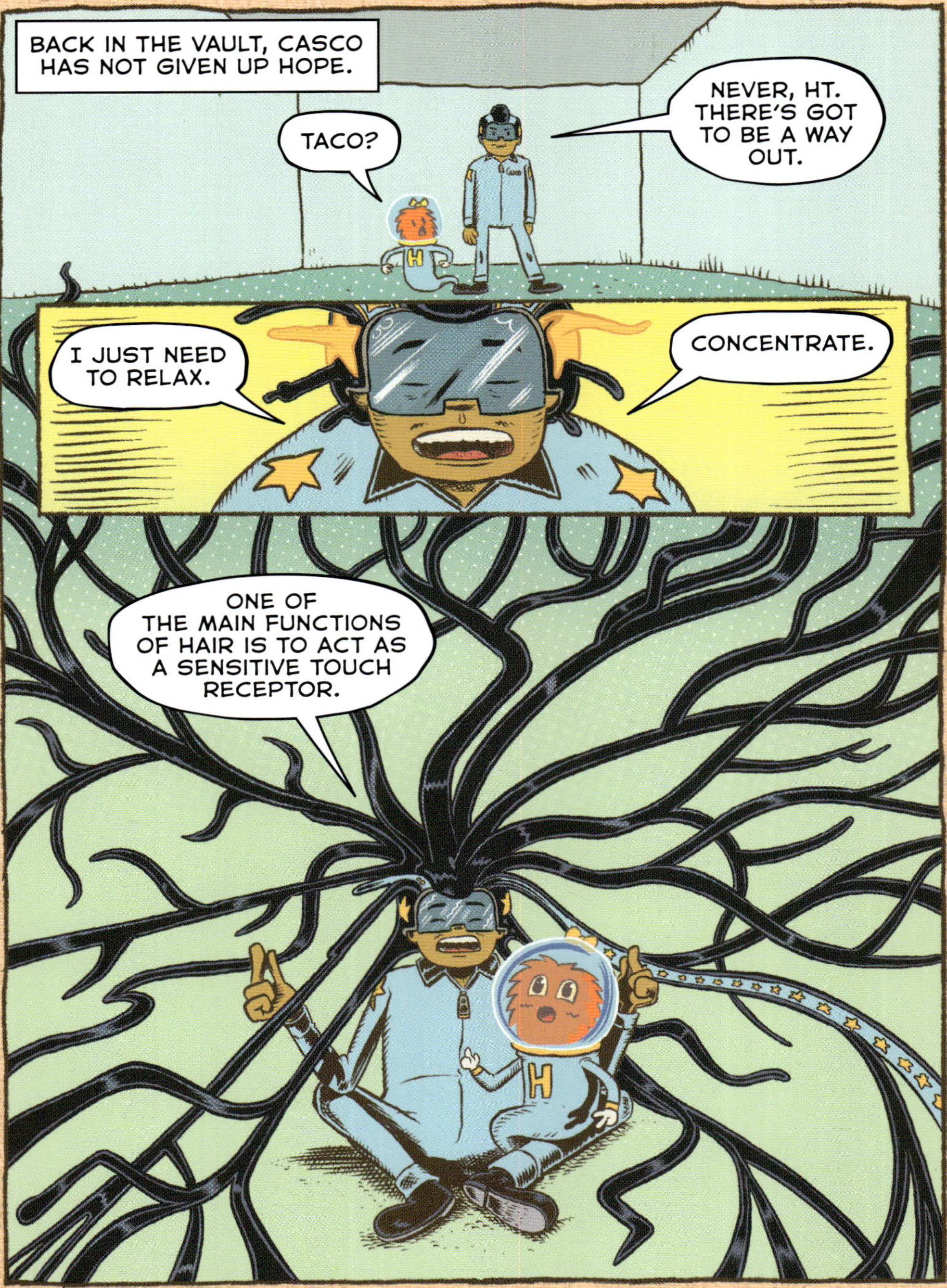

BACK IN THE VAULT, CASCO HAS NOT GIVEN UP HOPE.
TACO?
NEVER, HT. THERE'S GOT TO BE A WAY OUT.
I JUST NEED TO RELAX.
CONCENTRATE.
ONE OF THE MAIN FUNCTIONS OF HAIR IS TO ACT AS A SENSITIVE TOUCH RECEPTOR.

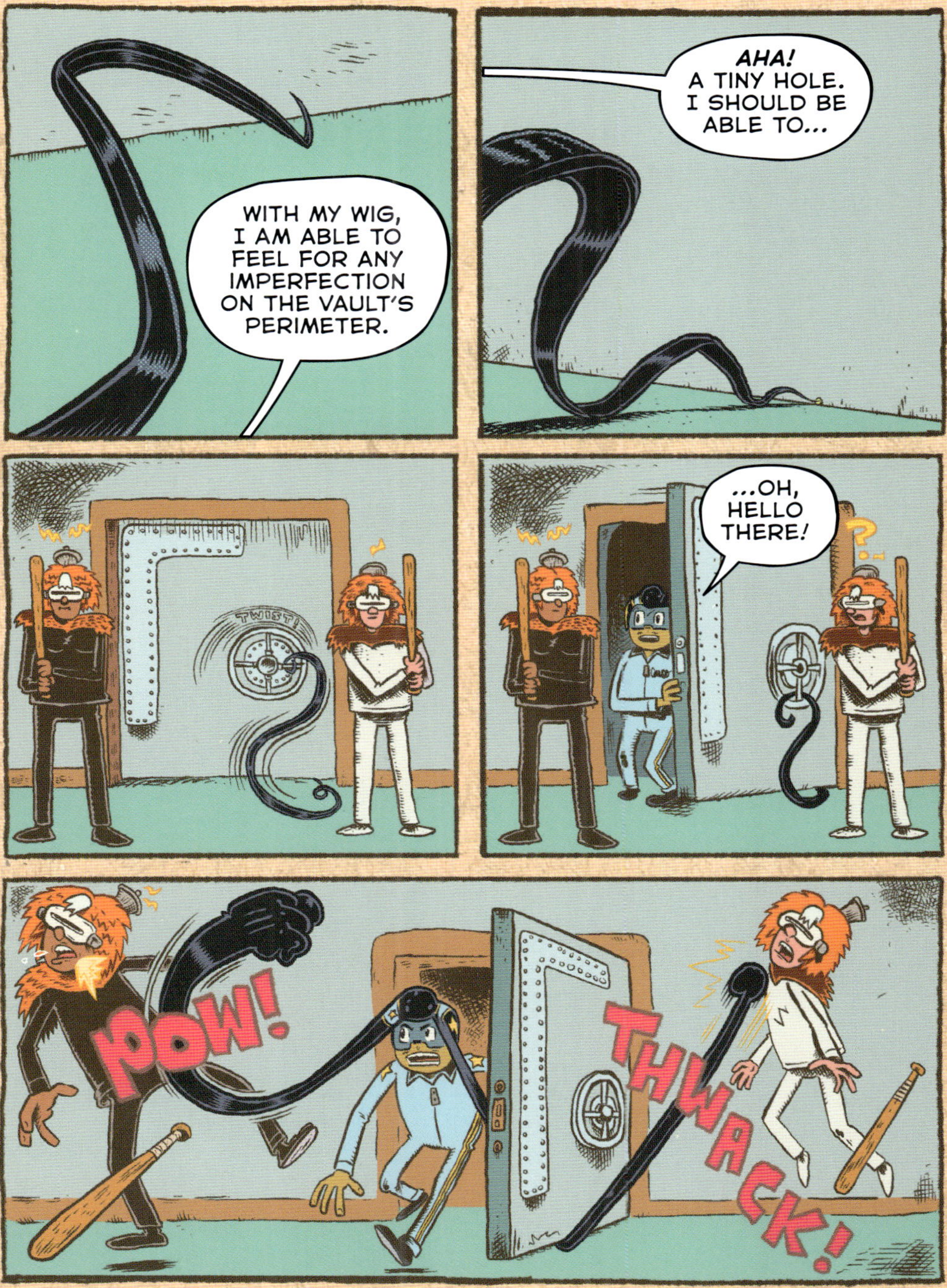
WITH MY WIG, I AM ABLE TO FEEL FOR ANY IMPERFECTION ON THE VAULT'S PERIMETER.
AHA! A TINY HOLE. I SHOULD BE ABLE TO...
TWIST!
...OH, HELLO THERE!
POW!
THWACK!

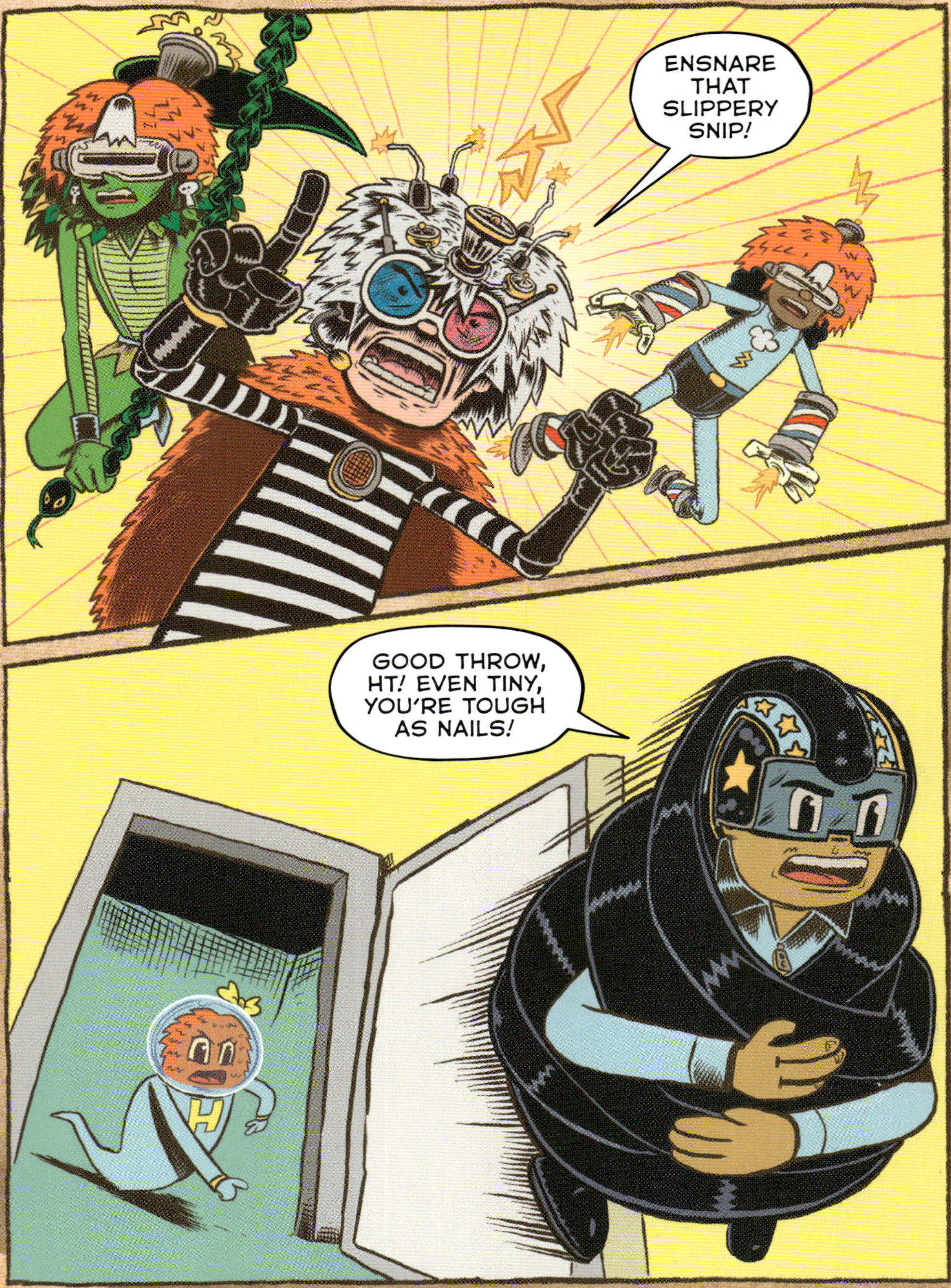
ENSNARE THAT SLIPPERY SNIP!
GOOD THROW, HT! EVEN TINY, YOU'RE TOUGH AS NAILS!

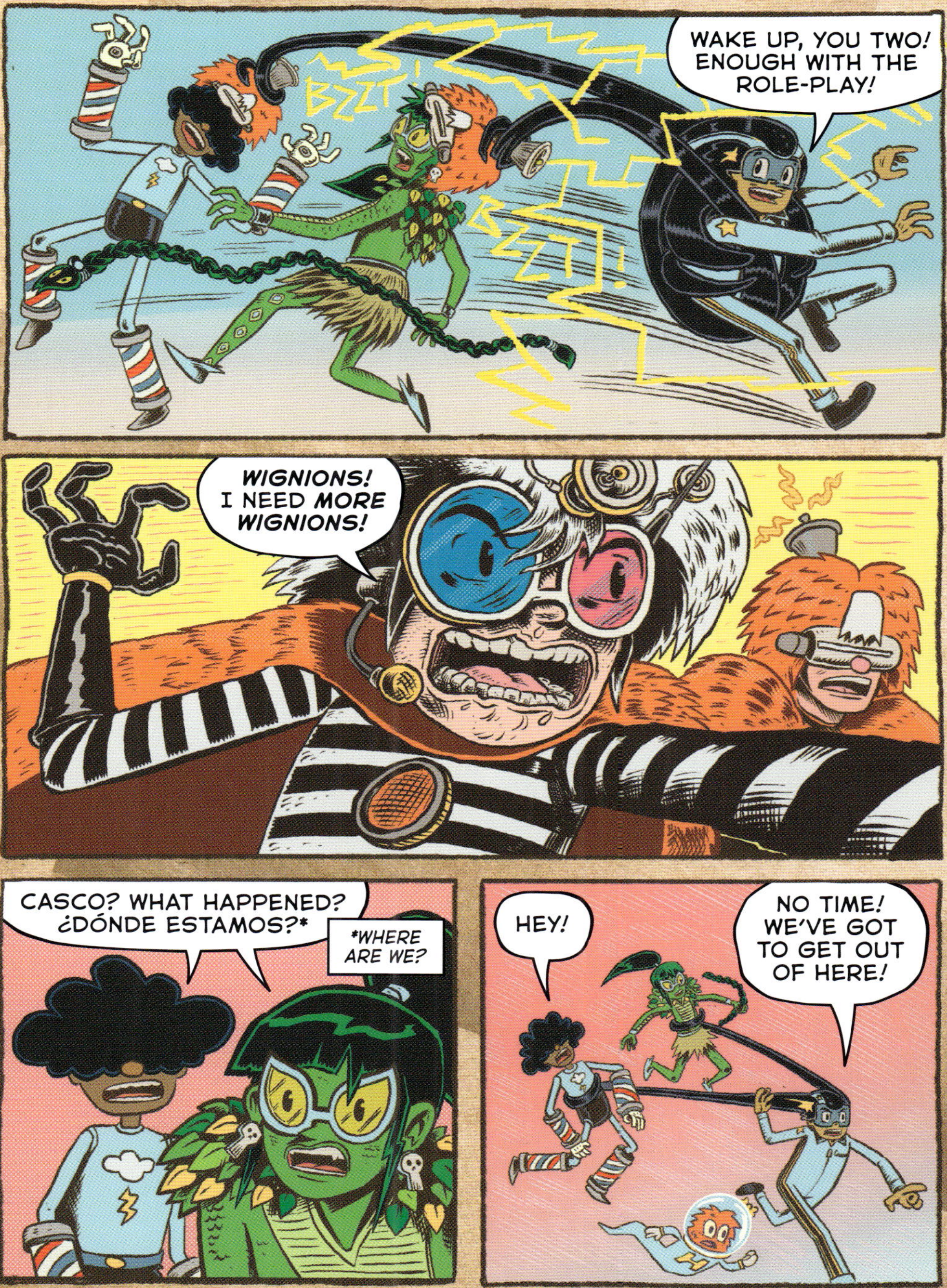
BZZT!
WAKE UP, YOU TWO! ENOUGH WITH THE ROLE-PLAY!
BZZT!
WIGNIONS! I NEED MORE WIGNIONS!
CASCO? WHAT HAPPENED? ¿DÓNDE ESTAMOS?*
*WHERE ARE WE?
HEY!
NO TIME! WE'VE GOT TO GET OUT OF HERE!

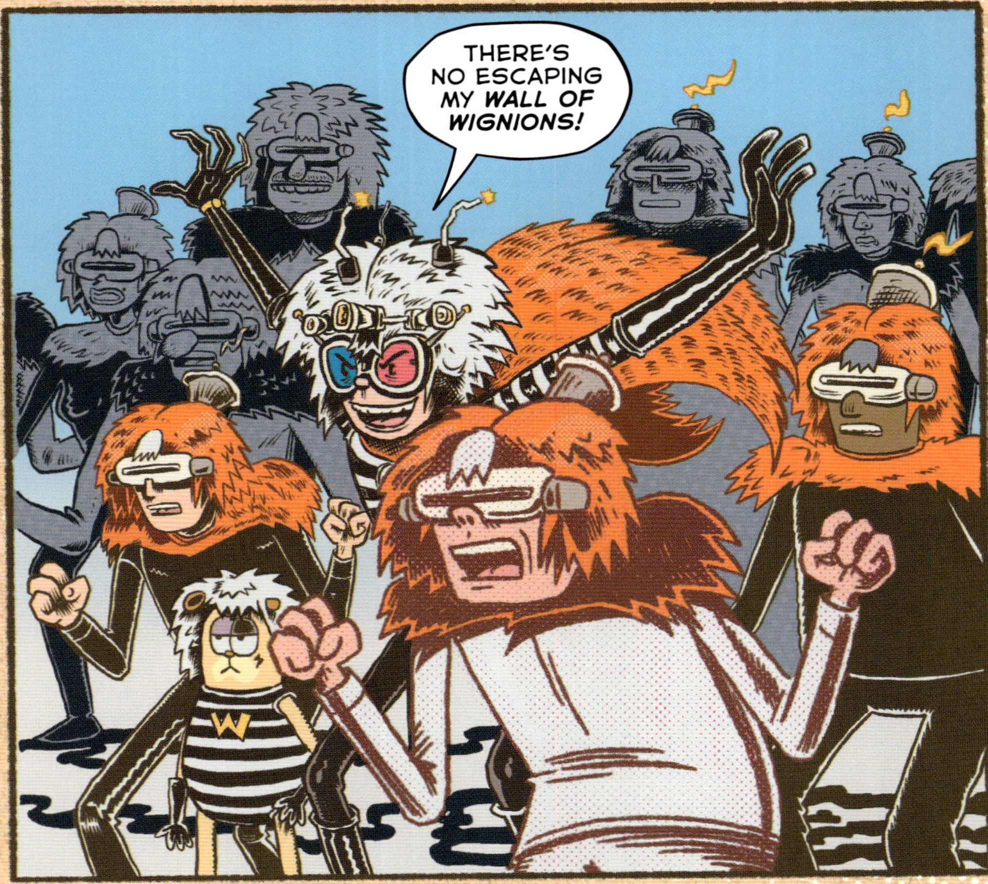
THERE'S NO ESCAPING MY *WALL OF WIGNIONS!*
W

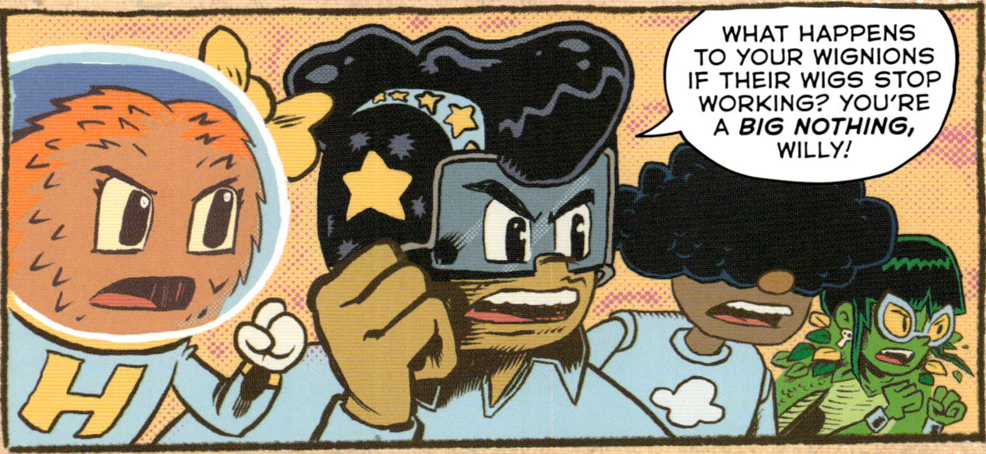
WHAT HAPPENS TO YOUR WIGNIONS IF THEIR WIGS STOP WORKING? YOU'RE A *BIG NOTHING,* WILLY!
H

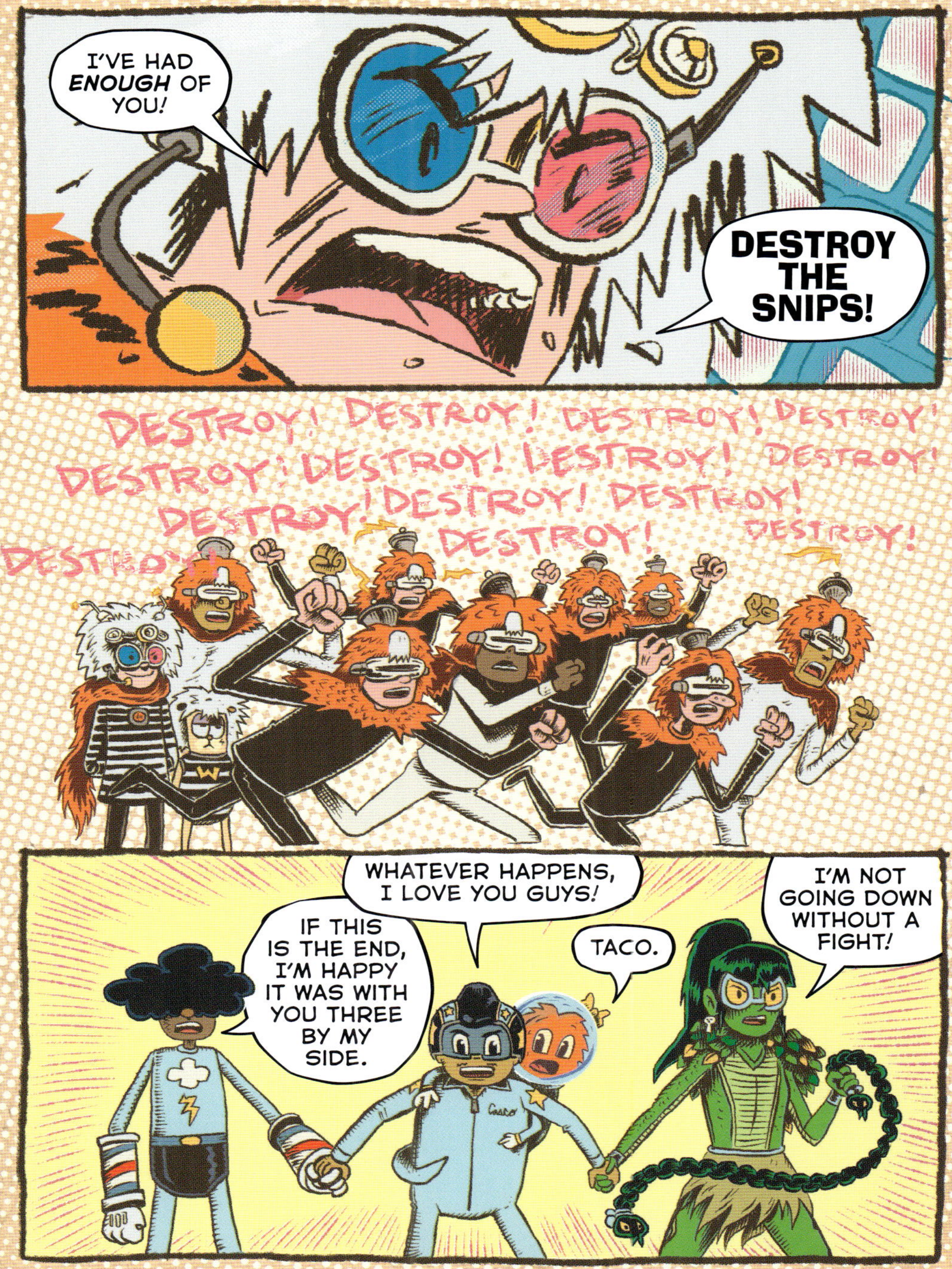
I'VE HAD ENOUGH OF YOU!
DESTROY THE SNIPS!
DESTROY! DESTROY! DESTROY! DESTROY! DESTROY! DESTROY! DESTROY! DESTROY! DESTROY! DESTROY! DESTROY! DESTROY! DESTROY! DESTROY!
IF THIS IS THE END, I'M HAPPY IT WAS WITH YOU THREE BY MY SIDE.
WHATEVER HAPPENS, I LOVE YOU GUYS!
TACO.
I'M NOT GOING DOWN WITHOUT A FIGHT!

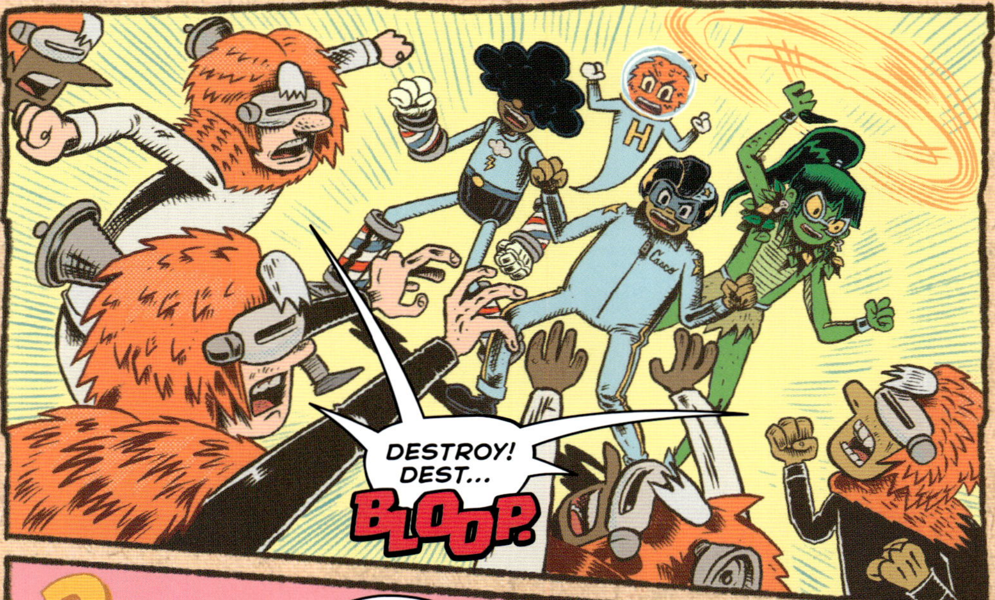
DESTROY! DEST...
BLOOP.

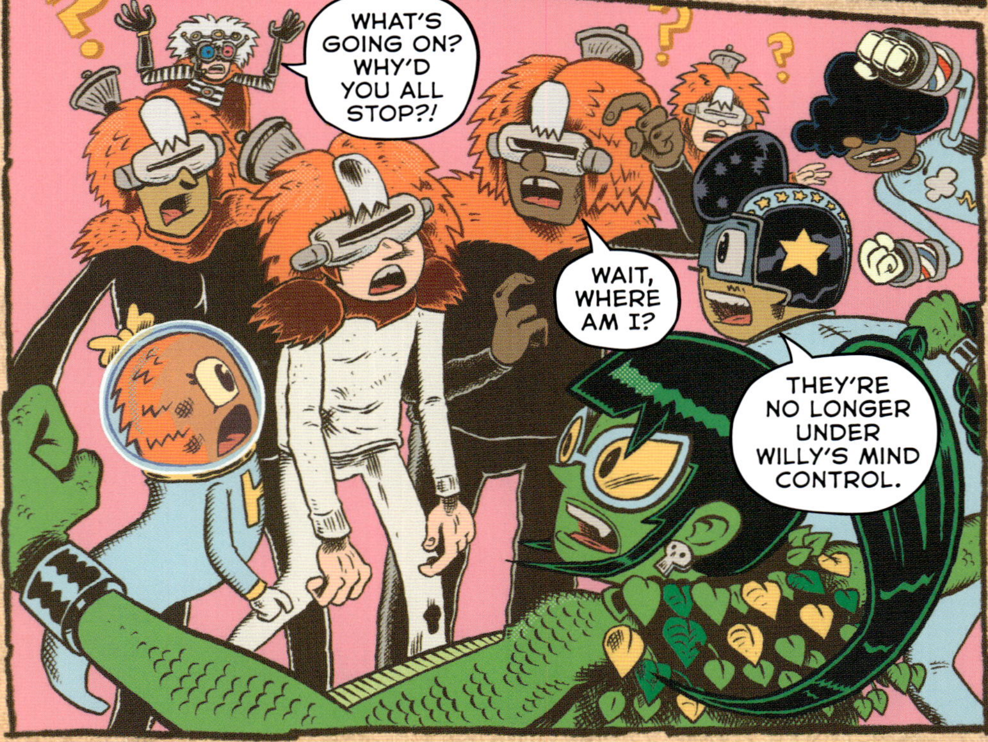
WHAT'S GOING ON? WHY'D YOU ALL STOP?!
WAIT, WHERE AM I?
THEY'RE NO LONGER UNDER WILLY'S MIND CONTROL.

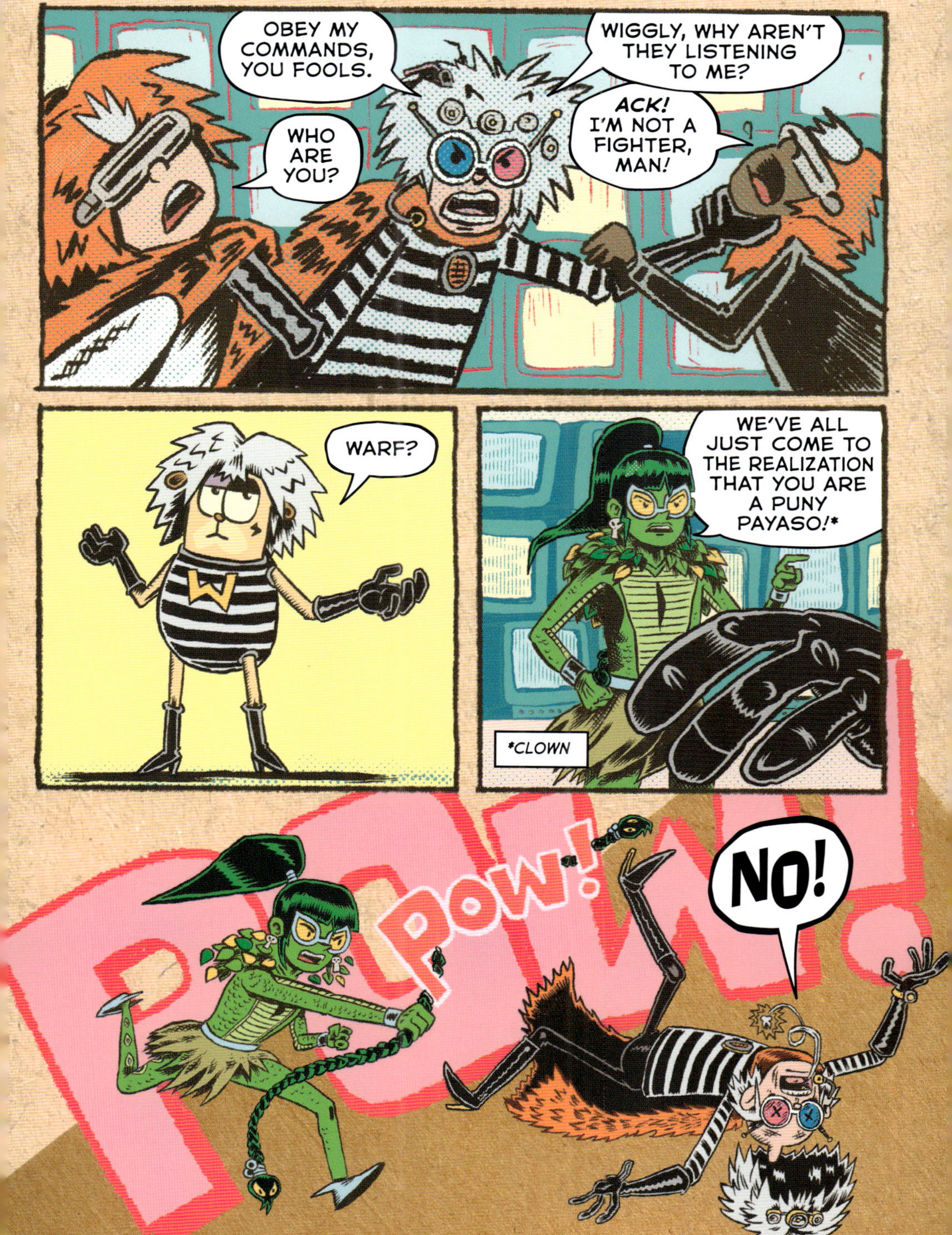
OBEY MY COMMANDS, YOU FOOLS.
WIGGLY, WHY AREN'T THEY LISTENING TO ME?
WHO ARE YOU?
ACK! I'M NOT A FIGHTER, MAN!
WARF?
WE'VE ALL JUST COME TO THE REALIZATION THAT YOU ARE A PUNY PAYASO!*
*CLOWN
POW!
POW!
NO!

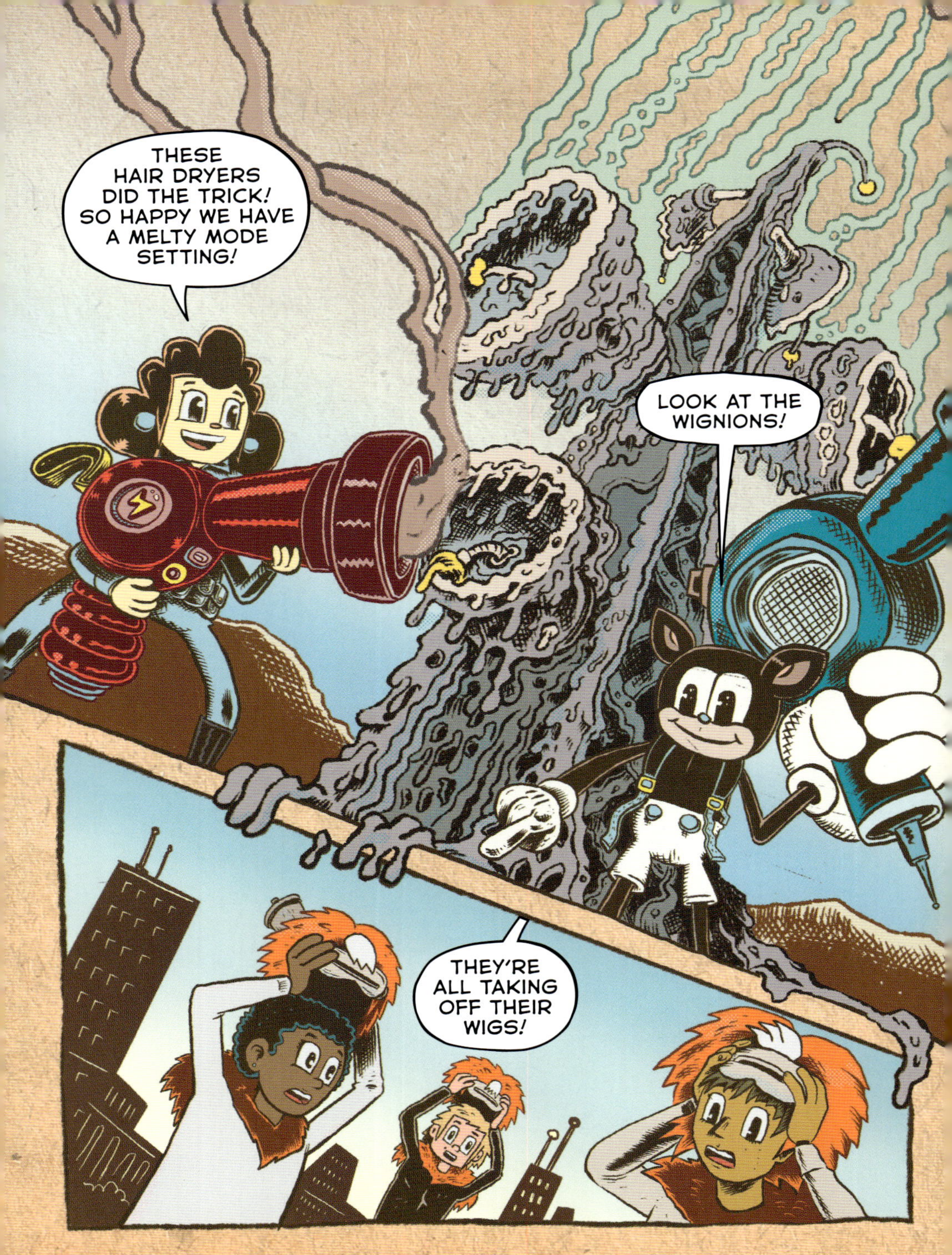
THESE HAIR DRYERS DID THE TRICK! SO HAPPY WE HAVE A MELTY MODE SETTING!
LOOK AT THE WIGNIONS!
THEY'RE ALL TAKING OFF THEIR WIGS!

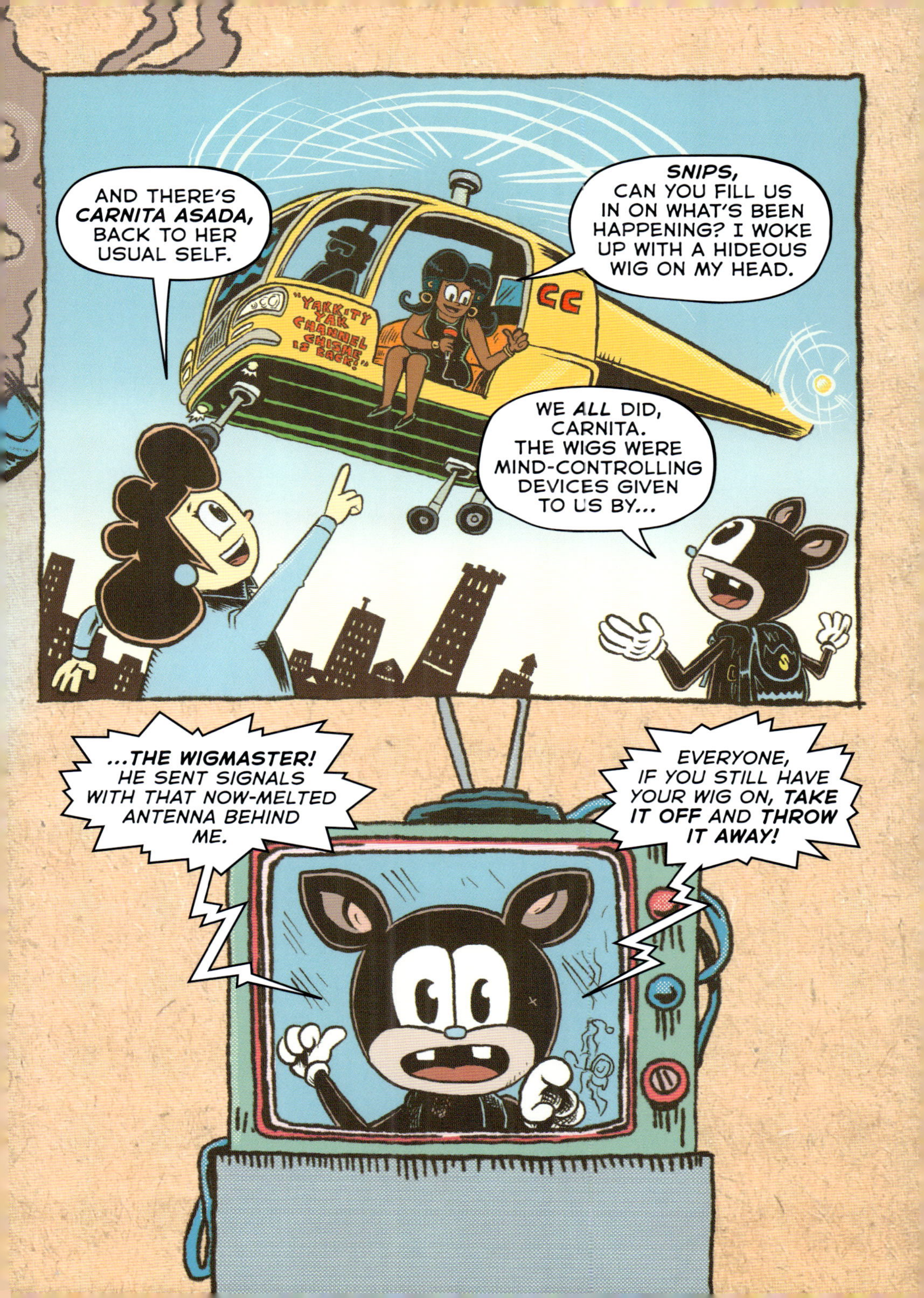
AND THERE'S **CARNITA ASADA,** BACK TO HER USUAL SELF.
"YAKKITY YAK CHANNEL CHISME IS BACK!"
CC
SNIPS, CAN YOU FILL US IN ON WHAT'S BEEN HAPPENING? I WOKE UP WITH A HIDEOUS WIG ON MY HEAD.
WE **ALL** DID, CARNITA. THE WIGS WERE MIND-CONTROLLING DEVICES GIVEN TO US BY...
...THE WIGMASTER! *HE SENT SIGNALS WITH THAT NOW-MELTED ANTENNA BEHIND ME.*
EVERYONE, IF YOU STILL HAVE YOUR WIG ON, ***TAKE IT OFF*** *AND* ***THROW IT AWAY!***

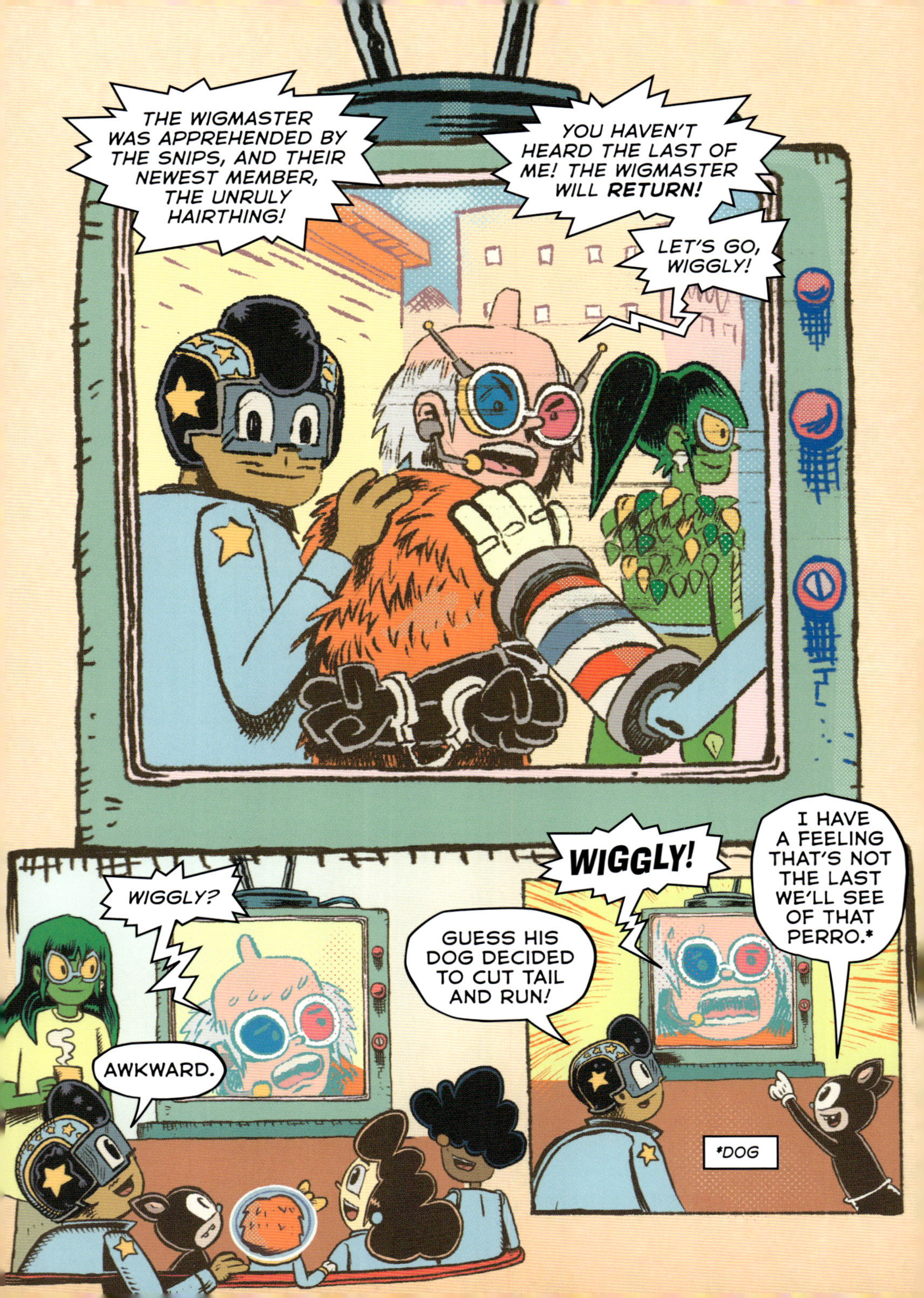
THE WIGMASTER WAS APPREHENDED BY THE SNIPS, AND THEIR NEWEST MEMBER, THE UNRULY HAIRTHING!
YOU HAVEN'T HEARD THE LAST OF ME! THE WIGMASTER WILL RETURN!
LET'S GO, WIGGLY!
WIGGLY?
AWKWARD.
GUESS HIS DOG DECIDED TO CUT TAIL AND RUN!
WIGGLY!
I HAVE A FEELING THAT'S NOT THE LAST WE'LL SEE OF THAT PERRO.*
*DOG

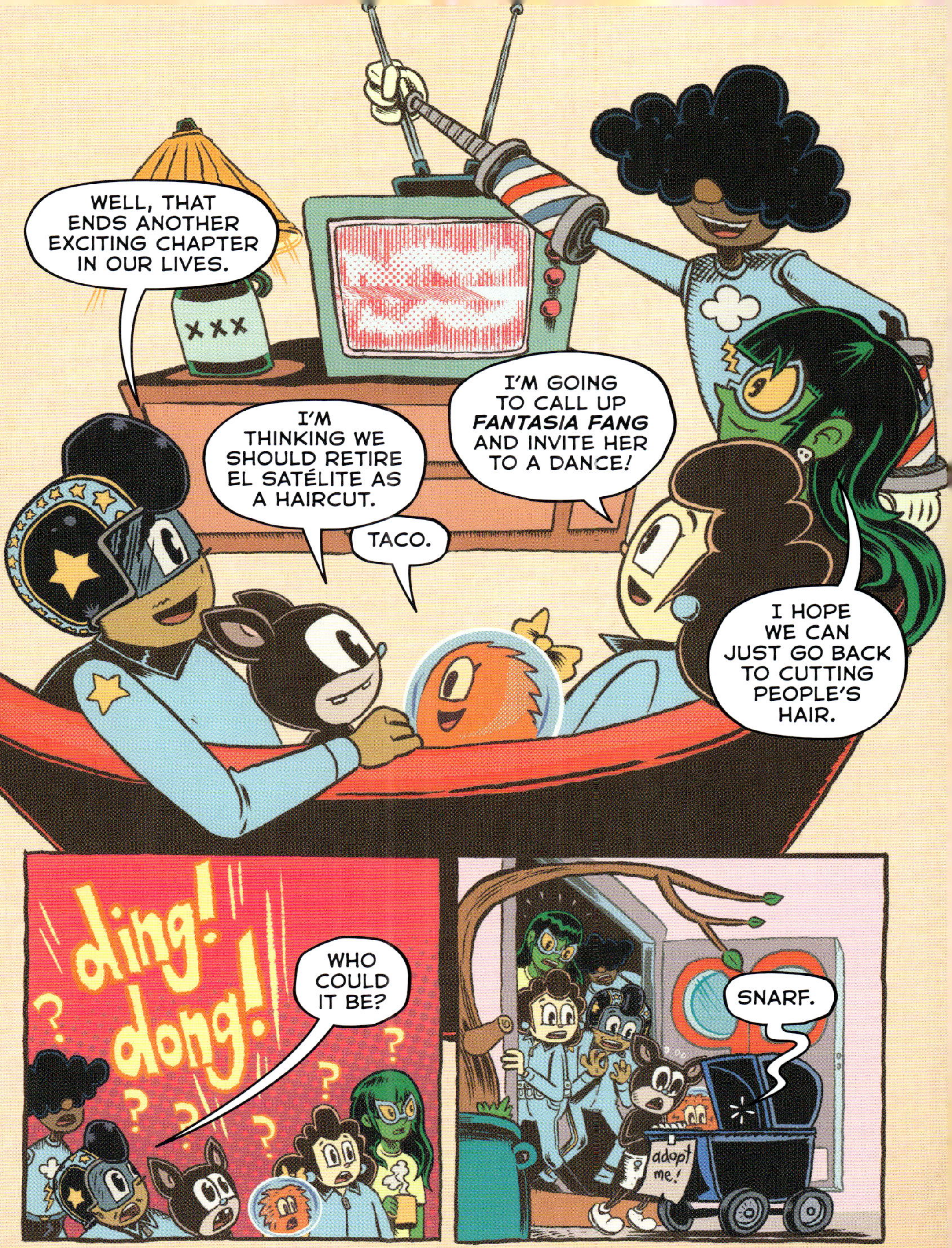

WELL, THAT ENDS ANOTHER EXCITING CHAPTER IN OUR LIVES.
XXX
I'M THINKING WE SHOULD RETIRE EL SATÉLITE AS A HAIRCUT.
TACO.
I'M GOING TO CALL UP *FANTASIA FANG* AND INVITE HER TO A DANCE!
I HOPE WE CAN JUST GO BACK TO CUTTING PEOPLE'S HAIR.
ding! dong!
WHO COULD IT BE?
SNARF.
adopt me!

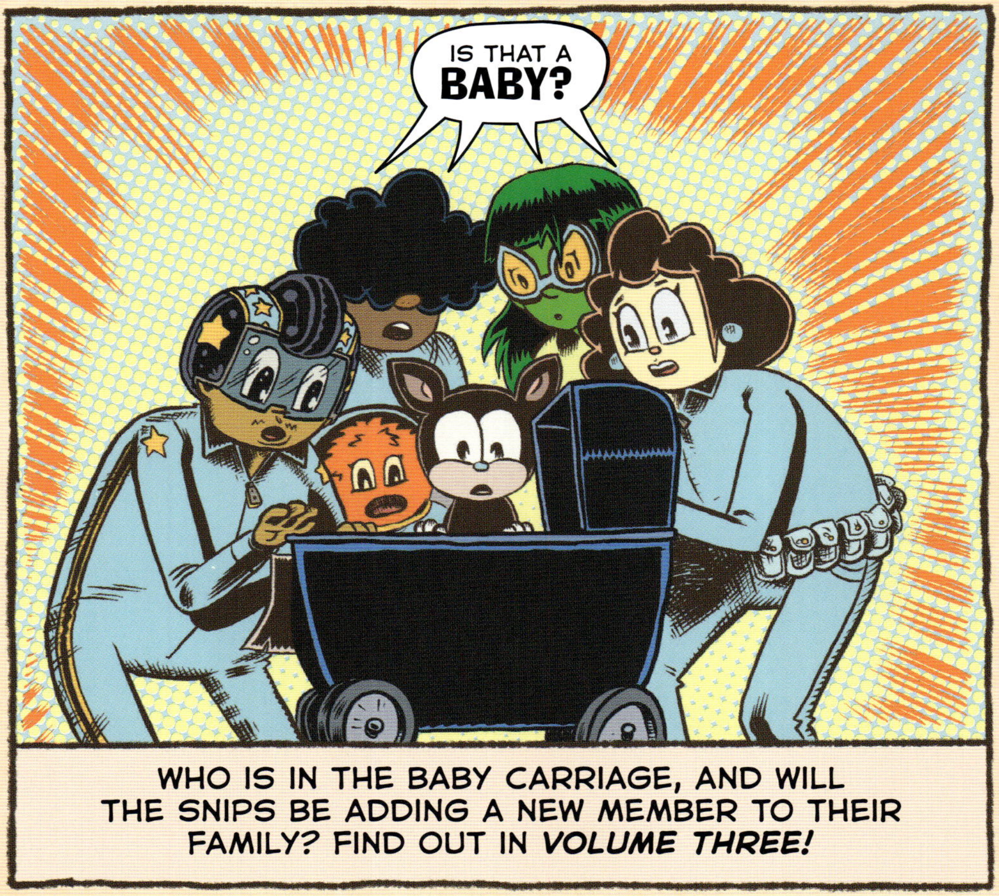
IS THAT A BABY?
WHO IS IN THE BABY CARRIAGE, AND WILL THE SNIPS BE ADDING A NEW MEMBER TO THEIR FAMILY? FIND OUT IN VOLUME THREE!

THE SNIPS

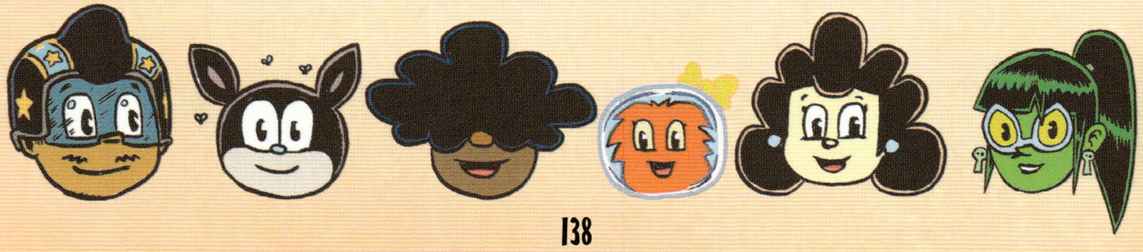

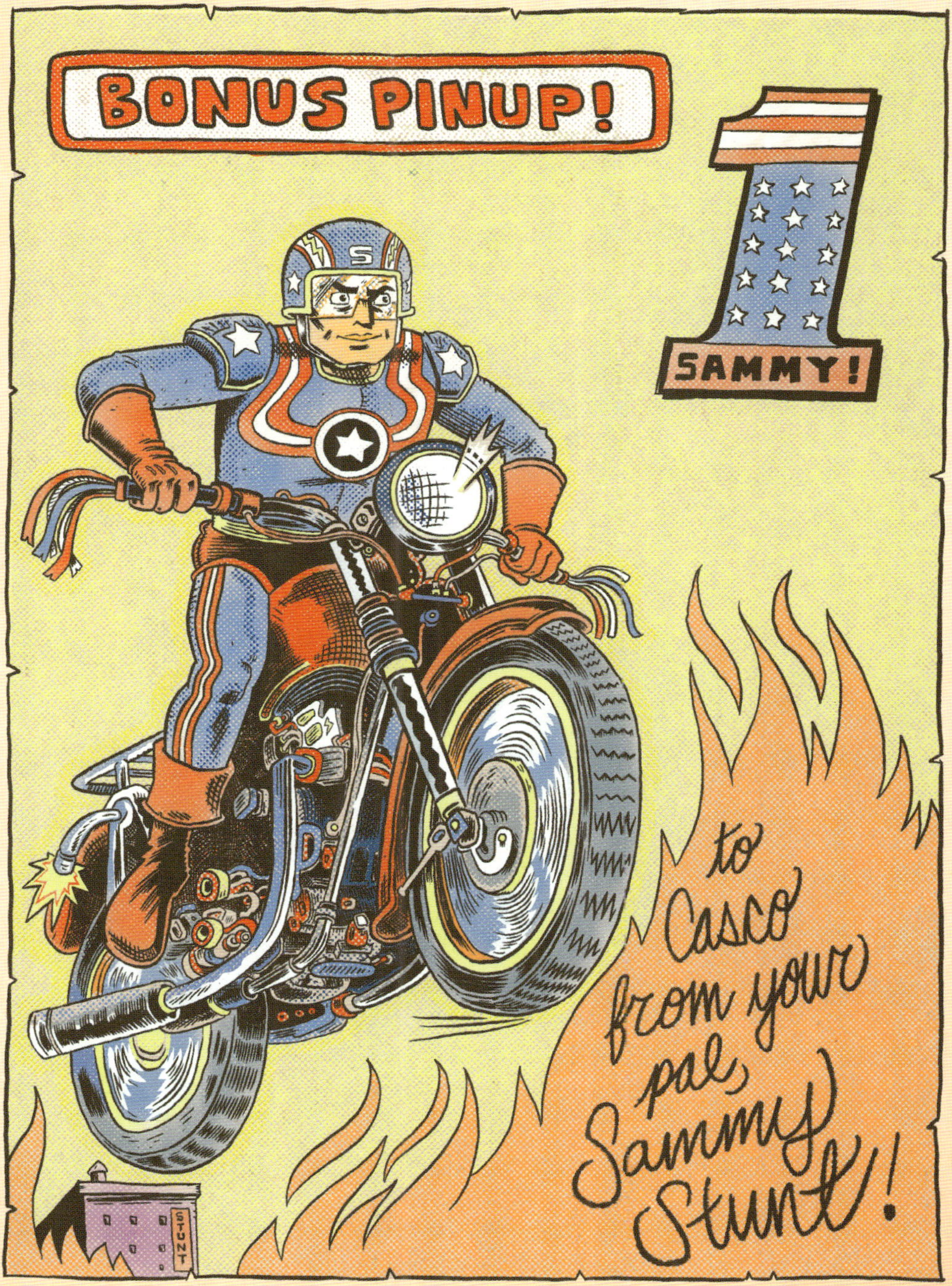
BONUS PINUP!
SAMMY!
to Casco from your pal, Sammy Stunt!
STUNT

ACKNOWLEDGMENTS

IT TAKES A TEAM TO MAKE A GRAPHIC NOVEL, AND THIS BOOK WOULD NOT HAVE BEEN POSSIBLE WITHOUT THE FOLLOWING PEOPLE. MY EDITOR, MARGARET RAYMO, WHOSE GUIDANCE OVER THE PAST TEN BOOKS HAS BEEN INVALUABLE! MY ART DIRECTOR, MEGAN McLAUGHLIN, WHO OVERSAW THE PROJECT AND KEPT IT FROM GOING OFF THE TRACKS. THANK YOU FOR YOUR KEEN EYE! ELAINE BAY'S PALETTE DECISIONS HAVE GIVEN MY WORK A DISTINCT LOOK FOR YEARS, AND HER WORK ON THESE BOOKS IS NO EXCEPTION. I COULDN'T DO IT WITHOUT HER! ELEONORA BRUNI'S COLORING IS EXCEPTIONAL AND HAS MADE EACH AND EVERY PAGE SING. AND LASTLY, ROB LEIGH FOR HIS AMAZING LETTERING. THANK YOU ALL FOR JOINING ME ON THIS ADVENTURE!

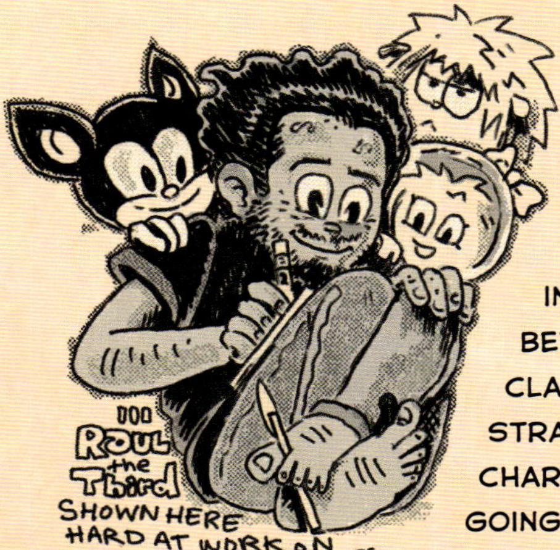
Raul the Third
SHOWN HERE HARD AT WORK ON THE SNIPS BOOK THREE.

RAÚL THE THIRD FIRST LEARNED TO DRAW BY COPYING THE CARTOON CHARACTERS HE SAW ON TV. HE LOVED THE SIMPLE SHAPES THAT MADE UP THEIR HAIR. IN SCHOOL, HIS DRAWINGS OF HAIR WERE ALWAYS MUCH BETTER THAN THOSE OF HIS FELLOW CLASSMATES, WHO DREW HAIR ONE STRAND AT A TIME, WHICH MADE THEIR CHARACTERS LOOK LIKE THEY WERE GOING BALD. SO HIS FRIENDS WOULD ALWAYS ASK HIM TO HELP WITH THEIR DRAWINGS, AND RAÚL BECAME THE HAIRSTYLIST FOR MANY A CHARACTER OVER THE YEARS—A POSITION HE TAKES PRIDE IN, ESPECIALLY NOW AS HE CONTINUES TO DRAW THE MANY ADVENTURES OF THE SNIPS. HE DOES THIS FROM HIS HOME IN MEDFORD, MASSACHUSETTS, WITH HIS WIFE AND COLLABORATOR, ELAINE BAY, AND THEIR SON, RAÚL THE FOURTH.

Snippets from Flealix!
LITTLE LORD
SCRAPBOOK
MEMENTOS
Tinta
COWBOY BOY
HEY!! KIDS COMICS

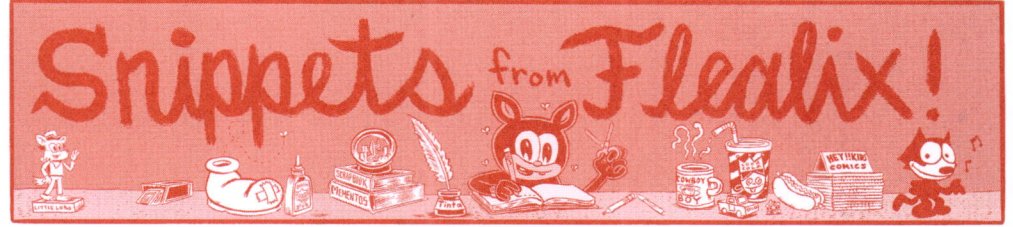

QUESTION of the WEEK!

"Are wigs made out of human hair?"
- Samson Delilah, age 7, Bangs, TX

IT ALL DEPENDS ON WHAT KIND OF WIG YOU WANT, SAMSON. WIGS ARE MADE OUT OF HUMAN, ANIMAL, OR SYNTHETIC HAIR. MOST OF THE HUMAN HAIR USED FOR WIGS COMES FROM CHINA AND INDIA! BARRISTERS (LAWYERS IN ENGLAND) USE POWDERED HORSE TAILS FOR THEIR WIGS. YAKS ARE BY FAR THE MOST POPULAR ANIMAL USED IN WIG PRODUCTION BECAUSE THEY GROW BOTH COARSE AND FINE HAIR. AND, SAMSON, IF YOU ARE EVER PLANNING ON CUTTING YOUR HAIR, YOU CAN DONATE YOUR LOCKS TO ORGANIZATIONS LIKE WIGS FOR KIDS. YOUR DONATION CAN HELP A FRIEND WITH HAIR LOSS FEEL CONFIDENT AND COMFORTABLE WITH A STYLISH WIG.

HEY, WIGGLY, CAN YOU BELIEVE I ONLY PAID ONE DOLLAR FOR THIS WIG?
WARF.
I THOUGHT IT WAS A GREAT PRICE TOUPEE.

HOW TO DRAW FLEALIX the DOG!
USE THESE SHAPES TO DRAW FLEALIX!
1.
2.
3.
4.
FIRST, DRAW A CIRCLE. NEXT, DRAW A LINE THROUGH THE CENTER OF THE CIRCLE.
DRAW SHAPES 2 AND 3 WHERE I DREW THEM. WE ARE ALMOST DONE!
ADD SHAPE 4 WITH A SMILE, AND BINGO! YOU ARE DONE!
DON'T FORGET TO FILL ME IN!
Flealix!

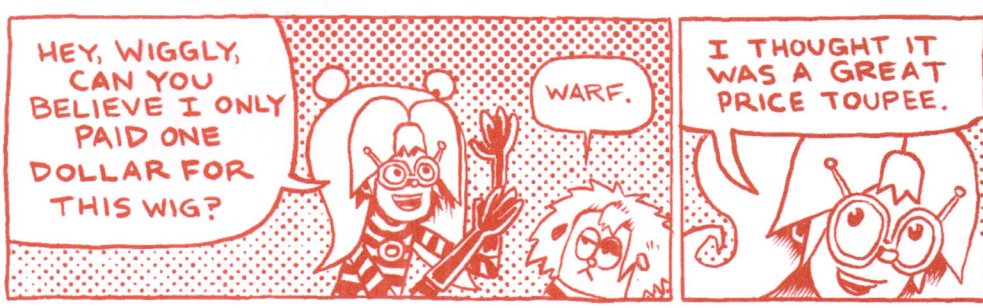

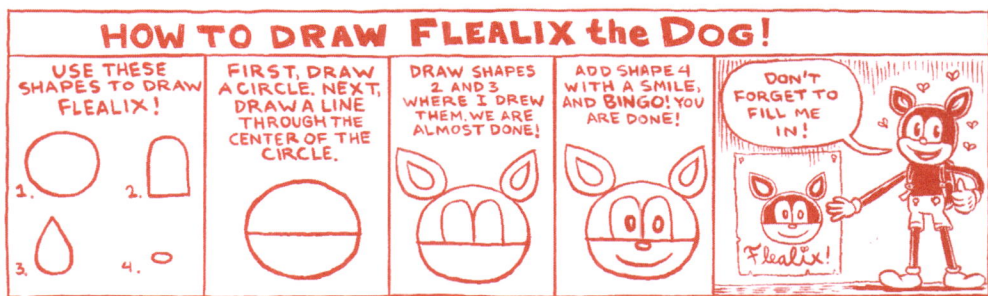

P.S. ADD A FEW OF THESE ♥♥♥ FOR ITCHY FUN!

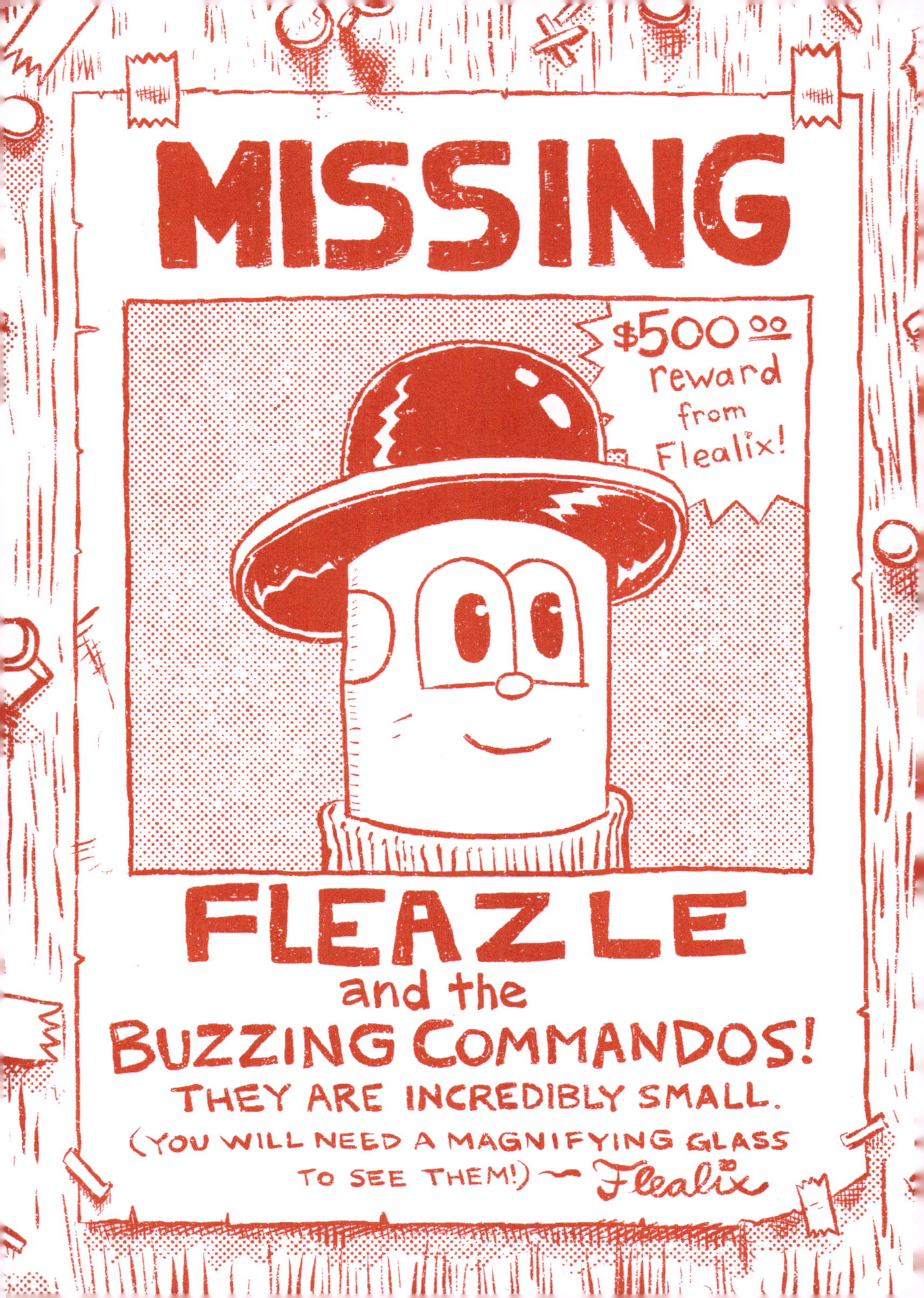
MISSING
$500.00 reward from Flealix!
FLEAZLE
and the
BUZZING COMMANDOS!
THEY ARE INCREDIBLY SMALL.
(YOU WILL NEED A MAGNIFYING GLASS
TO SEE THEM!) ~ Flealix